The Key of Ban

The Key of Ban

Published by Rockjack Books

Printing History

Rockjack Books
First Printing 2005

Cover illustration and book design by
Mark Kashino

Text illustrations by
Mary Blackeye

Rockjack Books, P.O. Box 170268
Boise, Idaho 83717

ISBN: 0-9719567-1-5

Printed in the United State America

11- 26-05

James Harshfield

The Key of Ban

James B. Harshfield

Rockjack Books
Boise, Idaho

Acknowledgement

With a twist of his nose, a look of disbelief and a sly smile, Bob Fahringer edited with gusto. Bob, thanks for your help.

The keen insights of Ann Fenley added enrichment and realism to the book. The world is a better place because of her caring and gentle presence.

A special thanks to Miriam Depew, Barbara, my wife, and the many people assisting in this project.

With pride I display the artwork of Mary Blackeye. Her talents add a special enchantment to the book.

Dedication

With love I dedicate this book to the heart of my life, my family: Barbara, Mark, Yeung, Amber, Greg, Lara, Tom, Tonya, Terry, Christopher and the mysterious K. & E.

Ancient Book of Lands
Roga of Tanz
2321 BK

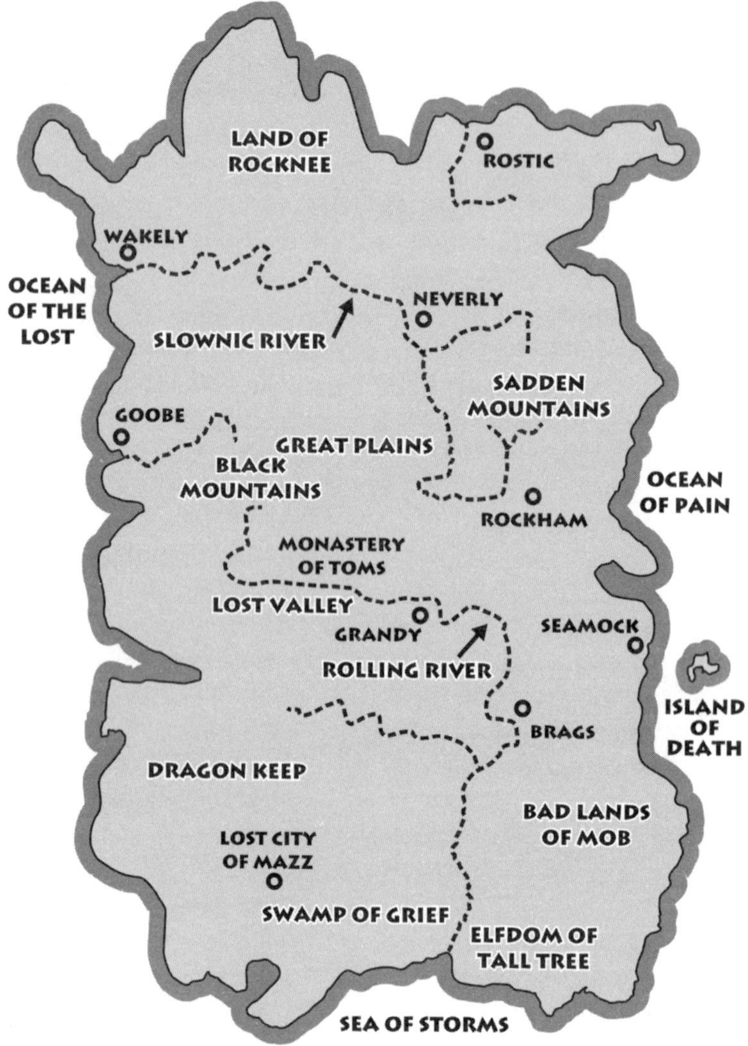

CONTENTS

Book I

Book II

BOOK 1

VOICES FROM THE OUTLAST

PROLOGUE

Hurricane-strength winds blew down the narrow canyon blasting Coaldon's face with punishing gusts. Sheets of rain pounded him with unrelenting force. The uninterrupted rumble of thunder and the flashing of lighting created the illusion of a war being waged against the walls of the narrow canyon. The unnatural intensity of the storm caused Coaldon to feel disoriented. The tempest seemed more like an unpleasant dream than a natural occurrence.

At first, he thought the storm would pass without interrupting his plans for a quiet stroll. Yet, the growing intensity of the cloud-burst created an inescapable reality. This was not a simple everyday incident, but the once-in-a-lifetime event of epic proportions.

He decided to escape from the canyon when the flow of water in the stream began to grow. With long steps he followed an animal path down the edge of the stream. He became concerned when he heard the distant rumble of water rushing down the gorge. The torrent of water raced faster and higher. He struggled to stay ahead of the rising surge of churning water. The rain had turned the normally shallow stream into a raging river.

With longer and longer strides he raced down the uneven floor of the canyon. A roaring sound drew his attention to a disturbance behind him. He turned just in time to see a wall of water towering above him. With a violent flick, the rolling water washed him off his feet and carried him down stream. Floating helplessly, he was uncertain if he would ever see his grandparents again. He felt like a tiny branch caught in a flood of fate rushing toward fulfillment.

As if it were meant to be, Coaldon was tossed into a grove of small trees. Groping, he used a branch to pull himself to higher ground. With all his strength, he clawed his way up the steep rocky canyon wall. He struggled to stay ahead of the rising torrent of water. Gasping for breath, he finally pulled himself onto a ledge above the devastating flood.

The pounding force of the wind battered him with flying debris. If he was to survive, it would be necessary to find shelter. Seeking protection, he crawled under an over-hanging ledge on the face of a cliff. From the safety of his vantage point, he watched the flood devastate the landscape. The shelter provided him with the opportunity to regain a sense of security. With a smile, he reflected, "At times nature has the ability to be more than enough and to demonstrate a boisterous, energetic personality."

The unbelievable turmoil of the flood heightened his sense of reality. His brush with death triggered a surge of memories to flow freely through his mind. He vividly remembered walking through the beauty of the Outlast. His responsibilities were light and peace was a faithful companion. He suddenly understood that he had lived a protected life under the guidance of his grandparents. The isolation of the farm provided a barrier between him and the influences of the outside world.

In three months he would be 18 years old, the traditional age for the transition into adulthood. He thought about what it would be like to leave the wilderness farm and be on his own. Yet, how would a half elf be accepted? He was told by his grandparents that only two half elves were known to live in the Empire. Would he be rejected or accepted?

Ideas continued to rattle around his head in unceasing circles of repetition. These images were then reduced to a single picture of an unending road extending before him. Coaldon saw himself standing in front of the farm house looking down the road. To his discomfort the peace and protection of the cabin melted away. He found himself standing alone with black, threatening clouds blanketing the distant horizon. His active mind associated the image of the flood with his future journey in life. He knew that life could be peaceful and secure. Other times it could be violent and unpredictable. His elfin senses detected a disturbance in his future. He thought, "Maybe this storm is a message to me. Is it possible that my peaceful life on the farm will soon be washed away?"

Lost Valley

Coaldon Rocknee awoke to the sound of talking. The morning sun was shining on his face through the dirty loft window. The aroma of ham and eggs cooking drifted from the kitchen. The cold air of late fall filled the cabin with the first signs of winter. The roaring fire in the fireplace would soon warm the cabin. He wanted to stay in bed, but fall was a busy time on the farm. His grandparents needed his help in gathering the crops and maintaining the farm. So, if he wanted to or not, it was time for him to face the new day. For the past few weeks, he had helped harvest the fruits of their summer labor. He smiled with satisfaction at the large crops that had been stored into the vegetable cellar.

Since he was first able to walk he followed his grandpa into the fields. This intimacy with the farm helped Coaldon realize the necessity of harvesting plentiful crops or face the danger of starvation. Winter in the Outlast was a time of deep snow and cold temperatures. Deep snow drifts created a barrier to the outside world. It was essential to have adequate food supplies to last through the long winter months.

Coaldon was a strong boy with black hair and a tall slender body. His hair flashed in the sun with broad bands of color. He walked with straight shoulders, high head and confident strides. His large bright eyes and curious mind did not allow anything to go unnoticed. Yet he had a gentle compassion for life. The kitchen often became a hospital ward for wounded animals. After many trial-and-error attempts, he had become proficient at doctoring his clients. His experience with death helped him to understand the frailty of life. He learned to accept death as a natural event.

Coaldon slowly rolled over and looked at his best friend. Sid's tail wagged at Coaldon's sleepy greeting. Coaldon felt the warm glow of happiness as he looked at Sid. Sid was a tall dog with long legs, muscular body, long hair and an alert personality. The dog and Coaldon spent many hours together roaming the endless playground of nature. On their long walks in the forest, Sid's dark brown fur would blend into the surroundings like a wild animal. Sid would frequently run ahead and hide in the brush, executing sneak attacks on Coaldon. This game would continue until Coaldon was knocked to the ground wrestling with a large excited dog. These happy moments rippled with fellowship and contentment.

Coaldon knew breakfast would soon be ready. He did not have time to waste on the comforts of his warm bed. Today he had to fix the fence on the north end of the farm. The cattle were escaping into the meadow through a hole in the stone wall near Rolling River. The cattle were safe as long as they grazed in the area near the cabin. They would become dinner for a large red wolf if they wandered into the forest.

Coaldon had lived 17 years with his grandparents in a narrow valley in the Black Mountains. The Outlast was the name of this isolated wilderness in the Northern Empire. Lost Valley was wedged between two towering mountain ranges. The lush green forest of the valley blended into the barren, rocky mountain peaks. Several times Coaldon hiked to the top of Lighting Point to proclaim, "I climbed to the top of the highest peak in Rocky Front Range." He enjoyed the physical challenge of testing himself to the point of exhaustion. While on the mountaintop, he looked over the splendor of the distant lands. He tried to imagine what it would be like to visit those far off places.

The forest surrounding the farm made it an island in a sea of trees. The road to the east led to the Village of Grandy, a small community that found contentment in its isolation and old family traditions. The village was the local hub for news, a center of commerce and a support in a time of need. The simple lives of its people were lost to the outside world.

The Rolling River flowed out of the Black Mountains, passed the farm, through the village and to the sea. It moved with the predictability of the seasons. The river could cascade with the power of an uncontrolled giant or wander with the slow current of a quiet breeze. The changing seasons determined the character of the river. It offered the floods of the spring and the gentle flow of late summer. Coaldon frequently visited the river to fish and swim.

A wide variety of birds flew overhead in perpetual search for food. The undergrowth was alive with the scampering feet of many animals. All the inhabitants of the valley shared in the bounty of nature. The alert eyes of the large black war eagles kept watch over the activities in Lost Valley. Coaldon often stopped from his activities to study their noble presence. He frequently thought, "Why are they called war eagles? Some day I want to talk with an eagle."

Often, during the summer months, evening storms bathed the valley with cleansing rains. These summer showers provided the needed moisture for the grain crops, lush pastures and vegetable garden. The showers washed away the dust of the day and sweetened the night air for pleasant sleeping.

The heavy winter snows made Lost Valley a home of frosty splendor. Winter was a time of peace, rest, reflection and study. Coaldon would often hitch the horses to the sled to gather wood. The prancing horses easily pulled Coaldon though the deep snow. He enjoyed being a part of the winter wonderland.

Coaldon could remember only a handful of people who ever visited the farm. These guests were friends of his grandparents. He loved to listen to their tales of the outside world. These visitors always took the time to talk with him and listen to his stories about life in the Outlast.

He knew the guests would spend several days in secret discussions with his grandparents. These visits had grown more frequent over the past few years. Recently, Coaldon noticed the guests were increasingly nervous, spoke in worried voices and wore grim faces. This climate of tension provided an overtone of impending danger. Coaldon was not allowed to listen to the confidential parts of the discussions. Yet, he knew he was part of the conversations. He heard his name mentioned in low voices, but paid little attention to their debates. Coaldon's life in the Outlast was the major focus of his special life.

Coaldon discovered at an early age he was not like the other kids in the village. He learned from his grandparents that he was half elf. At first he did not know what it meant. It was not until he was a teenager that he realized he was different from other youth. Coaldon discovered he could see better at night, hear unspoken voices and sense the power of the stars. At night he would feel the energy of stars flowing into his spirit. The strength he gained from the stars helped clear his mind and see beyond the present. The pulse of life spoke to him in a clear and understandable manner. He could feel the emotions of animals and hear the voices of their thoughts.

From his human grandparents he learned his father was human and his mother was an elf. His grandparents told of how his parents had fallen deeply in love at first sight. He learned that his birth was the greatest gift his parents had ever received. Their joy was written in the poetic verses in the Songs of Heaven. Sometimes Coaldon felt a great loneliness for his parents. He tried to imagine what it would be like to live with them as a family. These feelings quickly pass because of his deep love for his grandparents. Coaldon enjoyed the time when they told stories about his parents.

Even though he experienced time of peace and joy, his existence was not a life of complete freedom. Most of his time was devoted to his education and work around the farm. Most days had a set routine of activities: farm work, reading, writing, and swordsmanship.

His grandfather, Brad Rocknee, was a man of great knowledge, skill, strength, and patience. He was short and muscular with long gray hair. From his square face his deep blue eyes burned with a passion for life. His grandfather approached all situations with an air of nobility. He always expected Coaldon to act with discipline and caring.

Grandpa Brad, a master swordsman, taught Coaldon to handle the sword with expert skill. Coaldon enjoyed the challenge of trying to match the speed of his grandfather. He spent many hours perfecting the art of swordsmanship.

Grandma Ingrid was a woman of strength and kindness. Her gentle eyes and commanding spirit radiated the wisdom gained from a difficult life. Coaldon often thought she looked and acted like a queen. She always moved with a stately bearing and spoke with clarity and confidence. He was impressed with her ability to calmly respond to everyday events. He frequently talked with her about his dreams and goals. She would take the time to explain to Coaldon the difference between being average and living to a higher standard.

Grandma Ingrid kept the small cabin clean and pleasant. Meals were simple but good. She made the fruits of this wilderness taste with the flavor of a royal court. Her courage to withstand the hard life in the Outlast demonstrated her tough, resilient personality. Ingrid was Coaldon's academic teacher and advisor. She taught him to read and write in the common language, low elf and high elf. The common language was the speech used for every day communications within the Empire. Low and high elf were the languages of academic discourse used by scholars. Coaldon was required to be a star student and scholar. With the guidance of his grandparents, he became an adult in mind, body and spirit.

Coaldon's grandparents permitted him time to explore the wilderness. This freedom allowed him to grow in understanding of nature and himself. The isolation in the Outlast gave him the opportunity to talk with the animals and discover hidden secrets of nature. He loved the simple songs of the cugger birds, the quiet voice of the blue fox and the cries of the war eagles. He did not remember when he first talked with the wild animals of the forest. It was something that came natural to him. Each animal had its own special language. Coaldon possessed the ability to understand each of their unique voices. The energy force flowing from each animal was the medium of communication. The animals would share with him the events of their lives and the trials of surviving in a dangerous world. Coaldon was never lonely while walking in the distant mountains. His friends never failed to greet him with their songs, chirps, howls, roars and barks.

His hikes took him countless miles into the wilderness. The Outlast was crisscrossed with many animal trails and ancient roads. He found it fascinating that the abandoned roads could only have been made by people. Over time many of the old roads had been washed away through the erosion of water and wind. Once Coaldon tried to follow a road to its end, but only found an endless road stretching out before him.

At a young age Coaldon met the wandering folks. The wandering folks would walk and talk with him. He thought it was normal for all people to visit with these folks. The wood elves, dwarves and stone walkers would go out of their way to find him.

Wood elves were short, excitable, fun loving and shy. They enjoyed spending their nights dancing, singing and telling tales. Coaldon formed a unique attachment with elves because of his elfish nature. He viewed wood elves as long lost cousins, his extended family. Coaldon always had the feeling the elves knew more about him than he knew about himself.

Coaldon normally did not meet many dwarves on his walks. Dwarves usually traveled in groups of four or five with little time for idle conversation. They approached each event in life with serious intentions. Their short, stocky and muscular bodies were meant for hard work, not play. Their words spoke of wealth and the majestic caves hidden in bowels of the earth. The daylight world was of little interest to the dwarves. Only in times of grave danger would they join forces with the daylight people. During a recent visit, dwarves told him about an old man wandering in the Outlast. This was unusual because dwarves shared little about their activities.

Stone walkers were large folks that could only be detected in the shadows of the mountain. The constant struggle to survive in the harsh mountain environment prematurely aged their large strong bodies. The stone walkers were several heads taller than Coaldon. Their gentle faces radiated the peace of ancient wisdom. They wore leather clothing with boots made of heavy vine fiber. They walked with long strides that flowed like a quiet stream. They raised their families in the shelter of hidden places forgotten by time. Their gentle nature forced them to hide from incursion of people. Yet, when aroused they could be warriors of unchallenged skill and conquest. Coaldon found comfort when their calm voices told tales about ancient history.

During the summer the wandering folks would gather together to tell stories about the marvels of the past. Coaldon would sit under large trees for hours listening to their tales. Their words filled his mind with mystery and awe. He would often fall under the enchantment of their voices. He enjoyed creating visions of himself assuming the role of a great warrior or king. The difference between reality and fantasy often clouded his mind. The boy's thoughts would often be filled with images of evil wizards, grand palaces, noble kings and righteous wars.

The wandering folks did not like to talk about the future. The world of the past danced in their minds with images of greatness. Oddly enough, tomorrow was to be avoided. The present moment was the time to find peace and satisfaction. The wisdom of the ages was reflected in their quiet lives.

Life for Coaldon was not always bound by the isolation of the farm. Several times a year it was necessary to visit the Village of Grandy to sell produce and purchase supplies. The people of Grandy did not openly accept Coaldon because he was half elf. The villagers, except for two youths his own age, treated him with cold indifference. On his visits to the village, Raff and Paggy would meet with him in the woods south of the village. Raff, a tall 17 year-old boy, was a blacksmith's apprentice. Paggy, an attractive 18 year-old girl, dreamed of being a great singer. The villagers always looked forward to hearing her beautiful voice sing the ancient ballads. Coaldon always looked forward to having long talks with his wilderness friends.

The villagers would not journey into the Outlast. They heard rumors that the wilderness abounded with great danger and foul spirits. Brad and Ingrid's arrival in the community many years ago was still a major topic of discussion. The residents believed Coaldon's grandparents survived in the Outlast by using magic. It was finally decided that the newcomers were hiding from a great crime they had committed.

In order to help Coaldon understand the communities' negative response to him, his grandparents explained a unique character of human nature. They explained that the villagers were not comfortable with anything out the ordinary. Coaldon soon realized the community was not concerned about him, but rather wanted to protect themselves from the outside world. Coaldon was able to accept the villagers' rejections with little discomfort. By nature he was self-confident. His grandparents had taught him to make good decisions and stand up for himself.

Coaldon would be 18 years old in four days. He was becoming a young man with an increasing desire to face his own destiny. He was starting to feel a growing restlessness to be his own person. The outside world seemed to be calling to him. What was out there? He loved the farm, yet he had the need to reach beyond the farm. He was waiting for the day when the door to his future would be opened. He often wondered what would happen if something disrupted his peaceful life on the farm. Where would he go? How would he survive? Grandma Ingrid would respond to Coaldon's drive for independence by saying, "There will be many days in the future when you will pray to be back on the farm."

The Black Mist

Grandma Ingrid announced breakfast was ready. Coaldon had to force himself to leave his warm, comfortable bed. He slowly pulled on his leather pants and cotton shirt as he staggered to the kitchen. When he walked into the dining area, he felt a tension in the air. He paused to look around the kitchen. Nothing seemed out of the ordinary. He hurried to his place at the table and began to load his plate with tasty food. His grandparents joined him at the table.

Grandfather Brad said, "Coaldon, we have decided to take our produce to market. After breakfast please mend the fence in the North Pasture. Your grandmother and I will get ready for the trip to Grandy."

He and his grandparents visited Grandy to get supplies and sell produce. Coaldon was excited about the trip. He wanted to escape from the farm routine. He was ready for something different.

He finished his breakfast, helped with the dishes and pulled on his boots. Sid knew something was happening. With excited barks, he ran in circles. Coaldon's interest was on going to the village, not chasing stubborn cows. He walked into the meadow with Sid at his side. Coaldon sent Sid to his right to help push the fat cows back into the pasture. The cattle were happy with the plentiful grass in their new paradise. They did not want to cooperate. With tails in the air they rushed past Sid and Coaldon. In frustration, the young man waded back through the tall grass to head the cattle back toward the field.

When the cattle were finally turned, he once again tried to drive them toward the pasture. Coaldon learned from his grandfather to work cattle in a slow and easy manner. It was best not to push cattle too hard because of the added stress placed on them. This strategy did not work today because the cattle were not interested in leaving the bounty of grass. He laughed at himself for allowing the cattle to run the farm. At this point Coaldon decided to release the ultimate weapon, Sid the Marvelous Cow Mover. He gave the command to Sid with the motion of his hand.

Sid rushed toward the cattle with deep growls and snapping teeth. The cows knew their game was over. It was either go back into the pasture or feel the bite of Sid's sharp teeth. The cattle rushed back through the hole in the fence with the look of defiance. Coaldon followed the belligerent cows into the pasture and rewarded Sid with a pat on the head.

After mending the fence he returned to the barn to complete his morning chores. By midmorning he had packed his travel bag and the gemstones he would sell to merchants in Grandy. He had been collecting the gemstones for months from the local stream beds. These would give him spending money while in the village.

With the skill of a seasoned veteran, he hitched the two horses to the wagon. The family departed the farm late morning for the two-day journey to the Village. The wagon was loaded with Grandma Ingrid's hand made articles, sacks of grain and vegetable products. The two horses had to work extra hard to pull this heavy load.

The journey to town required traveling over rough roads along the banks of the Rolling River. Coaldon and his grandparents walked by the wagon in order to reduce its weight. A constant stream of conversation helped the trip go faster. They mostly talked about the unique characteristic of the surrounding area and wild life. Coaldon was especially interested in the different animals they observed. He pointed out a fox hunting in a thicket and a rabbit hiding in a log. At the end of the first day, they camped in a small meadow next to the river. Coaldon always enjoyed camping in open spaces and sitting in front of a campfire. At night he would lie on his back watching the stars. The starlight filled him with a pleasant sense of meaning and purpose. The stars made him feel close to unknown people, places and events.

After a long day on the road, Coaldon quickly fell into a comfortable sleep. This peaceful slumber was interrupted when an unsettling permeation touched his spirit. The night seemed like all other nights, yet a mysterious haze clouded his mind. As Coaldon drifted into an unnatural dream, he struggled to escape from the grip of the unwelcome trespasser. Dark shadows flowed out of a murky fog, filling his being with panic. Coaldon choked in horror as he experienced the violence of war. He saw many warriors fall in death before the hand of an unseen foe. Fear gripped him with oppressive dominance. He gagged in disgust at the foul smell of evil. His arms and legs desperately thrashed to escape from the hand of corruption.

The dream suddenly changed from the chaos of war into the picture of a tranquil forest meadow. A whisper flowed across the soft grass of the meadow surrounding Coaldon with a hint of words. This delicate murmur formed into a voice. The enticing words invited him to make a choice. It became a choice between following the quiet life of a farmer or facing the dangers of a noble quest. His youthful nature was attracted to the images of a grand adventure.

Coaldon was jolted back to reality when he felt the touch of his grandfather's hand. As he awoke, he felt sweat running down his face and his fists clenched. He looked around to see if any of his vision had come true. With relief, the face of his grandfather appeared before him, outlined by the rays of the early morning sun.

His grandfather said, "I heard you yelling and thrashing in your sleep. Is everything alright?"

Coaldon tried to talk, but he had difficulty in forming his thoughts into words. The ugly images of war and violence kept emerging in his mind. Coaldon was finally able to push aside the unpleasant images. He shared the account with his grandparents with the same intensity as he had experienced it. Telling the story reawakened the emotions of fear and anxiety. As he finished his story a strange thing happened, his grandparents looked at each other with sad expressions on their faces. Tears appeared in his grandmother's eyes. His grandfather lowered his head in despair. Coaldon could not figure out why a bad dream would cause his grandparents to respond with such strong emotions.

Coaldon questioned, "Why are you so upset? I only had a bad dream."

Grandpa Brad reacted, "We found your dream very powerful. Everything is just fine. I guess we had better get on the road."

Coaldon accepted this answer with obvious skepticism. He thought to himself, "I wonder if this has something to do with my birthday? I guess I will need to wait and see."

The travelers were greeted by a bright, sunny day. A breeze blew out of the west as the wagon lumbered down the road. As they drew closer to the town, the number of farms increased. Whiffs of smoke rose from the chimneys of small cottages surrounded by farmland. Each farm had a barn that was used to store hay and grain. These supplies would feed the livestock during the winter. The multicolored laundry waving in the breeze was a sure sign of civilization. Men, women and children were busy loading wagons with hay, grain and vegetables. Coaldon laughed when he noticed three children sneaking off to play on the banks of the river. Grandpa Brad stopped to talk with several farmers to gather local news. They learned the harvest was good in spite of a late spring. Also, the community was preparing for the annual Feast of Thanksgiving that would be held in several weeks.

The Village of Grandy, with a population of about 250 people, was located on the banks of Rolling River. A ferryboat crossed Rolling River on the north end of the town. The streets were narrow paths that joined the village into a web of commerce. The stores were made of unpainted rough cut lumber. Several large windows on either side of the door advertised the stores commodities. Large wooden shingles covered the roof of each building. Boardwalks connected the stores on each side of the streets to allow passage during the muddy seasons. According to the complaints of the local residence, the streets were either too dusty or too muddy. Large oak trees

spread their branches over the majority of the village. The trees provided shade in the summer and wood for winter heat.

Coaldon and his grandparents arrived in the Village during late afternoon. The wagon was left in front of the Log Inn and the horses were led to the local blacksmith shop for a well-deserved rest. Grandpa Brad tied a tarp over the top of the wagonload to protect the produce from the cold night temperatures. Mr. Baggy, the innkeeper, greeted the travelers with enthusiasm. He placed them in rooms on the second floor with a good view of the river. The rooms were furnished with several chairs, a table and a large wood framed bed.

After Coaldon had settled into his room, he went for a walk around the town. He sold the gemstones and bought two shirts, candy and work boots. He found the village to be the same each time he visited. The same people walked down the same street, lived in the same houses, shopped in the same stores and lived the same lifestyle. Change was not an acceptable part of village life. Whenever Coaldon arrived, he was always uncomfortable at being around so many people. Even though the village was small, it seemed large to Coaldon. His extreme isolation on the farm did not prepare him to live in a community atmosphere. Walking through the village helped him to adjust to people and the social environment. By dinner time, he was ready to face the crowds.

Dinner was served on a long table in the dining area. The robust atmosphere of the Inn added a measure of excitement to the dining experience. Businessmen from all over the Empire visited Grandy. The local farmers and craftsmen were famous for producing fine wines and quality leather products.

The dinner came with an extra helping of meat, greens, baked sweet roots, bread and gravy. Coaldon liked his grandmother's cooking, but he enjoyed the wide variety of new favors. After dinner Coaldon and his grandparents joined the local citizens in front of the large fireplace. The villagers talked about farming, kids, local events and the coming winter.

Mr. Baggy shared recent news about the Empire, "Emperor Wastelow sent out a decree to all loyal citizens to be on the outlook for rebels." With the flair of authority he stated, "Royal soldiers will be dispatched to all parts of the Empire to search for enemies. Crossmore the Wizard has learned that rebels are trying to overthrow the Empire. The decree states that these enemies must be destroyed."

Coaldon had a growing feeling that people were watching him.

Mr. Baggy continued, "Soldiers will arrive in several days to protect the village."

Coaldon and his grandparents retired early because the next day would be busy. The boy lay awake for several hours thinking about his future. He knew he could not stay on the farm all his life. The farm was a good place to live, but he wanted something else. He drifted to sleep thinking about the birthday party his grandparents were planning for him. Coaldon was awakened in the middle of the night by Sid growling at the door. He turned over in bed with no sense of urgency. He always felt safe while staying at the Inn.

A suddenly sense of panic drew his attention to Sid's behavior. Slowly he rolled out of bed and moved toward the door. He heard a throbbing sound in the hallway. A grip of fear clutched his body causing him to stand in confused silence. Coaldon decided it was necessary to do something. With uncertainty he turned to the table, grabbed his knife and approached the door with vigilance. With a swift motion, he jerked the door open and stood in the ready position to defend against any hostile action. To his surprise, a black mist was outlined by the light from oil lanterns in the hallway. Coaldon's heart raced as he watched the mist drift toward him. He felt it trying to reach into his mind. Coaldon backed into the room with his knife ready to attack. Yet, what was he to attack?

An intense feeling of fear gripped him when the black mist touched him. Coaldon experienced the vision of a hand reaching for him. On its palm he saw the symbol of a circle with a cross in the center. When the hand grabbed him, a flash of panic rolled through Coaldon's body. He realized the reaching-hand caused him to feel terror. In stubborn defiance, he was determined to not allow fear to control his life. He raised his knife and brought it down slicing into the black mist. At that moment an agonizing scream penetrated every fiber of the Inn. The black mist exploded into a blood red shower of wavering sparks. The sparks glowed briefly before floating to the floor as fine dust. Coaldon's knife glowed with a red tint. Shouts rang through the halls of the Inn. People rushed out of their rooms with looks of panic on their faces. Coaldon quickly shut the door. He hoped no one saw him. People ran up and down the hallway looking for the source of the disturbance. After a long time, Mr. Baggy suggested that everybody go back to bed. He told them he would investigate in the morning.

Alone in the room, Coaldon collapsed to the floor. His mind saw the reaching-hand clenched in anger. The power of fear and anger tore at the core of his mind. Without thinking Coaldon raised his knife in a gesture of defiance. The vision slowly faded into a black void.

As he opened his eyes, he heard a knock at the door. Sid's head was lying on his chest. As Coaldon pushed himself to his feet, he dropped the knife onto the floor. His knife hand burned with throbbing pain. Sid watched Coaldon with the look of curiosity. Again, Coaldon heard a soft knocking at the door, which cleared his thoughts. He opened the door to find his grandparents. They saw in Coaldon's face a look of distress and anguish. Upon entering the room they noticed the knife lying on the floor. His grandfather picked up the knife with a cloth, placing it in his pocket. His grandmother carefully examined Coaldon's hand. She left the room and returned with a small bottle of ointment. As she rubbed the salve onto Coaldon's hand, the pain began to ease.

Coaldon told his grandparents about the black mist, the reaching hand and the feel of fear. His grandfather listened with troubled thoughts. He finally said, "The time has finally arrived. Your recent dream plus this attack is not just a coincidence. We have been very lucky over all the years. I believe this is the beginning of the Age of Change. They know you will be 18 years old in several days and will be looking for you with increased intensity. Please do not ask us any questions because the truth can only be revealed to you at the appointed time."

The gentle voice of Ingrid injected, "Now, go to sleep; you will not be bothered again tonight. Tomorrow we will return to Lost Valley after we sell the produce. Do not say anything about what happened. We must hurry home. We have a birthday to celebrate. Good night, may the One Presence bless you."

Coaldon did not sleep for the rest of the night. The throb in his hand was accompanied by the burning memory of the black mist. He was still disoriented when the village roosters awoke the community to a new day. His mind kept reviewing the events of the night in vivid detail. On the way to breakfast, his grandfather reminded him to act as if nothing had happened. Following this recommendation, Coaldon ate his breakfast with a relaxed air of indifference, yet inside his body he was anything but casual. Mr. Baggy hurried around the tables with a look of frustration. The guests had been accusing him of not offering safe lodging. He repeated over and over, "Somebody must have had a nightmare."

After breakfast Ingrid and Brad began to sell the produce stored in the wagon. They had the reputation of selling good products at a reasonable price. They were happy when everything sold by noon. As Brad prepared the wagon and team to depart, Grandma Ingrid purchased the winter supply of dry goods.

During the morning Coaldon had free time, so he located Raff and Paggy at the dry goods store. They decided to meet at the old boathouse on the river. Raff and Paggy were especially quiet during the visit. Paggy finally said, "Several weeks ago representatives of the Emperor visited the village. These strangers asked many questions about any half elves living in the area. We were so embarrassed when the villager told the strangers about you and your grandparents."

Coaldon said, "Why would anybody be interested in my grandparents or me? We have nothing to hide."

Raff responded, "In the future, if we can help you, please let us know." Coaldon was pleased to learn about the loyalty of his friends. Yet, he had no idea how his friends could help him. They departed with hugs and the promise to meet again in the spring.

The trip back to Lost Valley was somber and restrained. Coaldon's grandparents were not willing to answer any of his questions concerning the events in Grandy. He had a growing sense of irritability over the shroud of secrecy covering his life.

The family arrived at Lost Valley on Coaldon's birthday. He reflected, "Today does not seem like my birthday." The boy's mind was in a downcast mood as the family arrived at the wilderness farm.

After unloading the supplies, Coaldon decided to go for a walk. He could not understand what was happening to him. As he entered the forest, he was surprised to find a wood elf waiting for him. It was unusual for elves to be this close to the cabin. This elf had an air of authority and mission.

He stated, "My name is Moonglow. Your time has come. You are now ready to take the rope. You are to tie the rope around your waist and allow it to lead you into your destiny. Please follow me."

Coaldon started to argue but decided to play along with the request. After a short walk the elf led the way into a cave hidden in the face of a cliff. The cave was lit by a large, beautiful fire. The fire burned with the glow of many colors and shapes. A strange and magical music pulsed in the cave with an ever-changing rhythm. With beauty and grace the wood elves slowly danced around the fire. Coaldon could see that the elves' eyes gazed far beyond the cave into distant realms. The dance and music created a mystifying sense of contentment and peace. Coaldon sat next to Moonglow as the wood elves continued to dance to an ancient rhythm. The cadence and movement of their bodies seemed to flow out of harmony with life.

He looked around the cave but could not find the source of the music.

Later in the afternoon each elf approached Coaldon with dignity and placed his right hand on Coaldon's left knee. In solemn voice each person declared, "I offer to you my loyalty as a citizen of the Empire." Coaldon viewed this event with a touch of humor. He could not image why they were offering loyalty to him. He was a simple farmer.

Coaldon watched these events through a fog of drowsiness. The elves' voices began to echo softly as if coming from a great distance. The songs of ancient lore faded into silence as his eyes drooped into a peaceful sleep.

He was awakened by Sid licking his face. He was lying next to the river in a sunny rock shelter. He laughed at himself for having such an odd dream. He speculated that he must have been more tired than he realized. As he walked back to the cabin, he felt his strength and attitude renewed. It was best to forget about all the unusual events of the past few days. It was time to celebrate his 18th birthday.

The Visitors

Coaldon entered the cabin with the intention of sharing the strange dream with his grandmother. To his surprise three strangers were sitting at the table with his grandfather. They stood in respect when he entered the room. His grandfather broke the silence by introducing the guests. Standing on his right was a tall, muscular and energetic man. He had been weathered by many miles of outdoor living. His dark face had brown penetrating eyes. He wore leather pants and a green cotton shirt. His boots were made of soft deer hide. His grandfather said, "This is Pacer, a wilderness scout and a very old friend. He has been wandering the Northern Empire for many years keeping an eye on daily events."

A short, stocky dwarf with long gray hair stood on his left. His deep-set eyes radiated intelligence and curiosity. He wore bulky cotton clothes and large leather boots. The heavy lines on his grumpy face indicated countless years of hard work. The wisdom of years added to his quiet posture. He gave Coaldon a stiff formal bow. Grandpa Brad said, "I introduce Earthkin, a dwarf of the family Cavemore. He is known for his ability to out-walk, out-lift, out-work, out-think and out-wit anybody I know. The events of the empire have forced him to seek council with me."

After a short pause he continued, "Last, I am proud to introduce Starhood, grand advisor to the Elfdom of Talltree. He has journeyed a long distance to meet with us." Coaldon had never seen or met a regal elf. Starhood was a tall, slender and dignified elf with long, black shiny hair and large, water pool eyes. The light of the fireplace shimmered in his hair like a flowing rainbow. His brightly colored clothes matched the sparkling radiance of his character. His yellow pants blended into his forest green shirt. Coaldon was attracted to Starhood's caring eyes. Coaldon felt a warm glow touch the center of his mind as he looked into Starhood's face. In some magical way, part of himself was found in Starhood.

At this point Grandma Ingrid started to load the table with a feast of food. The variety of meats, vegetables, breads and sweet drinks were eyed with great anticipation.

After everyone had gathered around the table, Grandfather Brad said, "Let us give thanks for this food and ask a blessing upon each of our lives. May our journey in life be in harmony with the One Presence. Amen." The room resounded in a long silence as a large quantity of food was respectfully consumed. After eating trail food for many days, the three visitors were hungry for home cooking. Grandma Ingrid was delighted to watch the food disappear with a loud chorus of satisfied praises.

After dinner their conversation centered about events in the Empire. Grandpa Brad was particularly interested in learning about the growing unrest in Neverly. Pacer said, "The increase in taxes by the Emperor is causing great hardship for the citizens all over the Empire. The tax money is being used to build a large army. Emperor Wastelow has not been seen for months. It is rumored he has fallen under a cloud of melancholy. The people on the streets of Neverly speculate Crossmore has been using magic to heal the emperor."

Starhood added, "Wizard Crossmore has assumed many of the emperor's social duties and decision making responsibilities. Crossmore might have the grand design of being emperor."

Grandma Ingrid brought in a large cake with 18 burning candles. A robust round of congratulations sounded as Coaldon blew out the candles with one healthy blast of air. At this point, Grandpa Brad stood and walked to the large, mysterious elfin trunk that had always been kept locked. He said several words under his breath and touched the elf runes on the lid. A flash of light lit the room as the trunk opened. Coaldon had never seen the inside of this trunk. His grandfather slowly pulled out a sword and scabbard with the reverence given to sacred objects. He walked over to Coaldon and placed the sword into Coaldon's hands saying, "This was your father's sword. It was made by the elves during the First Quarter Age in the forgotten Land of Westmore. Its name is the Blade of Conquest. It is endowed with the magic of Blessed Acts. If you use it for good and noble purpose, it will protect you from the power of evil. God bless you, my grandson."

Coaldon sat in absolute disbelief. As he held the sword, he felt energy pulsing within the blade. He noticed that the blade had a gray metallic color, a responsive feel and a slight vibration. He was unable to say anything because of the choke of emotions. As his hands slowly glided over the surface of the blade he experienced a strange event. He felt a stab of energy shoot into his body from the sword. The sword reached out to him. When Coaldon unconsciously returned the gesture, he heard the voice of the blade speak to him in mysterious bonds of oneness.

With natural dignity, Starhood withdrew a knife from his travel bag and placed it in Coaldon's hand proclaiming, "This knife will help protect you on your journey in life. Its name is Strong Edge. If you allow the power of the knife to assist you, it will bind you to the will of the One Voice. It will touch my heart if you reach to find my presence. May your quest be blessed by the One Source." Coaldon touched the knife with respect and awe.

Finally, Pacer and Earthkin stood and walked over to Coaldon. Pacer took a small package from his vest pocket. He said, "On this day of entering into your inheritance take the Gem of Watching as our gift to you. It will protect you in the face of danger. In times of doubt, look into its depths to find assistance. May the One Presence bless you." As Coaldon looked into the gem, a gentle blue light filled the room. The light penetrated deep into Coaldon's mind. A warm glow of peace filled the young man with hope and confidence. Earthkin commented, "The gem has claimed you as its own."

Coaldon was mesmerized beyond comprehension. His mind was struggling to maintain a sense of reality in the face of these unusual events. He said out loud, "I must be dreaming. I know I will wake up and find everything as it was yesterday."

At this comment the room was filled with laughter.

As Coaldon focused on his gifts, his grandfather rearranged the chairs in the room. Next to the elf trunk he set two chairs side by side. Several steps to his left he placed three chairs in a row. Facing the five empty chairs he placed a single chair in the center of the room.

Grandpa Brad requested Ingrid and the guests to join him in the living area. The guests took their places in front of the three chairs. He then directed Coaldon to stand in front of the chair in the middle of the room. Brad declared in a dignified voice, "As Emperor, I call the Royal Court of the Empire of Rocknee in session." He stood in front of the large chair with Ingrid at his right. Pacer walking in front of Emperor Brad, bowed and opened the elfin trunk. He took out a royal purple cape in a ritualistic fashion. He turned to Earthkin, handing him the cloak. He then removed a gem studded crown and held it in a stately manner. Earthkin was first to approach the throne. He placed the cape on Brad's broad shoulders. Then Pacer positioned the crown on Emperor Brad's head. Pacer and Earthkin then stood next to Starhood, bowed to the Emperor and were seated.

Coaldon remained standing in the center of the room in a state of wonderment. He looked around the room. It was still just a simple farm house in the middle of the wilderness. His head spun in a haze of confusion. He whispered to himself, "Why are they playing children's games?"

His grandfather proclaimed, "It is my honor this day to hold the first session of the Emperor's court in many years. Seventeen years ago an evil event ripped the Empire from my hands. It left me with a dead son, a deceased daughter-in-law, a granddaughter enslaved to the evil court and a grandson to raise. I escaped to this isolated place to find protection and to prepare a prince for his royal duties. With joy, I stand before you to open an Age of Justice."

Emperor Brad sat down with the flair of a noble personage. Pacer then stood up and said, "Prince Coaldon of Rocknee stand before your Emperor." With stumbling steps Coaldon approached the throne, gave a short head nod and stood in an awkward silence.

Pacer continued, "We realize this may be overwhelming to you. We needed to protect you from being detected by Wastelow. Please roll up the sleeve on your right arm and raise your arm with your palm facing us."

Without hesitation Coaldon responded just as he was instructed. On Coaldon's forearm was a small birthmark in the shape of a horseshoe. Coaldon had been aware of the birthmark but never put significance to it. Pacer pointed to the birthmark with a grand gesture.

He said, "Coaldon, this mark confirms your claim to the Throne of Rocknee. Please be seated."

Coaldon moved in a timid and indecisive fashion. He sat down in the chair located in the center of the room. Looking at Emperor Brad, he said quietly to himself, "Who is this man I have lived with all these years?"

Emperor Brad then stood with commanding authority. Pacer walked to the elfin trunk and withdrew a long sword that was set with many jewels. He handed it to the Emperor. The sword gave off a flash of light when Emperor Brad touched it. Emperor Brad said, "Coaldon, heir to the Throne of Rocknee, please approach the throne and kneel."

In helplessly obedience he stood up. With unsteady, hesitant steps he walked forward and knelt down.

The Emperor continued, "By my authority as Emperor, I place this sword upon your head and shoulders to establish your rights. By the holy power invested in me, I declare you as rightful heir to the throne of the Holy Empire of Rocknee. I declare you as an apostle to the One Source. I appoint you as council to the Emperor. You will act with honor, protect the weak, lead with authority, speak with wisdom and bring justice to the wicked. Let these words be witnessed by these honorable citizens under the watchful eye of the One Presence and by the spirits of our noble ancestors. Coaldon, arise and assume your royal duties this very day. We will guide, protect, instruct and correct you in your journey. You are to help lead the Empire into a new Age of Justice. Coaldon, greet your new subjects."

Each person, except his grandfather and grandmother, approached him, bowed and returned to his seat. Emperor Brad announced, "The court is now in recess until the next call to action."

At this announcement a loud cheer was raised under the humble roof in this far off land. Starhood added, "It is a pleasure to witness this new day in the life of the Empire. Coaldon, you are to act with courage in the presence of danger. You will be required to face unknown perils. You will need to grow in wisdom and knowledge. Please allow us to assist you in your times of need."

Coaldon said very little for the rest of the evening. Sweet drinks were shared with a round of story telling. The guests and his grandparents showed common enthusiasm on this happy day. For the first time in sixteen years the three guests and Coaldon's grandparents were together. The pleasant glow from the fireplace added warmth to their discussion. Coaldon, in complete exhaustion, went to bed early. As he left the room, his grandfather said to him, "Tomorrow we will hold council. Be ready to listen, learn and take action. Good night."

The Council

Next morning Coaldon slept in late. When he awoke, his thoughts jumped between excitement and uneasiness. He was excited about being an adult and facing his first real adventure. Yet, he feared leaving home and rushing into the unknown future. When he walked into the kitchen, he saw the sword sitting next to his chair and the three guests talking in front of the fireplace. This day would be like no other day in his life. He sensed that his whole life had change forever. The peace of the past would be consumed by the turbulence of the future.

Lunch was made from the birthday leftovers. The three guests proclaimed, "Good food yesterday, but better today." After finishing their meal, Emperor Brad called the council meeting to order.

He stated, "The purpose of this Council is to chart the course of action needed to reclaim the throne and remove the stain of corruption. We have much work to do. Where do we start?"

Starhood followed, "First we need to understand our enemy. Coaldon, will you please tell us about the appearance of the black mist in the village."

Coaldon stated, "At first I was surprised to find the black mist floating in the hallway. My confusion delayed my response to its potential threat. I was hesitant to do anything because I did not detect any danger. It was not until the mist touched me that I realized I was in trouble. I felt dread grip my whole being. If I had not resisted, I would have lost control to its powers. I found it difficult to move. Without thinking, I sliced into the mist with my knife. As the knife cut into the mist, I felt it resist the blade. I remember hearing an agonizing scream. An instant surge of heat shot into my knife. I believe the blade absorbed most of the energy before it got to me. Then the vision of the hand clouded my mind. I felt an evil presence reaching into my mind. In defiance, I pushed the reaching-hand away. The hand became angry when I rejected it."

Starhood asked to see the knife Coaldon used to attack the mist. Emperor

Brad laid it on the table. With caution, Starhood picked up the blade and examined it in great detail. After several minutes he passed it to Pacer and Earthkin. Starhood stared into the flames of the fireplace for a long time. At first he showed no emotion. Then a dark shadow of agitation began to cover his face. Starhood became more somber and grave the longer he reflected on the black mist and knife. A twist of his lips indicated he was ready to speak.

Starhood finally said, "Coaldon carried a very special knife. This is an elf knife from the First Quarter Age. It was infused with the power to destroy the evil creatures created by Doomage the Wizard. It is interesting that the knife was able to destroy the black mist. We need to remember the black mist had been imprisoned in the Chamber of Oblivion by the Key of Ban. This can only mean a doorway into the Chamber of Oblivion has been opened. Who could have done such a wicked thing?"

Starhood continued, "The lore of elf history describes the black mist in detail. It is an ancient evil that does not have a mind of its own. It must have a master to direct its activities. The black mist is sent by the master to gain information and to inject fear into its victims. It can easily enter the mind of a person without being detected. If it is not stopped, it will read the mind of the victim and create a deep sense of uncontrollable panic."

In excitement the dwarf stated, "I am sorry for the interruption, but I just remembered something I must share with you. The lore of my people tells of an age when a calamity from the past would revisit the world. We are required, as children, to memorize the following verse. The knowledge of this verse will alert us to an impending catastrophe. It states, 'Be aware when the Door of the Oblivion is opened. The immerging power will strive to destroy the Hand on the Sword. It will fill the brave with fear, challenge the powerful to action and encourage the wise to find the Key. The Hand is to enter the Cave of Hope in the Land of Westmore. The One Sword will open the Gate of Conquest.'"

A silence followed as each person digested this new information.

Coaldon's curiosity was challenged by this revelation. He questioned, "What is the Key of Ban?"

Starhood lifted his hand to indicate his desire to speak. "The Key of Ban is a book that was forged by the power of ancient elves. It was written to control and conquer the evil that ruled the world during the First Quarter Age. The power of the Key of Ban is activated by the actions of a wizard. The elfin runes of the book were so powerful they were able to drive Doomage and his army into the Chambers of Oblivion. This imprisonment has been forgotten except as recorded in the ancient Book of Lore. The Key to Ban was hidden to protect generations from misusing its power."

Emperor Brad followed, "Does the appearance of the black mist indicate that the doors to the Chamber of Oblivion have been opened? Never in the recent history of the Northern Empire has a foul creature like this invaded the land. I have fought the vices of mankind, not the vileness created by Doomage. If the black mist is a creation of the First Quarter Age, then it will be necessary to find the Key of Ban."

Earthkin entered the conversation; "The existence of the black mist could indicate the Empire is being flooded with Doomage's wicked creatures. We would be foolish not to take the black mist seriously. The wickedness, once released, will grow as it feeds upon itself. As my grandfather would say, 'Fear begets fear'. We must find the Key of Ban."

Pacer injected. "We will need a wizard to assist us. Has anybody heard anything about Topple the Wizard? The last time I saw him, he was wandering with a group of wood elves in the Wilds of Rognor. He was just as absent minded as you remember. That was about six months ago. By now he could be anywhere."

Coaldon was uncertain if he should make any comments. He finally took courage saying, "Several weeks ago I heard about an old man roving in the forest in the Valley of Nexter with a group of wandering dwarves."

Earthkin could not contain himself, "What are you talking about? What wandering dwarves? I do not know anything about wandering dwarves?"

Coaldon responded, "For many years I have talked with the wandering folks. The dwarves, wood elves and stone people are always traveling in the Black Mountains."

Earthkin sat in disbelief. "I thought I knew all about the dwarves in this part of the world. What does this mean?"

A broad smile grew across Brad's face. He declared, "As we have surprised Coaldon the last few days, so he has likewise surprised us. Pacer, do you know the location of Nexter Valley?"

Pacer responded. "I believe Nexter is an ancient title. I do not know its modern name."

Coaldon injected, "It must be in the Black Mountains. The dwarves indicated that they would see him in several days."

Emperor Brad followed, "Several weeks ago I remember reading in the Book of Lore about the Valley of Nectin. I believe Nectin could be the current name for Nexter. It is located northwest of here. It will be necessary to go over the Pass of Doom to reach it. It would be a tough three-day journey to get there. I believe we have no choice but to send a party to look for Topple. I suggest Pacer, Earthkin and Coaldon make the trip."

With nods, both Pacer and Earthkin agreed with the plan.

Pacer questioned, "Coaldon, are you positive about the information about the man wandering with dwarves?"

With confidence Coaldon nodded in confirmation. He added, "The dwarves said something about this person needing guidance. It seems he is very forgetful and possesses a most unique sense of humor."

Emperor Brad laughed saying, "This sounds like our dear friend Topple. I never met a person with such trust in the destiny of his life."

After a short pause, he continued, "Since we need Topple, we had better go looking for him. He could be anywhere, but I believe we have a strong lead. I suggest the team leave early in the morning to look for our old friend. The weather could turn bad any day, so you should take extra provisions and warm clothes."

Emperor Brad had been waiting for months to get information about his granddaughter. "Pacer, will you please tell us about Princess Noel."

Coaldon was thinking about the journey over the Pass of Doom when Pacer started talking. He did not hear the name Princess Noel.

Pacer said, "Last year I visited Neverly to gain information about Noel. She is still being held in the palace. She can only leave it under guard. I was able to visit Noel's guardian in the market place. This was dangerous for both of us, but I needed to gain information. The nursemaid is your loyal subject. She declares her allegiance to Wastelow, but in reality she claims you as her Emperor. Over the years she has revealed to Noel her true identity. Noel is in good spirits and ready to escape. I believe Noel is in great danger. The nursemaid told me that Noel is a robust, strong willed and determined young lady."

Coaldon's mind finally joined in on the conversation. He questioned, "Who is Princess Noel?"

Pacer gave a loud laugh, "I guess we have not done a good job of informing our new prince of his family. Noel is your twin sister. Wastelow captured her as a small child. He has the intention of forcing her to marry his son."

Coaldon felt a warm glow radiate from himself. He had a sister, a real sister! A sense of meaning and purpose blossomed within the young prince. He would never allow his sister to marry anybody without her consent.

Emperor Brad stated, "We must rescue her from the foul intentions of Wastelow. After you return from Nectin Valley we must pay the City of Neverly a long awaited visit. Coaldon, I am sure your sister would like to meet you."

Starhood stated, "I need to visit the Library at the Monastery of Toms. I want to search through the ancient books to find the location of the Land of Westmore."

Queen Ingrid had been showing growing frustration during the meeting. She injected, "I believe it is no longer safe for us to live on the farm. I heard rumors in the village about Wastelow looking for a half elf."

Brad suggested, "The Monastery of Toms may be a good location. We could live in the village next to the Monastery. The Wastelands will provide a barrier to anybody wanting to capture us."

Brad and Ingrid decided to start packing for the journey. It would be necessary to travel light.

The Pass of Doom

Anxious for the day to begin, Coaldon peeked out from underneath his blankets. Excitement pulsed through his whole body. His active mind fermented with many questions. He thought, "It does not seem possible I am a real prince. I wonder what a prince does to keep busy? Oh well, I guess I will find out soon enough. It should be an easy trip to find a wizard. Very little excitement ever happens in the Outlast. I wonder what a wizard is like? Will he be tall, stately and wise? Or maybe he will be short, quiet and noble?"

Coaldon's thoughts were transformed into raw reality of life as the cabin became alive with activity. A cold fog greeted the travelers as they prepared for their journey. At first light of day, the group was ready to depart. Extra care was taken to check the supplies before leaving the cabin. Pacer took command of the planning with the expertise of a veteran explorer. Coaldon's grandmother was concerned about him going on this expedition. Letting go was not easy for her.

Coaldon looked at Sid with a sad expression. "You are to stay at the cabin while I am gone. You may be needed to protect the place." Sid lowered his head with the look of dejection. Coaldon gave the dog a big hug and a kiss on his wet nose.

After a short farewell, the three men walked into the dense fog. Coaldon led the way up a hidden game trail with confident strides. The trail was narrow, rocky and cluttered with debris. Fallen trees and underbrush blocked the way. Carrying heavy packs quickly raised a sweat despite the cold temperature.

Coaldon easily selected the best path from a variety of choices. His knowledge of the wilderness eliminated many hours of searching for the correct trails. The shroud of fog started to clear midmorning. As they walked, nature greeted them with a show of grandeur. The sunlight, shining through the morning mist, created a wonderland of beauty. The orange and yellow leaves of autumn drifted to the ground in elegant grace. The rays of the sun were refracted through the morning dew into millions of glittering points of flickering lights. The crunch of leaves under the traveler's feet brought back memories of carefree childhood days. The sound of the woodland animals surrounded the travelers with a chorus of celebration.

They took a short noon break in a small meadow along the river. The heavy frost of the past few days had turned the meadow grass to a golden brown. Coaldon noticed elves had been following them for the past few hours. He was delighted to see their beaming faces in the underbrush. It was his elfin sight that allowed him to detect his friends skipping through the dense forest. Coaldon decided it was important to gather information from them about the current events in the wilderness. He used the excuse of looking for gemstones to take a short walk into the underbrush.

As he entered the forest, several elves greeted him. Coaldon was happy to see their smiling, robust faces. Each moment of their lives seemed to dance with excitement. They only stopped laughing long enough to answer Coaldon's questions.

He learned Emperor Wastelow was planning to arrest Brad and Ingrid. The wood elves had news about strange events in the Outlast. They talked about the appearance of a black mist that was searching the country side. Shadows in the night had been seen in the wilderness. Mysterious footprints announced the presence of unknown creatures in the high country. Without warning the wood elves leaped to their feet, listened to the wind and rushed into the brush. This sudden action was typical of the elves' excitable nature. Coaldon sat for several moments reflecting on this new information. It seemed unforeseen problems were being added to their agenda.

Upon returning to the meadow, Coaldon shared this information with Pacer and Earthkin. This news seemed to confirm their suspicion that an evil power was being awakened in the Empire. They were confident in their ability to handle any problems they might encounter.

Coaldon set a rapid pace for the afternoon. No sign of any unusual activities was found along the path. The trail became more difficult to follow in the dense undergrowth. The sun was setting when Pacer found a campsite. A large tree with drooping branches provided protection from any unwanted visitors. Coaldon's feet were sore from the long walk. After a hot meal the travelers rolled into their sleeping blankets. The night was filled the harmonious sounds of nature.

The following afternoon brought the first major decision. The group took a short break to decide which route to follow. They could take a longer, easier route to the West or challenge the unknown dangers of the Pass of Doom. A major winter storm could close the mountain passes any day. With a display of enthusiasm the group decided to risk taking the north trail to the Pass of Doom. The trail was shorter, but much more dangerous and demanding. It was rumored that spirits of the dead roamed trails of the Pass. Most people only laughed at this folk tale, while others claimed the Pass was haunted by revengeful spirits. After a brief discussion it was decided to challenge the Pass of Doom. The importance of their mission out-weighed the potential risk.

They crossed Rolling River in a wide, shallow section below a series of rapids. The most direct route required using the old North Ridge Trail. The group followed the steep rocky trail along a cascading stream flowing out of Silver Glacier. Many times they lost the trail in the maze of rockslides and washouts. Near the top of a ridge, Earthkin slipped on a loose rock with near disastrous consequences. He slid down the steep mountainside for fifty strides before he stopped his fall by grabbing a small tree. As he struggled to his feet, Earthkin looked over the edge of a sheer cliff several strides below him.

The dwarf said in relief, "That was too close for comfort. I have never had this happen to me before. I wonder if a shadow of danger is following us?"

When they reached the top of the ridge the travelers took an extended rest. The trail continued into a narrow ravine below a towering peak.

Darkness came early with the shortened days of early winter. They selected a campsite below a rocky shelf on the west side of the ravine. Pacer was happy with the second days progress. A fire was started to help drive away the cold night air and prepare a hot meal.

During the evening Pacer and Earthkin told stories of their adventures in far off lands. Coaldon realized he was traveling with men of vast experience and wisdom. He was surprised when they asked him to lead the party. Maybe they wanted him to experience the role of being a leader. He knew Pacer would step in if things got tough.

Pacer took extra time to express his fondness for fire. He explained a campfire was known as the traveler's companion. It protected, warmed, guided, healed, dried, inspired, enchanted and cooked. Before going to sleep, they divided the night watch.

Coaldon awoke from a sound sleep by a now familiar sense of fear. He felt, rather than saw, the black mist. He pulled on his heavy coat as he walked over to Earthkin. The dwarf was focusing his full attention on the sounds of the night.

Coaldon stated, "I detected presence of evil."

The dwarf declared, "I do not feel any sense of danger. Everything is all right. You can rest assured I am in control."

Before Coaldon sat down, he added wood to the fire. The extra heat was welcome to his cold body. Then, without thinking, he jumped up, automatically pulled his sword from its scabbard and stood in a ready position. Several steps behind Earthkin, he saw the black mist illuminated by the campfire. To Coaldon's surprise, he heard himself command, "Stop, by order of the Blade of Conquest!"

The black mist remained motionless. Coaldon shouted, "Who is your master? Speak!"

A moan of grief sounded from the mist. It hissed, "I follow the commands of Crossmore."

Coaldon stepped toward the mist ordering, "Tell me why you are here?"

With hesitation it responded, "The master is searching for Topple."

Coaldon struck the black mist with a quick stroke of his sword. A scream of agony penetrated the silence of the narrow valley.

Earthkin sat dazed with his eyes focused on the ground. The dwarf slowly raised his head looking at Coaldon with an empty gaze. With a jolt of awareness, he dropped his head into his hands.

As he collected his thoughts, Earthkin realized he had been in great peril. In a weak voice he commented, "I felt something beginning to probe my mind with small pulses of energy. The encroachment into my thoughts was so subtle that I was only vaguely aware of its presence. It could have captured me if you had not intervened. My head is beginning to hurt. It must have left some type of poison or vile residue." Earthkin stood up and walked with slow, uncoordinated movements.

He gasped, "I have never experienced such evil!"

Coaldon said, "It was the black mist. It was searching your mind for knowledge. I suggest we get some sleep because we have a long hike tomorrow. It is best to discuss this subject in broad daylight. We can do nothing more tonight."

Coaldon quickly fell asleep, but his two companions spent a restless night. The unusual events of the night brought the stain of fear to these brave hearts.

The morning sun shone directly into their protected campsite awaking the three travelers. Pacer braved the chilly morning air to rekindle the campfire. A cloud of fog covered the bottom of the narrow ravine. Below them the top of a fog bank stretched out like a soft, velveteen blanket. The delicate song of a mountain blue bird drifted over the campsite. Two rock squirrels scampered over Coaldon's legs. They both stopped when Coaldon extended to them a warm greeting. They stood on their back legs and chattered a happy welcome. The shadow of a red hawk sent the squirrels running for safety. Coaldon returned to a pleasant sleep as Pacer and Earthkin prepared breakfast.

For a moment Coaldon forgot he was an 18-year-old half-elf on a mission. He was once again a boy and Grandma Ingrid was calling him to get him up. He remained snuggled deep into his sleeping blanket until Earthkin's touch abruptly brought him back to reality.

The party consumed the morning meal knowing a difficult task lay ahead of them. The topic of discussion around the fire was the visit by the black mist. Pacer and Earthkin recognized they needed to prepare to fight a new enemy. Coaldon and

the sword were becoming valuable members of the expedition. The group realized the relaxed atmosphere of yesterday had been turned into the serious events of today. This was no longer a casual walk in the woods.

Pacer decided to take the lead. His eyes never stopped scouting ahead in search of anything unusual. The rocky trail switched back and forth up the steep hillside in a snake-like pattern. They soon reached the elevation where only scrub trees and brush could survive. The bare rocky hillsides offered a stark contrast to the green forest of the valley.

After hiking all morning the travelers saw the Pass of Doom dominating the landscape directly ahead of them. They discovered it would be necessary to climb a majestic cliff in order to reach the Pass. Coaldon felt a sense of elation at the challenge lying before him. The tops of the nearby peaks were covered with a fresh blanket of snow. Black clouds on the western horizon meant a snowstorm was developing. Pacer decided they needed a short break before tackling the pass.

Pacer commented, "I feel something is watching us. For some reason, it does not want to reveal itself. We could wait until tomorrow before starting the climb."

Earthkin injected, "If we are going to be attacked, it would be better to move quickly. Whoever is watching us will be better organized tomorrow." Coaldon said nothing but did feel the presence of evil.

The slope leading to the face of the cliff was a pile of large broken boulders. The trail was a maze of different paths branching across the rock field. By choice and by chance, the party finally ended up at the base of the sheer wall. After carefully studying the cliff, they saw a trail cut into rock. The narrow, treacherous trail angled upward toward the summit of the Pass. Upon investigation they saw the chisel marks made by the workers.

It was apparent by the piles of undisturbed dirt the trail had not been recently used. Large rocks blocked the path in many places causing delays in their progress. It was necessary to climb around jagged boulders with extra care. A fall would mean certain death. The trail had broken away from the face of the cliff in several places. One collapsed section spanned a distance of fifteen strides. After examining the collapsed section, Pacer took the ends of two ropes and inched across the sheer cliff wall with ease. His fingers and toes seemed to hold to the cliff like a spider. After reaching the other side, he secured the two ropes to an outcropping of rocks. One rope was tied higher than the other. Following Pacer's example, Earthkin tied the rope on their side of the collapsed trail. Earthkin was first to step onto the bottom rope while holding onto the top line. He carefully moved his feet across the rope with surprising skill and balance. He easily reached the other side.

Coaldon had never confronted such a challenge in his life. He gritted his teeth with uncertainty as he stepped onto the loose rope. The tension in his body caused him to move across the rope in awkward jerks. Half way across the rope he lost his balance falling backwards over the cliff. His feet slipped off the bottom rope forcing him to hang on the top rope for dear life. Swinging wildly, Coaldon's body smashed into the cliff. In terror he looked down to see piles of jagged rocks far below him. His mind and body froze in the face of impending death. It took several moments before he was able to push away the paralyzing grip of terror. He looked up to see Pacer's large hands reaching down to him. Hand over hand Coaldon climbed across the rope until he was able to grab Pacer's hands. Coaldon felt the strength of Pacer's powerful body pulling him up. He celebrated with a loud shout when he was again safely on the trail. Coaldon glowed in satisfaction at his ability to successfully overcome the challenge of a perilous situation. This achievement helped him find renewed self-confidence.

They reached the snow line about half way up the cliff. Pacer pushed the party to move up the trail at a steady rate. Coaldon's legs were starting to burn with fatigue as he neared the top of the grade. Pacer wanted to be over the pass before dark. The trail opened onto a wide expanse of loose granite and shale. Pacer, who was in the lead, suddenly dived for the cover of a large bolder. Coaldon and Earthkin followed without question or noise.

As they watched, five large beasts walked onto the path towards them. These tall, muscular beasts had brown leathery like skin. Their round flat faces were adorned with several small, curved horns on their foreheads. Their large yellow eyes squinted in the bright sunlight. Coaldon remembered seeing pictures of these beasts in children's books. Pacer started to talk in a low voice. "These beasts are called trogs in the ancient Book of Lore. They are very dumb, but were once known to be great warriors. I think they are looking for us."

The five trogs continued to walk down the path towards their position. Pacer whispered, "When they are past us, we will attack. Try to wound their legs first." The trogs were talking in deep guttural voices as they walked passed the large rock.

Coaldon attacked the first trog with the flash of his sword. The trog fell to the ground with a deep cut on his leg. The roar of pain shocked Coaldon. He had never attacked anything with intent to wound or kill. As he stood dumbfounded, the second trog took a wide swing at him with a long black sword. Coaldon reacted with the swiftness that his grandfather had taught him. He fell to his knees as the trog sword whistled over his head. With precision, his sword cut deeply in the bowels of the beast. A wet smelly liquid sprayed into Coaldon's face.

With his eyes covered with the foul liquid, he rolled several times to his right. He jumped to his feet, wiping the fluid from his eyes. He had no time to recover before the wounded beast again attacked him. He blocked a wild swing of the trog with a quick upward flick of his sword. While the beast's arm was in an extended position, Coaldon made a quick downward stroke. The sword cut deep into the trog's left legs. The beast fell to the ground in a heap of rolling flesh.

Coaldon quickly backed away from the battle scene to clear his vision. As he watched, he saw Earthkin and Pacer put down the other three trogs. The roar and cries of the wounded slowly melted into the quiet agony of suffering. It was not something Coaldon enjoyed.

After grabbing their backpacks and with their swords in hand, they moved swiftly up the trail. They stopped when they reached the summit. A foul aroma led them to a campsite in a sheltered area near the top of the pass.

Earthkin said, "The trogs must have been guards. But who would want them to guard the pass?"

Pacer searched but found nothing of any value in the camp. He did find a piece of leather with the symbol of a cross inside a circle. A large amount of foul smelling food was cached in a nearby cave.

Pacer said, "It looked as if they were going to be here for a long time."

Before starting down the northern front of the pass, the travelers took the time to look over the vast terrain. In all directions they saw the world falling away into a distant haze. Coaldon tried to estimate the location of his home. He felt sad that the grandeur of nature could be corrupted by evil. Darkness was approaching as small flakes of snow started to fall.

Pacer stated, "We have no time to waste. We must be off this mountain before the snowstorm entraps us."

Earthkin took the lead without any discussion. They walked with long strides until it was totally dark. The snow was about one hand deep when they stopped for their first rest. Earthkin took out a short rope from his backpack. He told Coaldon and Pacer to tie the rope around their waists in order to keep everybody together. Earthkin, being a dwarf, could easily see in darkness. Their progress slowed as the snowstorm became more intense. Strong gusts of wind blew snow into their faces. After an hour the snowdrifts were about four hands deep. At one point, Coaldon lost his footing on the steep slope. As he slid down the trail, he ran into Pacer and Earthkin. The tangle of arms, legs, ropes and packs created a turmoil of confusion. The narrow trail did not allow much room to get started again. It was a challenge for the travelers to keep moving. Cold and exhaustion were starting to affect their minds and bodies.

Earthkin stopped in the shelter of a rock face.

He declared, "It is good to be out of the wind! Should we stop here for the night?"

Pacer declared, "If we stop we may never get out of here. This storm could create drifts forty hands deep."

Earthkin and Coaldon agreed to continue after a short rest. Coaldon never believed hiking could be so difficult. He kept going with the doubt of survival growing in his mind. Each progressive step became more difficult. He started to hear voices talk to him. Coaldon kept hearing somebody inviting him to close his eyes and take a long nap. He knew he should not sleep but had to keep pushing his way through each snowdrift.

Many times Coaldon's tired body wanted to sit down and rest. In order to change the focus of his thinking, he established a cadence of words. "I can keep going! I will make it! I must keep going!"

These words were repeated over and over as he staggered down the trail. He was so focused on his struggle to survive that he did not notice when it had stopped snowing. Looking down, he realized the snow was only several hands deep. The trail opened into a small clearing with a stream off to the left. Earthkin and Pacer untied the rope and explored the area. Everybody was happy when Earthkin found a cave hidden by brush. Earthkin's earth-powers helped detect an open space in the earth.

Finding Topple

Pacer estimated it was about 3:00 in the morning when the weary travelers stumbled into the cave. Pacer had been a traveler for most of his life. Yet, he had never faced such a dangerous snowstorm. If he had been a superstitious man, he would have sworn that some unnatural force was fighting against them.

They were pleasantly surprised to find a pile of wood in the cavern. It was as if somebody had anticipated their arrival. The cave was welcome after a most difficult day. It was not long before the heat from a fire was drying their wet clothes and warming their deeply chilled bodies. Coaldon noticed the ceiling had been blackened by many fires over the centuries. He speculated the cave was well known as a safe haven. It had not been recently used as indicated by the undisturbed cover of dust on the floor.

The cooking pot was soon steaming with a warm porridge. Little time was wasted in eating the simple feast. The consumption of the delicious food, combined with the warmth of the fire, created a pleasant glow on the faces of the three tired men. Coaldon was the first to fall into a deep comfortable sleep. Pacer and Earthkin talked for a short time in the quiet of their safe place. They were impressed with Coaldon's performance. Pacer commented, "Brad will be pleased with Coaldon's endurance and determination. Coaldon has been well prepared for the challenges that lay ahead of him."

Coaldon was awakened about midday by a hungry growl in his stomach. He turned over to find Pacer and Earthkin sitting next to a crackling fire. The dim light of the fire gave the cave a feeling of mystery. The light of the fire projected Pacer and Earthkin's shadows on the wall with strange and eerie shapes. Coaldon's youthful imagination saw the shape of a dragon sitting on a mountain top.

Pacer poured Coaldon a cup of hot honey tea. Coaldon smiled as the hot liquid warmed his body. Coaldon reached into his travel pack and pulled out a loaf of hard bread. He softened the bread by dipping it into the hot tea. After several bites he felt the fog in his mind start to clear. He noticed Pacer and Earthkin were alert and in good health. He looked at them with admiration. Coaldon knew they would be stout companions and good teachers. He admitted to himself, "I have much to learn."

Earthkin said to Coaldon, 'We have been reviewing the maps. We believe it is about a half-days march to the western end of Nectin Valley. It will be a steep trail leading down the face of a mountain. Pacer and I have been debating if we should try to make the valley floor today?'

After a pause Coaldon stated, "It might be better to leave tomorrow morning in case we run into trouble. Besides it will be easier to set up camp in daylight." Both men nodded in agreement with Coaldon's logic.

Pacer suggested, "It might be best for us to scout the area before traveling into the valley. It would not be nice if we were greeted by an unfriendly host. I will head down the ridge to check out the valley floor."

Earthkin volunteered to scout the local area. Coaldon volunteered to keep an eye on the camp. After the two men departed, Coaldon patrolled the area for a short time but was soon drawn to the warm fire and his sleeping blanket.

The two scouts returned to camp at sunset. Coaldon had added wood to the fire and cooked the evening meal. The warmth of the cave and the aroma of cooking food welcomed the two scouts. Coaldon put several pieces of jerky into the broth to create a travelers' delight. They ate in the silence of their own thoughts.

Earthkin had found no sign of anybody in the area. He did locate an old stone building above the stream. It had been used as a shelter in the past.

Pacer said, "I discovered human tracks in the mud near the top of the ridge. I estimate the tracks are about two weeks old. Next to the human tracks, I found large trog footprints. I believe this person had been followed by the trogs. We will need to approach the valley with great caution. I discovered a sheltered route along the north face of a ridge leading into the valley. We can decide what to do once we have a chance to look things over."

Pacer pulled out the strip of leather he found at the trog camp. He handed it to Earthkin for his evaluation. Earthkin then handed the leather to Coaldon. Coaldon turned it over and noticed the hazy outline of words written on the back. For several minutes, he studied the words from different angles. Finally, he slowly read out loud, "Crossmore will lead to great glory."

Pacer interjected, "That explains part of the mystery. Crossmore must be the source of this evil. Somehow he has discovered a way to open the gates of hell. An army of evil has invaded the world. We already knew Crossmore was hunting for Topple. I assume Crossmore wants to kill him before we find the Key of Ban. Topple must be warned."

The mission of the three men to find Topple took on new urgency. The travelers spent a quiet night in the limited comfort of the wilderness cave.

The party was ready to move out at first light. The sunshine of yesterday was replaced by dark storm clouds. Pacer led the group down a ravine to the right of the main trail. As they descended the mountain, they could see a glimpse of a meadow through the trees. Pacer's sharp eyes detected movement on the valley floor. The trek down the mountain was made more difficult by dense undergrowth. Fallen trees and thick brush made progress slow and tedious. Even with the challenges of the hike, Coaldon enjoyed the view from the mountain. It was exciting to visit new places and taste the robust flavor of danger.

The travelers dropped below the snow line by mid afternoon. Near the bottom of the mountain, the forest ended. It looked as if a fire had burned off the forest below them. This was both good and bad. The open area allowed a good view of the valley floor, but they could not continue down the mountain during daylight without being seen. They decided to hike the rest of the way into the valley after dark.

The travelers spent the afternoon watching the activities in the valley. Coaldon noticed several black war eagles flying low over the treetops near the West End of the valley. From their perch on the mountainside, the travelers could see the movement of trogs around a stone building. The building was located in a small meadow near the river. It had several uncovered windows on the eastside. Two trogs guarded the building front and back. They counted ten trogs coming and going. Later in the afternoon a horse drawn wagon arrived from the east end of the valley. The empty wagon was driven by several trogs.

Pacer stated, "They must be guarding some one in the building. I would speculate that it is Topple. The wagon is probably going to transport him to Neverly. Crossmore must have found an ancient road leading into this isolated valley."

Earthkin agreed with a nod of his large head. "We must move quickly. Security will be increased when news of the battle at Pass of Doom reaches the valley. Right now, the trogs look like a very relaxed group of tourists. We must act tonight."

It did not take long to formulate a simple plan of action. Pacer concluded, "Let me summarize our discussion. After dark, Coaldon and I will watch the area around the building. Earthkin will approach the building to find out who is inside. If Topple, we will rescue him. Are there any questions?"

Smiling, Coaldon said, "Yes, we have not talked about one small item. How do we escape?"

Pacer laughed, "You are most correct. How could we forget this minor issue?"

He then continued, "The Pass of Doom has been closed by the snowstorm. We can either go east or west. The map shows high mountains along the western Front Range. To the east we have the long, open valley leading to the Great Plains and Monastery of Toms. We need to remember Crossmore will move mountains to destroy us."

Pacer paused, "Coaldon, did you once tell me there was a mountain pass going from here into Lost Valley?"

Coaldon responded, "Yes, I guess I am the only person who knows the route. A river flows from North Ridge Pass into Nectin Valley."

Pacer suggested, "Once we free Topple, it will be necessary to protect him. I am concerned about getting him safely out of here. I believe trogs are stationed through out the valley. I think it will be best for you to escape over the North Ridge Pass. I propose that I become the fox. I will lead the trogs away from your escape."

Earthkin challenged, "By now the pass maybe blocked by snow. We could be trapped in the mountains with no way to escape. I suggest we escape down the valley to the Great Plains. I estimate it will take at least two days of hard travel to reach the mouth of the valley."

Coaldon stated, "I do not believe the pass will be closed. It's not as high as the Pass of Doom. Furthermore, the valley is probably crawling with trogs. I agree with Pacer. I believe that going over the Pass offers us the best chance of survival."

After additional discussion the group agreed with this conclusion.

While waiting for darkness, Coaldon tried to learn the animal calls used by Earthkin and Pacer to send messages. He spent an hour attempting to hoot, bark, howl and whistle with little success. Pacer smiled, remembering his first humble attempts to learn animal calls. Coaldon's practice session ended when he finally mastered the hoot of a large tree owl.

At dark they slowly moved down the mountain side. The building was about 100 strides from the base of the mountain. While Pacer and Coaldon took up positions near the building, Earthkin moved noiselessly to the east side of the structure. First, he observed the guards in front of the building. They were sitting in chairs eating a plate of foul smelling food. Their loud voices could be heard over the roar of the river. Earthkin eased up to the window with quiet steps. After several moments he slowly peeked inside. He saw a guard seated on the floor eating from a grimy plate. Next to him sat an old man with a broad smile. He wore a dirty, ragged robe decorated with the stains of many meals and dusty trails. His wrinkled face was weathered by a long life. His small, withered body had the look of impending death. The old man glanced around the room without a concern in the world. He saw Earthkin looking in the window but ignored him with an air of indifference. Earthkin observed the old man had the ability to find satisfaction with his immediate situation. His eyes were not on the future, but found peace in the present moment.

Earthkin slipped back into the brush to give the report to his companions. They talked quietly with no fear of being heard. The river provided the noise to cover their conversation. The attack would take place once the guards became drowsy.

Coaldon had a hard time waiting for Pacer to begin the attack. He wanted to do it now. Why should they wait?

As Coaldon's mind drifted in boredom, he saw three trogs entering the building from the west. A loud exchange of ill-tempered voices roared in disagreement. A scream then erupted from the building. Shortly afterwards, the body of a trog was thrown out the door. The body lay in the light shining through the door. At this point something odd happened. The body of the dead trog evaporated into a cloud of black smoke.

In a quiet voice Earthkin said to Coaldon, "Trogs are evil spirits given a physical body by magic. Once the body dies, the trog returns to its spirit form. The magical power required to create the body is then released as energy. The spirit becomes a whiff of emptiness never again able to take on a physical body. It is difficult to comprehend how this happens. Just accept it as a fact. Do not burden yourself with attempts to understand."

Pacer moved closer to the building to hear the content of the argument. He heard, "I am the leader of this pack! I will take my prisoner to face his reward! We will not wait for instructions from your miserable master! I have my orders! You will follow my commands! There will be no more arguments! We leave in the morning!"

The commander departed, leaving behind additional guards.

When the full moon appeared over the eastern horizon, Pacer led the small group to the rear of the building. As the attackers passed under the window, they heard Topple joking with the guards. He said, "Do you ever use the horns on your head to hang decorations. I think I would use them to clean my fingernails. You must be proud of them."

The trogs ignored him with distain.

Pacer made a noise to attract the attention of the two guards standing in front of the building. As the guards walked around the corner to investigate, Pacer and Earthkin attacked with such swiftness the trogs never had a chance to even make a sound. The three attackers then glided to the door and rushed into the building. Death for the trogs was swift and painless.

Topple sat in a state of indifference. He treated the entrance of the three men into the building as an everyday occurrence. Death did not seem to impact him. He looked at Pacer and Earthkin with a broad smile saying, "My Lords, it is good to see you. What has taken you so long? I heard you were coming days ago. You are getting slow in your old age. By the way who is this handsome, strong, young man? He has been careless in selecting his friends." Topple then laughed with mirth.

The Escape

Standing in the cold night air brought the group back to reality. Pacer said to Topple, "We have been looking for you. It looks like you have made some disagreeable friends. I am glad we found you before you were sent to Neverly. It is our responsibility to invite you to join us on an urgent mission. Emperor Brad needs your help."

Topple sat on the wooden bench in front of the old building. The wizard had a passive expression on his face. He finally said, "I am going to write a song about three scrawny birds who sat in a tree. These birds decided to search for a big beautiful worm. They flew and flew until they saw a small ugly worm playing in a meadow. The three birds had to make a decision. Should they keep looking for a big fat worm or accept an old, tired creature? Guess what? I am the old ugly worm!"

He glanced at Pacer, then Earthkin and lastly at Coaldon. He stood up and walked over to Coaldon with slow easy steps. As he looked at Coaldon, his eyes burned with intense curiosity. With a burst of energy, he shook Coaldon's hand with great enthusiasm.

Topple said to Coaldon, "You have the distinct odor of destiny. Your elfin sword sags awkwardly at your side, your pretty knife awaits a mature voice and the gemstone in your pocket reaches beyond the strands of understanding. I see a strong young man wearing a big hat."

Topple then giggled as he gazed into the night. His face radiated confidence and understanding. His eyes revealed the calm wisdom of the ancestors.

Topple said, "My friends, the trogs are going to be very unhappy with you in the morning. Yes, yes, yes! Should we wait to tell them goodbye, or look for a nice, safe place to take a nap?"

He then looked at the building saying, "Goodbye, it has been such great fun, but I must go now."

After listening to Topple's rambling conversation Pacer said, "Topple, we will need to travel hard and fast. The trogs will be after us in several hours. Can you walk all night?"

With a big smile Topple responded, "I would rather be carried like a baby."Coaldon thought it was humorous response, but Earthkin did not. He grabbed Topple by the arm and threw him over his shoulder. (It should be noted that Earthkin had no tolerance for Topple's easygoing and childlike behavior.) Topple gave a loud screech of protest as his arms and legs flopped in the air. Earthkin jogged down the road with Topple bouncing along like a sack of grain. Earthkin stopped after they entered the forest on the east end of the meadow. He then laid Topple on the ground.

Earthkin said, "We have a long way to go tonight. What is your choice?"

Topple giggled as he sat up, "May I please ride piggy back?"

Earthkin was in agreement with Topple's request. He knew that Topple would not be able to keep up the pace needed to stay ahead of the trogs. Earthkin gave his pack to Coaldon. Topple climbed on Earthkin's back with the satisfied look of a knight mounting his trusted horse. The old road was surprisingly easy to follow. It was amazingly well preserved despite many years of abandonment. The trogs cleared the road of fallen trees and rocks.

They walked many hours without encountering any trogs. During this time, Topple talked in a steady stream of rambling words. Earthkin was getting tired of the constant hum of Topple's voice in his right ear. Pacer finally decided it was time for a rest. A cold breeze blew in their faces as the travelers listened to peaceful sounds of the night. They were aware that this calm was only the lull before the storm.

Coaldon suddenly sensed a surge of rage pass through him. He felt as if many needles had been pushed into his body. Coaldon's sword vibrated with rapid pulses.

Topple said, "Oh my, it is mad. You should never make it angry! This is not good!"

Pacer and Earthkin did not feel anything. Pacer said, "What are you talking about?"

Coaldon responded, "I believe we have stirred up an evil power."

Pacer suggested, "Let's keep walking until we find the river flowing from the North Ridge Pass."

As they walked along, Topple began to sing in a loud, cheerful voice.

"We dance; we dance so late at night,
just like mice running in fright.
We dance; we dance to make things ready,
to find our hands not so steady.
We dance; we dance weak and frail,
not the wind for us to sail.

We dance; we dance against tide,
but only for us to run and hide.
We dance; we dance with a slide and glide,
but hopefully never to be fried."

Topple smiled with delight. He radiated a glow of satisfaction at the completion of such a masterpiece. He, in a teasing manner, asked, "Earthkin, isn't it ironic that you look like a mouse running in fright? May I ask, 'Where do you plan to hide'?"

After these irreverent words, Earthkin struggled to control his temper. His serious nature was running out of tolerance for Topple. He was a no-nonsense man. No jokes. No humor. People were to work hard, no goofing off. He wanted everything to be neat and orderly. Yet, down deep he knew Topple was telling the truth. Earthkin was uncomfortable with Topple's free and uninhibited behavior.

The group was happy to find a river flowing out of the south. They assumed it flowed off North Ridge Pass. Pacer stopped as lights appeared on the road ahead of them. He ordered, "Topple, please be quiet! I see lights ahead of us."

Pacer had his companions hide in the brush while he scouted ahead. After he returned, he stated, "It is a camp of about 20 trogs. It is now time for us to go our separate ways. You must go to the south and find North Ridge Pass. I will become the fox. I am asking each of you to give me a piece of your clothing. I will drag it on the ground to act as your scent. I suggest we meet at the Monastery of Toms in several weeks. Travel with courage and faith. May the One Presence be with you." After collecting the clothing, Pacer disappeared into the underbrush.

Earthkin led the way to the river and found a path going upstream. He reached into his pack and pulled out a tube of grease. He told Coaldon and Topple to spread the grease on the bottom of their shoes.

"This grease" he stated, "will cover your scent as you walk. Do not touch anything with your hands. If you do, your scent will remain. Coaldon, I want you to take the lead. Topple, you must start walking. Please do not wander off. We do not have the time to spend looking for you."

The trail wandered through the trees in a southerly direction. The noise of the river covered the sounds of their steps. They entered a ravine with steep walls on both sides. Several times Earthkin had to grab Topple before he roamed off into the trees. Topple muttered to himself most of the way up the mountain. Several times he found humor with some unknown event. His laughter irritated Earthkin and delighted Coaldon. Topple's trust in life was a refreshing experience for young Coaldon. As the three fugitives struggled up the steep trail, Topple's rambling voice was swallowed up by the vast space of the wilderness.

The night prevented them from being seen by unwanted eyes. Yet, the moon provided enough light to see the trail. After three hours of steady hiking they were high on the mountainside overlooking the valley. Torches could be seen moving out of the west. The trog alarm had been sounded.

The trail rejoined the cascading river at the base of a steep slope. The light of a new day was bringing life to the surrounding world. Like watchful parents, the mountains towered over them. The dense forest of the valley thinned to scattered clumps of trees on the high mountainsides. Nectar Valley was hidden under a blanket of fog. A snowstorm moved in from the north during the night leaving only a skiff of snow. Daylight meant the travelers needed to find a place to hide from searching eyes. It would be too dangerous to travel in broad daylight. Earthkin was surprised to find an old stone building. It was located near the river at the junction of two trails.

Coaldon questioned himself, "Why would somebody construct a building at this elevation? I wonder what these people did during their lives? Where did they live? Were they my ancestors?"

The building provided adequate shelter. The roof, made of hardwood beams and shingles, was supported by thick stone walls. Several small windows opened with a view of the trail and valley floor. This was enough protection to keep out the snow and the bite of a cold wind. They built a small fire and cooked the morning meal. Coaldon went to sleep without any hesitation. Earthkin took the first watch. Coaldon assumed guard duties in the afternoon.

Late in the day he felt a chill go through his body. An evil presence started to cloud his mind and will. A stabbing pain shot through his body as he struggled to maintain self-control. He saw, in his mind, a circle of fire burning without source. Out of the circle a hand reached toward him. He saw the circle and cross on the palm of the hand. Fear raged through Coaldon's mind. He could only move in slow motion.

A soft melodious voice spoke to Coaldon. "I am Crossmore the Great. I offer you power and wealth. Come to me. Let me touch you. You will be safe with me."

Coaldon reached deep inside himself to find the strength to resist the smothering invitation. He was slowly losing the will to fight. Coaldon pushed away the alluring command but to have it return with increased power. The intensity of the struggle increased with each new attack. Coaldon was concerned that he could not endure much longer.

In a weary voice Coaldon spoke, "Please help me." Without thought, his left hand reached into his shirt pocket grabbing the Gem of Watching. Holding the Gem he shouted, "Crossmore, I command you, be gone!" A brilliant flash erupted from the gem sending out a streak of burning light. Within his mind he saw the Hand of Crossmore wither in pain as the light struck it. The light erupted into a torch of flame around Crossmore's hand. The charred remains of the hand quickly withdrew into the circle of fire.

The soft inviting voice of Crossmore was transformed into an eruption of anger. In agony he screamed, "I will find you, my foul enemy! You will pay for this crime against me! Your soul will burn in the fire of my wrath! I will send my special friend to destroy you."

Coaldon awoke with a yell of anguish. His body trembled in a cold sweat. He tried to stand, but his legs would not hold him. He fell to the cold ground in pain. Earthkin rushed to his assistance. As Coaldon's mind cleared, he saw the faces of his two companions. Topple said with a laugh, "My, oh my! Not bad my friend; not bad at all! You have placed a burning fear into his mind. His charred hand will be a painful reminder of you. He did not expect his power to be challenged. What a surprise!"

Coaldon tried to raise his left arm, but with no success. The gem was held tightly in his clenched left hand. His left arm burned with a deep throbbing pain. Topple looked into his eyes with a radiant compassion. With gentleness he placed his hand on Coaldon's arm. After repeating several words, Topple released a surge of energy. A flow of warmth moved up Coaldon's arm. The healing rapidly spread throughout his body. The pain disappeared, but his whole body and mind were consumed by exhaustion. Coaldon collapsed into a restless and haunting sleep. His dreams were filled with the reaching-hand, the magnetism of Crossmore's voice and the fight to resist the attack.

When Coaldon awoke, the shades of darkness were spreading across the mountains. Coaldon was happy to discover the stiffness and pain in his left arm had decreased to a dull throb. After a hot meal he felt much better. He told Earthkin and Topple the story of the Crossmore's reaching-hand.

Earthkin shook his head in doubt and suspicion. He commented, "If I had not seen your wild eyes and crippled left arm, I would not believe your story."

Topple's big smile danced with the joy of a child. "I have waited many years to share this moment with you. This is like a birthday gift."

Coaldon said, "Who is Crossmore's special friend?"

Topple joked, "Do not dance too closely to him. He might put the squeeze on you. By the way, he is big, ugly and has bad breath."

Earthkin could not tolerate any more of Topple's good times. In a grouchy voice he ordered, "What do we do now?"

Coaldon responded, "Early this afternoon I studied the two trails. The one on the left does not feel good to me. So, I choose the one on the right. Topple, what is your opinion?"

Topple's twinkling eyes watched Coaldon with delight. He said, "One to the left, one to the right. Of course I choose the right one." He quietly laughed at the wittiness of his joke. Topple found great pleasure in the simple and common events of life.

With disgust, Earthkin walked from the building.

Climbing in darkness was not an easy task for anybody. The steep, narrow and rocky trail showed the decay of many winters. The depth of the snow increased as they gained elevation. Walking in the snow added a measure of uncertainty. Each step became a guessing game. Earthkin warned his companions about any unusual obstacles. Progress was slow but steady. At midnight they stood on top of a long ridge.

Coaldon said, "We have assumed this trail would lead us to North Ridge Pass. I am not certain of our location. I do not want to go any further until the moon arises. I do not want to waste time going in the wrong direction."

Coaldon sat in the cold night air admiring the stars. He was happy when the full moon appeared in the eastern sky. The moonlight revealed the surrounding area. Within minutes he recognized several familiar landmarks.

He said, "It should take us about six hours to arrive at the pass. There is a cave near the pass where we can rest."

Earthkin was eager to reach the pass before daybreak.

He said, "Topple, get on my back, we are going to cover ground. Coaldon, you lead the way."

The night passed in peace. By morning light they could see the pass on the horizon. Coaldon commented, "It will take us another hour to reach the top of the pass. I think it would be best to continue walking until we arrive."

It was a relief for everybody to walk in daylight. The steep trail leading to the pass ended on a wide flat plateau. The area was covered with a deep blanket of snow. Several high drifts rolled across the summit. A panoramic view of Lost Valley opened before them in majestic splendor. The bright sunlight and blue skies added to the beauty of the surroundings. This was an adequate reward for all of Coaldon's hard work.

Topple hurried around the area talking to himself in an excited voice. He mumbled about the time an old friend accompanied him over the pass. In sadness Topple stated, "My friend's body and spirit were separated by Doomage the Wizard. He now wanders lost to himself." This statement did not make sense to either Earthkin or Coaldon.

Coaldon located the cave in a secluded area next to a rock ledge. Brush and rocks hid it from common view. A fire quickly warmed the cave and heated the morning meal. Coaldon took the first watch. From this location he knew it would take six hours to reach the valley floor He was anxious to be back home.

ᚹᚢᚴᚺᛏ

PACER

Pacer waited in the brush until his companions disappeared into the forest. He cut a branch from a nearby tree to wipe away footprints. He walked toward the trog camp dragging the branch and his companion's clothing. He hoped the clothing would provide enough scent to lead the trog trackers on an enjoyable game of hide and seek. Most of the trogs in the camp slept while several guards casually visited. Pacer quietly slipped around the camp on an animal trail. He continued to drag the branch and clothes behind him. He followed the animal path for a half hour before returning to the road. He hid the branch, picked up the clothing and started jogging down the road. In the distance he heard the sound of angry voices echoing in the valley behind him. Yes, the chase had begun. He continued jogging for several hours. He knew the trogs would be forced to pursue him at a run.

He finally stopped to catch his breath. As the sounds of the night entertained his senses, he developed a plan. With the clothing dragging behind him, he walked down a brushy trail. When he reached a small creek, he jumped across, walked 10 strides and stopped. He then picked up the clothing and walked backward in his own footprints to the small stream. Stepping only on rocks, he carefully walked down the creek. Pacer did not want his footprints or muddy water to show where he had stepped. He followed the creek until it entered the river.

Daylight was growing in the eastern sky when he reached the river. Distant voices alerted him to a large number of trogs running down the road. He knew he had to find shelter or face certain capture. Without hesitating he waded into the icy water of the river. The rushing water battered his legs, making it difficult for him to keep his footing. With steady steps he finally set foot on the opposite shore.

His attention was drawn to a tall evergreen tree with heavy branches hanging on the ground. He crawled under the lower limbs. The ground under the tree was covered with deep mounds of pine needles. No one could see his campsite from any direction. After changing his wet clothes and eating a cold meal he quickly fell asleep.

During the day he awoke to the shouts in the surrounding area. He could hear many loud voices talking on both sides of the river. He assumed the trogs were searching the area for him. Towards evening Pacer was jarred awake by several loud voices. He saw two trogs standing next to the tree where he was hiding. They searched the surrounding area for any sign of his presence. For some reason the small beast kept looking at the tree. A violent argument erupted when the large trog pointed down the river. The small trog was not interested in the dictates of his companion. The smaller trog stared at the base of the tree with riveted eyes. His attention was drawn to it like a magnet. The creature sensed something was not right. The small trog stepped toward the tree with the intention of looking inside the branches. In a state of rage, the large trog pulled his sword from its scabbard. Without hesitation it decapitated the other trog with a quick stroke. The trog laughed with robust satisfaction as he watched the body disappear in a cloud of smoke. With grim determination etched on its face, the large trog disappeared down the river.

Pacer watched this scene with relief. He said to himself, "That was too close for comfort."

A meal of hard bread satisfied his need for food. He was now ready to complete his escape. He prayed his little diversion had pulled the search away from his companions. Pacer welcomed darkness as a friend into which he could hide from his pursuers. He crossed the river, found the road and started jogging. He needed to escape the canyon as quickly as possible. The longer he remained in the valley, the lower were his chances of survival. The road was the quickest way to the end of the valley. Sooner or later he would be required to fight in order to escape. Danger was just a part of the game, a game in which life was the reward. As he jogged along, he noticed many large streams flowing into the main river causing it to becoming wider and deeper.

He did not encounter any trogs for several hours. When he did, their torches gave him ample warning. He hid in the underbrush until they passed him. The game of cat and mouse went on for most of the night. He hoped it was not much further to the end of the valley.

Pacer had mixed feelings when the light of the moon yielded to the sun's greater power. Daylight increased the risk of being seen but improved his ability to use the surroundings to his advantage. At a high point on the road he saw the end of the valley spread into the vast grass lands of the Great Plains. This moment of celebration was short lived. As a seasoned warrior, his instincts knew he was not yet safe. He sensed that pursuit was fast approaching from two directions.

As he rounded a turn in the road, he was greeted by a band of four trogs. With an easy motion Pacer pulled his sword. His major advantage was to attack first. While the trogs reacted in their usual slow methodical manner, Pacer killed the first two opponents. This aggressive strategy caused the remaining trogs to back away in surprise and hesitation, giving Pacer the opportunity to continue his attack. In his eagerness to end the battle he committed a cardinal sin of swordsmanship. He overstepped his ability to defend himself. He was too close to the trogs to effectively wield his sword. This mistake was almost fatal.

The trog on his left thrust his sword in an awkward forward motion. The feeble attempt struck Pacer's arm a glancing blow. Pacer dropped to his left knee, swinging his right leg in a roundhouse swing. The kick hit the trog at knee level. The trog fell onto his back. This allowed Pacer to regain his footing and defend himself against the other trog. With an upward swing of his sword he blocked a solid downward blow. Using the tip of his sword, he pushed the trog's sword to the side, leaving the center of the trog's body wide open. Pacer only had to flick his sword in a graceful forward motion to strike a fatal blow. Before the remaining trog could regain its footing, Pacer's sword ended its career as an evil warrior.

Pacer only stopped long enough to wrap the wound on his arm. He advanced down the road at a steady jog. The canyon road was an ongoing series of sharp turns.

When Pacer rounded a corner in the road, he was confronted by his greatest fear.

A band of trogs had placed a barricade on a narrow section of the road. He grinned, thinking, "I am now officially in trouble." Without counting, he estimated there to be about 30 trogs. At the sight of Pacer, the beasts gave a loud shout that echoed in the canyon. It was hopeless for him to continue down the road. He could not possibly fight such a large army. He turned and sprinted back up the road, with his eyes searching for a way to escape.

Pacer came to an abrupt stop when an equally large group of enemies appeared on the road ahead of him. He was now blocked from escaping on the road. The ground next to the road was bordered on one side by a sheer cliff and the other by the river. The only route open to him was the water.

Pacer hastily looked over the bank to find a suitable place to jump. Then with a short run, he leaped off the road into the river. He landed in a deep pool of water. The shock of the cold water caused him to gasp for breath. Recovering, he swam toward to the opposite side of the river, allowing the current to carry him downstream. Using strong strokes he reached the opposite bank.

The frustrated trogs stood hopelessly on the road above the river. At this moment Pacer felt jubilant as he remembered ancient stories about trogs fearing water. Many slow witted archers ran to the river bank. A cloud of poorly aimed arrows filled the air. As Pacer climbed onto the opposite bank he felt a sharp pain bite into his leg. A loud cheer went up from the trogs when they saw the arrow strike. After crawling into the brush, he gritted his teeth as he pulled out the arrow. He was not badly hurt, but was cold and wet. Pacer had to find a place to build a fire to warm his body and dry his wet clothes. Before continuing down the river, he put a temporary wrap around his leg to stop the bleeding and ate a handful of trail food. He prayed the trogs would not gather enough courage to cross the river.

He moved rapidly in order to maintain his body heat. After an hour of searching, he found the ideal resting place. The hollow remains of an old trapper's cabin was lodged against a stone cliff. The fireplace was still usable and the roof provided partial cover.

He was fortunate to find the cabin because the throb in his leg was intensifying. Dizziness caused him to stagger while entering the old building. After an inspection of the cabin, he stumbled outside to gather wood. Several agonizing trips provided ample wood for many hours of fire. He decided to start a fire and risk the chance of revealing his location.

As the warmth from the fire oozed into his body, the pain in his leg grew more intense. He was afraid the arrow had been poisoned. The wound was turning an angry red and draining a dark green ooze. He cleaned and applied a healing ointment to the wound. Suffering biting pain, he removed his clothes and hung them on a rope he had stretched near the fire. Wrapped in his sleeping blanket, he struggled to stay awake until his clothes were dry. After several hours, the blazing fire had transformed his clothes from soggy and wet into warm and dry. After putting on the warm cloths he drifted into a restless sleep. His mind rolled with violent dreams about war, anger and death.

He awoke in the night with a high temperature. The fever felt like a fire was consuming him from inside out. The pain in his leg was so severe he could only move with excruciating pain. After placing more wood onto the fire, Pacer crawled back to his bedroll before losing consciousness. He remembered nothing until the sound of voices and laughter entered his mind. The confusion of his dreams began to fade into conscious awareness of his surroundings. The light of a new day welcomed him as he opened his eyes. The heat of a newly laid fire greeted him with the cheerfulness of the special traveler's-companion. The bandage on his leg had been changed with the care of a healer. He looked around but did not find anybody in the room. Who started the fire and changed his bandage?

ᚲᚺᚢᚾᛁᛉᚹ ᚢᛉᚨ ᚱᚺᛋᚢᛉᚨ

Healing and Beyond

For a long time Pacer stared at the sagging roof timbers of the old cabin. The confusion in his mind continued to create a sense of fantasy and disorientation. He knew he had been unconscious for a long time but for how long? He had no way of knowing. His feverish mind began to search beyond the delirium to remember what happened to him. In his first image, he saw Topple standing in front of an old stone building. He also recalled fleeing from hundreds of trogs and jumping into the river. Finally, the memories of agonizing pain, a cabin, and a high fever helped refocus his mind. The past and present finally blended to a conscious whole.

He commented to himself, “Where are the trogs? They should have found me by now. The smoke from the fire can be seen for miles. Oh well, I should appreciate the fact that I am still alive.”

As the cloud in his mind cleared, he became more aware of his surroundings. Next to his mat sat a loaf of honey bread and a bowl of sweet fruit drink. The aroma of fresh cooked food lingered in the drafty cabin. After eating the meal he became dizzy and lost consciousness.

In the midst of his feverish hallucinations, he became aware of movement around him. He opened his eyes to see many small elves dancing around a magical fire in the center of the cabin. The flames burned with a stunning blend of bright colors. Fingers of vivid greens, blues, reds and yellows reached out and touched him. A warm sensation of healing flowed into his body. Looking away from the fire, he saw many smiling faces staring down at him. A gibberish of unrecognizable words floated from their mouths. He did understand one sentence. A gentle voice stated, “He is an important friend of Brad and Coaldon.” In the background he detected the smell of food.

A humorous voice recited, “Pacer, Pacer - with feet so base, with homely face, with clothes of lace, with mind of space, with wizards to chase, and with trogs to race.” The odd humor brought much clapping and laughter. At the sound of a loud clap, the room was instantaneously empty. Only a black void remained in his mind.

He awoke in the middle of the night to the warmth of the fire on his face. Again there was food and drink next to his mat. He sat up and ate but dizziness forced him to lie back down. With increased awareness he listened to the sounds of the night. The hoot of a large owl was answered by its mate. Several foxes scampered through the old cabin chasing one another. A breeze rattled a pile of leaves next to the door. The light of the full moon drifted through the window casting soft shadows. In the distance the rumble of the river offered a peaceful backdrop to the fogginess of his mind. Pacer tried to stay focused on his surroundings, yet the cloud of sleep slowly blanketed his thoughts.

He awoke with a cold wind blowing on his face. The light of a new day was shining into the cabin. He rolled over onto his knees in order to get up. As he rose to his feet, lightheadedness caused him to pause. He took several wobbly steps before he rested. A stack of wood was piled next to the door. With increasing strength and coordination, he carried the wood to the fireplace and rekindled the fire. He walked outside the cabin with his cooking pot to get water from a small stream. Within an hour he was eating a meal of hot trail food. He sat in front of the fireplace enjoying the feeling of improved health. He realized his next step was to go to the Monastery of Toms. He did not want to stay in the cabin any longer than necessary.

In the late afternoon he went for a walk around the outside of the cabin to build his strength and stamina. By evening he was tired from the physical activities. At sunset he collapsed into a deep, dreamless sleep.

The new day brought the demand for decisions. Should he leave, or should he stay in the cabin for another day? His food supplies were low. He was still very weak. The hike to the Monastery would take several days. He also knew that the trogs could arrive at anytime. After weighing the different factors, Pacer decided it was time to depart. He loaded his pack and set off at a slow walk. He found a path leading down a ridge top, descending onto the grassy plains. The ground was muddy from a recent rainstorm making walking difficult. He was thankful the ground had a rock base to keep his feet from sinking out of sight. He reached inside himself to find the additional strength to continue to walk. By noon it was time to rest his weary body. After a meal of hard bread, he sat with his back against a tree studying the surrounding area.

At this moment, the beauty of nature overwhelmed him with peace and wonderment. The ground fell away before him into a panorama of royal elegance. The deep blue sky blended into light green colors of the rolling prairie. The dark green forest of the mountains cascaded into the richness of a sea of swaying grass. He thought to himself, "The One Presence must have created the world in its own image. It is all so splendid."

As he continued to walk, the afternoon sun dropped into the west. The pain from his leg wound increased with each passing hour. The trees of the forest melted away into the flat lands. The tall grass supported herds of wild deer, horses and buffalo. A herd of horses could be seen grazing on a knoll to the east. To the south he could see the beginning of the Wastelands. The Wastelands surrounding the Monastery of Toms were a bleak and barren labyrinth of unending canyons and gullies. Many travelers died from starvation after becoming disoriented and lost in the baffling maze. The Monastery was built in the center of the Wasteland to protect it from the corruption of the outside world. This isolation helped maintain the purity of the Monks' contemplative lives.

He decided to make camp at the edge of the canyon lands. It took about an hour to reach his destination. This doorway into the Wastelands was bordered by steep walls towering high over his head. He took special care to find shelter that provided protection in case of attack. He selected a recess at the base of a cliff next to a small stream. The shelf opened into a small cave in the side of the cliff. His camp would be easy to defend.

His first task was to rest his weary body. His leg throbbed with pain. He wondered if he had pushed himself too hard. The long shadows cast by the setting sun brought him to an awareness of his present situation. It was getting dark. He was cold and hungry.

He gathered wood from several trees growing in the area. At sunset he built a fire. The warm flames, offered him a hot meal and relief from a difficult day. As he stared at the fire, the gentle flames mesmerized his mind and introduced a comfortable sleep. The insulating effect of the gully caused a dead silence. The cold night air forced Pacer to roll tightly inside his blanket.

Several hours before dawn, the silence of the night was broken by the snarl of several animals. Pacer's survival instincts put him on high alert. He quietly sat up with his sword in hand. His fire had died down to several hot coals. He crawled to the edge of the campsite to watch for any movement. He had learned that patience was the key to survival. He would have the advantage if he could outwait his opponent. After several moments four eyes appeared about 30 strides away from him. The light of the setting moon reflected off their burning, red eyes. The eyes slowly moved towards his location with stealth. He finally saw the bodies in the moonlight. Standing before him were two giant wolves. Their large heads had heavy eye ridges which dominated huge circular eyes. The long, broad, wrinkled noses lent emphasis to outsized mouths full of sharp teeth. The broad forehead was bordered by two long pointed ears. These were not ordinary animals. They were spirit wolves, a creation of evil. He watched as the beasts talked to each other in a series of growls.

As they came closer, he could hear their soft breathing and smell their foul odor. This was not the scent of nature, but the product of an evil creation and existence.

He patiently waited until they were within two strides before attacking. With a short stroke of his sword he decapitated the first wolf. The second wolf instantaneously began an aggressive attack. Pacer rolled to his left as the wolf lunged toward him. At the end of his roll, he brought the sword up in a swinging motion. As the spirit wolf leaped over him the tip of the sword bit deep into wolf's side. Pacer jumped to his feet ready for the next attack. To his surprise, the beast only stood watching him with hateful eyes. It was too dark for him to see if the beast was badly wounded. With a look of defeat, the creature slowly limped into the darkness. Pacer crawled back into his shelter to wait for sunrise.

He rejoiced when the daylight finally revealed the surrounding area. As he ventured out of his shelter, he could not find the remains of the dead wolf. This confirmed his assumption. The beasts were the product of evil. Once the spirit wolf died, its body evaporated into a cloud of nothingness. He saw the footprints of the spirit wolf lead away from the camp. The footprints disappeared in the tall grass.

Pacer knew he had to finish his journey to the Monastery before his health collapsed. After his morning meal, he spent an hour reviewing his map of the Wastelands. He did not want to get lost in the maze of canyons. The map showed a route starting in his present location. He mumbled to himself, "Am I willing to gamble my life on the accuracy of this map? Oh, why not? I have nothing else planned for today. Besides, waiting will only give the spirit wolves a better chance to nibble at my toes. No, I must go even though I am not physically ready."

With the map in hand, he began the dangerous trek into the Wastelands. It took great willpower to force his tired body and wounded leg to keep hiking. The journey down the canyons dissolved into a perplexing series of choices. Diverging channels took off in different directions at major intersections. Each junction had a right or wrong choice. The height of the canyon walls prevented him from gaining a view of the surrounding terrain. His mind melted to a state of disorientation after he made an infinite number of turns and followed endless trails. By noon he was convinced he was totally lost and heading for an early grave.

After a short break, he continued to follow the lines on the map. By mid-afternoon he collapsed into a heap of fatigue. Before continuing his trek, he closed his eyes for a short nap. The pleasant sensation of deep sleep caressed his mind and body. With a jerk he opened his eyes to see the fangs of a large mouth over his face. Saliva from the animal's mouth dripped on Pacer's face. The animal's hot breath warmed his cold cheeks. Any movement of his body was met with a vicious growl. Pacer said to himself, "I wish Topple was here to provide an appropriate response. As my grandfather said, 'There will be days like this'."

Welcome Home

Earthkin sat in the opening of the cave looking at the snow covered plateau. The fingers of darkness were slowly pushing away the fading glory of daylight into the western sky. Coaldon watched the spreading cover of darkness with eagerness. He was ready to go home. Yet, when he glanced at Earthkin, he detected a brooding concern. Earthkin's body twitched with tension. The dwarf had experienced something negative.

In a somber tone Earthkin said, "We can not wait here much longer. The trogs might be following us. I suggest we travel after the moon rises. I want to see where we are going."

Then he added, "I feel a disturbance in the spirit of the earth. Things are not well. A great power of evil has invaded a sacred temple. I am afraid we will be required to face a new danger."

Topple listened to Earthkin, but showed little concern. His relaxed smile beamed with a tone of assurance.

Earthkin looked at Topple with a disgruntled attitude. He assumed Topple's passive nature meant disinterest. Earthkin's concrete view of life demanded ridged conformity to an accepted standard of conduct. He could not understand how Topple could be so comfortable and satisfied in times of danger and distress. Earthkin believed concern and work provided the building blocks for tomorrow.

In a grave and philosophical mood he quoted,

"The stones of yesterday provide the foundation for today.
The rocks of today offer the building blocks of tomorrow.
The caverns of life are only empty space unless made alive
by purpose and action.
The power of each deed is a stepping stone in history."

Toppled chuckle as he responded,

"While kings rule by force,
clowns lead through weakness.

While kings command by dictates,
clowns dance with life.
While kings are slaves to time,
clowns celebrate each moment.
While kings are guided by rules,
clowns walk in faith.
While kings struggle for control,
clowns rest in submission.
While kings are captives of power,
clowns find peace in trust."

Topple smiled with satisfaction at his magnificent recitation. Earthkin shook his head in disbelief at the wizard's quick mind.

The rising moon signaled the time to depart. An ancient trail crossed the wide mountain side providing the best way down the steep slope. It was a challenge to walk on the snow covered slopes in darkness. Each step on the uneven ground required great caution. One false move would mean a dangerous fall. Coaldon followed a long ridge-line that seemed to go forever. His intuitive feel for the land successfully guided the travelers to the valley floor. The journey down a ravine did not allow a view of the valley. The sound of Rolling River indicated the end of the trek.

He led the way to a grove of trees next to the river. The glow of a new day came as the cold night air flowed into the valley from high peaks. As Coaldon stood in the tall brush he heard it.

Coaldon proclaimed, "The silence is deafening. I hear nothing. The usual morning sounds of the wildlife are gone. Something is wrong!"

Earthkin's grim face signaled trouble. Topple's soft grin was a bizarre discord to the stillness.

Without thinking, Coaldon ran to the riverbank. To his horror, his childhood home was a heap of ash. The bodies of half eaten farm animals lay scattered across the fields. The scene of death and destruction burned deeply into Coaldon's mind. He sat on the bank in a state of shock and disbelief. His world collapsed around him. The shock of the disaster slowly sank into his consciousness. His feelings of grief grew into a burning anger. Tears of rage rolled down his face.

Coaldon felt he was being initiated into his adult life by the ancient ritual of violence. He realized his vague goals of yesterday were being transformed into the clear and definitive goals of tomorrow. From this time onward his life would burn with the zeal for the conquest of evil.

Now What?

Earthkin, Coaldon and Topple sat for a long time as their eyes searched the surrounding area for signs of life. It was obvious something had caused the wildlife to leave the area. Nothing stirred or made a sound. As they were getting ready to begin their investigation, a crashing noise was heard in the underbrush. Something was moving toward them without any concern about being heard. The noise stopped for a moment then started again. A deep growl preceded its arrival. They pulled their swords as the noise got closer. With a giant leap, the growling animal landed directly in front of Coaldon. To everybody's surprise, Sid crouched ready to attack.

Coaldon spoke to him in a soft, gentle voice. Sid's stance relaxed when Coaldon's voice penetrated the barrier of his bewilderment. The dog seemed to awaken from a trance. He gave a yip of recognition. Sid danced around in a glorious state of excitement. As Coaldon rushed to grab him, the dog greeted him with barks. They jostled onto the ground. The dwarf and wizard smiled as the two friends were reunited.

After the reunion, Coaldon took a close look at Sid. The dog had many small cuts all over his body. Part of the hair had been ripped or burned away leaving scabs covering ugly wounds. Earthkin handed Coaldon his healing ointment. Sid did not resist as the ointment was applied to his wounds. He sat peacefully as the soothing cream sank into the inflamed flesh. Topple touched the dog's head with compassion. The soft touch gave Sid a charge of healing energy. Sid rubbed his nose against Topple's robes in friendship.

With eyes on the dog, Topple beamed in satisfaction. The tragedy of the farm became oblivious to him. He was not possessed by the future but found fulfillment in current events. His focus was consumed by his concern for Sid. He allowed life to take care of the small details.

As difficult as it might be, Earthkin and Coaldon knew it was necessary to cross the river. It was essential to examine the farm. Yet, how were they to do it? The water was high for this time of year. A warm spell in the west had melted part of the snow pack. Coaldon's only boat lay shattered on the opposite bank.

Earthkin finally said, "Coaldon, while you tend Sid I will think about how we will cross the river."

Earthkin's eyes shifted from Coaldon to the turbulent river. A churning sense of discomfort flooded his being. He had a fear of water. Dwarves did not like being in water, yet alone in a dangerous river. During his life, he did everything possible to stay out of water. Of course there were times when he had to get wet. Yet, as he looked at the river, his level of anxiety was overwhelming. He struggled to rise above his fear.

Earthkin grit his teeth, reached into his backpack and pulled out a rope. Without giving thought to his personal safety, he tied the rope to a tree and waded into the cold rushing water. His powerful body fought the current with staggering steps. It was not until he reached the center that fear finally overcame his courage. He felt lightheaded as panic slowly consumed his mind. He became disorientated, causing his foot to slip on a slimy rock. He fell backward. As he submerged in the water, panic limited his ability to move. The muffled sound of the churning water dominated his awareness. Out of some hidden part of his mind, a survival behavior took control. Still holding onto the rope he pushed his arms to the side and relaxed his body. The impact of going over a large boulder thrust him to the surface. Gasping for breath, he rolled over and planted his feet on the bed of the river. Pushing with all his strength, he thrust himself toward the bank. With uncoordinated arm strokes, he churned his away toward the shore. Finally, with heroic effort he crawled upon the opposite bank. He lay on the rocky ground gasping for breath and celebrating his success. Besides a wounded pride, he only suffered from a sore back and a cold body. Given a dwarf's innate fear of water, this river crossing was probably the bravest thing he had ever done. To his relief, he still held the rope in his hand.

Coaldon watched in horror at Earthkin's near disaster. His resurrection on the opposite shore brought an arousing cheer from Coaldon.

Not wanting to waste time, Earthkin tied the rope to a tree on the opposite bank. Earthkin signaled for Topple and Coaldon to cross the river. They could use the rope to stabilize themselves. Coaldon was not surprised when Topple shook his head. Topple's frail body was too weak to battle the force of the river.

Coaldon exclaimed, "We need to cross the river!"

With a sly grin Topple looked at Coaldon saying, "I will go piggy back."

Giving a deep, formal bow he said to Topple, "Your lordship, I offer you my service as your royal steed."

Topple climbed onto Coaldon's back with a flair of elegance. Topple's eyes danced with glee. With a grandiose wave of his arm Topple yelled, "Charge!"

In spite of himself, Earthkin could not help but smile.

Following Topple's command, Coaldon waded into the water. Coaldon used both hands to grip the rope. Topple had the responsibility to hold on for dear life. The rope provided the anchor enabling Coaldon to keep his balance. He carefully took one step at a time as the water rushed against him.

It took all of Coaldon's strength to keep his balance and footing. When Topple started waving his arms in wide circles Coaldon gave him a strong warning to be still. Topple stopped waving his arms, but continued an explosive outpouring of words. After a long struggle, Coaldon climbed onto the opposite bank in a state of exhaustion. As the young warrior fell to his knees, Topple laughed with delight. Topple had completed a most exciting adventure.

Sid swam across the river with little concern or effort. Earthkin was jealous of the dog's ability to swim.

The search of the area revealed no immediate threat. After examining the ground they decided a large army of trogs had attacked the farm. No sign of humans were found in the cabin. Part of the personal belongings from the cabin had been removed before the attack. There was no sign of a struggle or fight. The cold ashes indicated the attack took place three or four days ago. Like a dark cloud, the smell of death hung over the valley.

It was decided to set up camp in the root cellar. The travelers' cold bodies and wet clothes demanded immediate attention. After eating a hot meal in front of a warm fire, it was time to dry their wet clothes and to find sleep. Coaldon and Earthkin took turns on watch throughout the afternoon and night.

While Coaldon was on guard duty, Sid sat next to him under the bright stars. The depth of their friendship held an unspoken bond of intimacy. Even though no words were spoken there was recognizable communion.

During the night Coaldon thought about the forest being void of animals. Why would they leave? He concluded a great evil had driven them away. Over and over he kept seeing images of the destroyed farm. Mental pictures of the burned buildings, the dead animals and the destruction filled his mind with grief. In addition, he ruminated on the fate of his grandparents. The attack was so violent, how could they have escaped? Were they dead or dying, or maybe needing help?

Coaldon did not want to sleep in the cellar. He needed space and fresh air.

The morning light filtered through the holes in the cellar roof. The heat from the fire soon warmed the small room. Both Earthkin and Coaldon decided it was time to eat something other than trail food. They choose to put the remaining vegetables, stored in the cellar, to good use. Before long the aroma of bubbling stew excited their taste buds. The hot, tasty meal helped lift their spirits. Topple's broad smile was enough to express his appreciation.

The travelers held a short conference after breakfast to decide what to do next.

Earthkin said, "We need to leave this morning. We do not want to be caught here by the trogs."

Coaldon nodded, "I agree. We can not accomplish anything here. I suggest we go to the Monastery of Toms. Pacer said he would meet us there."

Coaldon suddenly became aware of a growing sense of discomfort. This was confirmed when he saw Sid cowering in the corner. Then his sword began to vibrate in rapid pulses.

Topple looked toward the door of the cellar with anticipation. He bent his head to one side with a look of curiosity. Then he said, "The watch dog has failed in his duties. I think we have visitors. This should be most entertaining!"

Coaldon and Earthkin knew Topple was serious. Earthkin carefully peeked out the door of the cellar. He heard the scream of many voices coming from across the river. Hundreds of trogs covered the opposite bank. They had followed the travelers over North Ridge Pass.

In a casual voice Topple said, "I guess it is time to go. Take your time getting your things together. No hurry, just a nice stroll in the woods."

Earthkin gave a shout of protest, "We need to move and move fast." Coaldon and Earthkin rushed out of the small room pushing against each other as they went out the door.

Topple found great humor at their show of panic. He laughed, saying, "Haste makes waste."

Coaldon and the dwarf stumbled into the bright daylight. They were greeted by the cry of hundreds of jeering trogs. Topple slowly walked out of the cellar and stood next to his friends. With a big smile, he gave the trogs a wild wave of greeting. The trogs responded with raised fists and foul curses.

Earthkin said, "I think it is time to get started. Let's take the east road towards Grandy. I hope the trogs do not find a way to cross the river."

Topple chuckled gleefully, knowing that the best was yet to come.

As they started to walk down the road, a loud clap of thunder rumbled across the Valley. The trogs started to chant over and over. "Gurlog! Gurlog! Gurlog!"

Topple said, "I told you our new friend was not nice. It wants to play with us. Let's extend our welcome."

Topple casually walked toward the river as Earthkin and Coaldon stood in disbelief. To them, running away seemed preferable.

Topple glanced backwards saying, "Let's not keep it waiting. Remember, fear begets fear. We must show courage and confidence."

A dark cloud appeared in the west end of the valley. It moved down the valley with unnatural speed. The cloud then abruptly stopped over the crowd of trogs. Another clap of thunder announced its arrival. The trogs fell face down onto the

ground in absolute terror. It slowly drifted across the river settling on the ground about 100 strides in front of the three men. The cloud swirled as it formed into a large black beast 10 strides tall. Its huge round body had two legs, two long arms, and a large head. Its face was blood red with tiny features. The small nose, lips and eyes were overshadowed by a large horn that jetted from its forehead. The horn curved down over its face giving it a grotesque expression of evil. With a loud roar of disgust, it focused its attention on the three people standing in the meadow. It turned its head to look at the trogs as if asking permission. The trogs yelled, "Gurlog! Gurlog! Kill! Kill!"

The monster started to walk slowly towards them with rumbling laughter.

Topple yelled, "Come no closer unless you wish to suffer death."

The beast thundered, "Who are you?"

Topple responded, "I am Topple the Wizard. This is Earthkin the Great Dwarf Warrior. This is Coaldon of Rocknee, the Hand-on-the-Sword. Go away and leave us alone. You are bothering us. We want to go for a nice morning stroll."

The monster stopped in its tracks. Its dense, slow mind worked to remember their names. With a loud shout of recognition, it took several steps backward. It leaned forward to take a closer look. A roar of flame burst from its mouth singeing the ground in front of Topple. In a casual manner Topple pointed his raised hand toward Gurlog. A bolt of lighting burst from his hand striking the beast with a shower of burning sparks. With a grunt of pain it shook with rage. Gurlog took several more steps backward. The trogs burst into a round of chants. "Gurlog, Gurlog, burn their flesh! Gurlog, Gurlog, evil lord!"

Gurlog stood in a state of confusion. It wanted to attack; yet, it felt a sense of doubt. It had never experienced uncertainty in its entire existence. The chants of the trogs enriched its confidence. It roared, "I will destroy this scum." With a burst of anger it lumbered forward.

Topple shouted, "Earthkin, you retreat backwards. Coaldon, you move to the right. I will go to the left. Coaldon, it is time for you to use the deadly power of the sword."

The monster took a wide swing at Earthkin with its giant arm. Earthkin had anticipated this move as he rolled to his right. Gurlog then fired a burst of fire from its mouth at Earthkin. Earthkin's right pant leg burst into flames as the giant pursued his attack. Gurlog burst into laugher as it saw Earthkin's pant leg burst into flames. Topple struck the beast with another bolt of lighting to draw its attention away from Earthkin. Gurlog staggered in pain when the bolt ripped into its soft underbelly. Roaring in frustration, it turned to attack Topple. This diversion gave Earthkin time to put out the fire. He received only minor wounds.

With Gurlog's attention on Topple, Coaldon drew his sword. He approached the beast from behind and pointed the weapon toward the monster. He released a surge of energy into the sword. The accumulated power turned the end of his sword into an angry red glow. Coaldon's knees sagged as a blinding streak of light erupted from the end of the sword. The energy hit Gurlog with such force the beast fell forward into a heap of thrashing flesh. The monster fell directly on top of Topple. A reverse surge of power from Gurlog hit Coaldon as he stood holding his sword. Coaldon felt the bolt pass into his body. A burning sense of evil griped his mind.

After a short pause, Gurlog slowly rose to its knees in a state of shock. With a surge of energy it staggered to its feet. Smoke started to pour from its large head. It made one step toward Coaldon before its head evaporated into black smoke. The life energy of the monster exploded in all directions. The monster dissolved into a faint whimper of distress. The remains of the beast drifted to the ground in wisps of dust.

The trogs on the far bank of the river stood in silence. Their source of power and leadership disappeared before their eyes. A few started to roam around as if lost sheep. Then one by one they walked into the forest without power or purpose. Trogs were mindless beasts requiring the will power of a master. A new master would need to gain power before the beasts could function as warriors.

A Time of Healing

The presence of evil limits the prosperity of life. It is like a cancer sapping strength from the very heart of being. Evil feeds evil as goodness nurtures goodness. The personal gift of sacrifice is essential in the conquest of iniquity."

Book of Enlightenment

The mark of evil had been removed from the surrounding area. The sound of returning wildlife emerged the moment the battle ended. The cleansing of the valley was greeted by an outpouring of energy. This burst of vitality spread like a strong wind.

Coaldon had been in a coma for two days. The blast of energy from Gurlog disrupted the half-elf's mind and body. His pale face, empty eyes and contorted facial features did not change. He often raved about a dark spirit. He moaned and thrashed in an attempt to escape from some unseen enemy. Earthkin watched him with growing concern.

Sid sat next to Coaldon with attentive eyes focused on his face.

Earthkin's burns healed rapidly after several applications of a curing ointment. The pain of the burn forced him to limit his activities.

Early evening on the third day after the battle, a horse returned to the pasture. The old animal had shaggy hair, friendly black eyes and a dirty white coat. Its short legs and round body moved with a lively, inquisitive, confident spirit. At sunset the horse trotted to the cellar to investigate the inhabitants. Topple rushed out to give the horse a warm welcome and a handful of carrots. The horse (Rose Petal) nuzzled Topple with gentle appreciation, blowing its warm breath on the wizard's hand. Topple and Rose Petal became good friends. It was not unusual to see them walking together over the battlefield of the farm.

While Coaldon was unconscious, Earthkin and Topple had time to talk. For the past few weeks an uncomfortable relationship had developed between them. Topple felt a responsibility to deal with the issue. So in an uninhibited manner, he opened a discussion with Earthkin. Topple spoke from his heart not his mind.

In unusual seriousness, Topple stated, "Over the centuries I have learned wisdom grows from trusting in the providence of the One Presence. Wisdom is not a word or idea but a gift. It is not a possession but an escape from the fears of life. What may look like craziness is in truth freedom from the enslavement to conformity. The unspoken voice of the clown is a protest of the empty values of self pursuits. The jester proclaims the values of humility, honesty, charity and honor. The clown dances in the face of the harsh winds of life. The face of my clown is the image of faith."

In a grim mood, Earthkin nodded in understanding. He realized Topple's inescapable personality was an expression of trust in the One Presence. To expect anything else was fantasy.

Earthkin responded, "My grumpy disposition grows from dissatisfaction. I am a person of action with little tolerance for the foolishness of wasting of time. My practical view of life could be described as Can do, Will do. I constantly rush to finish the immediate task in order to do the next. Your child-like behavior is difficult for me to tolerate. I expect adults to be serious and solemn. I need to learn to accept your unique behavior as you must learn to accept mine."

Then Topple and the dwarf hugged. This never-to-be-forgotten event opened the door to an unshakable friendship. The reconciliation helped paved the way to understanding, but did not put an end to the beautiful differences between the two men. Like two jagged rocks rubbing together, sparks would still be created.

Topple was most unhappy after his encounter with Gurlog. He constantly complained about the foul odor clinging to his clothes after coming into contact with the beast. Topple had to make a tough decision. He could wash his clothes or continue to smell the foul odor. It had been decades since he had washed his precious robe. He was afraid the robe might lose some of its old magic if it was washed. Topple sputtered around the cellar in total despair. Finally, with a look of determination, he decided to wash his clothes.

Soap was found in the burned-out cabin and an old tub located in the brush. Earthkin offered Topple a spare gown to wear while he washed his robe. Water, soap and the tub waited for Topple's dirty, smelly clothes. In moments of weakness, Topple changed his mind several times. He finally proclaimed that he could no longer stand the smell. With the courage of a great warrior he took off the old robe, put on Earthkin's short gown and walked to the wash tub. With tears in his eyes he dropped the robe into the soapy water. Topple treated the wet, soggy robe with the reverence due a valued religious object. With exaggerated and dramatic motions, he dunked the robe in a ritual of sorrow. The wizard portrayed an actor struggling to accept the tragic lose of a good friend. Topple removed the robe from the water and honored it with profound dignity as he hung it on a tree branch. When his clothes were dry, Topple put them on with righteous indignation.

Earthkin understood Topple's dislike of soapy water, but found no humor in his behavior. He thought Topple acted like a little child protesting the use of bath water. For Topple it would be weeks before the tragic pain healed. Topple referred to this calamity as the Tragedy of Soap and Suds.

The end of the third day, Coaldon was still trapped in his coma. Topple hummed around the root cellar with an air of carefree indifference. He placed an empty cooking pot on Coaldon's chest without thought or concern. There was limited room in the cellar so why not utilize all space to the fullest? Earthkin's tolerance for Topple's strange behavior was once again growing thin. Yet, what could he do? Topple had lived for many centuries with his eccentric personality. He was not going to change.

Sid remained at Coaldon's side with his curious eyes watching for any change in Coaldon's condition. Late in the afternoon the dog left Coaldon's side. He walked around the room in a restive state and then trotted outside. With impatience the dog walked in and out the cellar as if looking for something to satisfy some unknown need.

This uneasiness climaxed when Sid gave a sudden bark, placing his front paws on Coaldon's chest. Unconsciously, Coaldon grabbed his shirt pocket holding the gemstone. Moments later he shouted a command in an ancient elfin dialect. The authority of the words was so powerful it shook the ground and caused the cellar to rattle. Dirt fell from the ceiling creating a cloud of dust. Coaldon suddenly sat up coughing from the dust. He looked around the room with fear. The pot tumbled from his chest clattering to the floor. He relaxed when he saw Earthkin and Topple standing near him. He lay back on the mat and sighed in relief.

He said, "I have finally escaped from the beast. I feel so weak." Coaldon reached out to Sid giving him a hug.

He looked at Topple and Earthkin saying, "The spirit of Gurlog must have entered my body when it died. I have been fighting it. It tried to possess me. If it had not been for the power of the gemstone I would have been lost. I can still feel its ugly spirit pressing to gain control of me. The final battle consumed all my energy. I feel so dirty and lonely. Please stay close to me."

Earthkin poured Coaldon a hot cup of soup. Coaldon sipped the delicious potage with great relish. His hungry body craved food. He tried to get up, but did not have the strength. It would be days before he regained his old vitality. Without modesty, he consumed all the food placed before him. Coaldon was afraid to close his eyes, yet out of total exhaustion he slowly yielded to the gentle voice of sleep. He slept quietly through the night without any bad dreams.

Morning greeted the small party as they prepared to depart. Coaldon had gained adequate strength to walk out of the cellar.

Earthkin said, "I do not want to stay in the valley any longer. The potential of being attacked increases the longer we stay. Coaldon can ride the horse while Topple and I walk."

With a twinkle in his eye Topple asked, "Earthkin will you carry me piggyback." The dwarf growled several unsavory words in response. Earthkin's tolerance had not improved.

The journey made slow progress on the first day. It was necessary to stop frequently so Coaldon could rest. By the end of the day, black storm clouds were approaching from the west. Earthkin was happy to see Coaldon's body and mind were rapidly healing.

As the group traveled, Topple was well entertained. Different locations on the trip triggered memories of some past event. Topple's rich imagination would erupt with vivid enactments of events that happened centuries before.

The first night the travelers spent in a deserted stone house built into the recesses of a mountainside. They were amazed the old house was in such good condition. After cleaning out the fireplace, the dwarf built a roaring fire. Earthkin prepared a dinner with the touch of a seasoned wilderness chef.

After dinner Earthkin said, "Coaldon needs to have new shoes and clothes; plus we need to buy food. If we plan to go to the Monastery of Toms it will be necessary to cross Rolling River. Presently the river is too dangerous to cross on foot. The only ferry is at Grandy."

Coaldon suggested, "I believe it best to travel to Grandy by the Old South Road. People will be less suspicious of us if we arrive from the south. We do not want to be seen as strangers traveling from Lost Valley."

By morning a cold rain was falling. The solid ground of yesterday was turning into a sea of mud. It was difficult to leave the old house.

Topple smiled as he said, "Let's stay in this beautiful palace until the summer flowers bloom."

It took an hour of sloshing through the mud to reach the turn off to the Old South Road. The lightly traveled road to the south gained elevation in the foothills. The rocky soil made traveling much easier. The open land of the valley turned into the dense forests of the hill country.

The rain turned into a light snow by early afternoon. Coaldon decided to walk after developing several painful saddle sores. Topple graciously volunteered to ride

Rose Petal. With Topple on the horse it was possible to travel faster. By late evening on the second day of travel they stood on the southern slope leading into the Village of Grandy. Coaldon estimated they would arrive in the village by noon the next day.

The morning light found the three travelers shivering in the cold air. Topple gave a squeak of distress when he found that Rose Petal had disappeared. After a short investigation, they found the horses tracks headed east toward the river. Without a word, the travelers followed the tracks down a cattle trail toward Rolling River. Coaldon was happy when they saw the river in the distance.

Topple was overjoyed to find Rose Petal grazing in a meadow near the river. The horse welcomed them with a nicker. She trotted up to Topple with no fear or hesitation. Topple proudly climbed on Rose Petal's back and rode like a prince reviewing the troops. They followed the river until arriving at the outskirts of the village. Coaldon led his companions to an abandoned boathouse hidden in the trees.

Coaldon said, "People in the village do not visit the boathouse out of superstition. They believe the wicked Witch of Blacknose had cursed it with demons. The story tells how the previous owner had refused the witch's proposal of marriage. The Witch's anger raged in unholy torment. It is rumored the owner was drowned in the river by a demon."

Upon entering the cabin, Topple found an old trunk in the corner of the small room. A wide variety of usable clothing still remained in the trunk. Out of curiosity Topple rummage through the old clothes with an inquiring eye. With a gasp of surprise, he pulled out a green robe with a hood. The symbol of a dragon was on the front of the garment.

He exclaimed, "This is a robe of the Monks of Toms! I wonder how it got here?"

He looked at the robe for several moments before he spoke. "I have a plan. Since we do not want the villagers to recognize Coaldon, he can pretend to be a Warrior Monk of Toms. We can tell people he has taken the vow of silence. This would allow us to move more freely within the village. The monks are highly respected."

Topple suggested Coaldon rehearse being a monk. Topple said, "You are to stand erect and stately. Your hood is to remain over your head at all times. You are not to speak at any time. Your eyes are to remain focused on the ground in front of you except when listening to people. This should be fun."

Coaldon commanded Sid to remain at the boathouse to protect the horse. Sid's sad eyes followed Coaldon as he disappeared into the village.

The Village

Earthkin, Coaldon and Topple walked into Grundy from the south. The streets were deeply rutted pools of mud after a recent rainstorm. Boards had been laid over the mud to provide walkways. Normal business came to a halt when the villagers saw three visitors. No villagers had ever seen a dwarf. In their minds dwarves were only a legend. Amazement and distress clouded the villagers' faces as they gathered in the street. The appearance of a warrior monk caused gasps of fear and gestures of respect.

The world of the community had been turned upside down over the past months. The howl of strange wolves in the night, the rumors of war and the disappearance of a villager created a state of near panic. Now three strangers appeared.

The villagers watched with great suspicion as the three visitors approached the center of the hamlet. Topple greeted the crowd with a large smile and a vigorous wave of his arms. Coaldon gave the people a look of indifference from underneath his green hood. The symbol of the dragon provided an image of power, mystery and courage. Earthkin was the first to speak, "Good afternoon, people of Grandy. We come in peace. We seek food, rest and news of the world. We plan to stay only a short time. I am Earthkin of the Family Cavemore. This wise man is Ridgeway the Sage (Topple), who is traveling in search of new knowledge. It is my honor to present Rodney a Warrior Monk of the Monastery of Toms. He travels on a mission for the Abbot of Toms. We are very tired after many days of travel."

Topple walked into the crowd shaking hands. A small group began showing signs of hostility. Someone yelled, "Go away and leave us alone! We do not want you here!"

At this sign of disrespect Coaldon raised his eyes from the ground, he stepped forward and shot them a look of cold contempt. The small group of dissenters dispersed, melting into their daily routines.

Many villagers talked freely with Topple. The wizard danced around like an excited child. Mr. Baggy, owner of Log Inn, rushed out the door of the Inn to greet the newcomers. He invited them to spend the night, eat good food and share information about the Empire. The thoughts of a bed and home cooked meal convinced the travelers to stay. At first Coaldon felt uneasy about spending the night at the Inn, but the desire for a good night's sleep overcame the memory of the black mist.

As Earthkin paid in advance with the hint of a good tip, he noticed two men in dirty, ragged clothes. Their darting eyes, sluggish manners and constant smirks were out of character for the village.

Earthkin asked Mr. Baggy, "Who are those two men sitting in front of the Inn?" Mr. Baggy responded, "They arrived in Grandy several days ago. They call themselves the Royal Vigilantes. They have joined the soldiers in protecting the Empire from rebellion."

Meanwhile Topple was at the height of his glory. He moved through the community with a steady stream of words, laughs and excited gestures. His happiness attracted a group of adults and children. Topple performed a series of tricks that kept the audience spellbound. Even the villagers who protested their arrival enjoyed Topple's robust sense of humor and personality.

Coaldon stood like a statue by the door of the Inn observing Topple and people of the village. For once even Earthkin enjoyed watching Topple's antics. The dwarf decided to go to the dry goods store to purchase supplies. The soldiers watched him with interest as he entered. The owner was happy to accept cash in payment. Hard cash was welcome over the credit given to local patrons.

Upon leaving the store with his heavy bundle, Earthkin greeted the soldiers with a casual salute of respect. The soldiers responded with a look of relief. These troops were not interested in having a conflict with anybody, especially a seasoned warrior. On impulse, Earthkin stopped to visit. The lonely soldiers told the dwarf about their homes, families and their duties in Grandy. They had arrived a week ago under orders to protect the village and to arrest any half elves. A half elf was suspected of leading a rebellion against the Empire.

Leaving the soldiers, Earthkin deposited the supplies at the Inn. He then went back to the street to round up Topple. It was time for dinner.

The dinner at the Inn was roast goose, hot spice cereal, applesauce, and savory greens. The travelers ate at a slow, steady pace. Only necessary conversation accompanied the meal. Groans of satisfaction occasionally drifted from their table. They sat back in their chairs with the dazed look of gluttons.

The local people normally spend their evenings discussing current events and sharing stories in front of the large fireplace in the Log Inn. Tonight's crowd was especially large because of the three unusual visitors. Coaldon was surprised when Topple pulled a small flute from the folds of his robe. The flute was a deep silver color with elf runes inscribed on the barrel. The tone of the flute had a rich resonance and pitch.

Topple stood up with a grandiose flair, bowed and played his flute. The songs had ancient rhythms that brought claps and cheers from the crowd. He played nonstop for an hour, evoking sentiments of pleasure and happiness. With a loud trill of ascending notes the wizard ended his performance. He again bowed as he took his seat next to Earthkin.

Coaldon stood erect and motionless next to the exterior door. Mr. Baggy gave Topple a rousing cheer of appreciation. Musicians rarely visited the village. The local people expressed sincere appreciation before resuming a discussion of village problems.

Several travelers talked freely about the turmoil in Neverly and the unsafe conditions on the roads. The plague of criminal activities was creating instability in the Empire. Travelers were hiring guards to protect their caravans. Coaldon was particularly interested in the recent attack on Crossmore the Wizard. It was said the kind and gentle wizard had been attacked by an evil power, destroying his right hand. Topple quietly laughed at the story.

The major topics of discussion were the large wolf like animals in the forest and the rumors of tall ugly beasts in the wilderness. A story was told about a family being killed by spirit wolves on Rock Creek.

A man stated he had seen the beasts. He explained, "These spirit wolves were not natural. They look like wolves, but are much larger. These creatures have no fear of people and talk to each other in a growling language. I had the impression they were evil spirits dressed in wolves' clothing."

The crowd gasped in distress at this revelation.

A traveling salesman told about a robbery on the road to Neverly. A buzz of comments burst from the crowd concerning each bit of news. One man questioned, "I wonder if this has anything to do with the strange old man living in Lost Valley? Could he have started the plague of evil?"

A chorus of voices arose, some in agreement and others in opposition.

A Royal Vigilante jumped to his feet, yelling, "Foreigners are causing these problems! Three foreigners arrived today. They are polluting our fine community! They should not be allowed to stay!"

Jabbing his finger into Earthkin's chest, he demanded, "Go away and stop corrupting these good people!"

With that said, he drew a knife from his pant leg. Yet, before he could even raise his weapon, Earthkin's knife was pointing directly at the vigilante's throat.

The man yelled, "See what I mean. They are killers and thugs!"

Replacing his knife in its sheath, he raged out of the Inn. The crowd sat in disbelief and confusion. Sadly, some of them agreed with the vigilante. An argument between two men ended in a fistfight. The mood had gone from the beauty of Topple's flute to the evil created by the Royal Vigilante.

Earthkin stepped in between the two fighters, breaking up the fight. He proclaimed, "This is no way to solve problems. Do not allow violence to corrupt your fine community."

Pausing he continued, "We are tired after our long journey. Please excuse us. It is time for us retire to our rooms."

An hour before sunrise Earthkin awoke Coaldon from a sound sleep. The dwarf had everything packed by the time Coaldon and Topple were ready to depart. They ate an early morning breakfast in the warm kitchen. The kitchen was a stir of activities in preparation for the morning meals. Earthkin gave Mr. Baggy a generous tip for his excellent accommodations. While Topple and Earthkin talked to Mr. Baggy, Coaldon went to the boathouse to retrieve Rose Petal and Sid. The animals greeted him with excitement.

The three travelers were the first to arrive at the ferry. The ferry master accepted an extra fee to take them across the river before regular service hours. The early morning sun painted the scattered clouds in a beautiful blend of reds, oranges and pinks. This splendid backdrop of colors set the stage for Coaldon's new life. He was leaving the village of his youth and facing the hopes and dreams of his adult life.

ONWARD

Earthkin, Topple and Coaldon stepped off the ferry boat feeling despair. They stood on the shore of the river without saying a word. No words could describe their sadness. The peaceful village had been contaminated by the cancer spreading over the Empire. Crossmore's sickness infected the community. Either the citizens would fight the disease or all would be lost.

Gazing at the village from across the river Earthkin finally stated, "I am surprised at the disorder we found. Anger and frustration have literally exploded inside the village."

Turning away from the village, he continued, "I am tired. I believe we need to rest before going to the Monastery. Many small farms occupy the north side of the river. I suggest we find a farm family who will provide us with board and room for several days."

The small group followed the well-traveled road through the farmlands. They walked until there was only one farm left on the road. By this time Coaldon had removed the monk's robe.

With a giggle, Topple declared, "In my great wisdom, I select this farm. Matter of fact, we either choose this farm or we choose nothing."

As they approached the house, two large dogs greeted them with loud barks and growls. Topple walked up to the dogs in a carefree manner. He dropped to his knees and looked into the dogs eyes. Each dog gave a whimper of submission. Sid loped toward them in a playful mood. With a robust burst of energy the three dogs leaped off together. Topple enjoyed watching the dogs bounding around the yard. The dogs chased each other in circles and jumped to escape the pursuing animal. A small nip on the rump caused a frisky salvo of barking.

Earthkin approached the house in a casual manner. Several men with clubs greeted him at the front steps. A large man with a heavy black beard demanded, "What do you want?"

Earthkin bowed, saying, "We are in search of lodging for several days. We are honest travelers in need of rest. We will pay you well for your service."

The big man responded, "What did you do to my dogs? Nobody has ever gotten past them. They are vicious killers."

Earthkin continued, "They recognize we have no intention of causing harm. We come in peace."

The big man turned toward the door of the house as a woman stepped out. She looked with curiosity at the three travelers and the dogs. She smiled at the man saying, "Dod, it is all right with me if they stay for several days. We could use the company."

The big man nodded as he led Earthkin to a cabin next to the barn.

He said, "My wife likes you, so you are all right with me. You may stay in the cabin. Wood for the fireplace is behind the shed. The dinner meal will be served at 6:00 in the evening. If you need anything just ask. Good day."

The travelers gathered in the cabin to rest before the meal. It was pleasant to relax without being concerned about impending doom.

The ringing of the kitchen bell invited the guests to dinner. The three travelers sat down at the large table with Dod, his wife Doria, their daughter Rosa and a workman. The meal was pork, turnips and bread. Dod was interested in learning about the rumors of strange events. Earthkin told the stories he heard in Grandy.

Dod finally said, "We have heard the unnatural howl of wolves. I know they are not ordinary wolves. The calls are not normal. It cuts through my spirit with fear. Also, we have seen large foot prints near the farm. So far the dogs have kept unwanted visitors away."

Dod was uncertain if he wanted to ask the question burning in his mind.

He reluctantly stated, "We are just peaceful farmers. We have never needed to defend the farm with weapons. We are becoming concerned about our personal safety. Danger seems to be lurking at the edge of our farm. It has been many years since I studied the art of war. You appear to be warriors. Would you teach us to defend ourselves?"

Coaldon and Earthkin looked at each other with questioning eyes. Finally, Earthkin said, "We would be happy to assist you. What would you like to know?"

Dod showed them several old swords. Coaldon and Earthkin looked at the swords with surprise. Both were elfin weapons with unusual runes carved onto the blades in the ancient spiral script. Coaldon rubbed away the dust on one to take a closer look.

He read out loud, "The Sword of Truth will bless the hand that uses it in the defense of all that is good."

Coaldon could not read the writing on the other blade.

Earthkin said, "This sword is a weapon of great power. I am amazed you possess a sword of such great value. Remember, if it is used for righteous purposes it will assist you in fighting any evil."

Earthkin said, "Tomorrow we will teach you to use different weapons."

The next two days passed quickly as Coaldon and Earthkin explained how to use the sword, spear and bow in self-defense. By the evening of the second day the family members had been taught the basic moves in the use of each weapon. Doria and Rosa practiced alongside the men. They did not want to just watch, but desired to learn to defend themselves.

Coaldon explained, "It will be necessary to practice with these weapons daily. Only practice will prepare you to defend yourselves."

At dinner, Coaldon noticed that Rosa was watching him. Rosa was an attractive girl of 17 years. She had an outgoing personality with intelligence to match her strong character. The work on the farm had given her rough hands and strong muscles. Her mother taught her as a small child to read and write. After dinner Doria sent Coaldon and Rosa to take care of the evening chores. The two talked and laughed as they completed the tasks. Rosa was happy to meet someone her age, especially a handsome young man. They found it easy to talk together.

Rosa stated, "We moved to the farm from Neverly when I was a little child. My parents never told me why we moved here."

Coaldon responded, "That is strange. My grandparents also moved to the Outlast at about the same time. Maybe Wastelow drove your parents out of the capital?"

When they returned to the house, darkness was casting its long shadows over the land. Coaldon shyly promised he would visit her on a return trip.

The travelers left the farm at sunrise the next morning. Topple decided to leave Rose Petal at the farm in the care of gentle hands. Dod, Doria, and Rosa felt saddened to see their special guests leave the farm. Rosa and Coaldon touched each other's hands before they departed.

After leaving the farm, the travelers entered into a dense forest. They followed a seldom used road that wondered aimlessly in a westerly direction. Coaldon's attention was not on the journey. He could only daydream about returning to visit Rosa. The half elf felt a fire burning in his soul that he did not understand. For some reason the mysterious longing to be with Rosa had a bitter-sweet feeling. He experienced the longing to be with Rosa and the warm glow of her memory.

They had kept a steady westerly course all morning. The high peaks of the Black Mountains were looming on the western horizon. Coaldon's attention returned to his surroundings when the travelers walked out of the forest and on to the grasslands. He had never seen the Great Plains. The miles of grass and the openness was a feast to his senses. He could see for miles without anything obstructing his view. His feet sank into the rich soil that provided the basic nutrition for the abundance of life on the prairie. Large and small animals could be seen in all directions. Many small rodents scampered around in pursuit of some unseen destiny. Wild dogs could be seen hunting in small packs in the distance. Hawks and eagles circled in search of their next meal. Herds of horses and deer aimless grazed on the horizon.

After the noon meal, Topple said, "We should arrive at the Wastelands by nightfall. I have visited the Monastery several times. I remember how challenging it was to find my way through the puzzle of channels. I am looking forward to walking the twisted paths."

Topple's mood lightened as they approached the Wastelands. At dusk the grasslands abruptly ended at the boundaries of the giant labyrinth. In disbelief Coaldon stood before the barren and bleak maze of canyons. To him it felt as if the life force had been ripped from the land. Only a shell of existence remained in the form of desolation.

With reluctance Earthkin led the way into the badlands. He found shelter for the night in a dead end gully.

Coaldon commented, "I have found large wolf foot prints at the mouth of the canyon. We do not want to relax our guard tonight."

After dinner Earthkin and Coaldon took turns on guard duty. The steep walls of the narrow canyon created absolute silence. The whisper of bat wings could be heard in the muffled surroundings. Coaldon had never experienced such silence in his entire life. He developed a growing sense of entrapment within the towering walls of the canyon. He walked around to listen to the sound of his feet crunching on the rocky ground. He was happy when the morning light broke the spell of isolation. The voices of his traveling mates sounded like songs from heaven. The half elf looked forward to escaping from the absolute emptiness of the Wastelands.

Topple led the way into the maze of canyons with confident strides. He made the selection between canyons without pondering or breaking stride. The travelers made good progress as the morning hours passed. Sid, with his nose to the ground, suddenly left Coaldon's side. He ran ahead of the group to investigate the trail. Sid stopped with his eyes focused on the entrance of a side canyon. He barked a warning as three giant wolves jumped into the canyon ahead of them. These were not ordinary wolves, but something clever and wicked.

Topple exclaimed, "These are spirit wolves. They are intelligent and very dangerous. Spread out across the canyon floor. Let them come to us. Patience and confidence will be our best weapon."

The spirit wolves watched the group with hostile eyes. Their muscles rippled with anticipation. They waited for their victims to either run or attack. The three men looked at the beasts with calm self-assurance. Finally the creatures sprang forward with a burst of speed. The leader attacked Topple with a ferocious leap. Topple raised his hand, releasing a bolt of lightning. The spirit wolf froze mid-air dying before it hit the ground. Topple sagged with fatigue from the expenditure of energy.

The other two creatures lunged forward in unison. Coaldon paused as a giant beast rushed toward him. In hesitation he took a step backward tripping over his own feet. As he fell on his back, he had the alertness of mind to raise his feet to catch the forward motion of the wolf. With the push of his legs, Coaldon sent the wolf sailing over him. Coaldon jumped to his feet before the wolf could regain its footing. With a wide stroke, his sword nipped the top of the wolf's head. The spirit wolf's eyes burned with hatred. The cut on its head and the sight of Coaldon enraged the beast with an immeasurable passion to kill. Like an arrow being released from a bow, the massive beast sprang forward. Coaldon stepped forward with his sword pointing directly at the wolf's chest. The wolf hit him with such force that he was knocked to the ground.

With stars floating in his head, he tried to get up. To his horror he was unable to move. He looked up to see the wolf's mouth next to his face. With an explosion of energy he rolled to his left. The rolling motion allowed him to twist free of the heavy body. With a cat-like reaction, he sprang to his feet grabbing his knife from its scabbard. He held it in his shaking hand ready to defend himself. Lying on the ground, unable to move, the wolf looked at him in distress. Coaldon's sword was buried deep in the wolf's chest. As he watched, the wolf dissolved into a cloud of black smoke.

Coaldon looked around to determine what to do next. To his relief, all the spirit wolves were gone. He saw Topple sitting on a boulder with a broad smile on his face. Earthkin stood next to him with the look of satisfaction.

The dwarf stated, "I am glad there were only three of them. They are vicious fellows."

Topple glowing with excitement said, "That was fun! Fighting those nasty things provide good exercise and keeps our minds alert."

In frustration Earthkin erupted, "I do not need the exercise or the stimulation! But I do know we need to keep moving. There could be more of these creatures looking for entertainment."

After a short break, they returned to their trek. The wizard led the group like a blood hound sniffing out a trail. With a sense of calm assurance he made each turn in the labyrinth without hesitation. As they entered an especially narrow gully, Sid growled. He bounded forward at a full run. On the canyon floor they saw a body with Sid standing over it. Topple laughed as he trotted forward. Sid was growling as Topple approached the body. Topple giggled, "Now whom do we have here? Maybe it is a lost sheep or an orphan goat?"

Sid stepped back from the body with his tail wagging. With bewildered eyes, Pacer stood up with a look of disbelief. In delight he gave Topple a robust hug.

Topple squeaked, "I didn't know you cared. Now, let me go you big bully. I can't breathe."

Earthkin and Coaldon rushed to greet Pacer. The emotions ran high for several moments. Coaldon actually had tears of joy running down his face. He had missed Pacer's unwavering personality.

Pacer's face grew pale as he struggled to remain enthusiastic. He finally sat down with sweat pouring off his face.

He commented, "I was hit by an arrow. I think it was poisoned. Would you check my leg?"

Earthkin carefully pealed back the dressing. The wound was an angry red with puss oozing from it. He removed a small bottle of liquid from his side pouch. He rubbed a healing liquid into the wound. Pacer gasped with pain as the healing lotion ate away the infection. His eyes slowly closed as he lost consciousness.

Earthkin said, "It is best he passed out. This is going to hurt."

He lit a candle from the hot coals of his small tinderbox. He placed his knife over the flame to sterilize the blade. Topple and Coaldon held Pacer down as he lanced the wound. He slowly dug around in the wound with his knife to clean out the remaining infection. The dwarf smiled as he pulled out a small piece of metal.

He said, "This metal may be poisoned with the Curse of Death. I want to keep it for later examination." He reapplied the healing lotion and dressed the wound.

The dwarf smiled as he directed, "I will carry Pacer. Topple, you lead the way. "

The afternoon quickly passed. Coaldon noticed that Earthkin's massive strength was beginning to sag under the weight of Pacer's heavy body. As the sun was setting in the west, they walked out of the canyon into open fields. Several monks dressed in green robes were sitting on a bench near a stream. They stood to greet their guests.

The tallest monk said, "We have been waiting for you. Let us carry your wounded friend to the Monastery. We will take good care of him. We must hurry if we are to reach the Monastery before dark."

Coaldon stood in awe at the sight of the Monastery towering over the valley. It sat on top of a hill surrounded by cliffs. The Village of Toms was a collection of low buildings bathed in the shadow of the great Monastery. The Cathedral was constructed in a symmetrical blend of sweeping arches, tall towers, small chapels and majestic shrines. Earthkin commented, "This intricate stonework required the expert skills of many dwarf stonemasons. It must have been built in an age when the creation of beauty was of great value."

The road leading to the Monastery was narrow and angled upward across the side of a sheer cliff.

As Coaldon drew near the Monastery, he found himself relaxing. The peaceful surroundings helped him forget about the long, dangerous journey. He turned his head and looked at the beauty of the valley. He felt a swell of calm expand into his body and mind.

This moment was interrupted when he thought about his grandparents. He remembered leaving them on the farm only to return to find the farm destroyed. The charred ruins of the farm house did not leave any clues as to their fate. The memory of their smiling faces haunted him. At first, he wanted to rush off and search for them. Yet, he questioned, "Where would I look?" He finally decided he would trust the One Presence to bring them together.

ᚱᛏᚢᚨ, ᛁᛘᚹᛏᛁᚨ, ᚢᛘᚨ ᛣᚨᚢᛏᚲᚳᚳᚨ

Brad, Ingrid, and Starhood

Starhood stood in a detached mood as Coaldon, Pacer and Earthkin left on their journey to find Topple. To him, this was just another uneventful expedition. It was common for people to journey around the Empire.

On the day of the departure, Starhood sat in front of the fireplace for many hours. His thoughts drifted in a sea of free flowing ideas and images. The memories of many centuries churned in his mind. He realized success in defeating Wastelow depended on understanding the long history of the Empire. Human nature had not changed over time. The struggle was still between the quest to gain power and the pursuit of goodness.

During the early afternoon he drifted into an eerie trance. The events of the cabin were pushed aside as the flames of the fire captivated his full attention. He found himself floating in the tongues of the blaze. At first, he felt pleasure at this unique interlude, yet soon the intensity of the heat grew uncomfortable. Pleasure was replaced by growing turbulence. Within the flames he saw a peaceful meadow transformed into a battlefield. The flickering images, within the blaze, revealed a landslide of human events rushing toward unavoidable conflict. The impending collision was depicted by a hand crushing a gentle flower. Out of the hand flowed wicked beasts trampling and corrupting the beauty of nature. Then a group of ants immerged from the flames. These insects stood as insignificant obstacles to a towering giant. Yet, he sensed that success or failure was not a matter of size but an aspect of faith. Out of the flame burst a shower of blue and red sparks. These embers dusted the ants with hope, wisdom and courage. The irrelevant insects were changed into creatures of power and determination.

Starhood awoke from the trance with a warring contrast of dread and hope. The images of the dream disclosed prophetic illuminations of the future. He decided to keep this revelation to himself for the time being.

By late afternoon Starhood was ready for a break. Ingrid had prepared a light evening meal. The conversation at the table was limited to the weather and farm. Nobody wanted to talk about their impending destiny. The three adults knew the Age of Change would require them to confront the ugly face of violence and war.

After dinner, Brad and Ingrid joined Starhood by the fireplace. With the heat of the roaring fire warming their spirits, Starhood sang a song about the elfin Queen Lolia. His voice filled the cabin with mystery and wonderment. The magic of his words transformed the plain and simple cabin into a world of majesty and grace. As Starhood sang, Ingrid and Brad could visualize Queen Lolia as she conquered evil. The strength of her character extended into the fiber of the room. Brad and Ingrid found themselves absorbing the essence of Lolia's courage and conviction.

Starhood ended the song by singing these words:

"Queen Lolia held the rod of hope
with the courage of a lion,
and strength of a river;
She reached forth
with the touch of her power,
Not to destroy,
but to offer healing;
Her love gave presence to The Mantel of Wisdom.

She revealed,
evil manifests destruction;
love prompts forgiveness;
mercy empowers justice,
freedom sanctions choice.

She declared,
Blessed are the brave of heart who carry
the banner of righteousness.
Blessed is the glory of freedom
granting strength through choice."

The song ended, as it started, in the silence of the room. The depth of their friendship added determination to the goal of returning justice to the empire. Tomorrow would provide a path they could either accept or reject. Only by the courage of choice could they fulfill their destiny. The peace of the night invited restful sleep.

On the morning of the fourth day after the departure of the three men, Ingrid and Brad were busy packing for the move to the Monastery. Starhood decided to go for a walk along the river. As he strolled in the forest, he heard the excited voices of wood elves. Out of the brush a noble wood elf hastily greeted him.

The elf stated, "My name is Treeshine. There is great danger approaching this valley. You have until noon to leave or face death. The long arm of evil is reaching for you. We will help you escape across the river. A raft has been prepared for you. Remember, you must hurry."

Starhood bowed to his distinguished cousins and left without saying a word. He jogged back to the cabin to sound the alarm. Ingrid and Brad accepted the news with composure. Although their hearts were in anguish, their souls grasped the challenge. They packed their essentials in several large bags. With heavy hearts, they walked to the river.

The wood elves greeted the Emperor and Queen with dignity. Yet, formalities were limited to only a few words in order to make a quick retreat. A hastily constructed raft waited for them. Five wood elves stood ready to navigate the raft across the river. Sid, the dog, did not arrive at the bank of the river with Brad and Ingrid. Brad called for Sid several times but to no avail. The alarm of urgency was sounded when they heard a distant rumble.

Treeshine said, "I am sorry but we must go! The dog will need to fend for himself. They are upon us!"

The raft was loaded and pushed into the current. With long poles the elves guided the raft across the river. As they reached the opposite shore, the noise of screaming voices filled the valley. The passengers quickly unloaded the raft and hurried into the underbrush. It was necessary to find a hiding place before they were seen by the approaching mob.

Steep mountains blocked their escape to the north, while cliffs bordered the river to the east and west. This made it impossible to follow the river either up or down stream. The only escape route was to go over North Ridge. Brad led the group to the base of a tall cliff, allowing a view of the valley. He was angry with himself for not leaving earlier. Now, escape had become a life and death situation.

He asked himself, "How do we get out of here? We may have to hike over the pass."

The boom of a loud drum echoed in the valley. The beat of a war drum increased in tempo as a large number of ugly beasts swarmed over the farm. The cabin was set afire; the farm animals were killed and all the outbuildings were torn down. Shouts and screams fed the mass frenzy of the monsters. Many beasts feed on the raw flesh of the dead farm animals. Some used knives to cut large pieces of meat from the bodies. Others ripped and tore the flesh with their teeth. These evil creatures showed pleasure in destroying the farm.

The beasts carefully searched the area for any humans. Scouting parties were sent in different directions to find the escapees.

Starhood commented, "These are trogs. They have been released from the Chamber of Oblivion. This is a sign of great sorrow."

In disbelief and disgust, Ingrid and Brad watched the work of many years disappear in a matter of minutes. Tears ran down their sad faces. Ingrid quickly composed herself.

In angry words she responded, "I will never forget this moment. The enemy is real. The enemy will kill and destroy without conscience or caring. Our course has been set for us. We must do what is right and necessary."

A sudden silence interrupted the roar of violence. The trogs stood in fear as they watched a black cloud approaching from the west. A rumble of thunder rocked the valley as the cloud descended onto the farm. The trogs fell to the ground in dread and trembling. The cloud aimlessly drifted over the ground in search of something. It then paused over the remains of the cabin. After several minutes it moved in the direction of the river. At that moment Brad, Ingrid and Starhood knew the evil being was after them.

Treeshine yelled, "We must hurry! Follow me!" He ran along the base of the cliff. The underbrush, fallen trees and large rocks provided obstacles to the group's progress. The hasty retreat over the rugged terrain caused many bruises, bumps and scratches. The black cloud slowly floated to the river's edge while emitting deep rumbling sounds. It crossed over the river and settled on the ground where the party had landed.

Treeshine quickly entered a small crevice in the cliff wall. He then crawled into a hidden entrance like a rodent entering its burrow. The remaining elves crawled into the hole with grace and agility. The humans, because of their larger bodies, found the small opening a challenge to squeeze through. Ingrid wiggled through after a brief struggle. Brad got stuck half way into the entrance. With grunts, groans and moans he labored to squeeze into the cave. The dark cloud hovered over the side of the cliff in search of its prey. It gave a robust laugh when it spotted two legs protruding from the base of the cliff.

In a booming voice it declared, "Death is upon you!"

When Brad heard the message, he found renewed strength to push himself into the cave. He burst into the cave with clawing hands and digging feet.

A powerful force slammed against the side of the cliff. At the impact, rocks and dust fell from the tunnel ceiling. Again, the ground shook as the black cloud pounded the mountain side. Over and over the creature tried to reach the escapees by crushing the side of the cliff.

The dull witted monster proclaimed, "I will get you!"

A bolt of lighting struck the entrance to the cave. The blinding flash of light caused the escapees to turn their heads. Then, to their despair, a vaporous hand reached through the entrance to the cave. Its groping fingers nearly grabbed Brad before he escaped deeper into the tunnel. A repulsive feeling of evil began to over power them.

Treeshine said, "Elfin legend tells that this is an entrance to a massive tunnel system. I believe it is more dangerous to face the dark cloud than to confront the uncertainty of the cave. I suggest we follow the passage wherever it may take us."

With a nod of heads, they plunged into the darkness of the tunnel. The howl of anger slowly disappeared as the escapees trudged deeper into the bowels of the earth.

Starhood removed a blue elfin gem from his travel bag. After speaking several words in an ancient elf language, a light radiated from the stone. The gem provided adequate light to see where they were going. As they walked down the main passage, many openings appeared out of the darkness on both sides of the tunnel.

Starhood suggested, "We need to stop. I do not want to proceed until we make plans. I am not comfortable in this dark and damp world."

Brad agreed, saying, "I do not like this place. Worst of all, we are lost in the labyrinth of passages. It is best to stop and allow common sense to guide our way."

The wood elves were starting to show signs of distress at being trapped in the narrow tunnel. These delicate creatures found joy in the freedom of open spaces, the glow of stars and the beauty of nature.

Treeshine responded, "Legend tells there are many entrances in the mountain. We could search for a tunnel with fresh air flowing from it. We could follow it to its origins."

Feeling a flush of irritation, Ingrid stated, "Our mission will not be destroyed by this little detour. You can search for fresh air, but we will escape because it is our destiny. While you look for fresh air, I will claim the providence of my faith."

Starhood was paying little attention to the conversation of the group. He felt a growing discomfort. He was less concerned about the escape than actually living through this experience. Something evil was lurking in these tunnels.

The tunnel continued on a downward slope into an unknown world. To the frustration of the travelers, none of the tunnels smelled of fresh air. Rather, as they walked deeper, the air became increasingly foul.

While the others were concerned about survival, Ingrid felt a sense of excitement. Her life on the farm had offered a narrow exposure to the world. She submitted to her life with gracious acceptance, but always had a secret dream to step beyond the ordinary. She found it stimulating to look at the details of the tunnel. She noticed the walls and floor were smooth and even. She tried to imagine skilled artisans carving the tunnel and the sound of happy voices.

She asked herself, "I wonder what drove these people from their home. This must have been a beautiful place to live."

The tunnel abruptly opened into a large cavern. The light of Starhood's gem only reached a short distance into the vast opening. He signaled the others to wait while he investigated. The sound of his footsteps echoed in the vast cavern. Starhood stopped to listen. To his dismay, he heard the sound of deep, raspy breathing.

A melodious voice spoke, "Who are you? Why do you disturb my rest? You are trespassing in my kingdom!"

Starhood answered, "We come in peace. We only seek to escape from the mountain."

The voice laughed in response, "Nobody escapes from me. You are my prisoners. You will be my plaything."

Starhood continued, "I do not know your name. You speak with eloquence. I would assume you are a great leader and warrior."

The voice boomed in pride, "I am Gutrot the Great. This has been my kingdom for centuries. I possess great power. I have many slaves. You will soon be one of them!"

In a calm voice Starhood stated, "You should think carefully before attacking us."

The noise of crushing rocks filled the cavern. Starhood signaled his companions to step deeper into the tunnel.

He whispered to them, "I will delay Gutrot's attack. I will join you when I have given this creature something to remember our visit."

In the light of the gemstone, Starhood could see the approaching monster. Gutrot had the shape of a slug with tentacles lining the front of his body. It was covered with long, shaggy hair. Two massive arms were attached to its sides. Each arm had three long, claw like fingers. The arms were used to push its massive body forward. Its face was located high on the front of its body. One large orange eye sat above a flat nose. Its enormous mouth covered the center of its face. A long tongue darted in and out of its mouth with nervous regularity. Mucus dribbled from its nose in long, slimy strings. The beast's foul odor was overwhelming.

Gutrot's bloated body slithered across the cavern floor with grace and speed. Gutrot's waving tentacles indicated its excitement. It stopped in front of Starhood. Gutrot raised his fat, grotesque body in preparation for an attack on Starhood.

Starhood raised the blue gem into the air. He released a bolt of lighting into the beast's single eye. Gutrot fell forward as it gave a piercing scream of pain. Starhood stepped back into the tunnel opening just before the beast fell to the ground. Starhood narrowly escaped being crushed by its massive weight. Gutrot's tentacles reached into the tunnel. Starhood used his sword to attack the groping tentacles. With a wide swing, his sword cut several tentacles from the enormous body. The monster grunted in frustration as it continued to reach for its victim. Starhood leaped back several steps to remain beyond the reach of Gutrot. Starhood turned to face his companions.

Gutrot shrieked, "You have blinded me! I will get you! I will send my friends."

Starhood yelled, "Follow me! We must hurry! We will have unwanted visitors very soon."

Starhood led the way up the tunnel at a run. Brad fell back to guard the rear of the group. Ten minutes later, the group was forced to stop when the passageway forked into five different tunnels. Starhood looked at Ingrid with inquisitive eyes. It was time to use the intuitive power of this skilled lady.

He said, "Ingrid, which way do we go?"

Ingrid assumed the challenge with poise and assurance. She paused before the entrance to each tunnel before deciding. With decisiveness, she declared, "I select the center passage."

The central passage remained level for a short distance. Then to everyone's surprise they found a staircase. Without pausing, the group bound up the stairs. After an extended hike Ingrid demanded a rest. Her legs were burning with fatigue.

Starhood stopped at a wide landing. The landing was a large room extending back into the rock formation. He asked everybody to remain silent so he could listen. To their relief the passage remained quiet.

The climb continued uninterrupted until Ingrid again requested the group to stop.

She whispered, "I feel the presence of many creatures ahead of us. I expect an attack at the next landing."

Starhood did not question her insight. As they approached the room, he held a council of war.

He whispered, "I expect the landing to be a large room allowing space to fight. I will step into the space and release a burst of light from the gem. The light will cause confusion. Remember we are interested in defending ourselves. We only want to stop their attack, not maim and kill."

In silence the company approached the landing. Starhood leaped onto the landing with his sword in one hand and the gem in the other. He forced the gem to give off a bright flash of light. With shouts of pain, fifteen cave dwellers stood blinded. The attackers had a human appearance with extra large eyes, short muscular bodies, baldheads and pasty white faces. Their naked bodies were covered with black grease. The cave dwellers stood gaping at the light.

As Brad and the wood elves ran onto the landing, the battle began. With swinging swords Starhood and Brad were first to wade into the group of cave dwellers. The dwellers were so stunned by the light that they offered little resistance. After eight dwellers were wounded, the remaining attackers ran in panic. They ran into walls, fell down the stairs and attacked each other. The landing was cleared of cave dwellers in short order. Not one received a major wound. Treeshine had a cut on the leg, which was quickly bandaged. Brad had to contend with a bump on his head.

Ingrid said, "There is more evil. I can feel its presence."

Starhood responded, "I propose we continue climbing. I do not want to be caught by any more of Gutrot's friends."

The staircase continued its steady upward ascent. After a long climb, fatigue became an enemy.

The stairs finally ended on a platform with one tunnel entrance opening into darkness. Without hesitating, Starhood lead the group into the wide passageway. The tunnel twisted and turned in unusual patterns. At several locations it was constricted to small crawl spaces and narrow channels. The floor was uneven, with sections of steep inclines and declines.

Brad commented, "This tunnel was constructed to slow the advance of an invader. It was especially effective if a large army was trying to rush after the inhabitants. Somewhere in the area is a normal tunnel that was used by the defenders."

After an hour of struggling through the defensive barrier, a stream of light greeted the tired companions. Everybody gave a shout of conquest. The group entered a large cavern with a door on the opposite side. Bright sun light flowed through the opening, blinding their light sensitive eyes. Everybody sat on the floor with a sense of relief. Hope was a pleasant sensation.

In desperation, Ingrid leaped to her feet yelling, "We must go! It has arrived!"

As she spoke, a shudder throbbed throughout the mountain. A black, dense smoke poured out of the tunnel. The cloud moved across the floor with finger like probes. The outline of a face could be seen in the smoke. A whisper, as cold as ice, penetrated the cavern like a knife. It sliced through their souls, leaving a wound of fear. Each person heard a compelling voice command, "Do not move! Go to sleep!"

Before anybody could move the cloud surrounded them. With dazed eyes each adventurer was held prisoner by the commanding voice. The cold fingers of the smoke began to reach into their minds. The cavern became filled with coughing and gasping.

Breaking the trance, Brad yelled, "Hold on to each other's hands and follow me." With hesitant steps the group slowly moved across the room towards the fading light. Brad encouraged everyone to keep moving. A wood elf dropped to his knees in a deep sleep. Treeshine threw the limp body over his shoulder as he staggered forward. Starhood felt sleepiness creep into his mind. He had to fight to keep from slumping into unconsciousness. With heroic effort the companions pushed ever closer to the cave entrance.

Then, as so often happens in life, a miracle occurred. A sudden blast of air blew through the opening into the cavern. The dense smoke was pushed away from the struggling group by the burst of clean air. With a rush everybody staggered through the doorway to the outside. A cold wind washed over the adventurers as they fell to the ground. Several wood elves collapsed into a deep sleep. The other members lay gasping and wheezing. The smoke poured out of the cavern in pursuit of its victims. It did not move far before light of day attacked its presence. To everybody's relief, the smoke was vulnerable to light. The light of day consumed its energy, causing the smoke to dissipate into the morning air.

Journey to the Monastery

Brad lay on the cold ground as the morning sun warmed his back. He saw they were located on a small ledge facing south into Lost Valley. The ledge was about half way up the face of North Peak. The Monastery of Toms would be located to the east. The foul black smoke continued to flow in billowing puffs from the opening. Brad decided it was time to assess their present situation. The three wood elves and Starhood were starting to awaken from their sleep. Everybody else sat against the ledge wall in a state of drowsy confusion. The combination of fresh air and rest was the medicine needed to cure their disorientation.

When everybody was back to normal, Starhood said, "Gutrot may send his friends to find us after the smoke dissipates. I do not want to be here when they arrive. A trail descends the mountain in the direction of the Monastery of Toms. I propose we follow it until we find a good campsite. The farther I am from Gutrot the better I will feel."

With nods of agreement, the group readied to depart. The trail down the east face of North Peak was easy to follow. By late-afternoon the path entered a meadow with a small stream running through it. Brad sent Starhood and Treeshine to find a secure campsite. Shortly, Treeshine returned with the ideal location. It was situated in a small crevice against a low hanging shelf. If the group was attacked during the night the ravine would provide protection. A hot meal of trail food provided the opportunity to celebrate the group's escape from the cave. The festivities consisted of short speeches, humorous reenactments of the escape and time for causally talk. As darkness descended onto the campsite, the travelers rolled into their sleeping blankets. Under the watchful eyes and ears of the guards, the night passed with an uneasy tension.

After an early breakfast the party left the meadow. Brad wanted to reach the

Wasteland before night fall. A good trail helped achieve their goal. As the sun dropped low into the west, the escapees topped a rocky ridge. To their delight, the vastness of the Wastelands spread out before them. A hazy mist covered labyrinth's intricate pattern of channels. The distant horizon of the Wastelands disappeared into the haze of evening light.

The travelers arrived at the breaks of the Wasteland as the sun set behind North Peak. Brad selected a campsite in a steep walled gully. In spite of the wilderness conditions, a warm fire and hot food offered relief from the cold. Brad posted two guards to watch during the night.

At midnight Starhood was on guard duty. The light from the stars flooded his spirit with the warmth of an ancient rhythm. He added wood to the fire to provide heat and to keep wild things at a distance. He sat with his back to the fire to protect his night vision. He did not want to be night blinded by staring at the flames of the fire. As he sat in a state of alertness, he saw four sets of eyes appear in the distance.

Starhood gave a shout, "Be aware, my friends, we have visitors!"

Everybody in the camp bolted to a defensive stance. As the eyes drew nearer, they could see the outline of four large wolves with broad, flat faces.

He commented, "These are not ordinary wolves. These beasts have been brought out of the Chamber of Oblivion. These evil creatures are called spirit wolves."

Starhood pulled the blue gem from his pocket and walked toward the creatures.

He projected his thoughts at the wolves saying, "Depart from us and do not return."

The wolves backed away several steps. Then the largest beast leaped forward. Starhood raised the gem into the air and projected a strong beam of light at the lead wolf. The beast stopped when the light hit its eyes. The wolf gave a growl of anger as the light burned into its mind.

With contempt and arrogance the wolf responded, "The light is a nice trick, oh noble elf. We are not here to play children's games. We will destroy you, so beware. You will not arrive at the Monastery."

The wolves slowly turned, disappearing into the dark. The howl of the wolves continued throughout the night, but they did not return to the camp.

In the morning Brad told the wood elves they could return to their homes. Brad said, "I do not believe the wolves will bother you. They want Starhood, Ingrid and me. Go in peace. Without your help we would have died. I extend to you my thanks. Your noble efforts have allowed the conquest of evil to continue. Go in peace, for your courage has provided a chapter in the history of the Empire."

Treeshine said, "We accept your thanks. Your mission is also our quest. If you need help, the wood elves will stand by your side."

Brad responded, "We extend to you prayers for bright stars, warm fires, happy songs and clear trails."

After a round of handshakes the wood elves walked in single file toward Rolling River. Sadness gripped the remaining travelers.

Starhood stated, "I do not know the route to the Monastery from this location. We will let the One Presence provide for use. It is best to allow the route to the Monastery to find us."

Brad suggested they wait in their campsite until they received guidance. They spent the morning sitting in front of the fire talking about the adventures of the past few days.

At mid-day a stranger in a green robe walked into their campsite. He bowed respectfully and stood in silence until Brad recognized him.

Brad said, "Welcome to our most humble encampment. Would you like a hot drink and food?"

The monk responded, "Yes, I would. Thank you."

After finishing his meal, the stranger responded, "I am Brother Patrick, a warrior monk from the Monastery of Toms. I extend the greetings and blessings from Abbot Hugh. I have been sent by the Abbot to guide you to the Monastery."

Brother Patrick was a tall man with broad muscular shoulders, a black beard and long hair tied into a knot. He moved with the grace and confidence of a seasoned fighter.

Brad questioned him, "How did you know we were waiting for help."

He answered, "We received informed about the invasion of Lost Valley. Your escape from the mountain has been closely monitored. I was sent to you as soon as your location was confirmed"

Brother Patrick walked around the campsite examining the ground.

He then said, "The wolves have found you. These evil spirits have been sent to destroy you. We must be alert to a possible attack as we journey through the Wasteland. We have many hours of hiking ahead of us. We should arrive at the Monastery by midnight."

Brother Patrick walked to the fire, sat in a cross-legged position and mediated for several moments. He then led the way into the Wastelands.

As travelers proceeded through the maze, they paid little attention to the unending number of turns and corners. They placed complete trust in Brother Patrick's ability to guide them safely to the Monastery. Each person watched for any sign of the wolves. By late afternoon the traveler's alertness relaxed. The sun was getting low in the west when Brother Patrick paused. His eyes shifted back and forth with total concentration. Brad and Starhood were jolted into state awareness. They were embarrassed at being so lax in watching for danger.

Brother Patrick signaled the party to gather around him. He whispered, "I sense danger. We must find a place to defend ourselves."

At this point, a pack of spirit wolves appeared ahead of them. The wolves were in no hurry to attack. They slowly walked toward the travelers. When the wolves were about 20 strides from the group, Brother Patrick stepped forward, pointed his sword at the ground and gave a short command in the high elf language. To everybody's surprise, a giant wall of flame filled the canyon between the group and the wolves.

Brother Patrick said, "Please follow me. We do not have much time before the flames will burn out. I know of a place where we can make a defensive stand."

Brother Patrick jogged down a side canyon. After several minutes the group arrived at a wide clearing with a mound in the center. Brother Patrick led the way up the steep, rough path ascending the mound. Brad stood rear guard to protect the group's retreat.

The wolves burst into the clearing at a full run. Their large red eyes were burning with blood lust. To slow the wolves attack, Brad killed the first two beasts with a wide swing of his sword. He ran up the narrow path to the top of the mount as several wolves ripped at his feet and legs. Starhood and Brother Patrick grabbed Brad's arms and pulled him up before the wolves' jaws could lock onto his legs.

Brad rolled over and looked at his torn clothes and wounds. He had several large cuts on his left leg. Brother Patrick took a bottle from his side pouch. He opened the wounds with his knife and poured the healing ointment into each cut.

He said, "This healing ointment will kill any chance of infection. You must lie still for several hours to allow the healing to begin."

Brother Patrick wrapped the wound with a clean, white cloth and elevated Brad's leg. Brad tried to get to his feet, but Ingrid gave him a gentle push, forcing him back to the ground.

She said, "Lie still or I will do more damage to you!"

Brad and Starhood laughed at Ingrid's aggressive behavior.

Several wolves tried to run up the path, but ran into flashing swords. Two wolves rolled back down the hill and disappeared in a puff of smoke.

Brother Patrick said, "These wolves are evil spirits. They have no fear of death and feel no pain. They are difficult to defeat because of their intelligence. We must stop any attack before the wolves reach the top of the knoll."

Five wolves rushed up the steep path to initiate their second attack. The defenders killed the first four wolves before they could reach the top. The last wolf was able to leap onto the mound without being stopped. It ran toward Brad sensing his weakened condition. Brad jumped to his knees, raised his sword and thrust it at the chest of the charging beast. The forward momentum of the wolf carried it over the top of Brad. It landed next to Ingrid with a bounce and roll. The wounded wolf staggered to its feet, opened its large mouth and prepared to attack Ingrid. Its large, fierce eyes burned with the desire to kill. Ingrid did not back away but faced the beast with cold contempt. She drew a small knife from a fold in her dress. She raised the weapon in defiance. Yet, to her great relief the wolf was transformed into a shimmering vapor. She looked in awe at the empty space where the wolf had once stood.

She looked at her companions saying, "What type of evil could create such a foul beast?"

The spirit wolves backed away from the mound at a short distance and lay down. At sunset five more wolves rushed up the steep path. Three of the attacking wolves were destroyed, but two made it to the top of the mound unopposed. These two wolves started to move in a circle around the defenders in slow calculated movements. Then, five more wolves made a rush at the mound.

This attack came to a halt when a trumpet sounded in the distance. Out of the narrow canyon a group of fifteen monks in green robes entered the clearing with their weapons in the ready position. Without hesitation the monks attacked the wolves with a wide sweeping offensive front. Arrows were released as the first line of offense. Several beasts dropped to the ground with arrows protruding from their sides. As the front line of the attack reached the wolves, spears were released with pinpoint accuracy. Three wolves sagged to the ground with spears thrust deeply into their bodies. The remaining wolves' resistance crumbled in front of the assault of flashing swords.

In the mean time, Brother Patrick, Treeshine, and Starhood quickly destroyed the remaining two wolves on the mound. A great silence followed the conclusion of the battle. The few remaining beasts slinked away into the growing darkness. The monks formed a circle in the center of the battlefield, bowed their heads and gave thanks for a successful victory.

Brad learned later that Brother Patrick sent a mental message to the Monastery asking for help. To everyone's satisfaction the monks' arrival saved the day. Brother Patrick informed the travelers of the necessity to continue the trek immediately. Brad was carried on a stretcher to prevent the deep wounds on his leg from bleeding. He complained, but after several sharp words from Ingrid, he became much more cooperative. He humbly submitted to the wishes of his determined and caring spouse.

The moon rose in the eastern skies shortly after sunset. Starhood watched the moon with the appreciation of an old friend. His soul was warmed when the moonlight flooded his being.

He said to himself, "As long as the moon glows and the stars shine, I will have the courage and strength to continue this crusade."

After many hours of hiking, the twisting channels of the labyrinth opened into a wide expanse of fields and farmland. In the distance the grandiose presence of the Monastery of Toms could be seen. The light of the moon reflecting off the Cathedral towers created a mystical image. The travelers stopped to absorb the immediate splendor of the majestic view. The beauty of the Monastery was a striking contrast to the violence they had experienced in the Wastelands. The travelers only vaguely remembered the remaining journey to the Monastery. The hike through the fields, village and Monastery complex was only a blur of images to their exhausted minds. Upon arriving, a warm dinner was followed by soft beds and pleasant dreams. The end of the challenging day was blessed with the gifts of safety and comfort.

The Monastery

Brad, Ingrid and Starhood spent their time at the Monastery in a routine of prayer, conversation and research in the library. The musty library preserved the wisdom of the ages and the history of ancient events. Starhood wandered in the library stacks with the joy of visiting old friends. He was determined to find the location of the Land of Westmore and the Key of Ban.

Time passed in pleasant relaxation. Yet, the thoughts of Coaldon, Pacer and Earthkin were never far from the guests' minds. At dinner on a quiet evening the Abbot announced, "Four travelers will be arriving at the Monastery later this evening. Please welcome them with your usual warmth and courtesy."

After dinner Ingrid, Brad and Starhood helped clean the kitchen and dining room. Everybody staying at the Monastery was required to assist in housekeeping chores. The bell for evening vespers was sounded at 7:45. Vespers, a time of ritual prayer, was drawn from the Books of Praise. Starhood and his friends entered the Cathedral from a side door. Their seats were located next to the rows of monks' chairs and close to the sacred Table of Thanks. They arrived early to reflect on the mysteries of life. Many people from the Village of Toms crowded into pews to join the monks in prayer.

In another part of the Monastery the four new arrivals were sitting around a large table. Coaldon, Pacer, Topple and Earthkin were tired after the long hike through the Wastelands. Their packs had been stored in the sleeping area and a fine meal of fish and roots was served.

Topple talked to the monks about their funny looking green robes.

He declared, "I strongly suggest you change the color of your robes. Green is such a dull color. You should try bright red or yellow. I will design something for you. The kids in the villages would be so excited to see you in colorful, new robes."

After dinner the four guests were led to the Cathedral for Vespers. As they entered the massive church, the pipe organ was playing soft background music.

Coaldon stood in awe at the size of the church. The tall vaulted ceiling was painted with many scenes from the history of the Monastery. The walls were draped with large, colorful tapestries. Five stained glass windows graced each side of the massive walls. The images on the ceiling blended with the designs of the wall tapestries causing all eyes to ultimately focus on the Altar of Thanks.

As Coaldon stood at the door of the Cathedral, the music erupted into a robust song of praise. Goose pimples grew all over his body as the monks walked single file into the church. The long procession ended as each monk stood in front of his assigned chair. The hoods of the monks' green robes were pulled off their heads as they stood in quiet reverence. Abbot Hugh was the last to enter the Cathedral. He was a short man with a full body, round face and long brown hair. His gentle countenance was apparent through the language of his eyes. His green robe shimmered in the light of the candles. He stood in front of a chair located in the center of the chapel.

Coaldon became mesmerized with the richness of the environment. The music added a feeling of reverence. As he looked around, he became aware of the three people shadowed in the front of the church. Coaldon's eyes casually moved past them. Then their identity exploded in his mind. Without thinking he rushed down the center aisle of the Cathedral. Pacer, Topple and Earthkin watched him with smiles of delight. The music stopped at the disruption. Ingrid, Brad and Starhood turned to discover the cause of the disturbance.

The monks and villagers watched as the seven guests held a reunion in the center of the Cathedral. Vespers was delayed until the excitement of the celebration was finished.

After the reunion was completed, the organ burst forth in a hymn of triumph. The community joined in singing the praises of the One Presence. At the end of the liturgy, Abbot Hugh summoned the guests before the sacred Altar of Thanks. After the group knelt, he extended his hands over them. In his usual elegance, he offered a prayer of thanksgiving.

BOOK 2

CRIES FROM NEVERLY

ᛚᛞᚺ ᛟᚺᛣᛚ ᛚᚣᛟᚺᛏ

The West Tower

The West Tower of the castle was a constant topic of discussion by the citizens of Neverly. The tall, slender, stone spire had four windows at its top. The round windows faced east, west, north and south on a 90 degree axis. It was rumored the round windows were built to help gather energy from the forces of nature. This energy was then converted into the power driving the machines of magic. Even though the people on the street talked with authority, they knew nothing about the nature of magic or the forces that generated its power.

The magic from the tower was usually a product of the night and found its source in darkness. It was not unusual to see multicolored lights blaze from the windows of the tower. These lights would shift from green to yellow then brighten the night sky with blood red flashes.

The power of Crossmore's foul work acted as a mantle of gloom covering the city like a black pall. Fear gripped people every time the body of a complaining citizen was found in a state of unnatural death and decomposition. This often happened when people protested the reign of Wastelow or Crossmore. Blind obedience was expected, or a shadow in the night would end rebellious activities.

The West Tower was off limits to everybody except Crossmore the Wizard and Badda, his slow witted servant. The mindless servant could only follow the commands of Crossmore in blind obedience. Badda's cowering presence was a target for Crossmore's anger and hatred. Badda's short, anemic body supported a sallow face with pale, empty eyes. Ragged clothes hung on his body like a shroud lay over the top of the living dead.

Badda's unwashed body was covered with ages of dirt and filth. The odor of his presence was unbearable, except for Crossmore. Sadly, the servant's degenerated presence fed the wizard's own sense of power. Badda would sit for hours in a comatose state waiting for Crossmore's summons. The servant was often seen wandering the city at night on one of Crossmore's missions of dread.

Crossmore showed increased irritability during the months of spring. Budding leaves, green grass and spring flowers pushed him to fits of anger. Crossmore wanted destruction and fear to symbolize his existence, not hope and new life. Control was his sole quest in life. He diligently worked to gain the power needed to conquer all of creation.

On a warm spring day, Crossmore stood before a tall mirror attached to the wall in the tower. His tall, lean body was wrapped in a black silk robe that shimmered in the pulsating light emanating from a crystal ball sitting on a table. His dark eyes, pleasant smile and charismatic personality offered him the ability to convince people of his sincerity. Even though people sensed his corruption, Crossmore could convince them of his honesty and caring. People wanted to believe in his words and blame someone else for his deeds. The trap of his sweet voice was the death of many gullible individuals.

Crossmore glowed with pride at the grandeur of his power. From an outward appearance the room in the West Tower did not portray an image of magic. The small room had bare stone walls, a mirror, two plain chairs, several tables, a crystal ball and a large book sitting on a stand. A door opened onto a staircase leading to the bottom of the tower. The steps on the stairs were worn smooth by the feet of many wizards who had practiced their magic in the empowered environment of the tower.

Badda sat motionless in a chair near the door with a vacant expression on his face. He stared at the floor with no will to direct his behavior. Recently, Badda had begun to hear voices from the recesses of his mind. These voices were of happy children playing street games. He heard the voices but could not make any reference to their source or meaning. These voices wandered in complete freedom, weaving a tapestry of unknown patterns in the void of his mind.

Crossmore looked at Badda with satisfaction. He desired to have an army of people with the same void of will. They would do his every bidding with out question. Badda was a grand experiment in removing willpower from an individual.

Crossmore walked to the east window and looked over his future domain. He had two people to eliminate before he could become emperor. He smiled knowing Emperor Wastelow was slowly dying.

He thought, "For years I have increased the dose of the poison I give the Emperor. This charming drug has reduced his mind to the emotional level of a vegetable. Wastelow, the fool, is so naïve and stupid. He actually trusted me to nurse him back to health. It would only be a short time before Wastelow's destruction will be complete."

He chuckled, thinking, "After Wastelow's death I will use my usual grace, kindness and elegance to invite his son Regee into my confidence. I find Regee to be such a weak, spineless and pathetic life form. I will eradicate him in a most unique and unpleasant manner. I will have fun making dear Regee face his arrogance and stupidity."

He laughed out loud, admiring the wicked magnificence of his plan.

As Crossmore retreated from his daydream, the shades of darkness were starting to blanket the City. He stood in front of the window looking directly at the East Tower. He stared at the tower as thoughts of marriage entered his mind. Yes, someday he would marry a beautiful woman. His lustful intentions were anything but noble. He planned to entrap an honorable woman in his web of corruption. He felt his victory would be complete when Princess Noel was his wife to control and dominate until death they do part.

A burst of laughter illuminated his satisfaction with his plans to conquer Noel and the Empire. First, he would utterly destroy Brad and his rag-tag followers. Second, he would gain full control of the Empire. Last, he would have Noel for his bride. He smiled at the thought of dominating the worthless maggots of the Empire.

His gaze shifted from the East Tower to the East Gate of the city. The replacement of the guards was just taking place with the usual military formality. He enjoyed watching the soldiers march in cadence to his power. In confidence he declared to himself, "It will not be long before the whole empire will be my toy."

He was impressed with his great plans. Yet, he lacked absolute conviction. A shadow of doubt lurked in the depths of his mind. He could not forget his confrontation with the great power from the wilderness. The pain in his crippled right hand was a reminder. No matter how hard he tried to repress this doubt, it constantly resurfaced. He knew there was a challenge to his plan for conquest.

His childish pride could not accept anything but complete control. Frequently, his anger would rage in hatred of the enemy. No one ever dared to challenge his power. He vowed with evil curses to find and destroy whoever had turned his hand into a worthless stump. He questioned how it was possible for anything to match the Power of Reaching. Yet, it did happen without warning and under the protection of the Mirror of Farsight. For ages he used the magic of the mirror to reach into the Empire without any problems. The mirror gave him the power to touch the minds of his victims.

Recently, Crossmore spent many hours in his library studying the ancient books of prophecy to identify his enemy. In frustration, he found nothing. Was it a great warrior, a wizard, or maybe just an energy surge in flux of the mirror? Reports continued to arrive at the palace concerning strange events in the Village of Grandy and the Wilderness of the Outlast. A male half-elf and an older couple were identified as living in Lost Valley. Could this be the son of Rodney and grandson of Brad? The enchanted wolves from the underworld reported that great warriors defeated them in several battles in the Wastelands. These warriors arrived at the Monastery of Toms during early winter. He did not think it was possible for anyone to kill his partner in evil, Gurlog. He fashioned Gurlog from the very bowels of hell to be his commander.

Crossmore's mind could not accept the fact that something or someone was challenging his authority. Would it be necessary for him to reopen the doors into the Chamber of Oblivion to obtain more foul creatures to fight his war? Was it possible for him to lose control of the surge of evil escaping from the underworld? Crossmore knew he could not allow anything to stop him from fulfilling his dreams. He would need to depend on his intellect, magic and knowledge to guide him to fulfill his destiny. He decided it was time to reenter the life of the palace. As he left the tower, he threw Badda a piece of raw meat and a loaf of moldy bread.

He said, "Eat, Badda, because you will need energy to complete the work I have for you this dark and wonderful night." The people of the city heard Crossmore's laughter as he descended the steps leading into the heart of the palace.

ᚴᚲᚺ ᚺᚢᛚᚴ ᚴᛣᛟᚺᛏ

The East Tower

From a window high in the East Tower of the palace, the change in the seasons did not go unnoticed by Noel. She stared in wonderment at the splendor of spring. From the innate character of her half-elf heritage she found an affinity with the exciting pulse of new life. Her glowing eyes, pleasant smile and flowing black hair accentuated her natural beauty. Noel's dynamic personality, intelligence and enthusiasm radiated a zest for life that was uncharacteristic of most young adults in Neverly. Her tall, slender body was an expression of strength and grace.

She wore a simple, full-length peasant dress made from rough combed cotton. The dress had a light brown skirt and a woodland green top. The quiet shades of brown and green added softness to Noel's skin tones and luminous personality. She wore this style of dress out of protest to Emperor Wastelow's constant pressure for her to wear brightly colored silken court attire. This rebellion was a protest against her captivity and proclamation of her individuality.

As she stood, framed in the window, her mind drifted to thoughts of her family. At an early age she discovered her father was human and her mother was an elf. The title of half-elf provided her with a personal image of prestige and pride. Yet, it also offered a lingering uncertainty about her future. She realized only two half-elves lived in the Empire. She often questioned if people would hate or love her because of her ancestry. Would she be a target of prejudice from people who feared the unknown?

Recently, she felt a deep longing to share in the life of her family. She found comfort in knowing her parents shared a special love for each other. She was always delighted to hear stories told by Magee, her guardian, about the wonderful life shared by Rodney and Starglide. Their love for each other had grown into a legend told and retold throughout the Empire.

At age 15 years Noel learned from Magee that she had a twin brother. This knowledge provided her with an understanding of the mysterious void in her life.

Noel often dreamed about meeting her brother Coaldon. Today, as she stood before the window, she felt an unusual strong sense of longing for her family. Loneliness was an obvious product of her isolation and captivity. It was a sad day when Magee told her about the death of her parents. They had been killed by Wastelow in the bloody Battle of Two Thrones. She was excited to learn her Grandfather Brad was the true emperor.

For Noel springtime offered renewed hope of escaping from the East Tower. As she gazed across the changing landscape of spring, she was mesmerized by the unfolding beauty of nature. The sights and sounds of spring erupted before her like a volcano in the midst of winter winds. The daily struggle between the tides of cold air flowing down from the north and the warm breezes pushing up from the south formed a battlefield of conflicting weather forces. One day snow would force people into their houses to find comfort in front of a fireplace. Other days the warmth of the spring sunshine would encourage them to throw open their doors and greet life with renewed anticipation. The entrapment of winter created the need for people to escape from the confinement of four walls. Winter chilled the bones of each person like frost frozen deep in the soil. Tempers flared as the pressures of living close together for five long months erupted in conflicts. The regenerating powers of spring pulsated in the very soul of each individual in the community. The hope of earth's renewal created a subtle excitement in the spirit of each person.

On warm days children would roam the streets of Neverly in tides of happy voices. Men stared at the barren farmlands outside the city walls while women rushed to finish spring cleaning before the next blast of winter would strive to regain dominance. Newly stretched clotheslines flew the spring flag of blankets, clothing and linens being refreshed by the cleansing power of warm sunshine. Farm equipment was repaired; shovel blades were sharpened; and seeds were carefully inspected to help insure productive crops. The slow pace of sales during the last days of winter caused merchants to spend lonely days waiting for a healthy surge of optimism. They watched the amplified pace of spring with the prospects of increased prosperity.

Springtime offered Noel a feeling of resurrection from the hopelessness of her captivity. She was counseled by Magee to accept the limitations of her life with controlled impatience. The fear of being a captive for the rest of her life caused moments of anger and depression. Noel struggled to form a realistic balance between her present situation and maintaining hope for the future. This struggle would cause her moods to fluctuate between joy and despair. Some days the fire of her temper would repress her gentle smile and warm personality.

Noel's thoughts shifted from springtime to her immediate surroundings. She could see the open plains in the west blend into the great forest of the north. The

Slownic River ambled past Neverly like a large snake wandering into the distant horizon. Neverly was the capital city for the Empire. The four high stonewalls gave the appearance of gloom, dread and misery. The gray, dirty walls were smudged with the accumulated pollution of many centuries of smoke and grime. The city was a collection of rundown houses, narrow streets and dilapidated buildings. The litter-strewn streets were usually crowded with people pushing through the mob of shoppers and vagrants to reach their destination.

Noel used her vantage point in the tower to watch the flow of life in the city. She noticed the city was becoming more run-down and polluted by garbage. Even though she did not have the opportunity to talk with the citizens, she detected an increased sense of despair and discontent. A recent tax increase caused a swell in the poverty among farmers and city dwellers. A larger number of beggars roamed the streets and crime was escalating.

She turned to greet Norbert as he entered her chamber to begin her lessons. He tutored her in script, language, literature and numeric. Norbert was an old man with a gentle smile, long gray hair, frail body and sharp intellect. He never allowed Noel to neglect her responsibility to learn academic skills and to discipline her mind.

Norbert lived in the palace, but was not allowed to leave except under guard. Emperor Wastelow had a brooding distrust of Norbert's sense of independence. Noel was surprised Norbert was allowed to teach her because of his emphasis on teaching creativity and freethinking. Noel realized Norbert kept his views well hidden from everybody except Magee and herself.

Magee greeted Norbert with a warm smile. Their years of working together created an intimate bond of respect and understanding. Magee was a short, stout woman with a round face and quiet smile. Her long gray hair was pulled back to a tight bun. Her quick wit and easy command of words allowed her to dominate most conversations. Norbert usually yielded to Magee's aggressive nature until one of his values had been violated. At which time he would reestablish his position in their relationship. It was common for their lively debates to provide entertainment on dull afternoons.

Both Magee and Norbert escaped the purge of death that accompanied the conquest by Wastelow. The twin children of Rodney and Starglide were separated at the end of the War of Two Thrones. Emperor Brad and Queen Ingrid escaped with Coaldon in the confusion following the war. Wastelow held Noel as captive for the past 17 years. Noel, under the protective care of Magee, was raised as a subject of Emperor Wastelow. He determined she might be useful as a pawn. It was common knowledge that Wastelow planned for his son Regee to marry her. This marriage would help gain the loyalty of the people. This royal wedding would take place sometime during the next year.

It had been the secret duty of Norbert and Magee to prepare Noel to assume the role of princess after Emperor Brad regained power. Even though they demonstrated open allegiance to Emperor Wastelow, they were dedicated to Emperor Brad. The former emperor offered the only hope for citizens fleeing from servitude.

Norbert and Magee, under the disguised loyalty to Wastelow, instructed Noel in her history and responsibilities. She learned at an early age the truth about her captivity and her destiny in the new Empire. Thanks to Magee, Noel learned early in her life to play the game of cooperation, submission and courtesy with the Emperor and his staff. It was necessary to maintain an open and friendly relationship with the Emperor in order to remove any possible suspicion or distrust. Yet, her true commitment was to her family and the Empire.

Noel's eyes were glazed over in deep concentration as she looked out the window. She was startled when Norbert touched her shoulder. She paused before responding to his presence. She stated, "I love to go for my weekly horseback rides in the forest. I feel such freedom when the air blows through my hair. I wonder if Wastelow will continue to allow me to go on these rides outside the palace?"

Norbert looked out the window at the milling crowd in the city before he responded, "Something has happened to force Emperor Wastelow and Crossmore to increase security. I wish I had a source inside the Emperor's Chambers to provide us information about the events of the Empire."

Looking at Noel he continued, "I want to believe your grandfather has started his war against Wastelow?"

Noel glanced at Magee in anticipation of her response to Norbert's statement. Magee's eyes drifted away from her knitting to focus on Norbert's quiet face. She finally said, "This morning the Emperor's chamber maid told me Wastelow was still suffering from his depression and blue miseries. The servant said Crossmore continues to give Wastelow special herbs to control his illness. Some servants suspect the wizard is poisoning the Emperor in order to gain control of the Empire. During Wastelow's absence from the throne Crossmore has graciously offered to assist in the day-to-day operation of the Empire. Many people in the palace wonder if Emperor Wastelow will ever return to power."

Noel was slow to respond, "Crossmore has been showing an increased interest in my welfare. I believe that he would like to control me. The thought of that man touching me makes me feel dirty and ill. Is it possible Crossmore is striving to take over the Empire for his own evil purposes?"

Norbert looked at Noel and Magee with deep, probing eyes. He knew the time for immediate action had arrived. Noel needed to be freed from the palace before something terrible happened to her. But, what could he do? There were too many spies in the palace and in the city to make an escape.

Norbert questioned Magee, "Last spring you met with Pacer in the market. Did he say anything about an escape attempt?

Magee responded, "Yes. If you remember, Brad was waiting for Coaldon to turn 18 before he took action."

Norbert looked at Magee saying, "Did Pacer say when he would return to Neverly?"

Magee nodded, "Pacer stated he would meet with me in the market place on the first day of spring. He said he was planning to meet with Brad on Coaldon's birthday to make plans for the future. Rescue plans had not been made at that time. Pacer was afraid to talk to me too long because of fear of being detected by spies."

With a sly smile on her face, Magee continued, " Norbert, the spring equinox will occur in several weeks requiring the fulfillment of a most important event. I would be honored if you would accompany me on a trip to the market place to shop for Noel's new summer wardrobe. I know you will enjoy such a festive occasion?"

Norbert's expression changed from curiosity to a pretense of alarm. Magee learned how to create ripples of frustration in his crusty layers of bachelorhood.

He responded in contempt, "There is no way I will be seen in the market shopping for women's clothing. I will allow you to venture into the world of domestic pursuits while Noel and I study the verb tenses of the high elfin language."

Noel laughed loudly at the bantering between her two special friends. She paused as she heard noises outside her door. Several soldiers always guarded the door into her chamber. Under the orders of Wastelow, she could not leave her room without five soldiers guarding her every movement. On her horseback rides she was escorted by 20 guards.

She constantly prayed to escape from her dungeon. Over the past few months she had the strong desire to meet her twin brother and to share the bonding of their early life together. She knew a part of herself remained with Coaldon and vise versa. She also realized they needed each other in order to find fulfillment in life.

Decisions

The wind and snow from the storm blasted the walls of the Monastery with unrelenting pounding. Winter would not release its grip on the Monastery of Toms until the last great surge of cold and snow was spent. The monks, wrapped in thick coats and heavy boots, hurried between buildings. The Monastery was located in the heart of the Wastelands on the slopes of the Black Mountains. The Cathedral, cloister and workshops overlooked farmland and orchards. The rich farmland was watered by mysterious streams gushing out of the earth. It was assumed the water flowed from an aquifer originating high in the Black Mountains. The Village of Toms sat below the Monastery in a sheltered cove next to the Lake of Prayer. The villagers worked on the farms and offered many different services to the monks.

The founders of the Monastery realized it was necessary to protect the monks from the world by establishing the Monastery in the desolate Wastelands. The Wastelands, a vast area of gullies and canyons, was void of all manner of life. The many canyons of this forbidding land provided a far-reaching labyrinth of channels that resisted any intruder. This unfriendly ground was nearly impossible to cross, as testified by the bones of lost travelers and animals. In order to reach the Monastery, it was necessary to have a guide or map to show the way through the inhospitable maze. Many people believed a force of nature or magic actually resisted the intrusion of any living being into the Wastelands.

The Wastelands had been crossed several months ago by two groups of travelers seeking refuge. The monks of the Monastery received these travelers with open arms and provided them safe haven. Since their arrival, the travelers worked to gather knowledge from the monastic library and to make plans to conquer Wastelow. Starhood, the elf warrior, spent long days in the dingy stacks of the library searching ancient manuscripts for clues to the location of the Land of Westmore. The Land of Westmore was the ancient depository for the Key of Ban. This book of magic could defeat the forces of evil. The possession of the Key of Ban would be needed to crush the expanding influence of Crossmore. It would be necessary to have a benevolent wizard to control the power generated by the magic contained in the book.

Months passed without Starhood finding any information on Westmore. During this time of waiting, Emperor Brad required all of the warriors to spend time each day in physical conditioning and weapons training. Brad, the deposed Emperor, needed strong warriors if he was to regain the throne for his family. Even his wife, Empress Ingrid, joined the men in weapons practice. While the men would thrust and parry with swords, she refined the use of the bow & arrow and short spear.

Weekly conferences were held in a large room in the library. Brad led these meetings with the care of a gentle father. These discussions were attended by Coaldon, Earthkin, Topple, Pacer, Starhood, Ingrid and Brother Patrick. Recently, these meetings had deteriorated into a frustrating dialogue of meaningless bantering. The imposing restraints of winter and the lack of progress caused the group to lose the focus of their real mission. At one such meeting Coaldon's frustration finally burst into an explosion of angry words and red-hot temper.

Slamming shut a book, he yelled, "I am tired of just talking. We need to do more than just debate and argue. We are wasting our time. We need to have results."

In remorse, he continued, "I apologize for my anger but I am tired of just listening to words. We need to leave the emptiness of winter and greet the rebirth of spring with our actions."

The group quietly overlooked Coaldon's impatience and accepted his challenge as a wakeup call.

Brad interceded, "Coaldon, I agree with you. Words must be transformed into actions. We need to decide how to free Noel from her captivity in Neverly. We have pushed this topic aside for too long. It does seem impossible, but there must be away to complete the rescue. Today we must find it."

Pacer was first to speak, "Last spring when I made a trip to the capital I visited with Magee, Noel's nursemaid. I had a difficult time entering the city because of the large number of guards constantly patrolling the gates. I did not have the identification papers needed to pass through the gates, so I had to enter the city by using the old storm drain just south of the East Tower. This drain was closed many years ago because of decay and disuse. Only the royal family and their advisors had knowledge of the hidden channel. Seventeen years ago the drain was used as an escape route for Brad and his court. The main entrance inside the city is located in the old palace wine cellar behind the vats."

Pacer continued, "It is my impression the capital has become an armed fortress. Spies circulate in the city searching for any seditious activities against the Emperor. Wastelow and Crossmore have created a reign of terror. People are afraid to do or say anything against them. I did not see him, but people said a mindless creature wanders the streets at nights stalking the enemies of the Empire. Last year Wastelow increased taxes in order to support his army. These high taxes have forced many citizens into abject poverty. The streets of Neverly are full of homeless people struggling to find enough food to survive. I told Magee I would return to Neverly this year on the first day of spring. The first day of spring is only five weeks away, so if we are going to do something, now is the time to start."

Coaldon asked, "Do we have to enter the palace to free Noel, or is there another way?"

Pacer looked at Brad before he responded, "Last spring Noel was allowed to go on horseback rides in the forest north of the city. I observed that twenty guards escorted her on these rides. At first, I thought we could attack this mounted platoon, but now I have my doubts. We do not want to endanger the life of Noel by doing something reckless."

Coaldon leaned forward, asking, "Will it then be necessary to rescue Noel from within the palace? If so, will we need to enter her room to release her? Do we know the location of Noel's Chamber? Is the room heavily guarded? Is this room accessible to us?"

Pacer laughed as he looked at Coaldon with amusement.

He responded, "Whoa! You ask good questions. I will tell you what I know. I believe the only access we have to Noel will be within the palace. She is heavily guarded. It would take a large army to invade the palace and rescue her. We will need to develop a plan in which a small number of warriors under the cloak of secrecy rescue her. Last spring I learned Noel's room is on the top level of the East Tower. Guards are stationed at her door 24 hours a day. It is my understanding this room has no secret passages because of limited space in the tower. Brad, do you remember any secret passages that reach into the East Tower?"

Brad had been unusually quiet for the past few weeks. Some of his friends were starting to worry that the old king was losing his will to fight. In truth, Brad was not retreating from his devotion to the Empire, but striving to gain the proper mental focus. The old Emperor responded to doubting eyes in the room, "The events of the last six months have forced me to change from being a simple farmer to the leader of a rebellion. I have been required to regain skills I had long ago given up. Recently, the thoughts of Noel have been consuming my mind. I am ready to do my part in this great adventure."

Brad continued, "Yes, I believe I know of a way to enter her room by the way of a hidden passage. I have been thinking about this for the past several days. At first, I had doubts about accessing her room until I remembered an abandoned shaft passing on the inside wall of the tower. If my memory is correct, it passes next to Noel's chamber. This shaft was originally used to lift supplies to the top of

East Tower. It was sealed off after a section of a wall collapsed from a flaw in its construction. The shaft descends into the cellars of the palace. Yes, I know it does. As a youth I constantly searched the palace for secret passages. One day I found the opening of this shaft plugged by rocks and debris in the basement. I believe it would be possible to clear the rocks from the base of the shaft and climb to the top of the tower using ropes. It will take accurate measurements and calculations to know where to break through the wall into Noel's chambers. I can draw maps to help guide your way into the city, palace and shaft."

As the discussion progressed, Pacer's mind was alive with different ideas concerning the rescue. When he finally raised his head, he realized that everyone was watching him. He glanced at each person in the room before he spoke, "I believe we can get Noel out of the room without much trouble. It will be the escape from the city and journey to the Monastery that will be the major problem. What will we do with Norbert, the tutor and Magee, the nurse maid? Should we make arrangements for them to be a part of the escape plan?"

When Pacer finished with his statement, the room became quiet. Nobody knew what to say. Everybody knew Norbert and Magee would be killed if left behind. It was easy to talk about a rescue attempt until the real dangers grew into focus. Topple was the only person who did not have a distressed look on his face. Topple's infective smile and giggle filled the room with a cheery mood. He stood up with a robust explosion of energy, dancing around the room with happy steps. He turned his head to one side, laughed and said, "Can you imagine the effort it will take to lower our beloved friend, Magee, down a narrow shaft. If I remember right, she is a monument to good food. It would be worth the trip to see the wiggling, twitching and moaning that would be required to complete this gigantic task."

Earthkin could not contain himself from commenting, "Topple, I do not appreciate your light hearted attitude in such a time of serious planning. It's time you grow up and stop playing silly games!"

Topple looked at Earthkin for several moments before a wide smile enveloped his jolly face. Topple had a deep respect for Earthkin, but took great pleasure in frustrating his dear, grumpy friend. With a twinkle in his eye Topple finally quoted,

"As it is, it will be,
    with a laugh and a jolly glee.
We can sing or we can cry,
    just by the choice we can fly.
To dance in joy or mask in fear,
    the option falls so near.
To walk in peace or sag in pain,
    we choose a path to rein.

By thrill of life and eye to quest,
in faith we find our rest."

Topple gave a loud shout of elation when he had finished. He showed pride and satisfaction at his grandiose presentation.

Brad decided it was time to refocus the discussion before Topple and Earthkin got into one of their historic debates on the meaning of life. He finally said, "I agree with Pacer, the escape will need to be carefully planned. Also, we need to decide who is going on this rescue mission. I recommend Pacer, Coaldon and Brother Patrick form the team. I believe Earthkin, being a dwarf, would draw too much attention to the group. I want Earthkin and Topple to remain at the Monastery to help search the library for the location of Westmore.

At this point Topple stood up, staggered and fell on the floor. Everybody in the room stared in surprise at Topple's behavior. No one moved to assist him until it was determined he really had a problem. With his head on the floor, Topple opened his eyes and slowly looked around the room. He gradually sat up with a flair of melodramatic suffering. With a pathetic whimper and a look of wounded pride he said, "You just pushed me aside like a worthless old shoe. You put me out to pasture, cast me adrift in a river of pain and treated me as an elderly duffer. Oh, woe is me! Rejected in the prime of life! Where shall I turn to find peace in this moment of great tragedy?"

Topple tragically pushed himself to his feet in a slow, agonizing fashion. Everyone in the room, except Earthkin, watched his performance with a sense of appreciation and humor. From first appearances, Topple looked like a skinny, doddering, frail and feeble old man. Yet, on a second glance his strength was evident.

Pacer was the first to speak after Topple's grand theatrical presentation, "I agree with Brad's list of people to go on this mission. I also propose Topple join us on the trip. He could be a valuable resource if we needed magic in the rescue attempt. Is there any more discussion concerning this matter?"

No one commented, so Pacer said, "So be it! Now we must decide how to escape from Neverly and find our way back home, wherever home may be."

He stood with an obvious eagerness to add to the general discussion. Earthkin was usually passive in expressing his opinion and reserved when dealing with people. In his deep gruff voice he said, "I have been thinking of different escape routes the rescuers could use. At the time of the escape, it will be necessary for the team to leave Neverly in a hurry.'

Brad questioned, "If haste is a requirement, can Norbert and Magee handle a demanding escape?"

The dwarf responded, "I believe they will not be able to travel under excessive stress. A trek to the west across the Great Plains will be physically demanding and dangerous. A small party of travelers crossing the plains would be easily seen and captured."

Pacer injected, "Taking Norbert and Magee into consideration, what do you propose?"

Earthkin answered, "I suggest an escape route to the east. I believe Crossmore and Wastelow will expect us to flee to the west. We could use horses to travel into the Sadden Mountains and then south to the dwarf City of Rockham. The most dangerous part of the trip will be from Neverly to the mountains. If we choose the east route, I would need to be the guide once we arrive in the mountains. The Sadden Mountains can be a dangerous place. In the past, bands of thieves and murderers have taken up refuge in the north. Their strength and numbers have increased over the last ten years."

Nodding, Pacer followed, "I believe Earthkin has a good idea. Also, I am concerned about Magee's and Norbert's ability to physically handle a demanding journey. By using horses we could reduce the strain on them, plus make a quick retreat. I know of several hiding places east of the city where we could rest. Surprise and swiftness will be the key to our success."

Brad's face twisted as he contemplated Pacer's comments. He finally said, "We will have to take the chance. I may be wrong, but I believe Norbert and Magee will have the strength and determination to make the journey. We must provide them the opportunity to be a part of the escape. They will need to make the choice."

He then concluded, "The members of the team will be Pacer, Earthkin, Coaldon, Topple and Brother Patrick."

Brad continued, "You will leave in seven days. Pacer will be in charge of the planning. Coaldon will handle the supplies and equipment. I want a full report in four days. Thank you for your help."

Planning Stages

Over night the snowstorm changed into heavy rain. The cold winds from the north gave way to a warm front out of the southwest. The heavy snow melted rapidly, creating small steams of water flowing in all directions. The water running off the roofs pounded the ground in a mesmerizing rhythm. This time of year, rain had the special power to infect people with spring fever. The change in the weather brought a transformation in the monks. As they entered the dining hall, their normally stoic expressions gave way to smiles. The quiet, reserved voices of yesterday had been transformed into hearty voices of growing optimism. The monks chattered about cultivating the soil, the new seeds they had received from the south, the building of a new weaving machine, remodeling the west chapel, planting flower beds and weapons practice in the outdoor arena. The completion of these tasks was necessary for the overall survival of the Monastery.

This morning the visitors from the Outlast sat at a table in the corner of the dining room discussing plans for the journey to Neverly. It seemed Earthkin and Pacer had been debating how the rescue team should leave the Wastelands. Earthkin was in favor of departing to the east during the night. Pacer wanted to use a route to the north.

Pacer said in frustration, "The Wastelands are being watched on all sides by Crossmore's spies. No matter what direction we travel we will be seen and reported. We need to leave the Wastelands in a manner unexpected by the spies. Does anyone have a suggestions how we can do this?"

Brother Patrick said, "Maybe we can create a diversion that would draw Crossmore's attention away from the real escape route. I could arrange for a company of Warrior Monks to leave Wastelands to the east with covered wagons. It is about time for the Monastery to pick up farm supplies from the Dod Farm. We could have people dressed like us riding in the wagons. It will only be a short trip, but at least it will create confusion."

Brad nodded his head in agreement.

He commented, "That almost sounds too easy. Are there any weaknesses in this plan?"

Pacer reacted, "I think it is a great plan. The extra guards will give the impression of protecting people in the wagons. I support this plan."

Brad continued, "We will go with the diversion plan. Now we need to talk about how, where and when, the rescue team will depart.

Coaldon said, "We could travel from the Monastery during the cover of night in the opposite direction from the diversion team. After leaving the Wastelands, we could break up into small groups and travel in disguise? Maybe traveling as vagrants would satisfy our need for obscurity."

Brad questioned, "What route should you take?"

Before anybody could respond, several Monastery novices delivered two trays heaping with food to their table. The reputation of Monks being overweight was understandable because of the quality of food served by the Monastery. A bell rang in the dining hall, drawing the monk's attention to the front table. Abbot Hugh stood and signaled for everyone to stand. In a solemn voice, Abbot Hugh ask for a blessing on the food. Abbot Hugh was a short, rotund man with a gentle personality. His round, jolly face was alive with perpetual laughter and smiles.

The room was transformed from words of thanksgiving into the sound of clattering plates and robust conversation. Pork gravy over buttered honey bread was served. The monks enthusiasm indicated this was one of their favorite meals.

After the bountiful breakfast, Brad called the travelers to the library meeting room to finalize their plans. The group waited several minutes for Topple to arrive before starting.

Earthkin grumbled, "Now, where is Topple? Again, he has found something more important to do than attend this meeting."

Starhood explained, "Topple's values have been greatly modified over the centuries. The whims of the moment often dominate the focus of his attention. He can easily become engrossed in the sound of the wind blowing through trees, a beautiful sunrise, a bird singing in a tree, children playing games, a bug eating a leaf, or maybe rain water running off a roof."

With a smile Pacer added, "He follows the beat of a different drummer. His trust in providence fills every fiber of his body. We should not allow his unique personality to cause us to lose sight of his intelligence, wisdom and caring.

After the group finished talking about Topple, Brad stood up. He stated, "Let's get back to business. I like the idea of a diversion. This will allow the team to travel undetected. I also agree the group should travel under disguise. Now, we need to decide on the route of travel to Neverly. What direction will it be?"

Pacer responded, "We could go north along the slopes of the Black Mountains and take the road from Goobe to Neverly. Another possibility is to travel to Grandy and then travel to Neverly on the North-South Road. Do you have any opinions about these routes?"

Coaldon stood up in an uncharacteristic fashion. He looked around the room with a growing sense of authority and confidence. He stated, "I want to go through Grandy. I think this would be the last place spies would expect to find us. We can travel south out of the Wasteland under the cover of darkness, cross Rolling River and pass through Grandy as homeless seeking employment. We can cover our homely faces with dirt and grime. We can be among the many vagrants looking for a place to find shelter, food and work."

When Coaldon finished, Earthkin had a frustrated look on his face. He said with a tone of rebuke, "My face is not homely, but attractive and masculine. The rest of you are rather homely, but not me. We can not allow incorrect facts to cause misconceptions."

In a solemn voice Pacer intoned, "Coaldon must stand corrected in his observation. Earthkin's face is not homely, but he had better watch what he is saying. He is starting to sound like Topple."

Earthkin's eyes grew wide. "Now hear this! I may be charming, attractive and witty, but never accuse me of acting like Topple. I am a dwarf. I am not absent minded and irresponsible."

Brad interjected, "Earthkin, what disguise do you want to use while traveling? It will be difficult to cover up the fact that you are a dwarf."

Brother Patrick in a relaxed manner said, "Earthkin could act as a slave. A chain around his neck and ring in his nose would add credence to the disguise."

Earthkin was disgusted at the thought of being a slave. Everyone could see a tinge of anger ripple through his body. Yet in Earthkin's mind, he knew it was a good idea. After a moment of quiet contemplation, he said, "I will do it, but only if I am not a slave to Topple. That would be too much for me to handle."

In a tone of moderation Brad said, "I believe Topple is the only person who can play the role of a slave master. No one else has the character to convince people you are a slave. It may be challenging, but I believe it would be best."

Earthkin stared at the floor for a long time. He knew Brad was correct. He would need to convince himself that the rescue of Noel was worth the price he would pay. He finally said, "Brad, you and I will need to talk to Topple before I will say yes. This will be a sacrifice beyond the normal call of duty. I do not want to blow my cover because Topple over does it."

Brad responded, "That sounds good to me. I want the team to be ready to leave tomorrow night. I will talk to Abbot Hugh about sending out a wagon as a diversion. I bask in the dream of meeting my granddaughter and sending Crossmore a message concerning our intentions to defeat him. I take great pride in knowing each of you is willing to risk your life for my family and the Empire."

R

ᚴᛜᚺ ᛕᚣᛟᛏᛘᚺᛋ ᚱᚺᛈᛁᛘᛣ

The Journey Begins

It was dawn when the drowsy monks and the group of travelers gathered in the Cathedral for the morning prayer. The Cathedral resounded as the deep, melodious voices of the monks chanted the sacred stanzas. Abbot Hugh stood up, intoned an invocation and led the congregation in reading verses from the Book of Praise. Abbot Hugh invited the five rescuers to approach the Altar. With the flair of a grand master, he recited a prayer asking for a safe and successful journey.

Later in the day, final preparations for the expedition were completed. Brad and Ingrid held a party in the main dining hall for the men going on the mission. Ingrid prepared her famous pies, cookies and cakes. The mood of the rescue group was festive with many humorous comments directed at Earthkin and Topple.

Brad enjoyed watching the enthusiasm of the warriors. He thought about how many great accomplishments started with humble beginnings. Brad tried several times to get the attention of the robust and jesting crowd but to no avail. He laughed at himself for thinking he could interrupt this tide of good times with mere words. He then rang the dinner bell. At its sound the noise stopped with an abrupt closure.

He began, "The pages of history will measure our devotion and dedication. This noble quest will set an example to future generations to observe and follow. I extend to you my thanks, prayers and blessings. Go forth and let your courage be a light in the darkness of our times. May the One Presence be your guide and power."

Ingrid was next to speak, "The rescue of our granddaughter will send ripples of hope throughout the Empire. Thank you for risking your lives for a cause greater than any one of us. May you be blessed!"

At the close of these speeches, an enthusiastic round of cheers and clapping affirmed the crowd's agreement.

The meeting was interrupted by a monk delivering a message to Brad. As he read the note, the zeal of the moment drained from his face. A somber mood engulfed the room as the group realized something was wrong. Brad raised his head to look at the assembly. The sad gaze of his eyes revealed he had just been blasted by the hot breath of reality. He paused before he spoke, "I just received word that a monk, while on patrol, was killed this morning by trogs. A large company of trogs has invaded the prairie lands. There is no information on where the trogs are headed. We do know the beasts are still on this side of the river. I wonder if they are anticipating a move by us."

Pacer questioned, "Should we change our plans?"

In contemplative reflection, Brad responded, "No, I think its best to proceed as we have scheduled. You can adjust your plans to fit each new situation. We do not want to delay the team's exit any longer."

Pacer followed, "So be it. Let's get started. There is no use putting aside that which is destined to be."

With a solemn expression, Brad concluded, "It is necessary for us to face the truth. Crossmore will do anything to achieve his evil goals. I am afraid that danger and death will hound us on each step of our journey."

The weather was cool, dry and windy on the day of their departure. The diversion convoy left the Monastery early in the afternoon. Ten warrior monks dressed in green robes led the way. Each monk carried a sword, light shield, knife and short spear. Their restrained confidence and physical strength radiated superiority. With quiet steps and controlled grace they announced their refined fighting skills. The monks were followed by two wagons, each pulled by two large horses. These animals walked with pride and uplifted heads. These were not worn and defeated horses, but animals rippling with energy and strength.

At dusk the five travelers said a hasty good-bye and departed the Monastery. Pacer stated, "We are going to make a quick exit. We have no time to waste. The future of the Empire and the life of Noel hangs in the balance."

After a long personal debate, Coaldon decided to allow Sid to go on the expedition. Taking the dog offered many risks, especially if the dog should make a noise at the wrong time. Yet, Sid might also be an asset. He could provide a warning if unseen dangers were encountered.

Since speed was important, Brother Patrick set a rapid pace through the canyons. He wanted to be out of the Wastelands by daybreak.

When the sun rose in the east, the five travelers made a dry camp in a hidden alcove near the end of the canyons. The day was spent sleeping, talking and preparing their vagrant costumes. It was decided to break into two groups after they crossed Rolling River. Their first stop would be the Village of Grandy.

Darkness slowly swallowed the orange and purple sunset. The moonless night greeted the rescuers like an unfriendly acquaintance. The moon would not rise until after midnight. Pacer used the stars to guide their way to Rolling River. They were thankful the ground was flat with little to block their progress. By sunrise the roar of Rolling River could be heard in the distance.

The sound of the river triggered a vision in Coaldon's mind. He saw a watery hand from the river pushing him away from its banks. The hand directed him to stop. It then pointed toward the east. As suddenly as it began it ended. Coaldon tried to hold onto it, but it escaped into the morning light. His attention on the vision was interrupted by their arrival at the river. They found the river flowing at flood crest.

Pacer reacted, "We should have expected this. I was hoping the river would not be this high. I believe it will be too dangerous to cross. I think we should rest before we decide what to do."

An uneventful day passed, allowing the party to sleep and consider their next step. After a cold dinner Pacer called everyone together. He stated, "I do not want to risk crossing the river. We could follow the river until we reach Grandy?"

Earthkin had a passive look on his face as he spoke, "No one, except farmers, ever travel on this side of the river. There will be many questions asked if we approach Grandy from the Great Plains. We could visit Dod and ask for his assistance."

At this point, Earthkin told Pacer the story about their visit to Dod's farm while traveling to the Monastery.

Coaldon was uncertain if he should tell the others about his dream. He did not want to look stupid. Maybe it was just his imagination. Then something pushed him to state, "I have been debating if I should tell you something. This morning, before we reached the river, I had a vision. This may sound odd, but I saw the river pushing me away with a watery hand. Before the dream ended, the hand pointed to the east."

Pacer responded, "I am glad you did tell us. You have many talents you must learn to trust and honor. This is one of them. With this new insight, I suggest we travel to visit Dod and Doria."

Earthkin gave Coaldon a mischievous grin saying, "What do you think about visiting the farm?"

A shy smile crossed Coaldon's face as he thought about the possibility of visiting Rosa. She was the only child of Dod and Doria. Rosa was an attractive young lady who had the ambition of leaving the farm to find her place in the world. With dreamy eyes, Coaldon said, "I think it would be a good idea to check on the family. They might need our help. With trogs in the area we should check on them."

Both Topple and Earthkin looked at Coaldon with vivid memories of their own youthful excitement at meeting a special young lady.

Topple said to himself, "I have seen the passage of many seasons during my long life. Yet, it is always refreshing to see the power of infatuation blossom in the life of youth."

The night trek to Dod's farm was made under the soft light of the moon. Several hours before sunrise, Sid began to act strangely. Sid's uneasiness increased the closer they came to the farm. The dog started to walk as if he were ready to attack. His head swiveled back and forth looking for an unseen adversary. A deep growl rumbled in Sid's large chest.

Finally Coaldon said, "Sid is upset. I believe there is trouble ahead of us. We should proceed with caution."

Pacer directed, "We will break into groups and approach the farm from two directions. This will give us the chance to observe the farm from different positions. If there is any trouble, we can communicate by animal sounds."

It was decided Pacer, Earthkin and Topple would approach the farm from the north while Brother Patrick and Coaldon came in from the south. The teams carefully crept to the assigned areas and waited for daybreak.

An unnatural silence pervaded as the two groups approached the farm. Coaldon had a hard time keeping Sid from rushing toward the house. It was strange that Dod's vicious dogs did not bark. As daylight crept over the landscape, Coaldon caught his breath. He saw a group of trogs behind the barn and wood shed. The trog's muscular bodies and ugly round faces were highlighted by large yellow eyes. Just the sight of these beasts created a sense of fear and disgust.

In the distance Coaldon heard the sound of a barn owl. He responded with the sharp bark of the red fox. His animal calls had greatly improved over the past months.

After several more exchanges Coaldon spoke to Brother Patrick, "We will follow the cover of the rock fence until we are next to the wood shed. We will attack the trogs when Pacer gives the command."

Patrick nodded in agreement as they crawled down the slope behind the fence. Coaldon commanded Sid to stay in the bush until the attack began. Most of the trogs were sound asleep as the two warriors prepared to attack.

Coaldon whispered to Brother Patrick, "It is best to strike at their legs. Otherwise they are tough to bring down."

In the distance, they heard the howl of a wolf. Coaldon and Patrick drew their swords, jumped over the fence and swiftly attacked the unsuspecting group of trogs. Four trogs went down with four quick stokes of the warriors' swords. The remaining trogs jumped to their feet and were ready to fight. From the corner of his eye Coaldon watched in awe the speed and skill of Patrick's swordsmanship.

Moving with awkward strides, a giant trog rushed at Coaldon with a loud yell. Instinctively, Coaldon raised his sword in defense while taking a quick step to the right. The trog used its brute force rather than speed and agility in the attack. The power behind the trog's sword almost knocked Coaldon off his feet. As Coaldon struggled to remain standing, the trog made a wide swinging motion with its sword. The slowness of its actions gave Coaldon an opportunity to drop to his knee and thrust his weapon deep into the creature's massive leg. He then rolled forward to force the blade to tear the trog's leg muscles. The trog screamed as it fell to the ground.

Coaldon relaxed his guard as he watched the trog collapse. He realized too late that combat required total concentration and alertness. His grandfather had told him over and over, "Never let your guard down. One mistake will end your life."

Out of the corner of his eye he saw the blade of his attacker flashing in the sunlight. He dived forward as the trog's blade nipped the flesh on his shoulder. In an awkward movement, he rolled to his left and stumbled as he tried to get to his feet. The trog laughed as it stood over him with its sword ready to strike.

The trog's premature victory celebration gave Coaldon the split second opportunity to escape by crawling betweens its legs. The trog bent forward in an attempt to grab Coaldon as he scurried under its body. When the young warrior had passed the trog, he jumped to his feet. The dull-minded beast slowly turned to face his opponent. Coaldon challenged the trog by raising his sword in defiance. Coaldon gave a blood curdling battle cry as he attacked with three quick strokes of his sword. Coaldon's sword left three deep cuts in its arms and legs. The slow, cumbersome beast erupted into an uncontrollable fit of rage. With wild swings of its sword, the trog rushed at Coaldon.

Coaldon hoped this would happen. With agile swordsmanship he parried each savage stroke until the trog left itself open for a counter attack. The young half-elf drove his sword deep into the chest of the beast with pinpoint accuracy. The life of the beast ended as it had begun. Death greeting death. Evil meeting evil. At this point, the dead trog evaporated into a cloud of dark smoke.

Coaldon quickly turned in a circle to evaluate his surroundings. He saw that all the trogs were dead. Brother Patrick was leaning against the shed with his sword in hand. A smile crossed Brother Patrick's face as he stared at Coaldon with a look of satisfaction. The monk walked over to Coaldon, bowed and offered his hand.

Patrick said, "Let's check on our friends." As they arrived at the barn, a trog ran in terror with Topple following him. Topple raised his right hand and released a burst of flames at the trog. The trog jumped in pain as it raced over the hill on the west end of the farm yard. Topple laughed with satisfaction at his success.

Sid leaped after the escaping trog with loud barks. In the distance Sid's barking could be heard for several minutes. Later, Sid proudly returned at a slow trot. A piece of cloth hung from his mouth like a symbol of victory.

The wizard grumbled, "Look at the hole in my robe! That stupid beast cut a hole in my robe! I should have fried it! It got away, but it will not forget about me for a long time."

With swords in hand, Pacer and Earthkin walked around the barn.

Pacer proclaimed, "That was a challenge. We were victorious, but I do not like the odds of three to one."

The five warriors greeted each other with broad smiles and vigorous hand shakes. A noise from the house drew their attention. In a state of shock, Dod, Doria and Rosa staggered out of the house. The dazed family looked at the field of destruction surrounding the home. Doria's body was rigid with determination and her eyes burned with anger. Dod's face sagged with relief and fatigue after many hours of fear and doubt. Rosa, though tired, exhibited resilience in the face of death and violence. The family fell on their knees to give thanks for their lives.

Dod said in an emotional packed voice, "We gave up all hope of being saved. We were once dead, but now we live. You have given us back our lives."

Suddenly the family rushed to greet their rescuers with open arms and words of thanks. The rescue team did not feel any sense of heroism, just a flood of elation that the family was safe. Rosa threw her arms around Coaldon in a show of relief and caring. As she removed her arm from his shoulder, she noticed he was bleeding.

She proclaimed, "Coaldon, you are wounded! We need to stop the bleeding!"

Coaldon smiled, "It is just a scratch. I will be all right. We have more important things to do."

Rosa would not accept Coaldon's self-denial. She said, "We do not want you to get an infection. So sit down on the bench while we take a look at your little scratch."

Pacer and Rosa attended to Coaldon's wound, while the family started to put their home back in order. The warriors learned that Bob, the farmhand, died during the initial attack by the trogs. Dod, Doria and Rosa wanted to hold a funeral service for Bob at sunset. The long, grim day ended with the digging of a grave in a field south of the house next to a bubbling spring. The four warriors solemnly lowered Bob's body into the grave. The family's grim stoicism finally collapsed into an eruption of emotions. Their sorrow flowed like a burst dam. They sat before the grave holding hands in disbelief that such violence could invade their beautiful world.

The warriors waited patiently as the family expressed their grief at the loss of a good friend. After the anguish melted from Dod's body, he stood up and faced the group.

He said in a weak voice, "We commit Bob's soul to the One Presence. He was a good friend, a hard worker and a noble person. We know Bob will find peace in his final reward. On this day, I commit my life to find justice for his death. May peace and goodness return to the Empire. Amen."

The family returned to the house while the warriors covered the grave and placed a wooden headpiece on the mound of dirt. The words carved on the headstone stated, "Bob – A good man and a fine friend."

When the warriors reached the house, they found a meal of cold cut beef, bread and sweet drinks. The tension of the day dissolved as the family and warriors were bonded into lasting friendship.

During the meal Pacer kept looking at Dod with growing curiosity.

He said to himself, "I have met him sometime in the distant past. Who could he be? I must find out."

The simple meal seemed like a feast to everybody. The shared meal, casual conversation and mutual support provided healing. The soothing ointment of caring touched the family.

After the meal the group gathered around the fireplace to share an evening of reflection and discussion. Dod started by saying, "Several days ago two wagons from the Monastery picked up supplies from us. It was strange that ten warrior monks escorted the wagons. At that time I figured something unusual was taking place. Then yesterday evening we were attacked by the trogs."

Doria explained, "Bob held off the horde of beasts, allowing us to find the protection of the house. His heroic death gave us a chance to defend ourselves." Rosa added, "Mom and I used the bow and arrows to slow the first advance of the beasts. All the weapons practice paid off."

Dod continued, "All winter I practiced with the sword. I spent at least one hour a day working on swordsmanship. During the first battle, I grabbed the Sword of Truth and rushed out the door without thinking. I have no idea where my courage came from. I knew I needed to make a stand for the sake of the family. I was amazed at the power of the sword. I only needed to hold it in my hand and it did the rest. The tip of the sword almost dragged me around the yard. The trogs fell to the ground like grass in front of a scythe. They retreated when they realized they were facing a superior power."

After a pause he continued, "Last evening, they once again attack the house. The beasts started running toward the house screaming to build courage. I stepped out the door with the sword in hand ready to confront the assault. As the trogs drew near, I attacked them with either blind bravery or crazed stupidity. Again, the sword did its job. Another ten trogs collapsed on the ground before the remaining trogs backed off to where you found them. I was surprised the beasts did not attack us during the night. I thought they would take advantage of darkness to destroy us. We were waiting for the final attack when you arrived to save the day."

Pacer could not wait any longer to find out more about Dod. He questioned, "Dod, I have met you somewhere in the past. I cannot remember where or when. Can you help me?"

Dod responded, "I lived in Neverly before I moved to the farm. Maybe you saw me there."

Pacer looked at the sword on the mantle of the fireplace, "How did you acquire such a powerful sword? That is truly the Sword of Truth. I have searched for years to find it. The last person to possess this weapon was Emperor Brad. Now here it is in the hands of a farmer. Or maybe you are more than a farmer."

Dod had a sheepish look on his face as he commented; "This sword was given to me by a friend. I had no idea of its power.

Pacer debated with himself about what he should do next. He needed to find out how Dod came to possess the sword. Dod was keeping a secret. Pacer decided the best way to open the door to Dod's mystery was to reveal his own identity.

Pacer finally said, "Before the fall of Emperor Brad my name was Duke of Paulic. Does that name ring a bell?"

Dod's eyes grew wide as his face paled in disbelief. He was unable to speak for several minutes. His mind exploded in bewilderment. For seventeen years Doria and he had hidden their true identity from everybody including their daughter. The fear of being found and killed by Emperor Wastelow forced them to start a new life. Dod questioned if it was safe to reveal his true name. He looked at Doria for an answer. Her slow nod of approval allowed him to share their long hidden secret.

Dod said to Pacer in a confident voice, "I place my trust in your honor as Duke of Paulic. I remember the dignity and honesty of your father and mother. They were good and noble people who gave their lives fighting Wastelow at the Battle of Two Thrones. Your grandparents stand as living legends of devotion to the Empire. This is the first time in many years I feel safe in sharing my identity. I am the Duke of Slownic, first advisor to Emperor Brad. I escaped Neverly with the Emperor after the defeat. I have not seen or heard from Brad since that date. When we departed, the Emperor gave me the Sword of Truth as a gift. I had no idea it was anything but an ordinary weapon. By the way, do you know if Brad and Ingrid are still alive?"

Everybody in the room remained in stunned silence as they reflected on the new revelation. Duke Slownic was known for his wise counsel, deep insight and honesty, but not for his hand as a warrior. His short, round body was not the image of a soldier. Dod's plump, bearded face had penetrating eyes that seemed to reach into the very soul of the person being observed. Even though his body was soft, his mind radiated courage, intelligence and confidence.

Doria was a person of contrasting attributes. On one hand, she was a woman with gentle, motherly impulses and desires. On the other side, she was a lady with a quick mind and strong will. Without hesitation she would stand like a rock against any violation of her values. She was willing to fight for a good cause even if it meant endangering her life.

When Rosa learned of the identity of her parents, her emotions vacillated between anger and admiration. She was angry because her parents had not been honest with her, and yet, held high respect of them.

Looking at her parents, she finally said, "Why didn't you tell me about yourselves?"

With a sad face, Doria said, "Wastelow is a very wicked person. We could not take the chance that you might accidentally tell somebody of our identity. We are sorry to have hurt you. This was too much of a burden to place on you. We were planning to share this information with you once the rebellion started. We expected the revolt to begin once the male child of Rodney and Starglide turned eighteen. We always prayed that Brad and Ingrid's grandson survived the fall of the Empire."

Pacer stood up to reposition himself before the hot fire. He responded, "Coaldon you might have something to share with our hosts."

Coaldon was uneasy as he started to speak, "Recently, I learned I was more than a farmer from the Outlast. On my eighteenth birthday party I was informed by my grandparents that as a small child I had been rescued from the War of the Two Thrones. My grandparents had taken me to live in the Wilderness of the Outlast. For the last seventeen years Ingrid, my grandmother, taught me to read and write. My grandfather, Brad, taught me to be strong, independent and honest."

Duke Slownic (Dod) jumped from his chair with an uncharacteristic burst of enthusiasm.

He said with excitement, "Then you are the crown prince! Thanks be to the One Presence! The time has come to begin the rebellion!"

Dod and his wife kissed and hugged with a joy they had not felt in seventeen years.

Coaldon was startled by their happiness. He said to the family, "I have a twin sister who is being held captive by Wastelow in Neverly. We have been commissioned by my grandfather to rescue Noel from her prison. We stopped here to ask for your assistance on our journey to Neverly."

Dod exclaimed, "Brad and Ingrid are still alive! Noel is alive! How wonderful!

Coaldon continued, "My grandparents are presently living at the Monastery of Toms. Crossmore's army of trogs forced us to seek the safety of the Monastery. My grandparents are healthy, of good mind and are ready to conquer Wastelow. Would you like to join us?"

With excitement, Duke Slownic proclaimed, "I would be honored to be a part of your noble army. Please tell us about your life, your grandparents and how you got here."

Coaldon, Pacer and Earthkin spent several hours reviewing the events of the empire. As Dod and Doria listened to the story, they felt reborn with renewed hope.

Rosa watched the reactions of her parents as they listened to the story of Coaldon's life. She said to herself, "Who are these people I call my parents? Where did all this energy and excitement come from? As I watched them, they seemed like strangers to me. I guess I have a lot to learn." She also began to watch Coaldon thoughtfully.

When the light from the new moon flowed through a south window, Topple drifted into a deep sleep.

Pacer said, "I think it is best we retire for the night. I am very tired. We have all been awake for many hours. Before going to bed there is a topic you need to consider. I do not think it is safe for you to remain on the farm. The trogs will return to avenge the death of their companions. Next time they attack you might not be so lucky. Maybe you should move to Grandy. We can finish this conversation in the morning. Guards will be stationed throughout the night in case the trogs return. Good night."

Return to Grandy

As the light of the new day reached into the bunkhouse, it received an unwelcome reception. The warriors wanted twelve more hours of sleep. Yet, they knew there was a difference between fantasy and reality. By lying in bed they were wasting valuable time. The warriors were interrupted when Sid started to bark and scratch at the closed door of the bunkhouse. Coaldon staggered to the door to let his friend in. Sid nearly knocked Coaldon over as he bounded into the room. Barking loudly, he pounced on Topple's huddled body. A deep rumbling sound emitted from Topple's chest. With irritability, he slowly opened his eyes. He was preparing to transform Sid into a lizard. Sid paid no attention to Topple's threatening behavior. He tugged on the wizard's clothes with his teeth.

At that moment, a horse whinnied nearby. Topple's eyes opened wide. He jumped out of bed and rushed out the door. Rose Petal greeted him with a loud whinny. The horse wheeled and kicked. Rose Petal's short legs supported a round body showing many years of hard service. Her brown, black and white coat had the pattern of a rose petal over her hindquarters. Her head was short and wide, with a lazy downcast appearance. Topple grabbed Rose Petal around the neck and kissed her. He would not leave Rose Petal to join any of the group's activities for the rest of the day. Topple and Rose Petal had a mysterious bond that went beyond normal communication. They walked around the farm sharing their friendship. Words were not spoken, yet they found understanding just being together.

After a big breakfast, Pacer called everybody together. He started, "What do we do now?"

Dod responded, "Doria and I agree the farm is no longer a safe place to live. We will move to the Village of Grandy. We will only take what is essential. Coaldon, would you please go with Rosa and find the horses that were scattered when the trogs attacked." With smiling faces both Rosa and Coaldon nodded in enthusiastic agreement.

Pacer interjected, "We need help leaving the Great Plains undetected. Every effort must be made to eliminate suspicion while traveling to Neverly. Noel's safety cannot be jeopardized by any mistakes. If the rescue team approaches Grandy from the Great Plains, we will be subject to scrutiny by Wastelow's spies. Can you help us?"

Dod paused before he spoke, "Two of you can act as our hired hands. The move to the village will justify the help of two hungry vagrants. The others can hide in the wagons until we arrive in the village."

Pacer commented, "You plan sounds great to me. We need to leave tomorrow if we plan to arrive in Neverly by the first day of spring."

The farm was busy with people moving back and forth preparing for the trip. Dod and Doria had to make many decisions on what would stay and what they would take. Several times Doria blinked back tears when she had to sacrifice a personal treasure. Yet, she knew necessity dictated austerity. She did keep several keepsakes as mementos of their good life on the farm. By evening everything was ready for the trip. The family spent a restless night dealing with the changes in their lives.

When the morning sun spread over the farm, everybody gathered for the final farewell. With tears in his eyes, Dod set fire to the buildings. He burned the buildings to keep the farm from becoming a staging point for trogs. Without looking back, the family climbed onto their wagons and started towards the village. From this moment on, the family would look to the future and not dwell on the past.

All the warriors, except Topple, had dressed in vagrant clothing. Their beards and old clothing, plus a coating of dirt gave them the appropriate appearance. Topple could not understand why he should be anybody but himself. Pacer tried, without success, to convince him to put on clothing that would change his appearance.

Topple clearly stated, "I will not cover my gorgeous face with dirt or wear anything but my precious robe." Topple believed there was some old magic in his robe. He clung to it like a child holding on to a special blanket.

Pacer and Coaldon assumed the role of being hired hands for Dod. They drove the wagons and assisted with repairs. While riding in the wagons, Topple, Brother Patrick, and Earthkin were ready to hide under a tarp to escape detection.

The road to Grandy improved as they traveled closer to the village. It took several hours of steady traveling for the party to reach the first farm. Dod decided to visit with the Rosic family to find out the latest news. The Rosics were happy to see their distant neighbors, but saddened to hear that Dod and his family were moving to Grandy.

Dod stated, "We were attacked by beasts from the wilderness. It is too dangerous for us to live on the farm."

He advised Jeffda, "You should set up a militia to protect yourself."

Jeffda responded, "I do not believe a militia would be necessary. We will be all right. Empire Wastelow and his soldiers will protect us."

With unfriendly glances, Jeffda watched Coaldon and Pacer. Strangers, especially vagrants, were viewed with contempt and hostility.

Dod left the Rosic farm with a sense of despair.

He stated to Pacer, "The people of the Empire have lived in peace for many years. For most citizens, war is only the subject of ancient stories."

Pacer followed, "Maybe, we have taken too much for granted. We have had it too easy."

Dod responded, "Sadly, people do not seem to appreciate their simple blessings. The emphasis has been on personal gains, not the betterment of the Empire."

Pacer concluded, "The Empire may pay a terrible price for becoming so complacent."

As the wagon slowly lumbered down the road, they passed many small farms spread across the horizon. The farms were a beehive of activity as farmers prepared for spring planting. The reinvigorating warm spring air purified and refreshed the farm houses. Farm women worked to remove the staleness of winter and replace it with the freshness of spring.

The wagons, pulled by four large horses, made better time as the road improved. The local farmers banded together to put down a rock base under the road to insure year round travel. The sun was setting as the party approached a forested area. At this point the farmlands gave way to the gullies and woodlands bordering Rolling River. Dod suggested it was best to set up camp for the night in a secluded area. The campsite was blanketed by the lush spring grass and surrounded by a wall of trees. A small, gurgling creek meandered through the clearing.

After a quiet night's sleep, the party was ready for an early departure. The sun rose as the wagons headed down the road. The descent from the plateau into the river basin was steep and winding. A long, narrow tunnel of trees enclosed the road. The quietness caused by the cover of trees created a sense of entrapment. A feeling of isolation and loneliness grew as the travelers went deeper into the forest and dense undergrowth. Coaldon and Pacer noticed the quietness of the forest became deafening. There were no sights or sounds from the birds, insects or animals. When Pacer and Coaldon reached a wide clearing, they pulled their wagons to the side of the road. As Coaldon stepped down from the wagon, a sensation of evil passed through him. He walked several strides from the wagons, but could not detect anything unusual. Each member of the party was happy to take a break from the bone-jarring impact of the wagons.

Dod was checking the horses when a black mist flowed around him. He shouted in fear when he started to lose control of his thoughts. Coaldon was the first to identify what was happening. Coaldon observed the mist penetrating Dod's body. Coaldon pulled the Blade of Conquest from the scabbard and pushed its tip into the mist.

He ordered, "Be at my command! Remove yourself!"

The black mist slowly flowed out of Dod's body. Once the mist withdrew, Dod collapsed to the ground in a state of shock.

Coaldon said to the black mist, "Open your consciousness to me!"

The black mist gave a grunt of resistance as it slowly yielded its power to Coaldon. As the mist succumbed to Coaldon's control, it changed colors from black to a bright red. Coaldon formed a mental link, through the mist, to its master.

Coaldon said in a commanding voice, "What do you want?"

The vision of a charming face clouded Coaldon's mind as an enticing, gentle voice engulfed him.

It said, "With whom do I have the pleasure of sharing this most fine moment? Do not be bashful. We can be good friends."

Coaldon responded, "Greetings! I am a beggar wandering the Empire."

The melodious voice probed, "You hide from me. I wish to know your name. I offer you the gift of my great wisdom and friendship. Join me."

Coaldon started to feel himself drifting into the grip of the wizard's magic. He held his sword with renewed strength saying, "I locate myself in the heart of the One Presence. I am the nightmare you search to conquer. Your hand aches from our last meeting. Why do you try to entice me with empty words and vile actions?"

Crossmore understood he was being challenged. His brooding pride could not allow any challenge to his power. He erupted, "You dare play games with me! You must be a bumbling fool! I am Crossmore the Great. Your simple mind is only child's play for me. I look forward to enslaving you as one of my pets."

Coaldon responded, "You must not understand the danger you are facing. Your defeat is like a storm on the horizon."

Crossmore's sweet voice responded, "Oh simple child, do not bask in empty arrogance. You will be mine to destroy."

His voice then changed from the coo of sweet enticement into the tone of wicked authority. In a booming voice, Crossmore commanded, "I order you to release your soul to me!"

Coaldon fell to his knees as the surge of Crossmore's power overwhelmed his mind and body. As Coaldon knelt on the ground, his pale, trembling face grimaced in pain. He knew he had to defeat Crossmore's attack or lose his soul to darkness. He desperately hunted to find a way to escape from the attack. As he searched, a stir of awareness drew his attention to the hint of a blue light. This light illuminated from deep within his being. He cleared his mind of all thoughts except for his focus on the light. Out of the haze grew a quiet pool of blue water. Guided by an unknown impulse, he drank from the pool's refreshing water. As the water flowed into his spirit, he felt a pulse of power.

Coaldon looked up from the pool to see Crossmore's hand straining to grab the essences of his soul. He knew he would need to strike a blow against Crossmore. As he watched, the pool of water was transformed into a reservoir of blinding light. This expanding surge of power pushed and pulled violently within him. He felt as if he was being torn apart. Coaldon realized an enormous flood of energy was trying to escape from him.

Out of fear of being consumed, Coaldon raised his sword into the air, focused his attention on Crossmore and released the throbbing force. A bolt of lighting erupted from the tip of Coaldon's sword and disappeared into the blue northern sky. The blast of energy was so powerful that each person standing next to Coaldon was knocked to the ground. A clap of thunder shattered the silence of the forest.

In the West Tower of the Palace in Neverly, Crossmore stood with sweat running down his face. He looked into the mirror, straining to control Coaldon. He had never faced a person with such power. Then without warning, a bolt of lightening shattered the mirror and exploded in the room. It emitted a blinding flash of bright colors. Crossmore was blown backwards into the opposite wall of the tower. He sagged to the floor in a state of agony. He could smell the odor of his burning hair and clothing. He stumbled across the room, grabbed a pitcher of water and poured it over himself. His clothes and face were powdered with black soot created by the explosion. He staggered to the window to escape the toxic fumes.

As he stood by the window, rage dominated him. The tremor of Crossmore's anger sent an earthquake rattling through the tower and into the city. People stood in fear as the black smoke boiled out of the tower windows. The citizens measured the degree of Crossmore's anger by the power of the earthquake. They rushed to find shelter before Crossmore released his vengeance on whomever was nearest.

As Crossmore's anger dissipated, he looked over the city and into distant lands with a growing uncertainty about his new opponent. His trembling body was bruised, battered and burned. His mind was in a tormented fog of confusion. He had trouble just walking across the tower to the door.

As he stumbled down the long staircase, he said to himself, "It is good for me to have an opponent worthy of my great magic, intellect and strength. I will destroy this slimy blob of scum. I will dominate all living things. Next time, I will be ready for him."

Coaldon remained on his knees with his head drooped onto his chest. He felt a void of awareness. He was empty of the life energy needed to survive. He could not hear the voices of his friends or perceive his own substance. The surge of energy had literally drained him of all presence. His attack on Crossmore was an undisciplined and reckless release of his essential life matter.

He finally collapsed onto the ground in a pile of ruin. With a serious expression on his face Topple sat next to Coaldon. He realized Coaldon had nearly destroyed himself. Topple placed his hand on Coaldon's head with the gentle touch of a new mother. He began to chant a litany of words from an ancient elf language.

Topple said, "I hope I can reach deep enough into your soul to pull you out of your nothingness."

After Topple had struggled and toiled for an hour, Coaldon slowly opened his eyes. He looked around the meadow and gave a sigh of relief. He gave Topple a smile and drifted into a peaceful sleep.

"We won" said Topple in a quiet voice.

Coaldon was loaded into the wagon, and the trip to Grandy continued with a renewed sense of urgency. It took several hours to navigate the road through a series of curves, ruts and potholes before entering a meadow next to Rolling River. The North South Road could be seen in the distance with the usual flow of horses, wagons and hikers. The tree covered banks of Rolling River were attached to the horizon.

Pacer parked the wagons in a clump of trees to rest the horses. When the wagons stopped moving, Coaldon awoke with a gasp of breath, sat up and looked around. As he stepped from the wagon, he was greeted with excitement and big smiles. He had a difficult time remembering what had happened.

It was not long before a crackling, warm fire lapped at the bottom of the cooking pot. Everybody watched with anticipation as the midday meal of meat and vegetables slowly simmered. Dod sat next to the fire with glazed and anxious eyes.

He finally looked toward Coaldon, saying, "What happened when the mist attacked me?"

Coaldon was slow to answer, "Crossmore uses the black mist to search the Empire for news and information. The black mist is an ancient evil Crossmore retrieved from the Chamber of Oblivion. The Chamber is located in the center of the earth where evil creatures and spirits are imprisoned by an elfin power found in the Key of Ban. Crossmore uses the mist to enter his victim's minds, seeking knowledge and control the unsuspecting person. You are lucky he did not inject his poison of hate and anger into you. By the way, what did you experience?"

Dod's confused thoughts and emotions limited his ability to answer clearly. "I just remember a dark – ah – cloud – no, spirit – oh, something dirty entering into my mind. I remember hearing a sweet voice inviting me to become his friend. I do not remember telling the voice anything."

Coaldon said. "You heard Crossmore's voice. He uses the mist to reach across the Empire. It is difficult to fight off the enticing call of Crossmore's evil seduction."

At this point Coaldon proceeded to tell the group about his battle with Crossmore. The young half elf explained, "Once I had gained control of the black mist, I challenged Crossmore without thinking about the consequences. As Crossmore reached into my mind, I first felt the magic of Crossmore's alluring presence. This attraction must have been enhanced by a magic spell. Several times during the battle, I felt I was losing control to his overwhelming power. Not until I reached for my inner strength was I able to resist his attack."

He paused before he continued, "At this point, I began to search for a way to strike a blow against him. For some reason, I found a deep pool of peaceful blue water in the core of my being. As I drank from this pool, a swell of power began to grow within me. At first it appeared like streams of light expanding in ever-widening circles. Finally, the pressure of the energy began to rage out of control. I remember releasing the expanse of energy into the face of Crossmore. At that point, everything became deathly quiet. A void of emptiness replaced the force of the light. I looked around, but I could not see, feel, hear, smell or taste anything. I was not conscious of myself until Topple pulled me from my world of empty realities."

Topple said, "I will call this most interesting encounter The Battle of Two Minds. By the way, young man, you almost died from the battle. You must learn to use your powers in a controlled manner. I will talk to you later about what you must do to survive such surges of energy."

Pacer followed, "After the meal, we must leave for Grandy. I suggest Topple and Earthkin wait in the forest for our return. There is no reason for you fine gentlemen to take the risk of visiting the village. I also believe it would be best for Rose Petal to remain in the village with Dod. The danger we will face on the road and in the mountains will be too much for this gentle creature. We will return tomorrow morning."

The meal was consumed with the casual conversation of good friends. Topple and Earthkin took the needed camping supplies and found a comfortable hiding place. Sid remained with the two campers. The two wagons traveled across a wide expanse of open ground before reaching the North-South Road. Pacer and Coaldon sat in the driver's seat as they approached the ferry crossing the Rolling River into the Village of Grandy. When the wagons pulled to a stop, the ferry attendant looked at Pacer and Coaldon with contempt. Dod stepped down from the back of the wagon to negotiate the price for the use of the ferry. The attendant recognized Dod, but continued to glance at the two vagrants driving the wagons.

The attendant said to Dod, "Who are these two miserable creatures? Where did you find them?"

Dod responded, "Good evening. It is good to see you. They are just hired workers helping me move to the village. Evil beasts from the mountains attacked us several days ago. It is no longer safe to live on the farm. Do you know of any houses for rent in the village?"

The attendant confided, "I would imagine those beasts were the handy work of the old couple living in Lost Valley. The old man and his half-elf grandson are bad business. By the way, check with Dame Rocksmith about a house to rent. She lives on the south end of Apple Street."

Dod paid the attendant his fee and crossed the river without delay. The streets of the village were empty of people except for several children chasing a chicken through the grass in an empty lot. Pacer and Coaldon drove the wagons directly to the house of Dame Rocksmith. After introducing himself, Dod chatted with her about the rental. He accepted her terms of rent and directed the wagons to a house next to the river. The old, brown, two-story house was sheltered under a cover of many large oak trees. It was well maintained, with a flower garden and a comfortable porch. The interior was clean and ready for the occupants. Pacer and Coaldon helped unload the household goods from the wagon and into the house. The sun was setting when Pacer, Coaldon and Brother Patrick said farewell to the family. Dod and Doria had long faces as the three warriors slipped out the back door and into the night.

Rosa's heart sang after she hugged Coaldon goodbye. "I am worried about him," she thought, "but I feel so happy. What is wrong with me?"

Unpleasant Welcome

The three warriors held a short meeting in the tall grass next to the river. They agreed upon a simple plan to gain information about the Empire. Each of the warriors would enter the village alone and snoop around. They would meet at the old boathouse south of town at midnight to share their findings.

Coaldon, wearing ragged clothes, wandered into the streets of the village. As he slowly ambled down the street, two pale faced and shabbily dressed men confronted him.

The taller man said, "We are Crossmore's vigilantes. We are here to protect the village from rebellion. What are you doing here?"

Coaldon lowered his head as he stammered, "I am just passing through the village. I am on my way to N-N-Neverly to find work. I will be leaving tomorrow. I only wish to find a meal and a place to sleep."

The narrow faced vigilante gave Coaldon a swift kick sending him to his knees. He then jerked up Coaldon by the collar as he threatened, "Be out of my sight, or I will turn you over to the soldiers. Now get out of here!"

Coaldon limped into the shadows of a building while the two men laughed at his cowering behavior. He watched as the two of them slouched down the street toward the Inn. Coaldon slipped around the back of the clothing store and sat below an open window of the Community Room in the Log Inn. The community room was the social gathering place where villagers came to discuss the events of the day, drink ale and enjoy a good meal.

Coaldon pulled his hood over his face to hide himself in the shadows of the building. From his position under the window, he could easily hear the conversation coming from the Inn. At first the discussions were the usual: farm, family, friends, crop prices and weather. Coaldon's thoughts drifted until he heard the name Wastelow. He abruptly became aware of the conversation.

"I heard Emperor Wastelow is very ill and is not expected to live. I wonder who will be crowned Emperor if he dies?"

"I am sure it will be Prince Regee."

"I would support the wise leadership of Crossmore. He would be reluctant to be Emperor, but he would help the common person."

Crouched outside the window, Coaldon had to bite his lip to keep from responding.

"I saw ten new soldiers arrived in the village today. This means we now have twenty. Why do we need so many troops to protect us from nothing?"

"I heard troops are patrolling the North South Road to guard the Empire from rebels. Have any of you traveled the road lately?"

"Yes, I just arrived today from Neverly. I went through five checkpoints to get here. I was amazed at the number of vagrants looking for food and shelter. I believe the high taxes are draining the wealth from the Empire."

"Well, it is hurting farmers for sure."

A loud crash interrupted the conversation. Coaldon took a chance on a peek through the window to observe what was happening. The tall vigilante stood in front of an overturned table with a knife in his hand.

In an angry voice he declared, "Do not question the wisdom of Wastelow and Crossmore! Say one more word criticizing our noble leaders and you will be sent to Neverly in chains. Or maybe, I could take care of any rebellious attitudes right here and now? I have sworn absolute obedience to the Emperor and Crossmore. I will accept no more words of descent. Ah! Ah! Ah! The vigilantes support the Empire with knife and sword. Long live Crossmore!"

The room became silent after the vigilante's outburst. Most villagers quickly left the Inn in small groups.

Coaldon heard a man say, as he stepped into the street, "In the old days we could speak freely without threats. Now fear and death seem to be the tool used to control the Empire."

"You had better be quiet, or you will face the power of the knife."

Coaldon had heard enough. He retreated to the back of the Log Inn and walked several blocks to a small hut standing recessed in a grove of trees. The young warrior approached the hut silently and peered into a window to gain a view of the room. Seated in a wooden chair was a large, muscular, young man with brown hair and blue eyes. Raff was the local blacksmith.

Coaldon walked to the front of the house and knocked on the door. After a long pause the door slowly opened. The young man stood in the doorway ready to defend himself with a short sword. He looked down at Coaldon with the authority of a massive body.

He growled, "Go away! I have no extra food or drink! I will use this sword if you try anything."

Coaldon regarded the young man in silence.

He finally said, "Raff, it is good to see you. I have missed you."

Raff's mind struggled to remember the name of this beggar.

Coaldon said, "How is Paggy? Is she still singing like a song bird?"

Raff only stood in silent frustration.

Coaldon finally said, "It's me, Coaldon."

Raff's eyes widened as he recognized his dear old friend. He hugged Coaldon in a burst of happiness.

Raff responded, "I am so happy to see you. I thought you had become one of Wastelow's dead or missing. Why the disguise and secrecy? What has been happening?"

Coaldon said, "May I come in before someone sees me talking to you?"

Raff blushed as he recognized he was not being a good host. He responded, "Come in and please forgive my mess."

Coaldon sat in a straight back, wooden chair next to the stone fireplace.

He commented, "I do not have enough time this evening to discuss old times. I want to talk with you about the future of the Empire. There is growing rebellion against Wastelow's violence and lies. I am here to ask for your help. You must maintain complete secrecy about this visit. A great deal has happened since our last visit. I am a member of a group willing to risk our lives to save the Empire. I can say no more, but I am asking you to consider helping us."

Raff sat quietly absorbed in Coaldon's comments. He looked first at Coaldon then at the flames flickering in the fireplace. As he again looked at his friend, he abruptly smiled.

He responded, "I have feared only a rebellion could end this reign of terror. I fully support and encourage your efforts. I will hold this conversation in complete confidence. You are my best friend. I would trust you with my life. Through my work in the blacksmith shop, I know of many people in the village who would agree with you. I will start gaining support from people in the community. Secrecy is essential."

Coaldon nodded, "I must go, but I hope to return to see you in several months. Please tell Paggy hello for me. You can make a difference."

The men shook hands before Coaldon walked out of the hut. Without looking back, he headed down a dark side street to the edge of the river.

He followed a narrow path until it passed a clump of trees and brush near the river's bank. Using the underbrush as a cover, he walked until he saw the old boathouse. He was guided by the firelight shining through the open door. As Coaldon entered the small room, Pacer and Patrick casually greeted him.

Pacer leaned forward, "How did it go?'

Coaldon took a seat on an old wooden box next to the door.

He responded, "I learned the community is being controlled by fear and intimidation. The vigilantes are running things with a rough hand."

Stirring the fire, Pacer asked, "Anything else?"

"Yes, I visited with my old friend Raff. I have known him since I was a small child. He is interested in joining the rebellion. He assured me many local people are becoming frustrated by the taxes and violence. I also learned the Empire has set up road blocks along the North-South Road between here and Neverly."

Both Pacer and Brother Patrick agreed that fear and anger were evident in the village. They had also noticed an obvious conflict developing between the people who supported the Emperor and those who did not.

Pacer commented, "If this frustration and anger continues to expand, we will have the army we need to face Wastelow. We can talk in the morning. Our hike to Neverly will offer us many hours to grow tired of each other's conversation."

On the Road to Neverly

The morning sky was dark with storm clouds as the three vagrants approached the ferry from different directions. Pacer faced the ferry attendant with a lowered head and hat in hand.

He said, "Good sir, I need to cross the river. I desire to travel to Neverly in search of work. What is your fee?"

As Coaldon and Patrick arrived, they voiced the same request. The attendant was torn between letting them cross and refusing their request. He finally demanded a fee double the normal price.

Coaldon responded, "We are just poor beggars. We cannot afford such a high fee."

The attendant's face grew red with anger as he yelled, "What can you pay?"

With trembling hands, each of the three vagrants reached into their money pouches withdrawing several stonas. The attendant laughed with contempt when the beggars could only produce 6 stonas to pay for the crossing.

Finally he yelled, "Get on the ferry before I call the soldiers to have you arrested! It is cheaper to get rid of you than to pay for your food in prison."

Meekly the vagrants climbed onto the ferryboat. The trip across the river was slow and rough because of the high water.

As the three travelers left the ferry, the attendant muttered, "Get out of my sight and do not return!"

The three travelers were happy to escape from the oppressive atmosphere of the village. As they approached the secluded campsite, they heard laughter. Topple and Earthkin were casually talking and giggling about some humorous story.

Pacer joked, "We will not tell anybody you were seen laughing and joking together. We do not want to give either of you a bad reputation."

With a grin on his face, Earthkin answered, "We just had a weak moment. It will not happen again."

It took about an hour for the three warriors to share with Topple and Earthkin what they had learned. After a meal the group was ready to begin their trek to Neverly. Topple and Earthkin would go first, followed by Pacer, and last would be Coaldon and Brother Patrick.

The trip to Neverly took eight days of hard walking. The first five days of the trip were uneventful other than the usual bantering among themselves and the occasional insults they heard from passing travelers. Many people showed contempt for the homeless. The guards at the checkpoints showed open hostility at having to talk with them.

Topple was exquisite in playing the role of a pompous slave owner. Earthkin rather enjoyed cowering in such a subservient and pathetic manner. Rain fell on the second day, but the roads remained in good condition. Mud was not a problem, but a brisk cold wind blowing out of the north stung their faces.

Each evening the five travelers gathered in an isolated campsite. It was enjoyable to talk about the events of the day and the exploits of Topple and Earthkin. Topple had the ability to gather a crowd with his bombastic behavior even on the empty road. On the morning of the sixth day, warm sunshine was reason to celebrate.

Topple and Earthkin began their daily journey with brisk steps and a loud introduction of their presence. After walking several hours, the two men were confronted by ten heavily armed men wearing ragged clothes. A short man with a black beard approached them with a sword in his hand.

He bowed deeply and said, "I am Robbet. These are my friends. Give me all your money!"

Topple also bowed and laughed as he threw Robbet his money pouch.

He said, "As you can see, I am a poor man. Maybe I can pay by offering you something special."

The wizard did not give Robbet time to respond before performing his first magic trick. A flash of light shot from the tip of his nose as he dramatically waved a silk cloth over his head. After several such tricks the bandits relaxed and enjoyed the show. Topple continued his act with tricks and songs until Pacer, Coaldon and Patrick joined the small group.

Robbet suddenly realized three more travelers had arrived without being noticed. He ordered his men to surround the five travelers with swords drawn.

Robbet again bowed and said, "That was a great act my good friend, but it does not put food in our stomachs. We are taking up a collection. Please, put all your coins into my hat."

Coaldon stepped forward, drawing his sword. With a quick flick of his wrist the tip of his bright sword rested on Robbet's throat.

The young half elf said in a calm voice, "We do not want to harm you. We are just beggars on our way to Neverly to find work. Please let us pass in peace."

He ended this statement by giving his sword a small twist. A tiny trickle of blood ran down Robbet's neck.

Robbet said in a loud voice, "Truce! We wish to have no problems with you"

Coaldon lowered his blade and wearily took several steps backwards.

Robbet then yelled, "Attack! We need their money!"

Before Robbet could even move, the flat of Coaldon's sword hit him across the head. He collapsed to the ground unconscious. Pacer and Earthkin only had to threaten an attack before the other bandits threw their weapons on the ground. Nobody was hurt except for a large knot on the side of Robbet's head.

The warriors realized these bandits were hungry men looking for their next meal. It was obvious the thieves were not warriors, but farmers, merchants and laborers. The high taxes demanded by the Emperor forced them to use whatever means available to survive.

Coaldon said, "Again, we do not want to harm you. You face death if you continue your attack on us. Stand down, declare a truce and we shall be friends. We only desire to continue on our journey to Neverly."

The thieves nodded dumbly.

Staggering to his feet, Robbet stammered, "I apologize for our rudeness. We are hungry men with hungry families. We are desperate. We have been cast into poverty for the sake of Wastelow's greed for power and wealth. I was a teacher in the Academy before being forced to resign. Many of my men were merchants and leaders in Neverly. We would not cower to the Emperor's quest for dominance. We were forced to escape or be killed.

Coaldon responded, "This is a grim story you share with us."

Robbet continued, "May I be so forward to ask your names. I know you are not ordinary travelers. You handle your swords with the grace of expert swordsmen. Your gentle character speaks of nobility. "

The other thieves shifted their eyes from Robbet to Coaldon in anticipation of his response. These men had the look of people searching for a glimmer of hope. Their miserable lives were a series of tragedies. The selfish, inhumane policies of Wastelow created a living nightmare for these men and their families.

Coaldon smiled as he said, "Names are only a handle to a limited reality. Names are symbols; whereas, character shares true identity. We offer the shadow of a greater truth. A truth that will blossom when the proper season arrives. I believe it is possible to find hope in our presence."

Everybody including the warriors regarded Coaldon with curiosity. All eyes remained on him waiting for something to happen.

Robbet was the first to breech the silence, "I am spellbound by this encounter. The character of your rag-tag group radiates power and dignity. You offer a silhouette of hope into the world of our impoverished existence. You extend a ray of sunlight into our darkness. I do not know your mission, but pray it will provide a small step toward justice."

In unison, the band of thieves nodded in agreement with Robbet's statement.

Robbet continued, "We will make no reference to this chance meeting to anybody. We will keep our lips sealed to everybody, but each other. There are many spies looking for information to give to Wastelow. The reward of food is a powerful motivator to desperate people. We do not want to endanger you in anyway. We offer our bond of trust."

Individually, each thief swore an oath of secrecy and fidelity.

Coaldon said, "Thank you for your assurance. I am pleased to find men of honor in this wilderness. I wish we could talk longer, but must be about our business. If we wished to contact you in the future, how can we communicate with you?"

Robbet said, "We will contact you once you arrive in Neverly. I extend my blessings to you and your friends."

Coaldon reached into his pocket and withdrew a coin. He stated, "I give you this gold coin as a bond of our fidelity. This should feed your families for many days. We place our lives into your hands. Your trust will reap rewards. May the One Presence bless you."

When the travelers had resumed their journey to Neverly, they talked openly about the grim situation of the thieves.

Pacer commented, "I hope you did not reveal too much to the thieves. We must be careful not to give away our mission. I believe Robbet will have someone follow us. We must not alienate these people. Somehow, they may help us achieve our goal."

On the eighth day the team approached the last checkpoint on their journey. Over the past several days the landscape changed from forested bush lands to open expanses of farmland. At first these farms were few and far between. As the group came closer to Neverly, the number of farms increased. It was obvious to the travelers that poverty was rampant. Many farms were over run with weeds and infected with decay. It saddened the warriors to see empty farmhouses standing as a tribute to the destructive policies of Wastelow. At the checkpoint a large number of travelers waited before being allowed to proceed. The five friends sat close to each other in anticipation of their turn at the checkpoint.

As the sun set in the west a soldier signaled them to step forward. The tired soldier sat behind a wooden table with a large book lying in front of him. He said in an impatient tone, "I have sat in this chair all day long. I do not like you. I do not want to talk to you. So answer the following questions quickly."

The members of the team did not hesitate to provide the information in a courteous manner. The soldier seemed reluctant to let the five vagrants past the checkpoint.

The guard then stated, "So you come looking for work and food. We have neither. People are starving to death on the streets of the city. Move ahead, but remember we will not allow dissension against the Emperor. Death is the price for the crime of sedition."

Neverly

The sun was setting as they looked for a place to spend the night. On both sides of the road groups of beggars could be seen huddled around fires. The warriors became aware they were being closely watched. As Coaldon glanced over his shoulder, he noticed a group of beggars following them.

He said to the team, "We are being followed. I suggest we turn and greet our new friends. This will help dispel any misconceptions."

The travelers stopped and turned to face the group. They were a motley group of poverty stricken men. Their thin, haggard bodies and hollow eyes reflected their need for food. The warriors knew hungry men could be dangerous. Pacer stepped forward in a slow, casual manner. He raised his hand as a sign of welcome.

He said, "Greetings, we travel to Neverly looking for work and food. We desire to avoid any conflict."

Loud, sarcastic laughter erupted from the unsavory group. In an arrogant and defiant manner, a short, thin man walked toward the five travelers.

He said, "You offer us great humor. All we ask for is your money. Then, we will leave you alone. Now save yourselves grief by handing over your coins."

Pacer responded, "Again, we seek no trouble with you. As it has been said, 'Live and let live'. Let it be known, we will ably defend ourselves."

The vagrants raised their arms in mockery and gave cynical shouts of fear. The group advanced on the five warriors with clubs and rocks in hand.

Coaldon stepped forward, declaring. "We come in friendship. Do not waste your blood by attacking us. Be wise. Leave us alone."

Before anybody could act, a yell came from the crowd watching the impending disaster. With long strides, Robbet stepped from the bystander. He ordered the advancing group to stop. The thief walked forward with the confidence of a commander. His eyes flashed with intelligence and his body moved with authority. The advancing vagrants showed respect to his invisible influence. The group stopped and held a short meeting with Robbet. Several beggars looked up at the five travelers with suspicious glances as the conversation continued. Finally, the cloud of hostility dissolved from the vagrants. The character of the mob shifted from aggressiveness to reconciliation.

With downcast eyes the man leading the mob approached the rescuers saying, "We extend salutations to you. Your friends from the forest have offered you safe passage. Go in peace."

The mob quickly dispersed into the fading light of day. No further attention was given to the newcomers.

The five travelers continued down the road with no desire to talk with anybody. They did not want to draw any attention to their journey. As darkness blanketed the area, they spotted an old barn in a weed choked field. Alert to any possible encounter with the local homeless, the travelers carefully approached the barn. The inside was littered with old fire pits and garbage. After consuming a warm dinner, they had a peaceful night's sleep.

At the first light of day, the group continued their trek toward the capital city. As they topped a knoll, the walls of Neverly could be seen in the distance. The two towers of the city dominated the skyline. The gray, dark walls of the city framed the west gate in a vivid outline. The Slownic River, with its tree covered banks, snaked across the land forming a barrier between them and the city. The five travelers could see the West Road join the North-South Road in front of the famous Talking Bridge.

The Talking Bridge, spanning the Slownic River, was the magnificent creation of the dwarves and elves. Marble and granite blocks, quarried in the Sadden Mountains by the dwarves, were used to build the foundation. It was the architectural miracle crafted by the elves at the height of their genius. The beautiful bridge stretched across the river in a graceful series of arches with no obvious means of support. The magic of the elves was infused into each block of the bridge, allowing it to stand against the force of gravity. The interlocking bonds of magic within the bridge created a flow of energy that sounded like whispering voices. This sound would often cause people to run across the bridge in fear of being cursed by the murmuring resonance. The warriors stopped to marvel at the splendor of the bridge. Even though corruption abounded, the elegance of the Talking Bridge stood as a testament to potential goodness in the world.

With reluctance the rescue group lowered their eyes from the majesty of the bridge and focused on the road descending to the river. As they approached the Talking Bridge, small bands of beggars were making their daily migration into the city in search of food. The homeless mixed together as they crossed the bridge without being aware of its beauty or miraculous creation. The crowd of people walked with fatigued steps up the narrow road leading to the city's west gate. The five travelers, in their ragged clothes, blended into the milling crowd of people as they approached the city. On both sides of the large metal gate, vagrants huddled in small clusters watching the arrival of the tragic parade of poverty. The soldiers pushed the beggars into large holding areas to have better control of them in case trouble erupted. This mass of humanity looked like a tide of misery washing up against the wall of the city. At the appointed time, several wagons arrived from the city with the daily ration of food for the homeless. Wastelow determined it was better to feed the crowds, rather than face a rebellion.

The warriors stood in disbelief as the vagrants made an uncontrolled rush at the wagons to gain their share of the food. Coaldon saw how poverty had driven normal people to act like wild animals. He noticed how the weak and ill beggars were pushed aside with little or no concern for their health or safety. The soldiers advanced on the mob with lowered spears to regain control. As the hungry mob formed into orderly lines, the distribution of food began. The five travelers found a place at the end of the line. When their turn arrived to be served, each received a small ration of bread, cheese and watery soup. Pacer led the group to a secluded location next to the city wall. The mob became quiet after the food was handed out. Several beggars roamed around the crowd stealing food from the weak. If individuals protested, the thieves would cuff them. Bullies had a free-hand to do as they pleased. The ability to remain human was a challenge in the face of lawlessness.

The new arrivals were so engrossed by the churning mass of people they did not notice an old blind lady approaching them. The decrepit woman had a small, skinny body with wrinkled, brown skin. Her weathered face emitted the solid strength of the earth. She wore a ragged dress stained with many weeks of collected grime. Her white empty eyes were directed towards some unseen reality. She approached the team with the guidance of her walking stick. The hair on Sid's back stood up as he gave a deep growl of warning.

She pointed the stick directly at Coaldon saying, "What has taken you so long to get here? I expected you several days ago!"

Coaldon looked in disbelief at the old woman. He finally said, "I do not know what you are talking about."

The old woman gave a loud cackling laugh as she lifted her arms into the air. "My, you have the same temperament as your father. I can feel his presence stirring in your body and mind. Yes, this should be a most enjoyable adventure. Pacer, it is my pleasure to welcome you to Neverly. I extend my greetings to Brother Patrick and Earthkin. Your reputations stand as monuments to your fine character. Oh, and if it isn't the unfortunate Topple. You must be the most worthless person in the world. I should have drowned your sorry soul when I had the chance."

Topple's eyes sparkled at the unexpected challenge. He slowly stood up, spread his feet apart and placed his open hands on his hips. He said, "It has been a long time, Hilda. The last time we met, your uncensored words created a rebellion in the Empire."

Hilda pointed her walking stick at Topple saying, "Why must the world be tortured by such a marginal example of humanity?"

The flicker of a smile grew on Topple's face. He finally said, "You have tormented many people with the emptiness of your mind."

Hilda arched her back as she prepared her next rebuttal. With clearly articulated words she said, "The simplistic nature of your foolish personality is found in the acts of little children."

Topple's face finally blossomed into a broad smile. He countered, "It would seem your mouth continues to control your common sense."

Topple and Hilda then rushed forward into each others arms. At this signal, all the members of the group except Coaldon started laughing and clapping with pleasure.

Coaldon questioned, "What is going on with these two?"

Pacer laughed as he said, "Hilda and Topple are brother and sister. They have not seen each other for many years. This bantering is their special way of saying hello. I was hoping we would find her here. She has magical powers we can use."

Several beggars sitting in the area of the encounter started to stare. Hilda had the reputation of being a strange and dangerous person with few friends. People believed she could cast a spell of misfortune, merely with the look of her blind eyes. Nobody, out of fear of being turned into a toad, rat or maybe a snake, ever went near her hut south of the city.

Pacer finally said, "We need to be more discrete. Spies could report us to Crossmore. We could visit with Hilda, but I believe it is time to start our investigation of city. Let's meet here at sundown. Hilda, we will visit you this evening."

Before departing, Hilda gave directions to her home.

As she walked away, each member of the group began to mingle with the crowd of vagrants. Coaldon and Sid walked north along the city wall until they reached the edge of the crowd. Coaldon sat down next to a small group of individuals talking in quiet voices. He pulled his hood over his head to offer an image of disinterest. He removed his knife from its scabbard and held it loosely in his hand under his coat. Being prepared for an unanticipated threat was becoming second nature to him. As Coaldon listened, the conversation of a small group shifted from topic to topic without any direction or purpose. It seemed the meaningless discussion helped fill the void between sunrise and sunset. The elf soon lost interest in the discussion.

Coaldon's attention was reawakened when the subject changed to Wastelow and Crossmore.

"I heard that Wastelow died today. Did anybody else hear this rumor?"

"Yes, it is true. Wastelow is dead. They say he will be buried tomorrow in the royal crypt.

"I believe that Prince Regee will be crowned by authority of the five royal advisors. The Empire is in deep trouble when Regee takes the throne. He is so pathetic."

"Ruffor, you should not speak out against the new Emperor, or you will face retaliation."

Coaldon saw people looking around to see if anybody heard the seditious comment.

Finally someone with a soft voice commented, "Did you hear that Crossmore has not been seen for nine days? I heard he received wounds when he was attacked while working in his tower."

"How could he be attacked in the tower?"

"I don't know, but I would like to thank the person for performing such an important service for the Empire. The power of the wizard is increasing every day. I believe Crossmore will ultimately eliminate Regee. If Crossmore takes power we will be given food, but in the process we will sell our souls in his evil plan. I believe I have said too much, yet I feel so helpless."

Moaning in agreement, everyone again looked around for spies. At this point, somebody noticed Coaldon sitting next to the group.

A loud voice shouted, "Hey you, what are doing there?"

The young half elf ignored the question.

Again he heard a voice say, "I am talking to you. Who are you?"

Coaldon heard someone walking towards him in slow, deliberate steps. Finally, he felt the pain of a solid kick to his side. Coaldon looked out from under his hood with sleepy eyes.

He said, "Why did you do that? I was just resting."

The man pulled his knife and pointed it at Coaldon. He ordered, "Stand up and let us get a look at you."

Coaldon slowly stood up, keeping his knife concealed. He responded, "I just arrived yesterday from the Village of Grandy. I came here looking for work. I do not know anything about this city."

The man advanced on Coaldon with his knife raised.

He exclaimed, "You must be a spy. Otherwise, why would you be sitting next to us?"

Suddenly he thrust his knife at Coaldon's chest.

As Coaldon stepped to the right, the knife tore a hole in his clothing.

Coaldon declared, "I am not a spy."

Sid walked to a position putting him between the two fighters and the crowd. As several men stepped forward to help their friend, Sid bared his teeth and growled. Sid's threat of attack forced the crowd to stay back.

The man laughed and made a slashing motion with his knife. Coaldon darted to his left and grabbed the man's arm as it passed in front of him. With a swift twist of his body, he flipped his assailant on the ground.

The half elf repeated, "I am not a spy. I come in peace. I do not want to hurt you!"

The man jumped to his feet and made a running dive at Coaldon. Coaldon stepped to the side and intentionally made a small cut on the man's forehead. The man fell to the ground in an uncoordinated tumble. He gripped his head to stop the bleeding. Coaldon stood over him with a stern face and a dominate posture.

Coaldon said, "Next time you attack me, you will die."

With Sid at his side, he turned his back to the bleeding man and walked into the milling crowd of people.

With a look of dejection, the man yielded in defeat. He felt a twist of admiration at Coaldon's courage and noble character.

Coaldon spent the rest of the day exploring the area around the city. He examined the ancient walls and watched people moving in and out of the massive gates. He took special note of the movement of the guards. He memorized where the guards stood, the number of guards at each station and how people gained access to the city.

The young half elf took the time to visit with people as they waited to enter the city. On his walk around the outskirts of the city, he observed the features of the land surrounding the walls.

As the sun set, Coaldon gathered with his friends at the West Gate. Little was said as they walked south from the city to a hill surrounded by a thick grove of trees. A twisted trail led up the knoll. It was difficult to walk up the path because of the dense cover of thorny bushes and brambles. When the group approached the top, two large dogs rushed at them barking frantically. The dogs stopped when Sid leaped in front of them. The two dogs positioned themselves to attack Sid. Topple, with a casual motion of his arms, pointed his right hand at the dogs.

In the distance they heard a voice yell, "Don't you dare fry my dogs. They are only happy to see you."

With an air of pompous arrogance, Topple released a small burst of energy at the two dogs. As the surge hit the animals, a dancing light flickered around their bodies, ending with a burst of red sparks shooting out the dog's noses. The dogs yelped in terror and ran back into the trees with tails between their legs. In the distance a tall woman walked from the trees with the two dogs cowering behind her. With long, confident strides she approached the group. She had a pleasant face, long brown hair, a slender body and sparkling eyes.

With indignation she looked at Topple saying, "If my dogs do not recover from this shameful attack, I will singe every miserable gray hair on your body."

Topple smiled as he responded, "I was just offering the world a special service. The dogs were being rude and disrespectful. In the future, their manners will improve. I know you will learn to appreciate my gift."

Coaldon's four traveling companions greeted the woman with obvious friendship and warmth. Coaldon looked at her with bewilderment. He detected something familiar about her, but could not identify it. With understanding, Pacer turned to Coaldon with an open smile.

He said, "I know you must be thoroughly confused by now. I want to introduce you to Hilda, Topple's sister. She is of the Order of Glad. She can change the way people perceive her in order to hide her identity. Everyone in Neverly, including Crossmore, can only see an old blind lady. For us she appears as her true self."

Hilda approached Coaldon with a warm glow.

She said to him, "It is my pleasure to meet you. I have waited a long time for you to assume your role as Crown Prince. I realize you are confused by the change in my appearance. I must change shapes to protect myself. Crossmore tolerates me because he thinks I am harmless. Anyway, it is good to keep Crossmore guessing about my identity."

The group walked a short distance to an opening in the side of the hill. The entrance into her home led into a pleasant dwelling furnished with wooden furniture and woven wall tapestries. A fragrant dinner was simmering on a large stove under a window overlooking the city. Without interruption, two young ladies wearing bright green uniforms served the meal in exquisite style. Hilda introduced the two helpers as her apprentices. She explained they were the best candidates she had ever instructed.

The meal was simple, yet elegant. Sweet roots were cooked in a light sauce of red watercress, sugar maple and green bitters. Roast duck was marinated in sweet rose oil and slowly cooked over a low fire. The vegetables were flavored with a delicate coat of honey and tart rootmeg. Coaldon had never eaten a meal with such robust flavors.

After the dinner, Pacer called the group together to discuss the rescue of Noel. Pacer carefully explained to Hilda the history of the past year. Special emphasis was spent on Coaldon's adventure with Crossmore. He concluded by reviewing the plan to rescue Noel.

After Pacer had finished, Hilda carefully probed each of the five rescuers with her penetrating eyes. Coaldon responded to these nonverbal inquiries with his own nonverbal examination of her character. As he looked deeply into her eyes, he detected a rich wealth of knowledge and wisdom. He relaxed as the truth of her nature flooded him with understanding.

Hilda finally stated, "It sounds as if you have developed a good rescue plan. It will not be long before it will be the first day of spring. Please do not rush any part of your planning. I invite you to meet with me in four days. May the One Presence bless us in our mission."

The group left Hilda's home in a different direction than they arrived. After they walked a short distance, Pacer stopped and listened. He signaled the group to proceed while he hid in the brush. Several minutes later the four men heard a shout of surprise. The group returned to find a man lying on the ground with Pacer's sword pointed at his chest.

Pacer demanded, "Who are you and why are you following us?"

The trembling man said, "My name is Bodso. Robbet has assigned me to follow you. He is concerned about your safety."

Pacer removed his sword and invited the man to stand.

Pacer said, "We can take care of ourselves. We do not need your help at this time. It is dangerous for you to follow us. Please extend our thanks to Robbet, but we must not be limited by your interference. How can we contact you if we need your help?"

Bodso responded, "I will give your request to Robbet. We will have a friend stationed at the West Gate at noon each day. He will be wearing a red hat. Just say 'spring is beautiful' as the password. He will say 'the flowers are red'."

Bodso departed, and the group found shelter in an abandoned cabin near the river. This location would act as home for several weeks.

The death of Wastelow was a major topic of discussion throughout the area. On the day after his death, Wastelow's body lay in state in the Church of the One Presence. Only the people with money and position were allowed to view the body. Late in the afternoon Crossmore and Regee arrived for a short memorial service in honor of the dead Emperor. The church was full of people who expressed little sorrow over the death of Wastelow. The service was performed in a dignified manner, lasting about thirty minutes. Crossmore dominated the funeral with his overpowering charm. He fronted his counterfeit grief by giving an emotionally laden eulogy of Wastelow's service to the Empire. Regee remained quiet and offered bogus tears of mourning. After the requiem was sung, a solemn procession took Wastelow's body to be buried in the Hall of Emperors.

After the internment, Regee called a meeting of the Council of Advisors. Regee demanded he be immediately crowned Emperor. The members of the council protested, but Regee was surprisingly supported by Crossmore. The coronation was held in the Grand Hall of the Palace with only twenty people in attendance. After the coronation Regee sat on the throne with the look of benevolence, but in reality he felt only contempt for his subjects.

Petra, his loyal attendant, waited on him with complete servitude. The servant enjoyed being the head butler for the new emperor. Petra submissively nodded in approval at anything Regee said or did.

He listened carefully as Regee told him, "I feel sorrow at the death of my dear daddy. I will suffer this loss with the dignity of a true gentleman. Thankfully, I can now fulfill my destiny. I will act with humility when people of the kingdom bow to me in homage. I have always wanted to live a life of luxury and power. I will demand complete obedience. Ah! Ah!"

As Regee basked in his new found glory, events in the city were unfolding according to plan. Each day, the members of the rescue team learned more about the city. Coaldon always spent some time watching the windows in the East Tower. He was pleased when a young woman appeared at the window. She did not see him among the crowds of people, but at least he saw the reason for his quest.

Topple and Earthkin were gaining near celebrity status in their performance as master and slave. Topple's grandiose behavior was complimented by Earthkin's subservient groveling and whining. Topple was especially good at throwing scraps of food onto the ground with an eccentric flair. Earthkin was then forced to crawl on the ground grasping for the food. Coaldon noticed the crowds were starting to support Earthkin. At times groups would boo Topple for being so cruel to pathetic Earthkin. Topple responded to the crowd's boos by bowing in a grand, theatrical fashion.

The next meeting with Hilda included a lengthy discussion of the many different aspects of the rescue attempt. Hilda ended the meeting by talking about the escape from the city.

She said, "I do not believe you can make a clean escape unless a diversion is created. Do you have any ideas how this could be accomplished?"

Brother Patrick stated, "I wonder if we could use Robbet and his band of thieves to create a distraction south of the city? He might be willing to help us. If we use him, I suggest we do not give him any clue about the time, date or reason for their involvement. At the designated time and date, his small army will make hit and run attacks against the royal troops. We will only give him several hours notice before they are to attack. We should offer him a reward in gold for his cooperation."

Hilda and Pacer were pleased with Brother Patrick's plan. Coaldon volunteered to contact Bodso to begin negotiations with Robbet. The next item on the agenda was the decision to send a reconnaissance group to check out the tunnel under the palace. Coaldon, Brother Patrick and Pacer were assigned the responsibility to make the first venture under the palace. The group would enter the tunnel the next day to begin the exploration. Finally, Topple, Earthkin and Hilda were given the job of locating horses for the escape to the mountains. The final details would be worked out just before the actual rescue operation.

Under the Palace

Pacer, Coaldon and Brother Patrick departed the cabin an hour before daylight. They took a round-about route to the tunnel entrance to avoid being detected. When the team was within 20 strides of the entrance, Brother Patrick scouted the area to make sure they were alone. The rock slab covering the entrance was lifted from the opening and set aside. A steady flow of rank, unpleasant air blew out of the dark hole.

Pacer commented, "This flow of air means the tunnel is not blocked." Pacer was the first to walk down the stairs leading into the tunnel. He removed burning coals from his tinderbox to light a torch. After entering the tunnel, Coaldon and Patrick carefully pulled the stone back over the entrance.

Coaldon felt an instant sense of entrapment. At first he wanted to rush back to the entry way and push the stone away. He craved to see the daylight and breathe fresh air. He clenched his fists and closed his eyes. He did not expect to feel so ensnared. To his relief, the desire to escape passed quickly. With lingering discomforts, he was ready to begin the adventure.

Pacer's torch provided a flickering image of a rounded passageway, lined with stones and mortar. The floor was layered with many years of dirt and rocks. Over time stones had fallen from the roof creating an uneven walking surface. Water dripped from the ceiling forming puddles. A dull light emanated from the gray moss growing on the passage walls. No extra light was needed, so Pacer doused his torch.

A musty, foul odor filled the travelers' minds with unpleasant mental images of its source. Pacer waited for his two companions to arrive before starting down the narrow passage. The explorers walked slowly to keep from tripping over large rocks and to listen for any unnatural sounds. After fifteen minutes the group arrived at a junction in the tunnel. Without having a good reason they decided to follow the passageway to the right. After several minutes, they found the tunnel blocked by a collapsed wall. Returning to the junction, they proceeded down the left passageway.

As the group advanced down the tunnel, Coaldon started to have odd sensations. He finally said, "Let's take a break. I am experiencing something unpleasant. Are you feeling the same thing?"

Pacer commented, "No, I feel nothing. It has been rumored Crossmore placed evil creatures in these tunnels to protect against invasion. The last time I went through here I had no problems."

Coaldon felt his sword vibrate in a slow steady rhythm. He responded, "I believe we will have visitors before we depart from the tunnel. If we are attacked, we must kill all the creatures. If one should escape, our mission would be jeopardized. Maybe we should set a trap for our hosts. By forcing them to come to us, we can control the attack."

Brother Patrick said, "If we are going to set a trap, then we must find a location in the passageway that will fit our fighting style. Let's continue walking until we find a place where we can launch a surprise assault."

The group continued down the tunnel until they entered a section having a series of collapsed walls.

Pacer stated, "We can have a person hide behind the walls of dirt at three different locations. After the inhabitants of the tunnel enter the trap, we can attack simultaneously. The gray luminous moss on the tunnel walls will provide enough light for us to see our opponent."

The three men placed themselves in protective positions along the passageway. As Coaldon waited in his hiding place, he grew impatient for the plan to unfold. He wanted to keep moving and get things done. After an hour, his mind drifted into lazy day dreams. He remembered the Outlast and the many hours he explored the wilderness. His usual state of alertness had been compromised by his youthful restlessness and the stale, foul air.

He was suddenly jerked back to reality when he heard raspy breathing and the crunching of rocks under padded feet. His sword was alive with a pulsing rage. To his shock and dread, the beast standing in front of him was a huge, black, hairy monster that nearly filled the tunnel. Pacer gave the command to attack. Coaldon held up the Gem of Watching to begin his assault. At Coaldon's command the Gem released a blinding flash of light. The monster screamed in pain as the light burned into its sensitive eyes. In rage, the monster reached out for anything to release its anger. Before Coaldon could move he found himself being swept up by a giant hand. As he was yanked through the air, he lost the grip on his sword. The sword rattled to the floor as the beast wrapped its powerful arms around Coaldon's body. The smell of the creature's nauseating breath caused Coaldon to gag. With unbelievable strength the muscular beast squeezed Coaldon. Coaldon heard his bones begin to crack under the pressure of the squeezing arms.

His terror was compounded when he looked directly into the mouth of the beast. The large, scum coated teeth were dripping with a black, slimy saliva. The beast's long, narrow tongue darted in and out of its mouth. Coaldon had to jerk his head back and forth to escape the slashing motions of the tongue. Luckily for Coaldon, the beast's agony caused it to lose focus of Coaldon. As Coaldon started to lose consciousness, he made a desperate attempt with his free arm to reach for his knife. As the monster thrashed around, Coaldon could not find the blade. Finally, he determined it had shifted backward on his belt. With an exaggerated twist of his body, he was able to grab the knife with his finger tips. He held on to it with claw-like determination. He was relieved when the knife released from the scabbard and dangled from his fingers. With a quick upward flip of his wrist he was able to grasp the knife in his hand. Bearing unbelievable pain, he raised the knife over his head and plunged it forward into the beast's hairy chest. The magical powers of Strong Edge discharged a searing burst of energy into the beast. The beast screamed as the power of the knife attacked its evil nature. The last thing Coaldon remembered was collapsing onto the floor.

In a nightmarish state, Coaldon kept seeing an angry beast reaching for him with long arms. He felt the terrifying slow movement of his hand reaching for his knife. He saw a large mouth, with black teeth, trying to bite him. Out of the monster's mouth, he beheld the presence of death looking at him. With a shimmering glow, death assumed a human form. Its body, covered with a radiant white robe, filled Coaldon with a sense of peace. Its quiet face glowed with warmth and understanding. He heard death's gentle voice extend a pleasant greeting. It offered a hand, inviting Coaldon to follow it into lasting peace. Coaldon found himself drifting toward eternal happiness. Then with a burst of awareness, he remembered Crossmore, his grandparents, friends, the empire and Noel. Death reentered his awareness offering him a choice. He could join death or return to his former life. Coaldon was offered a hazy glimpse of his future life filled with trials and pain, happiness and fulfillment. Over and over the choice demanded a response.

With a sudden jerk, he forced himself to awaken. Pain enveloped him as he regained consciousness. He did not know which was worse, his encounter with the monster or his aching body. As he opened his eyes, he saw the light from a torch. Pacer and Brother Patrick were rubbing a healing lotion all over his body. Coaldon tried to speak, but only a dull groan passed through his lips. He felt his pain slowly diminish as the ointment soothed his sore muscles. After several moments he was able to move slowly and say a few words.

He asked, "Did we destroy the beasts?"

Pacer answered, "Those two cute, fuzz balls wanted to play with us. You destroyed one, and we put the other beast out of its misery. I have never seen so much strength bundled into one package. I was hoping we could get by without another fight. No such luck. After the beasts' death, it was fascinating to watch their bodies melt into piles of slime. I never imagined evil could be reduced to such a small, meaningless residue."

Coaldon slowly forced himself to sit up and stretch his arms over his head. As he reached into the air, his back realigned itself with a series of popping sounds.

He commented, "I think I can walk, but not too fast."

Pacer said, "We will go as long as you can keep up."

After a short distance, the tunnel split into three different passageways.

Pacer said, "I remember Brad telling us about this junction. We are to take the one on the right. We can explore the others if we have time."

The tunnel to the right ended with a manmade stone wall. The wall was a combination of old and new construction. The ancient mortar on the left side of the wall was crumbling into a powdery dust.

Pacer commented, "The reconstruction on the right side of the wall must be where Brad concealed his escape seventeen years ago."

The three warriors started to dig at the old mortar and rocks with sharp metal tools brought by Brother Patrick. After a short time, Pacer broke through the wall. A dim light could be seen penetrating through the hole.

With great care Pacer removed the stones from the edge of the hole. When the gap was several hands wide, Pacer looked inside with hesitation.

He commented, "Brad was correct when he told us the wall was hidden behind a wine vat."

He reached through the hole and touched the old vat. It was about one arm's length away from the wall. The explorers decided to remove the stones below the hole in order to keep it hidden from view. The warriors were delighted to smell the cool, fresh air flowing into the tunnel from the old winery. When the hole was large enough, Pacer pushed his way into the space between the vat and the stone wall.

He crawled around the vat and into the room. The large room looked as if it was a storage area that had been forgotten over the ages. Many boxes, pieces of furniture and piles of rubbish were randomly stacked and covered with a thick layer of dust. Several small windows with iron bars were located high on the wall straight ahead of him. A large door on their left had been boarded shut. On their right, a small, solid wooden door entered into the palace. He signaled the others to follow him into the old winery.

As they gathered next to the vat, Pacer stated in a soft voice, "I am concerned about disturbing the dust and debris. When we move through this room in preparation for the rescue, we could be detected. What can we do?"

Everybody stood silently observing the room for any clues to solve the dilemma. Finally Brother Patrick said, "We can create the impression somebody is once again storing things in the room. Every time we enter we can bring something into the room and pile it in front of where we are now standing. This will give the impression that the disturbed dust is a normal activity of palace life."

Coaldon looked at Patrick saying, "Patrick, I am happy you are on our side. I believe you would be a dangerous enemy."

Pacer nodded in approval as he walked across the room to the door. He put his ear to the door to listen for sounds in the hallway. After several minutes of concentrated listening, he decided it was safe to take the next step. He reached down and tried to open the door by pulling on the handle. The door did not open. He assumed the dead bolt was in the locked position.

Brother Patrick stepped forward to examine the lock.

He commented, "This will be easy unless the mechanism is rusted together. One of my jobs at the monastery is being a locksmith. I have worked on all kinds of locks."

Brother Patrick pulled out a small kit from an inside pocket. He carefully looked at the lock, then selected a specially designed tool to manipulate the latch. After several minutes they heard the loud click of the bolt retracting into the lock. Brother Patrick stood back as he allowed Pacer to approach the door. Pacer opened the door with extreme caution. The dark hallway was covered with litter and waste. A pathway down the middle of the floor indicated people were still using the hallway on a regular basis. To his left, Pacer noticed light filtering from the end of the hallway. As he looked to his right, the hallway disappeared into the darkness.

Closing the door behind them, he said, "Coaldon, how are we to get to the plugged shaft?"

Coaldon pulled out Brad's hand-drawn map from his pouch. He said, "First, the map shows we are to turn right after we leave this room. The hallway will then come to a staircase going down into the basement of the palace. At the bottom of the stairs we are to follow the hallway until we reach a junction. We are to go down the hall to the left. This passageway will open into a large room. The plugged shaft should be in the far left hand corner. Shall we give it a try?"

Pacer chuckled as he responded, "I guess that is why we are here. We could wait, but what would that accomplish. Let's go!"

As the warriors walked down the hallway, Coaldon noticed rooms lined both sides of the passageway. He saw signs where several of the doors had been opened recently. Footprints in the dust led into the rooms. Pacer waited until they were walking down the stairs before he opened his tinderbox and lit a torch. The deteriorated stairs descended down steep steps. Each step brought the possibility of falling. The men were surprised at the length of the staircase. Coaldon never imagined the palace could house such a deep and forbidding place. At the bottom of the stairs, a small room opened into a hallway bordered by empty cells on each side. The rusted iron doors hung open in a state of corrosion. As the group passed down the hallway, Coaldon was shocked to see human bones scattered on the floor.

He thought to himself, "These bones should not surprise me. People are only objects to Crossmore. These people were killed to satisfy his greed for more."

The rusted remains of a large metal gate lay on the floor at a three-way junction. Pacer carefully examined the floor for signs of anybody walking through the area. He commented, "I see no signs of people entering this area in many weeks or months. We are now to take the passage to the left. We should be careful because it was the practice to construct traps to discourage anyone from entering certain areas. These traps can be pits, falling gates, or collapsing floors. Brad told me this hallway might still have a concealed trap. We have come to far too make a silly mistake now."

Pacer held the torch high in the air as he probed ahead of himself with a pole. The hall narrowed to a small doorway opening into a large room. Pacer stopped in front of the door to examine the door frame. He carefully studied the area. He started to move forward when Coaldon commanded, "Stop! I have a strange feeling." Pacer stopped in his tracks. He looked over his shoulder at Coaldon to gain some idea what he should do.

Coaldon continued, "Pacer, back up and let me check things out. I have never felt this tingling sensation before. It feels like something is reaching out to me."

He stared into the room with curiosity. A strange vibration began pulsing in the pouch where he kept the Gem of Watching. Out of curiosity, he reached into his pouch and removed the Gem. As he held it in his hand, it released a peculiar light. The bright light reached through the empty doorway. In the area illuminated by the light, a shimmering image took form. At first it was a round shapeless accumulation of particles. The transparent mass started swirling faster and faster in a circular motion. The three warriors could actually feel a breeze from the rotating particle cloud. In a burst of light, the nebulous mist assumed the proportions of a human body.

A yell of happiness suddenly sprang from the wavering shape standing before the three men. The transparent image drifted loosely in the doorway. A big smile and excited eyes radiated from the face of this most unique presence. It proclaimed, "Hello! Hello! Helloooo! I am so happy to meet you! I have been so lonely for the past few centuries. Do you have time to talk? It has been a long, long, long time since I have talked to anybody. Where should I start? I am just delighted you would stop by to visit with me. Well, tell me all about the weather, news about the Empire

and the Emperor. Wait just a minute; I do not know you gentlemen. Before you arrived, I was thinking about going for a walk, but I forgot that I couldn't walk. Silly me! I know that I can only float along. You stand there looking at me as if you are seeing a ghost. Wow! Wow! That is what you are seeing! Were you surprised when I appeared? Oh, I heard you coming down the hallway, but I did not expect to talk with you. By the way, what are you doing down here? The only people I get to see are the weak, wicked and miserable. You do not look and feel evil. That must mean you are good. That is excellent! Have you ever met my good friend Topple? He is such a special person. I miss him."

Coaldon finally injected, "Stop talking!" The spirit stood in shock at actually hearing a voice. Normally he could only hear a soft muddled mixture of gibberish when people talked.

The ghost responded, "You mean you can hear what I say? Well, that is such a treat. Now what do I do? I think I only know how to talk and not listen."

Coaldon continued, "I will try to answer several of your questions. We are the three who have come to find the way. Our names only provide a vague hint to the hidden nature of our being. We step into the battle between that which consumes and that which gives. The villain feeds on the pain and agony. In answer to this infection, we are called to action. The wind blows with passing opportunities. The lofty eagle beholds the presence of choice. Our journey will offer substance to the lasting power of justice and mercy. It will be fulfilled as we drink from the cup of faith and eat the food of truth."

The spirit was obviously confused by Coaldon's words. It shifted back and forth in discomfort. His facial features twisted and contorted as he struggled to understand Coaldon's statement. The waving figure slowly disappeared, then reappeared in a different location. Groans of uncertainty poured from the apparition. Finally, it looked directly at the three warriors, saying, "My brain is lazy and my will power has lived in an empty land. It is easy to become undisciplined in a place with no choices or challenges. I believe I am being called to become something more than I was yesterday. Yes! Yes! Yes! I accept your summons. Anyway, it will be my honor to join you on this worthy endeavor. My word is my bond. Oh, this has been such fun. Thank you for visiting me! Before I go, do you have any questions?"

Without thinking Pacer asked, "Is it safe to enter the room?"

The spirit said, "No harm will befall you. Now I must go to my new home."

The spirit smiled, waved goodbye and closed its eyes. With a burst of light, it flowed from the top of its head into a narrow, pencil-like stream across the hallway and into the Gem of Watching.

With stunned disbelief Coaldon watched the spirit flow into the Gem. He put the Gem up to the torchlight and saw a cloud flowing in the center.

The young elf looked at his two companions saying, "What just happened?" Brother Patrick responded, "I have heard stories about wizards who had their bodies separated from their spirits by Doomage the wicked wizard. The spirit wanders in the world until it is reunited with its body. This might be the case. Anyway, it is now a part of our journey if we like it or not. I would recommend we do nothing until we talk with Topple. It might be dangerous to try to intervene without getting more information. Let's go inside and look around."

The large room had many piles of unused equipment and supplies. These remains were scattered across the room in a disorganized jumble. Pacer went directly to the left hand corner of the room to look for the abandoned shaft. Several times he tripped over the piles of litter as he struggled to wade through the giant mess. He cheered as he stood before a pile of rocks clogging an opening in the wall. He signaled the others to join him and help clear the area around the opening. The hole stood about two strides high and one stride wide. Most of the stones were about the size of summer melons.

Pacer commented, "This is better than I thought. The rocks will be easy to remove. Where can we hide them?"

Coaldon's searching eyes detected a shadow in the wall next to the door. He found a small room containing cooking supplies. He said, "I think I have found the solution to the problem. We can pile the rocks in the room and then cover the entrance with rubbish when we are through."

Pacer responded, "I like your suggestion. I am hungry, so let's take a break to eat. I would like a few minutes to think before we make our next move."

The room was quiet as each rescuer reflected on the events of the day. Coaldon vividly remembered seeing the spirit entering the gemstone. He pulled out the Gem and watched the cloud slowly float in a circular motion. He could almost hear excited laughter and see a smile glowing from the center of the stone.

After eating his meal Pacer said, "I suggest we go back to the junction. I would like to explore the left passageway before we return to the outside world. I need a better picture of our location."

The group took every precaution to cover any sign of their intrusion into the underworld life of the palace. Upon returning to the winery, each man deposited several pieces of equipment and furniture next to the wine vat. They locked the door, scattered the dust and crawled into the passageway. They returned to the junction and began to investigate the tunnel to the left. After ten minutes of stumbling through the rocky passageway, the tunnel suddenly ended. A stonewall blocked the tunnel.

Pacer said, "What do we do now? We could go back to the original entrance, but I would like to find a second escape route. It looks as if the builders just quit work. I don't understand; I thought this was a storm drain."

While Coaldon and Pacer walked up and down the passageway looking for an exit, Brother Patrick sat and studied the wall. His eyes wandered over the inside of the tunnel with curiosity. It suddenly occurred to him that after each ending there is a new beginning.

He said to himself, "All the signs in the passageway indicate the tunnel continues. The way the rocks have been cut can only mean the tunnel extends beyond this point. Yes, I believe magic is at work. Magic can be understood as the distortion and manipulation of reality. Too often we think magic is something solid, rather than an idea viewed as reality. The solid curtain of magic can be walked through when we understand it is an idea made real in the mind of the beholder. To break through this magic it is necessary to accept the illusion as a projected thought. Yes, many years ago somebody found it necessary to block this tunnel with a curtain of magic. I can just walk through the illusion."

Brother Patrick stood up, walked forward and passed through the magical curtain at the end of the passageway. Both Pacer and Coaldon stood in amazement as Brother Patrick disappeared into the stone wall.

Coaldon said, "I do not believe what I just saw. My mind can not comprehend Patrick walking through the wall."

Pacer then laughed with embarrassment.

He responded, "Our good friend, Brother Patrick, did not rush around looking for the answer, but rather allowed the answer to come to him. Let's go!"

Pacer stepped forward and also disappeared through the wall.

Coaldon looked around the tunnel with the desperation of a person trapped within his own limitations. Sweat rolled down his face even though the tunnel was cold and damp. His heart raced in fear of being left alone in the miserable tunnel. He was alone with no one to help him. No one was there to ask for guidance and assistance. He had to figure this out all by himself.

He finally said, "I need to gain control of my mind. I can do nothing in this state of panic. I need to get my thoughts in order. First, I saw my friends walk through that wall. Second, people cannot walk through a solid wall. Therefore, the wall is a product of magic. If the wall is only an illusion, then I can also walk through it. So why am I just standing here?"

Coaldon started to walk forward, but when he arrived at the wall he stopped. He put his hand on the wall and felt the surface of the stones. His mind reeled in panic as he faced the conflict between what seemed real and what was actually real. His eyes saw a wall and his hands felt the stones, but his mind knew it was an illusion. Coaldon was in a state of paralysis as he stood facing the wall. He needed to force his mind to look beyond the illusion and take control of his behavior. Several times he tried to step forward, but to no avail. He finally closed his eyes, allowing himself to relax. Slowly the panic of the moment retreated from his thoughts. He calmly reviewed the reality of his situation. He slowly opened his eyes, saw the illusion of the wall, and stepped forward. To his total delight he found himself standing in a passageway with Pacer and Brother Patrick looking at him.

Coaldon shouted, "I did it! I did it!" With a sense of pride both Pacer and Brother Patrick shook Coaldon's hand. Coaldon faced and conquered a giant within himself.

The Room of Magic

The three warriors continued down the tunnel until they reached a collapsed wall that blocked the passage way. A loose mound of dirt and rocks created natural steps up to a ceiling of the tunnel.

Pacer laughed, "Well, Brother Patrick, can you pass through that wall?"

Smiling, the monk commented, "No, that is the real thing. I would get hurt if I tried to walk through the rocks."

In a serious tone, Coaldon stated, "I feel the presence of magic. Not the minor energy of an illusion, but something of great power. Can any of you detect what it might be?"

Brother Patrick responded, "Look! There is a door over our heads.

The door was hidden in a recess and difficult to see. Pacer lit his torch to get a closer view of the door.

The door was made of a hard, smooth metal that reflected a bluish tint from the light of the torch. The door had no keyhole or any sign of a lock. Pacer walked up to the pile of rocks, examined the door and gave it a hard push with his arms. He then spread his legs apart, bent his knees, took a deep breath and gave a mighty push with his shoulder. The door did not move or bend.

He said, "I wonder why the door will not open? Let's take a closer look."

He lifted a burning torch up to the door to look for any evidence of a latch. He noticed a dull flash of light flicking off the symbols inscribed into the hard metal. The script had long, delicate, sweeping marks flowing in a beautiful pattern. Pacer looked closely at the inscriptions, but could not decipher the unusual markings. He invited Brother Patrick to look at the script, but even Brother Patrick with his strong academic background could not translate the script. Without including Coaldon in the dialogue, Brother Patrick and Pacer began to talk to each other about the symbols.

Coaldon ignored the two men, as he crawled up the mound to examine the script. Holding a torch, he turned his head in different angles to gain a better view of the strange markings. As Coaldon's eyes shifted back and forth over the inscription, he detected a pattern of script he had seen before. Grandma Ingrid had insisted Coaldon learn different elf dialects during his education in Lost Valley. He knew this ancient writing was the foundation for Roseland High Elf Script. The longer Coaldon looked at the pattern, the easier it was for him to translate the script. He was amazed at how the meaning of the ancient script was revealed to him. Coaldon heard about a living language, but had never experienced it. After several minutes, he was satisfied he understood the meaning of the inscription. He looked at Pacer and Patrick saying, "I believe I know the meaning of these inscriptions. I learned this dialect from Grandma Ingrid. If you look carefully at the scrolling pattern, you can see the same shapes as Roseland High Elf. At first, I was confused by the reversed characters and rotating sequence. It made sense once I detected the overall pattern of the symbols. It reads something like this, 'Blessings to you. In the Book of Time, your arrival has been foretold. You will be the first allowed to pass through this door. You are to retrieve the Scroll of Revelations. The scroll will be a guiding light into the shadows of the future. Only the Grand Advisor to the Elfdom of Talltree will be able to share its words. The door will open at the name of the spirit within the stone."

Brother Patrick and Pacer listened to Coaldon's presentation with fascination.

Brother Patrick was the first to speak. "I have heard about the Book of Time. Yet, I have never seen a copy. Is it possible our journey was prophesied centuries ago? I find this difficult to understand."

Pacer responded, "I agree with you, but I do not want to speculate about walking in parallel paths of reality. My mind cannot comprehend such a mystery. I am only interested in knowing more about the scroll inside the room. It sounds as if we will need Starhood to interpret the scroll. It must be our responsibility to rescue the scroll from the room."

Coaldon followed, "I wonder what the inscription means, 'The door will be opened at the name of the spirit within the stone?' What stone and what name is the message talking about?"

Pacer commented, "Since our presence here was known long ago, it would mean the prophecy also projected our present circumstances. The only stone we possess is the Gem of Watching."

In an excited voice Patrick said, "If this is the stone, we can assume the name of the spirit present within the gem would be our new friend. What do you think?"

Coaldon replied, "I know of nothing in the Gem other than our happy, smiling tag along."

Pacer concluded, "If this is true, then we need to find out his name."

Coaldon pulled out the Gem of Watching from his money pouch. He received the Gem as a gift on his 18th birthday. He lifted it to the light of the torch to watch the white cloud flowing around the center of the stone.

Coaldon questioned, "I wonder if spirit will appear when invited?"

Pacer responded, "Let's give it a try."

Coaldon said in a hesitant voice, "Spirit in the Gem, please join us."

The three men watched the Gem to see if anything would happen. The Gem began to vibrate and grow warm. With a blue flash, a cloud flowed from the Gem in a slow, gentle stream. The first image to appear was a happy, smiley face, followed by a wispy body.

The spirit declared. "I am so happy to see you gentlemen. It is nice to travel with you. I see you have arrived at the Room of the Scroll. I was here when they built it. It seemed like it was only yesterday. Oh, I have been thinking about going on a vacation. Would you take me on a trip? Maybe, we could go to the mountains or maybe visit the ocean. I would like to go fishing. By the way, why did you call me? Wow! Wow! Would you like to join me for dinner on the veranda?"

Coaldon finally interrupted saying, "What is your name? It would be nice to place a name with your face. Or maybe I should say 'a name with your smile'."

The spirit developed a thoughtful look on its face. He twisted his face in strange and contorted shapes. At one point the spirit's smile actually drifted to his forehead.

Then he said, "It has been a long time since I thought about my name. Let me think about it. Could it be? No, Potdog is my cousin. Hidy! Hidy! Hidy! This is most embarrassing. I cannot remember my name, but I keep hearing the phrase, 'Cando More."

In confusion Coaldon replied, "What are you talking about? What can you do?"

The spirit responded, "No, Cando More."

Brother Patrick asking, "Cando More?"

The spirit replied, "Yes, you are most correct."

Coaldon looked at the spirit with frustration pasted on his face. He asked, "What are you talking about? What can you do more?"

The spirit laughed, "Not Cando What, but Cando More!"

Finally Brother Patrick looked at Coaldon smiling, "We are trying to figure out the name of our new friend. So think about what we have been talking about."

In aggravation Coaldon erupted, "I don't get it!"

The spirit exclaimed, "Yes, now I do remember, it is Cando More."

Coaldon's face grew red with embarrassment as he hung his head. He responded, "Could your name be Cando More?"

His companions gave a hearty cheer. With a rousing burst of amusement, the spirit flowed back into the Gem.

Pacer said, "We could spend a long time talking about the strange events of today, but we have more important things to do. We must gain access to the room and get the scroll. Now that we have Cando's name, our next step is to open the door."

Coaldon walked to the door and said, "Cando." Nothing happened. Coaldon then looked at Pacer and Brother Patrick.

Patrick commented, "Coaldon look at the writing on the door again to see if you might have missed something."

Coaldon positioned himself to gain a good view of the inscriptions. He held the torch to his right side to obtain the best reflection off the ancient symbols. He was quiet for a long time before he gave a yelp of satisfaction.

He said, "I found the answer. The last line of the script has an unusual ending. I thought it was only a farewell statement. It reads, 'Farewell and blessing you. Allow the Gem to guide your way.'"

Pacer commented, "Then we are to use the Gem of Watching while opening the door."

Coaldon raised the Gem to the Door saying, "Open in the name of Cando."

A loud snap was heard as the door opened inward. A gentle, fluctuating light flowed from the room. Pacer slowly raised his head into the room. The room was about 8 strides square with a door exiting to his right side. The white stucco walls were embedded with many sparkling gemstones. The light source was a round ball buried in the ceiling. On the floor to his left, was a trunk with elfin script decorating the top and sides.

The three warriors entered the room with respect for the power maintaining its presences. All three men heard a deep humming sound created by the throb of magic. Coaldon looked around the room in awe. Everybody was concerned when the trap door closed with a sudden snap. The outline of the door blended into the pattern of the floor. The three men became uncomfortable as they watched the walls change color. The room became unbearably hot and humid. With a sudden jerk, the room began to slowly vibrate and shake. Plaster fell from the ceiling in large chunks. Large cracks appeared in walls as the floor crumbled into small pieces.

Coaldon closed his eyes to focus on the sources of the problem. He detected the blackened hand of Crossmore trying to penetrate the magic protecting the room.

He yelled, "Crossmore is attacking the room. He knows something is here but he cannot break through the magic. We need to rescue the scroll and get out of here. We must use the side door."

Coaldon hurried to the trunk and said, "Open in the name of the Gem of Watching." Nothing happened.

Finally he commanded, "Open in the name of Coaldon of Rocknee, heir to the throne and master of the Gem of Watching!"

He saw a ripple pass through the trunk as the lid opened. He grabbed the metal tube lying on the bottom.

Under the power of Crossmore's attack, the walls of the small room began to sag into molten rock. The light in the room dimmed to a dull, eerie glow. The red-hot heat in the room was starting to cause the three men to grow faint. Pacer rushed to the side door and threw his shoulder into it. The door swung open without resistance. Pacer looked into pitch-black darkness.

Pacer yelled, "Follow me!"

The three warriors rushed into the unknown dark tomb without considering the consequences. As they stumbled into a dark room, they tripped over a pile of wooden boxes. The men landed on top of each other with their arms and legs kicking and flailing. Lying on the dusty floor, they struggled to gain their bearings. Small, delicate shafts of light filtered into the room. The small beams outlined what appeared to be a large door. They could smell the musty odor of decaying materials. Coaldon still held the long tube tightly in his right hand.

The room looked like an old storage shed with large double doors opening to the outside. They could not see any sign of the door through which they had escaped. It was as if they had just walked through solid rock.

Pacer said, "We must be inside the city walls."

Brother Patrick was first to approach the double doors. He discovered the doors were held shut by a long board placed into several brackets bolted to the inside of the door. He lifted the board from the brackets and placed it on the floor. He cracked the doors to look outside. The monk could only see a weed-choked courtyard surrounded by stonewalls. The courtyard had not been used in many years.

After a long day in the tunnel, the three explorers welcomed the blue sky and refreshing air. The long shadows of early evening were spreading in uneven lines across the yard.

After entering the enclosure, they noticed the East Tower looming over their heads. They ended up in a courtyard next to the palace. On the north wall, the vague outline of a small door could be seen through dense underbrush. Pacer pushed through the brush, pulled open the latch and pushed the door open. He looked down an empty street.

Pacer said to the others, "Are we ready to enter the city? I guess we do not have a choice because we cannot go back into the tunnel. Let's go. We can decide what to do when we reach the market place."

Each of the warriors assumed his role as a vagrant. With hoods pulled over their heads they slowly entered the flow of people moving through busy streets. People walking in the narrow street pushed away from the undesirable vagrants. The travelers entered the market square as the sun was setting in the west.

The marketplace still had several booths open after a long day of trading. Coaldon noticed that certain homeless people jealously claimed the best locations for begging. These beggars would throw rocks and wave sticks at any vagrant who got too close to their territory. Against the walls on the main streets, the homeless built rough shelters out of old pieces of lumber and tarps. The warriors found an empty space along the north wall of the marketplace in an isolated alcove. From this position they had a good view of the street and the West Tower. The three men sat in silence as they observed the flow of life in the square.

Several local citizens, walking down the street, were having a loud conversation about events of the afternoon.

"Crossmore must have had a bad afternoon. Seldom have I seen him so angry."

"I actually heard him cursing and yelling about discovering a room. Did any of you notice the earthquake? It was like a raging battle between opposing forces. It gave me an uncanny feeling."

"Yes, I felt a tingling in my body. Something strange must be taking place. I believe an unknown power has been challenging Crossmore. Maybe the rumors about the Age of Change are true. I often wonder if Emperor Brad is still alive. I hope so."

As the people disappeared into a side street, the three vagrants could not hear any more of the conversation. Coaldon looked at the West Tower with growing concern.

He told his companions, "Our encounter in the Room of the Scroll was noticed. I hope we have not made ourselves too obvious? Could we have jeopardized the chances for the rescue of Noel?"

Pacer and Brother Patrick sat quietly as they considered Coaldon's questions.

Pacer finally said, "Coaldon, we need to have a meeting with the group to discuss your concerns. We do not want anything to threaten the rescue of Noel. It might be a good idea for us to hide out until the rescue."

In the distance the cackling laughter of an old woman could be heard. To the three men's surprise, Hilda marched down the street, waving her walking stick in front of her. Several people ran away to escape a glance from her blind eyes. Her friends watched as she approached them with sure, steady steps. She then paused in front of them with her face contorted in irritation.

She yelled, "How dare you stare at me! I am just an old, blind lady. I do not need your disrespect."

She caught her breath before she commanded, "Be gone from the city!"

Pacer led the group as they rushed down the street toward the West Gate. Hilda waved her arms over her head, as she hobbled with amazing speed after the men. When they reached the West Gate, several guards tried to stop them, but the group pushed past the guards with Hilda in hot pursuit. Hilda pointed toward Coaldon, as he tripped over some unseen obstacle. He fell to the ground with his arms and legs flopping in spastic twists. He stumbled to his feet and hastily ran away. Hilda laughed in triumph. She was still cackling as she walked out of the city with impunity. The guards found great humor in the comical escape of the three vagrants. The three men disappeared into the darkness as the people settled into another night of terror.

Return to the West Tower

Crossmore had been agitated for the past few weeks. The wounds from his recent battle were healed, but not his attitude. While resting in the tower he continued to search the Empire for information about the identity of his enemy. The battle with the unknown warrior was interfering with his ability to plan for conquest. Several months ago he knew exactly how he would gain control of the Empire, but now he was feeling uncertainty and confusion. The old books of legend told how the Age of Change would infect the Empire with turmoil and rebellion. He was concerned that the Age of Change might challenge his dream for control.

While Crossmore recovered from his wounds, he had time to evaluate his present circumstances and make four major decisions.

First, he was going to remove Regee from power. Within the next week Regee would disappear. He would direct the blame for Regee's disappearance to the enemies of the Empire. He would graciously assume the throne out of the generosity of his heart. Anybody who got in his way would join Regee.

Second, he knew it was necessary to destroy his unknown enemy. He would alert his vigilantes to look for new signs of rebellion. Any rebellious attitudes and activities would be crushed by the power of the Imperial Army.

Third, he would expand his power base in the Empire as quickly as possible. More army units would be stationed throughout the Empire to maintain his influence. The sooner he gained control the sooner he would be the source of history. He would use cruelty and fear as his companions. He would take delight in watching people cower and grovel before him. He often dreamed about requiring people to genuflect when he passed in the street, or demanding criminals beg for his mercy.

Finally, he needed to start making wedding plans. He knew Noel would ultimately give into his proposal of marriage. He would take pleasure in slowly crushing her strong will and personality. Just the thought of her submitting to him added pleasure to his life.

As he looked out the tower window, his thoughts were interrupted. Without warning, a sudden surge of magic flooded his being. He staggered back into the center of the room. He had seldom experienced such a powerful discharge of magic. As the force clouded his mind, his knees grew weak. He visualized a small room with a metal tube stored in an elfin trunk. He reached out his hand to combat the energy released from the room. He closed his eyes and pushed his magic against the throbbing force. He felt the small room collapsing under the pressure of his magic. He saw the vague outline of three men rushing from the room as it burst into fragments. As suddenly as the power surge had begun, it also ended.

When the magic force abruptly ended, Crossmore nearly fell to the floor. He desperately searched for the source of the disturbance. The magic left no trace to follow. He could not tell if it had come from near or far. Crossmore's inability to control the situation caused his frustration to burst into unusual violence. As his anger exploded, Badda was thrown to the floor. Fire burst from the tower windows in large orange flames. Crossmore's voice erupted with uncontrolled torrents of cursing and yelling. After the anger had drained from his body, he sat on the floor holding his head in his hands. He always felt better after he released his pent up rage.

Crossmore remembered when he did not always have these fits of rage. The purge of energy opened his mind to memories of his youth. He saw himself as a child playing alone in the streets of Goobe. He remembered the pain of being teased by other children. He never knew when a rock would hit him or a gang of kids would strike and kick him. He discovered that the captivity of his personality was inescapable. His gentle nature, frail body, pockmarked face and shyness were target for constant mistreatment. In his loneliness and pain, he soon developed a seething hatred and distrust of people. His sense of inadequacy was compensated by an over powering desire to demonstrate his self worth and supremacy. This quest for power was fulfilled through the use of magic. He used magic to hurt and control his enemies.

As a youth he repeated over and over, "I will prove that I am the best. I will punish people for what they did to me. I will be the most powerful wizard in the world."

These thoughts faded as the sight of Badda drew his attention.

With inquisitive eyes Crossmore looked at Badda lying on the floor. He was pleased how Badda had injected terror into the hearts of local residents. Yet, Badda had been slowly changing over the last several months. His servant had been showing signs of childish emotions. He was considering reprogramming Badda with a new mind purge but it needed to wait. Presently, he did not want to lose focus on the events surrounding his quest for power. He was then reminded of the special evening he had planned for the new emperor.

Crossmore had invited Regee to a dinner to celebrate his coronation as Emperor. He had also invited Noel to join them in recognition of the festive occasion. The main dishes would be savory duck cooked in wine with fresh sautéed vegetables and creamed fottee roots. The wine was imported from a winery in the Village of Brags. Crossmore knew the dinner would be a great success. Regee would find the evening a life-changing experience.

Crossmore smiled to himself as he thought, "My dear Regee, you will not have to wait long to meet forces much more evil and corrupt than you."

The dinner party was held in Crossmore's lavish apartment in the south wing of the palace. The dining room was adorned with colorful tapestry, crafted furniture and plush carpets. Regee was first to arrive followed by Noel and Magee. Noel would only attend the dinner if Magee would act as her escort. Two waiters from Crossmore's staff served the four course dinner. Crossmore dazzled his guests with his charm and wit. He told light jokes and shared humorous stories about events in his life. The evening was interspersed with pleasant conversation, a toast to the new Emperor and words of praise for the splendid dinner. As darkness covered the palace, Magee and Noel departed Crossmore's apartment. They were relieved to escape the arrogance of their two dining companions.

After Magee and Noel left the room, Crossmore invited Regee to sit with him in front of the fireplace. Crossmore stared at the leaping flames in a relaxed, peaceful mood.

He finally said to Regee, "I am so proud of you. I feel like a father sitting with his son."

Crossmore's melodious voice dripped with charm and sincerity.

He continued, "Over the years I have watched you grow into a strong, intelligent and skilled leader. I know you will be one of the outstanding rulers in the history of the Empire."

At the sound of these words, Regee's face glowed with self importance.

Crossmore followed, "I have always thought you would be a greater emperor than your father. May he rest in peace. Your insights into human nature will help the Empire grow and prosper. I am volunteering myself to be your advisor and friend."

Crossmore's charismatic personality and sweet smile were drawing Regee into his trap.

Regee responded, "I accept your offer of support. I agree with you about my potential to be a great leader. I have often watched in disbelief at my father's miserable management of the Empire. It was time for him to die so I can fulfill my destiny."

Crossmore said, "I was saddened by your father's death, but it is now time for you to stand in the glory of the throne."

"Yes," said Regee quietly to himself.

Crossmore continued, "I suggest we construct a monument to you. A tribute to your greatness should not be delayed."

Regee commented, "Where could we build this monument? Maybe in the market place or outside the West City Gate?"

Crossmore responded, "I want to share with you a bottle of wine I have been saving for such a special occasion. This important moment should be celebrated with the very best wine."

He rang a bell and a waiter entered the room carrying a bottle of wine and two glasses on a small tray. With the skill and grace of an elegant gentleman, Crossmore poured the wine into the glasses.

He raised his glass to Regee, saying, "Regee, to your success. May you always remember this day."

Regee grinned with conceit as he swallowed the wine in one loud gulp. His pale, pimple infected face gleamed with a scornful smile. Regee's greasy hair and hairless face framed his lifeless eyes. He looked at Crossmore with contempt.

Regee thought, "I will make Crossmore my tool. He is such a fool to believe he can trick me with his dumb magic."

Crossmore followed, "Have you ever seen my black ring?"

Regee's eyes were becoming lackluster and glassy, as he responded, "No, I have not seen it before. What can it do?"

Crossmore laughed to himself as he thought, "The power of this ring will soon perform its magic. This poor fool will face a new future."

Crossmore answered, "The power of the ring will open your mind to new and exciting opportunities."

Regee was starting to feel uncoordinated as he looked at a shaft of light flowing from the ring. With a burning sensation the light penetrated deep in Regee's mind. Before Regee could fight off the magic, he was enslaved. The poison in the wine held Regee in a state of submission, thereby allowing the light from the ring to gain control. Regee understood everything that was happening to him, but he could not fight back. Crossmore looked at Regee with disdain. His smug smile erupted into uncontrollable laughter and celebration.

He looked at Regee, saying, "You will have the opportunity to hate me for eternity. The image of my face will stand as a reminder of what I have done to you. I will enjoy knowing your abhorrence of me will last forever."

Crossmore raised the ring high in the air, saying, "By the power of this ring, I cast you into the Chamber of Oblivion. You will live in the torment of your own creation. Your self indulgence will be the master of your hell."

Thoughtfully he continued, "Thankfully, I am beyond such trivial limitations. I take pleasure in knowing that my supremacy will shift the balance of power from the weakness of decency to the glory of evil. I will make wrong right. I will crush the roots of goodness. I will validate my own destiny. The future will be justified according to my wishes and commands."

With every fiber of energy in his being, Regee struggled to escape his bondage. He listened to Crossmore with disbelief, hatred and anger. Regee knew he had been drawn into this trap by his desire for self glory. Blackness filled his mind as he whirled in a downward spiral into nothingness. As he convulsed in rage, he fell into a bottomless pit. His freefall into emptiness continued for what seemed an eternity. In panic Regee reached for something to hold on to. His hands only passed through the illusions of reality.

After a long terrifying period of frantic despair, he found himself facing many ghostly images. Their faces were long and narrow, characterized by large round mouths and eyes. With anticipation the red eyed demons anxiously waited to torment the new arrival. The mouths howled an unquenchable thirst to inflict pain. Long fingers grasp at Regee seeking to assert dominance and control. The quest to destroy or maim was the unending motivation of these vile spirits.

As these evil spirits attacked Regee, they faded in and out from different locations. Reaching hands ripped at his flesh and violently poked at him. Their taunting voices belittled every characteristic of Regee. Ghostly laughter mocked his failures, weaknesses and limitations. Regee fought back with violent gestures and words. His imprisonment would be the perpetual battle between himself and forces striving to control him. He did not know that his only escape was to accept his limitation and yield to the powers of humility and forgiveness.

Crossmore watched Regee disappear into a cloud of smoke. He looked into a mirror on the wall with personal satisfaction at his handsome appearance. He was now ready for the next step in his plan. First, he needed Badda to visit the city to begin a new reign of terror. Crossmore's spies had reported many rebellious comments needing an answer. He again glanced into the mirror and thought about preparing for a wedding.

He laughed to himself as he said out loud, "How could Noel possibly resist a refined gentleman like me? Ah! Ah! Ah! Ah! By the way, I will miss you, Regee! Ah!"

ᛚᚣᚹᚹᚦᚺ ᚢᛘᚨ ᚠᚢᛘᚨᚣ

Topple and Cando

The campsite was a welcome sight for Pacer, Coaldon and Brother Patrick after their adventure under the palace. Topple and Earthkin had a hot meal ready for their friends. Coaldon was especially hungry and ready for a good nights sleep. As he sat in front of the fire, his thoughts stormed with the events of the day. He kept reliving the battle with the monsters, the appearance of Cando, the escape form the room of magic and of course the encounter with Hilda.

Hilda arrived at the camp shortly after the group had finished eating a hearty dinner. She found great delight in describing how she had helped the three men flee from the city. Coaldon listened for several minutes before he collapsed into a deep sleep while Pacer and Brother Patrick told the story of their adventure under the palace. When Topple heard the account of Cando, he jumped to his feet shouting with happiness.

He exclaimed, “Cando was my best friend! We shared many adventures together. I thought he was gone forever when Doomage the Wizard separated his body from his spirit. I have heard stories about a spirit in the palace, but I did not relate it to Cando. It will be wonderful to meet him again.”

Pacer said, “We are tired, so let’s meet tomorrow morning to make plans for the rescue. It is only three days before the first day of spring and we have many things to do before we can complete the rescue.”

The next morning the group met at Hilda’s home. She demanded all five men take baths before they could eat breakfast. She decided the cause of the rebellion would not be hampered if the men would submit to the cleansing power of hot water and soap. Nobody complained about bathing except Topple. He finally submitted after seeing the plentiful food awaiting him if he took the plunge. Hilda’s acolytes served a large breakfast of boiled grains, honey and cooked pork roast.

The meeting of the rescuers was held after breakfast. It was decided that Earthkin, Pacer and Brother Patrick would return to the palace to remove the rocks from the shaft. Coaldon would meet with the Robbet's messenger at noon to start making plans for the diversion on the day of the escape. Topple and Hilda would continue to buy horses for the escape to the mountains. Topple explained in great detail how they had purchased five horses. These horses were being kept on a farm under the pretense of being used by merchants going on a trip. Saddles and tack were stored at the farm. After Coaldon had told the story of finding the metal tube in the Room of Magic, he pulled it from his pouch for everyone to examine. The tube had a bright silver color with elf script inscribed into the metal.

Coaldon said, "The elfin writing on the chamber door stated only the Grand Advisor of the Elfdom of Talltree could read the scroll. We will need to protect the tube until Starhood can open it and share the contents with us."

Pacer looked at Topple with a sly grin saying, "Coaldon, will you please remove the Gem of Watching from your pouch and invite our new friend to join us."

Coaldon raised the Gem of Watching into the air so everyone in the room could see the cloud rotating in the center of the stone.

He requested, "Cando, please join us."

A deep rumbling noise rattled through the house. The pleasant scent of roses flowed across the room. Then a yellow cloud of smoke shot from the Gem forming circles of rotating rings. Cando's face appeared from the center of the cloud surrounded by a sparkling halo. His smile literally spread from ear to ear. Cando gave a loud shout as his transparent, ghostly body leaped from the smoke.

He shouted, "Hidy! Hidy! Hidy! I have always wanted to make this type of grand entry. How did I do? Did you like my introduction? Topple, I am so happy to see you. It has been a long time since we have had the opportunity to talk. What have you been doing for the past several centuries? I have missed you! You have not changed one bit. You look just as homely as ever. They rescued me from the basement of the palace. I like my new home in the stone. I have decided to remodel the whole house next week. The present décor is too simple and basic. I want something more formal."

Interrupting Cando, Topple said, "If the present company will excuse us, Cando and I have many things to catch up on."

Coaldon followed, "Well, we have work to do. Each of us has an assignment, so let's get started. We will meet here tonight to make plans for tomorrow."

It was late morning when Coaldon casually walked into the crowd of vagrants milling in the area near the West Gate. The soldiers were late arriving with the daily ration of food, causing the crowd to begin protesting. The guards warned the crowd with uplifted weapons. The threat was enough to force the crowd to return to an uneasy state of submission.

Coaldon walked through the crowd to the area next to the gate. He saw a man wearing a red hat sitting by the wall. Coaldon sat next to the man saying, "I have been sent by Bodso."

The man looked at him with questioning eyes, responding, "What are you talking about?"

Coaldon answered, "Bodso said a messenger would be stationed by the West Gate wearing a red hat. By the way, 'spring is beautiful."

The man replied, "I have noticed that the flowers are red."

Coaldon sat for a long time watching the crowd grow in size and irritation.

He finally said, "We will need your help within the next few weeks. We are asking you to create a disturbance west of the city by making three or four hit and run attacks on military targets. We will only be able to give you a few hours advanced warning. We will pay you well for your services. I would like to arrange a meeting with Robbet."

The man replied, "We have been waiting for you to contact us. You can meet with Robbet in two days in this same spot and time."

The two men walked away from each other in opposite directions. Several men in the crowd were encouraging the vagrants to attack the soldiers. The guards were starting to advance on the crowd with spears and swords when the food wagon arrived. The arrival of food was enough to return order to the volatile situation.

Coaldon thought to himself, "The Empire is ripe for rebellion. We need to put a plan into operation to tap into this growing state of dissatisfaction. We cannot wait for Crossmore to crush the life out of the people before we act."

As Coaldon was getting into the food line, he heard a booming voice. An officer of the Emperor's Court was standing on the food wagon waving his arms.

He yelled, "Emperor Regee has disappeared from the palace. We believe enemies of the Empire have kidnapped him. Crossmore the Great will assume the role of Emperor until Emperor Regee can be rescued. Long live Emperor Crossmore!

This announcement was greeted by both cheers and boos. Several fights erupted between groups of differing opinions. Order was quickly restored by the point of a spear.

Back into the Tunnel

With growing anticipation of the rescue attempt, Coaldon left the cabin to help Hilda and Topple. Meanwhile Pacer, Earthkin and Brother Patrick departed for their expedition under the palace. After a search of the area around the tunnel entrance, the team removed the flat rock, entered the opening and replaced the stone cover. The luminous moss provided adequate light in the tunnel.

After an hour of steady progress through a maze of collapsed ceilings and walls, they entered the old winery. Pacer's investigation revealed the room had not been disturbed since their last visit. The three men crossed the floor, careful not to disturb anything as they passed. They left the winery, locking the door and walked into the basement of the palace.

The group stopped before entering the hallway leading into the old guard quarters. With vivid memories of Brad's warning of ancient traps, they cautiously proceeded into the passage. Pacer, followed by Earthkin and Brother Patrick, slowly progressed down the narrow passageway. Brother Patrick paused half way down the tunnel to study several old paintings on the wall. The vague images of the Cathedral of Toms could be seen outlined by the maze of canyons.

As Brother Patrick continued to walk down the passageway, he stepped on a large flat stone. With a loud crack the stone floor collapsed under the monk's feet. With a shout of surprise, he fell out of sight into a black gaping hole. A dull boom resonated throughout the tunnel as the hole consumed Brother Patrick. Pacer and Earthkin rushed to the hole in the middle of the hallway.

With a strong sense of guilt, Pacer said, "I should have been more careful. I hope Brother Patrick has not been hurt."

Pacer and Earthkin lowered their torches into the black, empty space. Below them they saw Brother Patrick's unconscious, crumpled body lying on the floor of a large room with two doorways on opposite sides. They saw a puddle of blood next to his head.

Earthkin commented, "The latch on the trap door must have been old and rusty, causing it to stick. I have heard about this type of trap. In ancient times beasts or evil spirits were placed in these rooms to kill anybody unfortunate enough to fall. An evil spirit may still haunt the chamber. One of us must climb down into the room to help Brother Patrick. I volunteer. You can stay here and watch the hallway."

Earthkin found a metal hook to attach a rope. He tossed the rope into the hole and used his powerful arms to lower himself into the chamber. Pacer dropped a lit torch and a bag of medical supplies to the dwarf. Earthkin discovered that Brother Patrick had no broken bones, but the monk had received a cut on the back of his head. He concluded Brother Patrick must have hit his head on the edge of the trap door when he fell. Earthkin stopped the bleeding by applying a generous layer of healing ointment. He then wrapped Brother Patrick's head with a bandage.

Opening a small jar of medicinal cream, Earthkin spread it under the monk's nose. The cream had a powerful herbal ingredient that would stimulate the mind and body. With a sudden jerk Brother Patrick opened his eyes. The monk tried to sit up, but Earthkin pushed him back onto the floor. The dwarf realized Brother Patrick needed to rest and regain his orientation before getting to his feet.

As Earthkin attended Brother Patrick, he felt extreme fatigue slowly envelop his body. The suddenness of this weariness seemed unusual. He struggled to keep his eyes open, but soon drifted into an uncomfortable sleep. As he slept, a swell of fear crept into his mind. In a dream he saw a grotesque creature approaching him with its arm extended. It touched Earthkin with the tip of a deformed finger. The dream escalated into waves of dread. Fighting off the fear, the dwarf forced himself to awaken. His body was trembling, his clothes were drenched in sweat and his face was contorted into a grimace.

His burning torch still lay on the floor of the chamber. As Earthkin looked around the room he saw the outline of a figure step from a doorway into the chamber. A short, hairy beast with a round body, black scaly face and large teeth moved toward him. Earthkin tried to stand up but discovered his body was paralyzed by panic. He knew he had to gain control of his emotions or face death. The beast moved toward him in slow, deliberate steps. As it drew closer, the dwarf lost control of his thoughts. The more he struggled against his panic, the more he became confused. His entire body was a massive knot of cramped and distorted muscles. As his heartbeat became uneven, he gasped for breath.

In a weak, desperate voice, Earthkin pleaded, "Help me, or I am lost!"

A sensation of hope filled his mind. He felt a warm breeze sweep through his spirit. The power of the One Presence answered his call for help. A quiet whisper flooded his mind with a gentle caress of peace. At first, Earthkin thought he had died, but realized he was still conscious. The monk lay on the floor with the trap door outlined over his head. The vision of the beast became transparent in his mind. Unexpectedly, he remembered, as a youth, reading an ancient story about this creature. He relaxed his thoughts in an attempt to remember the details of the story. Eight fuzzy letters took shape in a recess of his mind. These letters drifted in random order in an eerie, yet beautiful dance. Suddenly, in quick rotation, the letters formed into a sequence. The letters created the word FEARNUMB.

He thought, "I remembered reading stories about fearnumbs. They are ancient spirits that use fear to entrap their victims. It transmits the sensation of terror into the victim's mind. The spirit projects the image of it being a vile, vicious beast. The victim is lost, if he yields to the crippling grip of dread. Yet, outside of creating the illusion of fear, the spirit is totally harmless."

With this new insight, Earthkin relaxed his muscles and mind. He remembered that there was more to the story. Fearnumbs can be released from the spell of evil by offering it understanding and compassion.

Earthkin stood up and pointed his index finger at the spirit saying, "I release you from your enslavement to evil. You no longer need to roam the world as a captive to the forces of wickedness. Go in peace."

Earthkin watched as the spirit grew into a bright light, then dissolved into a blue mist. After the blue mist disappeared, the dwarf could detect the faint odor of carnations filling the chamber.

Brother Patrick lurched into a sitting position with an expression of fright on his face. He said, "What happened to me? I thought an evil spirit had possessed my body. I was terrified."

Earthkin responded, "It was a fearnumb. The spirit uses fear to control its victim. How do you feel? We need to get out of here and back to work."

Brother Patrick commented, "My head hurts; my body aches; and I feel terrible. Other than that I am doing great."

Earthkin smiled, saying, "Do you think you are capable of climbing a rope?"

With reluctance, Brother Patrick responded, "It will be a challenge, but what choice do I have. There is no use babying myself. I am ready."

The dwarf yelled, "Pacer, are you there?"

With sleepy eyes, Pacer's face appeared in the trap door opening. Pacer said, "I can not believe I fell asleep. I had such a bad dream. I am sorry, but I lost track of you."

Earthkin responded, "We are going to climb out of here. We will need your help when we get to the top."

Brother Patrick was first to climb out. He had to try several times, but he was finally successful. Earthkin easily climbed the rope and crawled through the trap door.

He commented, "Pacer, I have a good story to tell you, but it can wait. Let's get started removing rocks from the shaft. Brother Patrick can rest while we work."

The three men entered the room at the end of the hallway. Brother Patrick sat next to the door to allow the dizziness to clear from his mind. Pacer led the way to the plugged shaft. He pulled rocks from the hole and passed them to Earthkin. It took several hours to remove the stones from the base of the shaft. Earthkin carried the rocks to the side room for storage while Pacer struggled to loosen the stones still tightly wedged inside the shaft.

Finally, Pacer could not reach any higher up into the shaft without stepping inside. He started to step inside the shaft, but paused to consider the consequences if the rocks should accidentally break loose. He stepped back to consider the next step.

He invited his companions to sit down with him to discuss the problem of the plugged shaft. As the group consumed the meal sent by Hilda, they heard a loud rumbling. The floor shook as rocks and dirt collapsed down the shaft, releasing a cloud of debris into the room. The dust was so dense nobody could see anything. Gasping for breath, each person was forced to cover his face with a piece of cloth. The team instantly knew that one problem was solved, but another one had been created. The plug in the shaft had broken loose, but the sound of the collapse would have been heard in the palace. Somebody would be sent to investigate.

Once the dust had settled, Earthkin said, "This dust will cover any trace of our visit. I suggest that we leave the palace immediately. I do not believe we have any time to waste."

Each person took special care to cover his tracks by dragging a piece of tarp behind him. Each warrior carried a piece of furniture from the dungeon and deposited it in the winery. As Brother Patrick locked the winery door from the inside, the sounds of many feet could be heard rushing down the hallway. After the three men entered the tunnel behind the wine vat, the door to the winery was thrust opened with a bang. The scuffle of feet could be heard in the room.

A deep voice said, "I didn't know this room was again being used for storage. I don't see anything out of the ordinary. Let's check the rest of the rooms. I want to find out what caused the noise."

After a short time, Pacer left his hiding place and stood with his ear to the door. After a long wait he heard the soldiers returning from the basement. The sounds of laughter echoed as the soldiers joked with one another.

"I did not know that the basement had traps. I almost fell into that hole. I do not want to go back down there again."

"The noise must have come from rocks falling down the shaft in the old guards quarters."

"I agree with you. The basement is a spooky place to visit. By the way, what do you think happened to Regee?"

"Wherever he has gone, I am glad. He is so worthless."

The voices drifted away as the soldiers marched up the passageway into the palace.

Pacer walked back to his friends in the passageway and shared the content of the soldiers' discussion. After listening to Pacer's story, the group hurried through the network of tunnels to escape the repressive atmosphere of the palace basement. As they left the tunnel, the cool air of night greeted them like an old friend.

Earthkin was the only person who had enjoyed the underground journey. His dwarf instincts found comfort and security in the confined, closed environment of the tunnel. Brother Patrick had forced himself, in spite of the pain, to walk the full distance in the tunnel without help. Yet after emerging from the passageway he lay down on the ground to regain his strength. Pacer and Earthkin put their arms around Brother Patrick's shoulders and carried him to Hilda's house. Pacer hoped Hilda would have the power to assist Brother Patrick in his recovery.

Final Plans

It was late morning on the first day of spring when Coaldon departed for the West City Gate to meet with Robbet. As he approached the gate under the watchful eyes of the guards, the crowd of vagrants was finishing their meal. He felt uncomfortable because more guards were patrolling the area than usual. The seething animosity of the crowd was barely contained by the threat of military intervention. Coaldon had no doubt Crossmore would crush any further rebellion by the beggars.

The man wearing the red hat sat against the city wall. Coaldon reclined next to him. Saying nothing, Coaldon pulled the hood over his head and watched the crowd. A loud shout drew his attention to the west gate. As he watched, he saw Blind Hilda standing over Topple next to the guard station. Her anger was directed at Topple, who had just kicked the cowering dwarf.

The crowd showed distain for Topple's unmerciful treatment of the poor dwarf. The guards supported Hilda with shouts of approval. As the guards focused their attention on Topple's punishment, Pacer slipped past the guards and sauntered into the city. Hilda's wrath ended as quickly as it started, allowing Topple to crawl into the crowd on his hands and knees. The crowd laughed at Topple being humiliated by the old blind woman.

Finally, Coaldon said to the man in the red hat, "Should we meet here?"

The man responded, "Yes, this is a good location. Robbet is sitting next to you."

Coaldon glanced to his left to see Robbet wearing a black robe.

Coaldon asked, "Can you help us?"

Robbet did not respond for several moments. He slowly replied, "What are you willing to pay?"

Coaldon said, "We will pay you two gold pieces now, and five after you have completed your task."

Robbet's body jerked in surprise when he heard the large amount of money he would be paid.

Coaldon continued, "If you fail us, your price will be painful and tragic."

Robbet smiled as he responded, "You have nothing to worry about. We accept your offer. We will be ready tomorrow morning. We have already picked the targets for our attacks."

Coaldon slipped Robbet two pieces of gold, "Here is the down payment for your services. We will ask you to attack within the week. We will only give two hours' notice. We will fire off several skyrockets over the city. The burst of the fireworks will indicate you are to attack within two hours. Your final payment will be found under a pile of rocks next to the entrance to Ringbond Cave on the day of the attack."

Robbet nodded in agreement.

He responded, "It will be my pleasure to do something other than hide in the grass like a baby deer".

With a broad smile on his face, Robbet stood up and disappeared into the crowd. Coaldon walked back to the campsite to rest in preparation for the ordeal looming before him.

In the center of the city, a different scene was being played out. Pacer walked slowly up and down the rows of merchants in the market place. After he had carefully examined most of the products for sale, he decided to sit in an obvious location next to the water fountain. The sun was exceptionally warm for the first day of spring. As he sat with his back against the base of the fountain, the warm sunshine massage his body into a tranquil state of serenity. Even though he had many concerns, it was pleasant to allow the problems of his life to melt away.

His eyelids were closing when someone kicked him on the leg. As he opened his eyes, he saw Magee standing over him.

She yelled at him saying, "Just don't sit there! We have work to do. I am not paying you to sleep. Now grab these bags and carry them to the palace gate for me."

Pacer jumped to his feet in a gesture of submission to Magee's demands. He followed several steps behind her with his head bowed and body hunched over.

After they had entered a side street leading to the palace, Magee turned to him and said, "Well, what do you have to say for yourself?"

Maintaining his submissive pose, Pacer quietly responded, "We are almost ready to rescue you, Noel and Norbert. We have found a way into the palace and located a shaft in the East Tower next to Noel's chamber. We have started to clear out the rocks plugging the shaft. Tomorrow we plan to clean the remaining rocks and locate Noel's room."

Magee realized several people were watching their exchange.

She ruffled in anger, saying, "No more excuses! Why are you doing such a poor job?"

In a whisper, Pacer continued, "We will tap on the wall of the shaft to locate the room. When you hear the tapping, please return the tap with a solid object. If there is an emergency, tap three times. We want to make the rescue within the next few days. We will escape the city on horseback. Do you and Norbert want to go with us?"

Feigning disgust Magee replied, "Of course, now get to work?"

Pacer said, "Once we break through the wall of the room, we can make the final arrangements for the rescue. While in the palace, please do not say anything about the escape without using noise as a cover. Spies might be listening anywhere. We will see you in two days. Tell Noel that her brother is anxious to meet her."

As several people approached them on the street Magee yelled, "Now pick up these bags and follow me."

Pacer delivered the packages to the palace and returned to the marketplace. The sun was setting when he saw a crowd of people walking toward the West Gate. He joined the group, working his way toward the middle of the crowd. He left the city without being challenged. He returned to the campsite as darkness captured the last rays of sunlight. Later, as the group ate their evening meal, everyone shared the events of his day. The level of excitement was growing among the warriors as the actual time of the rescue grew closer.

On the following morning Pacer, Brother Patrick, Coaldon and Earthkin left their campsite before dawn with a full load of equipment and supplies. They arrived at the entrance to the drain tunnel at the first light of day. The journey under the palace and into the basement was uneventful. The group took extra care to examine all aspects of the winery and hallway leading into the basement for signs of any recent activities. Pacer's expert tracking skills revealed that the last people to enter the basement were the soldiers three days ago. Upon arriving in the old guards' quarters, the four men wasted no time in clearing the remaining rocks from the shaft. By mid morning the shaft was ready for someone to begin the ascent to the top of the East Tower.

Earthkin could hardly contain his excitement, "I want to climb the shaft. This is my type of job. I have the strength and skill to accomplish the task. It may take a while for me to complete my task, so you can relax."

Earthkin loaded his chest pack with climbing supplies, food, a long rope and the pulley. Several days before, he had a rope specially made that would be twice as long as the tower was high. The dwarf crawled into the shaft, placed his back to one side and his feet on the other. With a grunt, he started to climb by rotating the pressure between his feet and back to slowly creep up the shaft. Earthkin's strength made it easy for him to make steady progress. About half way, he found the area where the wall had collapsed. Using a torch he discovered that three sides of the wall had buckled under an unknown pressure. The collapse had created a large, open space that halted Earthkin's progress. As he studied the area behind the collapsed wall, he realized it was part of a secret system of tunnels used to move covertly around the palace. By all indications it had not been used for many centuries. Out of curiosity he wanted to follow the passageway, but reluctantly decided it was best not to venture from the agreed upon plan.

In the rubble, he found several old oak beams that had supported the shaft wall. He propped one end of the beam onto the opposite wall of the shaft above the collapsed area and the other end on the floor of the passageway. He decided to climb up the beam, get above the collapsed area and continue his climb. As he crawled onto the old beam, he felt it shift and slide down the wall. He prepared himself for a fall, but the beam lodged in a hole. Earthkin gave a grunt of relief as he looked down into the black pit below him. With a renewed commitment he finished climbing up the beam, carefully positioned his body and again wedged his feet and back on opposite sides of the shaft.

The climb up the remaining section went more quickly. When he reached the top of the shaft, sweat was dripping down his face; his muscles were tired; and his fingertips were raw from pushing against the wall. Beyond that, he was having a wonderful time. Even though he had to fight unending spider webs and many bugs, it felt good to be back in his natural element. The dark, cramped quarters of the shaft offered him a sense of security and belonging.

At the top of the shaft, Earthkin found a metal door. On the underside of the door he found several heavy metal support straps. He noticed there was a gap between the door and the straps. This would provide him a place to attach the pulley. He hoped the metal straps would support his weight.

He grabbed a strap, allowing the full weight of his body to test its strength. To his, relief the bar held. He made every effort to eliminate any unnecessary noise. He placed a piece of leather around the metal strap before attaching the pulley. He threaded an end of the extra long rope through the pulley, attached a weight to the end of the rope and lowered it down the shaft. The rope finally stopped dropping at approximately half its length. He felt a tug on the rope from his companions in the basement. It had been agreed that Pacer would anchor the rope to something solid at the base of the shaft.

Earthkin let his body weight test the strength of the rope. To his satisfaction the rope held.

Using the rope for support, Earthkin lowered himself down the shaft to a point where he thought Noel's chamber might be located. Taking a metal spike from his chest pack, he struck the wall a sharp blow. He waited for several moments, but did not hear a response. He dropped down the shaft in sections and repeated the process of hitting the wall with the spike. At last he heard a tap in response.

Earthkin used a hammer to drive the metal spike into the mortar of the stone wall. He placed a piece of leather over the head of the spike to diminish the sound of each hammer blow. The rough surface to the wall broke away easily. Earthkin used the spike to loosen the rocks. After working for a half hour, he had progressed about four hand lengths into the thick wall. He was concerned about the noise caused by rocks falling down the shaft, but there was nothing else he could do. He paused to rest his arms and to readjust his awkward body position in the shaft. He had placed his legs and back into a wedged position allowing his arms to work freely. Earthkin's physical strength and endurance were starting to fade. As he rested, he heard several male voices talking at the top of the shaft. He guessed the men were soldiers using the tower as a lookout. He listened to the muffled conversation of the guards.

One guard said, "Do you think the tower is haunted? I keep hearing sounds coming from somewhere in the tower."

The other guard laughed saying, "With Crossmore in the city anything is possible. Maybe the ghost is a victim of Crossmore's magic. It might be a spirit looking for someone to haunt. Ah! Ah! Ah! Maybe its Regee."

The first voice responded, "Don't be silly, I am serious. I do hear strange sounds."

The second voice answered, "I was just joking. I agree with you; I think the tower is haunted by something unnatural. I would like to get a transfer to another unit, but we will be stuck up here for another three days. Let's get something to eat and stop talking about ghosts."

With renewed effort, the dwarf hit the spike an extra hard blow with the hammer. The spike met little resistance as it penetrated into the room. He saw a small point of light pass through the hole. He used the spike to quietly open a small hole. He did not want to create any more noise in the room than was necessary. When the hole was about the size of his fist, he paused to allow someone inside to respond.

Finally, he heard a woman say, "Good afternoon, how may I help you?"

Earthkin was so stunned by the welcome, he could only pause in silence.

The voice continued, "I am very busy today, please state your business or be on your way!"

Earthkin had been so focused on achieving his goal of accessing Noel's chamber that he found no humor in the situation. Yet, after several moments he had a shift in attitude.

He responded, "I am sorry for bothering you, I must have the wrong address. I will try next door." After saying this, he plugged the hole with a rock.

To his delight, the rock popped out of the hole as he heard giggling erupt from the room.

A voice inside the room said, "My name is Magee. We will help you open the hole. Please be very quiet. We do not want to arouse the suspicion of the guards in the hallway. We think they are already suspicious."

It took 10 more minutes to finish opening the hole. The dwarf crawled into the chamber and stood in amazement at actually being in Noel's room. For months he had only dreamed of being in the room, now it was a reality. Magee, Norbert and Noel greeted him with enthusiastic handshakes and hugs. After the rush of emotions had passed, Earthkin bowed and whispered, "My name is Earthkin. I am a Warrior from the Dwarf City of Rockham. It is my pleasure to be at your service. I have been accompanied by Prince Coaldon, Pacer, Brother Patrick and Topple. Your grandparents send their love."

Without further discussion, the dwarf rested while Magee and Noel silently cleaned up the debris and placed a large tapestry over the hole into the shaft.

In a quiet voice, Magee stated, "The change of the guard will take place in several minutes. They check inside the chamber to make sure we are present. You can hide in the closet until the room check is completed."

With a nod of understanding, Earthkin found a comfortable position in the small, dark closet. Moments later, he heard a door bang open and heavy foot steps invade the quietness of the chamber.

He then heard a loud male voice dictate, "Emperor Crossmore has requested your presence at a formal dinner in his apartment tomorrow night. You are to come without your guardian."

Noel answered, "I will not attend without my escort."

The voice commanded "You will attend the dinner as ordered. You will be ready at 7:00 tomorrow evening. May the Light of Crossmore shine on you."

Earthkin heard the door slam with an abrupt echo.

He slowly opened the closet door and saw the three captives sitting around a table in shock. Noel's angry face was blanched with helplessness, frustration and desperation. Her eyes were not focused on the room but gazed off into the world of her thoughts. After several moments, her attention returned to room. Never before had she faced such a dangerous and humiliating situation. She knew it was necessary to act in a decisive manner. She had to establish what she would accept and reject. With her eyes staring at the floor she proclaimed, "I will not go to Crossmore's apartment as directed! They will have to take me screaming and kicking! He is not my master! I must do what is right, not what Crossmore tells me to do!"

In an unusually soft voice, the dwarf said, "I compliment you on your resolute attitude. You are responsible to do what is correct, not convenient. I must say this adds a new complication to the rescue. It will be too dangerous for Noel to be alone with Crossmore. I believe we must make the escape tonight."

This declaration caused the three captives to show anxiety at the new turn of events. The thought of escape had always been a dream. Yet, to actually face the escape was disturbing and frightening. In silence, Earthkin allowed time for the three captives to adjust to the rapidly changing circumstances.

In a positive tone, Noel finally declared, "I am ready to go, but I will not leave my friends!"

The dwarf responded, "They are invited to join us."

Decisively, Noel followed, "Then let's get started. How do you plan to get us out of here?"

Earthkin responded, "You can climb down the shaft by rope. We will need to figure out a way to get Magee and Norbert out of the palace. We entered the palace through the old winery in the basement. You could escape the same way."

Magee answered, "Yes, but very few people ever go down there. We would create suspicion if we were seen in the basement."

Earthkin said, "Maybe this evening you can make a trip to the old winery using the excuse of needing to put old furniture into storage. You will not return to the room, but join us on a vacation trip to the mountains. How does this plan sound to you?"

The three captives glanced at each other. Then Noel said, "What choice do we have."

She looked Earthkin in the face, proclaiming, "We accept your gracious invitation."

After a small meal, Earthkin stated, "Noel, I will need to prepare you for the descent down the shaft. Have you ever repelled down a cliff?"

Shaking her head, Noel responded, "No. I have lived a very sheltered life. I have not been allowed to learn anything that might increase the possibility of escaping."

Earthkin followed, "Well, it is time to learn a new skill. You should wear pants and a loose top. You will need to move freely."

He reached into his pack and pulled out a rope. With expert hands he tied together a harness for Noel to wear around her waist and shoulders. After Noel put on the harness over her dress, Earthkin adjusted it for a snug fit. He explained how the rope was to feed through several metal clips and wrapped behind her body. Earthkin threw the rope over a beam in the room, requiring Noel to practice repelling down the wall of the chamber.

When Noel had performed to Earthkin's expectation, he questioned, "Well, are you ready? Is there anything else we need to consider before I return to the basement?"

Magee responded, "We can not begin the escape until the guards do their last room check. That is usually at 9:00 o'clock."

Looking at Noel, Earthkin concluded, "When you enter the shaft you can brace yourself by placing you feet on one side of the shaft and your back on the opposite. This well give you time to attach the rope and prepare for the descent. You can practice by using the walls in the closet. It is best to slowly descend down the shaft. It will take time for you to learn to coordinate releasing the rope and walking down the shaft wall. You can do it, but do not panic if you have a problem. We will be ready to help you. Also, the wall of the shaft has collapsed about half way down. You will only have one wall to place your feet. So be ready for this obstacle. When you are ready to begin your descent, drop a rock down the shaft. Please be careful. We want to present you to your brother in one piece."

With the plans in place, Earthkin quickly climbed down the rope in a hand over hand descent. When he arrived in the basement, he provided the details of his day to his three companions. He said, "There has been a change of plan. It is necessary to complete the rescue tonight. We cannot allow Noel to fall into Crossmore's hands."

The room was quiet for several minutes before Coaldon responded, "I suggest I go to Hilda's home and let her know of the change of plans. We will need to get the horses ready. Hilda can make the arrangements to shoot off the rockets and pay Robbet."

After a short pause he continued, "Brother Patrick, please wait in the winery for Magee and Norbert. You can escort them to Hilda's house. I will ask Topple to keep a magical eye on Crossmore. We do not want him to do something that would endanger our plans. Pacer and Earthkin will wait here for Noel. If there is no further discussion, then let's rescue my sister."

Let it Begin

Coaldon and Brother Patrick left together. Brother Patrick waited in the winery for Magee and Norbert while Coaldon hurried down the tunnel. When the young warrior arrived at Hilda's, he created a commotion with the change in plans. Hilda and the two apprentices spent the rest of the evening gathering horses, arranging tack, organizing supplies and loading the pack horses.

Topple accepted, with obvious delight, his responsibility to monitor Crossmore. He opened his mind to detect if any magical activity was emanating from the West Tower. As he relaxed, he paid little attention to the confusion surrounding him. He wanted to focus his full attention on his opponent. In the beginning, he found only small pulses of magic flowing from the West Tower. At sunset, he felt the touch of magic brush his mind. He sensed the reaching hand. He slowly opened his mind to the intrusion. He found an enticing invitation to open a dialogue with Crossmore. The evil wizard had accidentally contacted Topple. Topple did not reveal his identity, but only remained silent.

Pushing aside this request, he detected Crossmore had inadvertently left himself unguarded. Topple giggled as he found that his adversary had carelessly opened himself to a mind search. With the skill of a great artisan, Topple slowly reached into his opponent's mind. A flood of anger and hatred greeted him like a blast of hot air. At first Topple sagged in bewilderment at the intensity of Crossmore's emotions. With caution, Topple pushed aside Crossmore's passion, allowing his thoughts to be heard.

He heard Crossmore talking to himself, "I know a rebellion has started somewhere. I feel a stir in the flow of magic. I cannot find it! Why? Why? Could it be the power of the Great Warrior? I feel something close to me. No! That is not possible. I have too many spies in the city. Or perhaps, I should look closely in my own backyard."

Topple withdrew his probe from Crossmore's mind. He did not want to be detected. He quickly developed a plan that would draw his opponent's attention away from Neverly. First, he wove a wall of magic to protect himself from Crossmore's power of enchantment. Then, with a gentle probe, he touched his adversary's mind with a distorted series of words. Topple felt the evil wizard's instantaneous attention to the words. Topple gently projected a simple message. The words sent by Topple were, "The warriors are ready ----- leave tomorrow ------four days to Neverly-----attack-----surprise is important------we must be successful."

He felt a pause of relief come from Crossmore. Topple was elated that his adversary was so gullible as to accept such a phony message. This was uncharacteristic of Crossmore's usual efficiency. Topple sensed that his enemy's attention was distracted by thoughts of Noel. Topple laughed, "If this is the case, then Crossmore is creating his own downfall. This might be a weakness we could exploit."

In the wine cellar Brother Patrick rested in a state of meditation. He thought, "Why did I become a monk? I guess I need to discipline myself away from the things of the world." As he drifted into a deeper contemplation, he felt himself blend into a pleasant harmony with the general flow of life. He knew he had to offer the world an image of the Truth. His example needed to reveal the existence of the One Presence. He recognized the importance of offering his life to something greater than himself.

The monk was drawn away from his reflection by noise coming from the winery. He heard a woman say in an uncertain voice, "Is anybody here?"

Brother Patrick came out of his hiding place to extend his greeting, "I am Brother Patrick, a warrior monk from the Monastery of Toms. It is my pleasure to be your escort this evening." He noticed both Magee and Norbert had small traveling bags and wore clothes suited for life in the palace.

The monk continued, "In the future, you will need to wear rugged traveling clothes. Be careful while walking in the tunnel, your shoes do not offer much protection from sharp rocks."

He locked the door to the old winery and led his two guests down the tunnel to freedom. It was a slow trip because Magee and Norbert's feet had become sore from walking on the rough surface of the tunnel floor. The soft life in the palace had not prepared them for the trials of this strange night.

Upon arriving at the house, Brother Patrick introduced them to Hilda. He said to her in private, "It will not be long before we find out if our two guests are tough enough to survive the challenges of the escape."

In the basement of the palace, Pacer and Earthkin waited for Noel.Earthkin said, "Even though we have taken every precaution, something may go wrong. I hope we are ready for the unusual."

During the evening Noel's thoughts ranged from joy about the rescue to panic about the trip down the shaft. Several times she looked down the narrow shaft into the black emptiness. To her, the darkness of the shaft symbolized her mysterious future. After Magee and Norbert departed for the basement, she was forced to act on her own. This was a new experience. In the past, she could always turn to her guardians for support. In truth, she liked the feeling of independence and the power of making her own decisions.

The guards checked on her several times during the evening. She was haunted by the fear they suspected something. She did not want anything to go wrong. She had dreamed of this moment all her life. While waiting for her escape to begin, anxiety nearly overwhelmed her. Her distain for Crossmore provided the motivation to continue. This was not just an escape attempt, but also a personal challenge. The journey down the shaft had become the door way into a new life. She had to prove something to herself.

After the final room-check by the guards, Noel changed her clothes, crawled into the climbing harness and sent a rock clattering down the shaft. With shaking hands and paralyzing fear, she grabbed the rope hanging in the shaft and crawled through the wall feet first. This allowed her to place her feet on the opposite side of the shaft. With her feet firmly planted on the wall, she slid her back onto the opposing wall of the shaft. Firmly holding the rope in her right hand, she slipped the rope into the two locking rings and pulled the rope around her waist with her left hand. The clips would allow the passage of the rope for normal descent, but lock in case of a free fall. With the right hand, she gripped the line over her head. With her body trembling with anxiety, she took an uncertain breath and lowered her weight on the rope. This was one of the most difficult things she had ever done. She was hanging onto a rope in a pitch black shaft. She could only depend on herself and the rope to reach the bottom.

With trembling arms, she pulled up on the rope over her head with her right hand, allowing the resistance clip to release its hold. This movement permitted a short section of rope to pass through the grip of her left hand. This allowed her to drop a short distance down the shaft. She was slow in moving her feet down the wall causing her to hang in a precarious head back position. She quickly lowered her feet to compensate for the awkward position. It was not long before she mastered the fundamental of repelling down the wall. Her confidence increased as she moved down the cavity. She began to assume an overly confident attitude at her accomplishment. With her increased coordination and self assurance, she increased the speed of her descent.

Feeling good about her achievement, she momentarily forgot Earthkin's warning about the collapsed tunnel wall. The consequence of this oversight was soon made apparent. As she repelled downward, her feet shoot into the open space of the collapsed wall. This motion caused her feet to shoot upward and her weight to shift backward. This action forced her to fall into a head down position. Her weight shifted against the shoulder straps of her handmade harness. In panic, she released her grip on the rope. She gave a yelp of fear.

Noel's body swung wildly in the open space. Her head violently slammed into an obstacle in the shaft. For several moments she remembered nothing. Then, in dazed state, she realized she was hanging head down in darkness. The shoulder strap of the harness was the only thing keeping her from falling head first into the cavity. Fright gripped her. She thrashed wildly in an effort to find something to hold onto. To her relief, she grabbed a wooden beam next to her head. This offered her a sense of security, but did not solve her problem. She was still hanging upside down. Fear became the master of the moment. The use of reason and self-control played second hand to terror.

Through the haze of her mind, she heard a muffled voice. Abruptly, she realized someone was calling to her. Refocusing her attention, she listened.

In the distance she heard Earthkin ask, "Are you all right?"

In a weak voice she answered, "I'm upside down and don't know what to do. I am scared."

In a gentle voice, Earthkin directed, "You will need to rotate yourself to an upright position. Reach up, grab the rope and pull yourself up. Give it a try."

As her thoughts cleared, she did as Earthkin had advised. She grab the rope and pulled up, but she was not able lift herself into the upright position. She tried several more times with the same results. She did not have enough strength in her arms and shoulders. Doubt dominated her thinking.

Then she demanded of herself, "I must do something. What can I do? Maybe, I can use the beam. The timber reaches across the shaft at an upward angle. If I grab the beam and pull myself up the plank, I might be able to put myself into the upright position."

Hugging the timber with both arms, she slowly climbed up. With each pull of her arms, Noel moved up the beam. After several minutes, she realized her body was level. She grabbed the rope with her right hand. Pushing off the timber with her left hand, she rotated into an upright position.

With a squeak of joy, she whispered, "I did it! I did it!"

With a throbbing head and trembling muscles, she slowly repelled to the bottom of the shaft. When Noel crawled out of the shaft, it was apparent she had had a difficult trip to freedom. Her clothes were ripped and she had a large bump on the side of her head.

Pacer bowed to Noel saying, "I am Pacer, a good friend of your grandfather. It is my pleasure to welcome you to your new life. It looks like you had a rough trip down the shaft. Please sit on the floor so I can attend to your wounds."

Noel smiled in greeting as she allowed her shaking legs and body to rest. Without talking, Pacer quickly applied bandages to Noel's wounds. Finished, he said, "You have a spectacular black eye, fat lip and a large bruise on your face. I would not call them beauty marks. Are you ready to go?"

Noel nodded, "Thank you for helping me. I have waited a long time for this moment. I will follow you."

It was midnight when Pacer, Earthkin and Noel walked into Hilda's home. Magee, sitting by the fireplace, gasped in horror when she saw Noel's wounds. Noel ignored Magee's mothering. She proudly treated the wounds like a badge of courage. Noel, Magee and Norbert's reunion was caught in the midst of chaos.

People rushed around the room to complete the last minute preparations for the departure. In this confusion it did not take long for Noel, Magee and Norbert to feel an added sense of insecurity. The excitement of the escape was replaced by the reality of their new situation. The narrow confines of Noel's past life had just exploded like an out-of-control horse. The new surroundings and the unfamiliar sense of freedom, only added to her feeling of anxiety. She felt like dancing and laughing, yet at the same time she wanted to cry. Rather than doing either, she just sat in front of the fireplace and closed her eyes.

When she opened them, Noel found herself gazing at herself in the face of the young man standing before her. She knew she was looking at her twin brother. Without pausing, she leaped to her feet and threw herself into his arms. At that moment all her frustrations and confusion melted away. The security of Coaldon's presence was enough to provide her the courage and strength to do what needed to be done. Their childhood bond was rekindled into a powerful union of hope and support.

Escape from Neverly

Coaldon said in an excited voice, "It is time to go. We have many miles to travel before sunrise. Your horses are in the barn. It would be nice to stay, but Crossmore will be in a foul mood in the morning."

Each person was provided with a horse to assist in their escape. Everybody mounted their horses except Topple. Coaldon looked at him asking, "Are you going with us?"

Topple smiled as he responded, "I have some business to attend to before I join you. I need to borrow the Gem of Watching for a short time. Hilda, Cando and I need to have a short visit with Crossmore before we leave Neverly. We will join you once we have completed our task."

Coaldon nodded as he handed Topple the Gem of Watching.

Coaldon then said, "Hilda, thank you for your hospitality. You are a part of our team. Your help has been important to our success. Please remember to fire off the skyrockets and to pay Robbet for his services. Pacer, please lead the way to our new destiny? Until we meet again."

Pacer selected a route to the east that would draw the least attention and leave a poor trail to follow. He realized they needed to set a modest pace to allow Magee and Norbert to adjust to the physical demands of riding horses. After several hours the group heard a distant boom. Turning, they saw several beautiful fireworks blossom in the distant sky. To their surprise, a third rocket burst in the sky forming the shape of a dragon. The red dragon flew over Neverly several times before it burst into a cloud of red and green balls of fire.

Pacer said, "The dragon must be Topple's handy work. I knew he would add something to frustrate Crossmore."

Coaldon knew Crossmore was angry when his sword jumped in its scabbard. He realized gaining distance from Neverly was their best defense.

When the morning light greeted the travelers, Pacer decided they should take a short break and eat a meal of hard bread and honey. Pacer invited Earthkin, Brother Patrick and Coaldon to join him for a conference. As the men huddled together, Noel joined the group.

She looked directly into the eyes of each man, "I may be a woman, but I do expect to be involved in decision making." The men laughed at Noel's boldness and happily invited her to join them as they discussed their next move.

Brother Patrick began the discussion by saying, "By now Crossmore should have discovered that Noel has escaped. He is probably having a temper tantrum. I know Topple will compound Crossmore's problems somehow. I believe Crossmore will send out scouts in all directions to locate his lost prize. I assume he will focus most of his attention west and south of Neverly. But once he has had time to consider all possibilities, he will look in our direction. Our journey to the mountains will take several days. We will face greater danger every hour. I suggest we ride all day to increase our distance from Neverly."

Pacer responded, "I agree with you. We might consider going north, traveling through the rugged hill country. It will be longer, but less obvious."

After seriously considering the suggestion, Earthkin looked at the group saying, "I do not believe Magee and Norbert can handle the hardships of the hill country. We need to go directly to the mountains as fast as we can travel. Once we are in the mountains we will have the advantage."

Coaldon looked at Noel, saying, "Crossmore will destroy anybody or anything to capture you. After listening to this conversation, I say we go directly to the mountains. I see no advantage to taking a side trip. Crossmore will use all the power in the Empire to catch us."

All members nodded in agreement.

Coaldon continued, "Pacer, do you know of a place we can safely spend the night?"

"Yes, I do." commented Pacer, "We need to start now if we plan to be there before dark. I suggest we place several blankets on Magee and Norbert's saddles to help prevent saddle sores. We can not afford to be slowed down by anything."

With their horses moving at a steady pace, the group looked at the hazy outline of the Sadden Mountains in the distance.

As the group traveled across the wide expanse of grass and woodlands, the scene in Neverly was a picture of turmoil. The fireworks had initiated widespread assault outside the city. The well coordinated early morning attacks had been directed at army outposts. The Imperial soldiers were so poorly prepared for an attack, they were literally defenseless. The rebels did not want to kill, but only to create disorder.

Many soldiers were hurt, but few received serious wounds. Several barracks and military camps were burned to the ground; weapons had been taken; and the pride of the burly, arrogant soldiers had been crushed. It became a silent joke among local residents that the soldiers had received most wounds on their backsides because they ran away from the fighting.

Not until midmorning was order restored to Neverly. Crossmore's elite Palace Guards rallied the troops to seek out and destroy the attackers. The rebels had disappeared into the west with the soldiers in hot pursuit. The city gates that had been closed earlier in the day were reopened. The city dwellers started to venture into the streets to gather information about the early morning's events. As life returned to normal the final blow hit. Word leaked out that Noel, Magee and Norbert were missing. The city gates were quickly closed, people were herded back into their homes and soldiers began a house by house search of the city. By early afternoon the shaft in the East Tower had been discovered by guards searching the palace. It was not until later afternoon that the tunnel entrance into the old winery was found.

Crossmore's frustration increased as he received each additional piece of information about the escape. By early evening, he had gained a good picture of the events of the past 24 hours. He decided to make a personal tour of the escape route to help him better understand his opponents. He looked down the entrance to the shaft from Noel's room, walked through the basement, crawled through the hole in the winery wall and followed the tunnel to its end. Crossmore could not find Goo and Gor, anywhere in the tunnel. At one point in the passageway he found two dried globs of slime on the floor of the tunnel. This was all that was left of his dear friends. These two companions had been like children to him. He was amazed that the rescuers had destroyed the monsters. He assumed it had been the work of the great warrior. The emotional impact of Goo's and Gor's deaths was quickly transferred into a renewed resolution to avenge their destruction.

Crossmore decided he needed time to think. With slow deliberate steps, he climbed the long staircase to the safety of the West Tower. Upon entering the tower, he sat in his favorite chair, allowing the events of the day to filter through his mind. He needed time to think. He closed his eyes, relaxing into a quiet state of contemplation. The quiet void of his mind allowed ideas to surface in a free and random order. It was not long before memories emerged from the deep recesses of his mind. He remembered the discovery of a young half elf and old couple in Lost Valley, the escape of Topple, the destruction of Gurlog, the unusual gathering of people at the Monastery of Toms, his battles with the unknown warrior, the mental message he received about a rebellion and the well planned rescue of Noel.

Crossmore's eyes popped open as the meaning of the sequence of events became clear. His preoccupation with being in control had caused him to lose track of what was obvious. Even though he had received news from all regions, he had not seen the big picture. Now he did. Brad was still alive; the Prince freely roamed the Empire; his opponents had the skills to rescue Noel; and the rescue party was within one day's travel from Neverly.

As Crossmore's attention was drawn back to his present situation, he realized the tower was flooded by moonlight. The large, orange moon was just rising from its cradle in the eastern sky. Crossmore finally understood why the activities of the day were focused west and south of the city. Noel's escape team was heading east toward the Sadden Mountains.

He thought to himself, "My, this might get interesting very soon. It is premature for my little secret to be discovered. I must immediately send a cavalry unit to capture the group before they reach the mountains." As Crossmore prepared to stand up, he detected a stirring of magic around him. He quickly prepared himself to combat whatever magic was being directed at him.

While Crossmore had spent the evening evaluating his present circumstances, elsewhere Topple had been making plans to add an interesting twist to his life. Earlier that evening, Hilda and Topple, plus the transparent presence of Cando, had gathered around a table in Hilda's home.

Topple said, "My nap today was wonderful. I have not slept so well in months. The escape went off as planned. I am most pleased. Now we need to discuss the reason for this meeting. It will not be long before Crossmore puts all the facts together and figures out what has been happening. He will even determine the escape party is heading east. We need to detain him for several days."

Hilda responded, "Crossmore will not be easily delayed. What do you have in mind?"

Topple answered, "Have you ever heard of Triangulation Magic?"

Hilda injected, "No. Is it a secret wizard thing?"

In a state of enthusiasm Cando followed, "I have always wanted to try a triangulation spell, but the magic was always too complicated and dangerous."

Hilda showed frustration as she asked, "Topple, are you going to wait all day before you tell me about this magic?"

Topple sat back in his chair, looking at Hilda with teasing eyes, "Why would I want to tell a mere shape shifter about top secret wizard magic stuff? It might confuse your simple mind."

Without warning Topple found himself lying on the floor with his chair sitting on top of him. With an injured look on his face, Topple removed the chair, stood up and sat down.

"How's that again?" Hilda asked sweetly.

Topple looked at her saying, "My, Hilda, you have such a fragile temperament. I did not realize you are like a delicate pansy on a hot summer day. You just melt away when put under a little stress."

Hilda's face wrinkled as she prepared to release her next assault. As she prepared to speak, her mouth froze wide open. Her tongue suddenly stuck out of her mouth and began to flop up and down. Hilda jumped to her feet waving her arms in distress while yelling incoherent sounds. With one hand she grabbed her wagging tongue and with the other she grasped her frozen jaw. Hilda's bulging eyes searched the room looking for help, when they finally rested on Topple's smiling face. She abruptly understood the source of her problem. As she relaxed her tension, the paralysis of her mouth slowly disappeared and her wagging tongue stopped flapping. As she realized the humor of her panicked reaction, her anger was transformed into robust laughter.

She looked at Topple saying, "That is one of the best tricks I have ever seen. My response was absolutely perfect. You can be such a wonderful brother."

Topple beamed in triumph. Yet, he didn't see the purple wart appear on the end of his nose.

Cando found great humor at the perpetual sibling wars between Hilda and Topple. Yet, he also believed the group had something to accomplish, so he said, "We need to hear about Topple's plan for triangulation."

Topple looked at Hilda, as he spoke, "Triangulation is a powerful spell requiring three wizards to perform. In our case, I believe one superior shape changer and two brilliant wizards can pull it off. I will explain what each of us needs to do for the magic work. This triangulation spell will cause the affected person to go into a state of hibernation for several days. Crossmore will not be hurt, though he is apt to be a little angry when he comes out of hibernation. By the way, if the spell fails to work, we will inadvertently reveal our location. A horde of Crossmore's troopers will descend on us like a cloud of locust. Is everybody in?"

Cando and Hilda nodded in approval.

Topple carefully explained what each person needed to say and do for the spell to be successful. The three participants spent an hour practicing their individual role in creating the spell. It was dark when they were finally ready. While standing, each person took their position. They formed the shape of a triangle, standing one stride from each other. Each person raised their arms and touched the fingers of the other. In sequence, going around the triangle, each participant intoned a series of elfin words. This rotation of words completed a series of sentences. Even though each individual had limited power, the effect of triangulating magic allowed the spell to develop into a significant force. They could feel the surge of their combined energy vibrate in the room. With the wave of his hand, Topple sent the pulsing force directly at Crossmore. The old wizard was delighted when he felt Crossmore resisting the spell.

The old wizard grinned, "This is going to be fun. A scrapping battle with Crossmore will make my day."

Once Crossmore realized he was being attacked by magic, he directed a lethal surge of energy at his attackers. The channel of magic created by the triangulation spell offered the conduit to direct his assault. As the three braced themselves for the counterattack, Crossmore's magic hit them like a tidal wave. The triangle effect of the spell dispersed his attack among the three persons. This caused the power to be diluted into tolerable doses. As the pressure of Crossmore's counterattack waned, Topple injected the spell directly into his mind. Crossmore forcefully resisted the assault, causing the two wizards to grapple for control.

Crossmore's arrogance quickly dissolved as he lost control. Sweat ran down Topple's face and his body trembled as he worked to maintain his edge. After a long grueling struggle, Crossmore could no longer resist the command of the triangulation spell. As he drifted under the influence of the spell, Topple slowly relaxed his control. When Crossmore finally succumbed to his fate, Hilda, Topple and Cando smiled in satisfaction at a job well done. The apprentices clapped in glee at the success of the magic. Crossmore would be out of circulation for several days, allowing the escape party to reach the mountains before he could interfere.

Hilda knew Crossmore would take action against her. Her direct attack on him would not go unanswered.

Taking this into account, Hilda said, "It will no longer be safe for me to live in Neverly; may I join you on your holiday trip to the mountains?"

With a broad smile on his face, Topple nodded in agreement. After Cando was safely tucked away in the Gem of Watching, the two walked out the door arm in arm. Topple and Hilda found great satisfaction in facing the future together. The two apprentices happily joined Hilda and Topple as they rode their horses eastward under moonlit skies. The brother/sister team would add new pages to the history of the Empire.

BADDA

As the first light of day filtered through the tower windows, Crossmore remained slumped in his chair. Even thought his advisers and army generals desperately needed his command, they dare not enter the tower out of the fear of death. Crossmore never allowed his subordinates to enter the tower or make major decisions. The business of the Empire would need to wait until he returned to the throne room.

With the turmoil of the past day dominating the attention of the citizens, little thought was paid to the absence of Badda. The foul slave of Crossmore served his master as an executioner and fear monger. He could only act under the direction of his master. His visits to the city created terror in the minds of all people. The sight of Badda on his nightly missions left a feeling of corruption in the hearts of the observers.

Today, something was different. Crossmore rested in a magical slumber, while Badda remained inactive. Badda stared at Crossmore, waiting for a command to cause him to act. Crossmore's silence allowed space for a tiny swirl of thoughts to grow in Badda's mind.

The light of the new day was accompanied by the muffled sound of words within his head. The words cascading through his thoughts remained only symbols without comprehension. Badda's empty consciousness found no way to transform words into a framework of knowledge. Words filtered through Badda's mind, echoing like shouts in the dim recesses of a cavern. As the hours of the day extended into evening, the resonating pulse of words was transformed into voices. Then, like a sudden shout, the sound of a woman's voice filled his mind. The face of the woman flashed into a vivid picture. He had known this person.

He heard a child's voice saying, "Mom, may I go outside and play?"

The word mom reverberated while the face of the woman grew in familiarity. He developed a connection between the word mom and the face. He understood that the face was mom. Yet, he could not bridge the gap between the woman and himself.

He asked himself, “What is a mom?”

A puzzled expression grew on Badda’s face, as he looked around the room. He sensed he was something other than nothing. A tiny corner in the vast emptiness of his mind was now occupied by understanding. Like a grain of sand on a vast beach, a single symbol had gained power. A crack had been made in the wall of his memory. The barrier created by Crossmore had been breached, allowing past memories to once again be experienced.

A glimmer of light radiated out of the grotto of his mind. With an infantile power of choice, he followed the beam to its origins. Words, faces and events blossomed into his thoughts like a light passing through a prism. Each filament of light was a memory striving to find meaning in the disorder of a nebulous mass.

A turbulence of frustration rolled though him like an earthquake. The tremor radiated from his struggle to create order out of chaos. The essence of his creation was calling him to wholeness.

This confusion was followed by the eruption of words.

“Bobby go wash up, it is time for dinner.”

“Grandma is coming for your birthday party.”

“Bobby, do you want to go fishing?”

“Let’s go play in the forest.”

“Why do you keep visiting with Wizard Crossmore?”

“Magic is too dangerous. Why do you want to be a wizard?”

“Crossmore taught me some magic today.”

“I talked to Topple this morning? He told me I was in great danger.”

“Crossmore told me he wants to talk to me tonight in the tower.”

“Topple told me not to visit Crossmore.”

“I can think for myself!”

The flow of memories had started as a small trickle of names, places, people and events. At first, his struggling mind was unable to develop associations between the bits and pieces as they seeped through the crack in his memory. As the night progressed, the flow of information increased. It was like opening the floodgates of a dam.

His stunted freewill could not restrain the flow of reawakened memories. Badda was like a ship without a rudder. He grew increasingly disoriented as his thoughts interacted freely. His mind raced to keep up with the expanding flow of information. Several times he tried to tame his mind, but he only collapsed in distress. His willpower was like a shriveled muscle, weak from a lack of exercise.

The night passed with Badda facing ever increasing contact from his past. The light of a new day found him lying on the tower floor in a state of exhaustion. He was grinding his teeth. His muscles flexed in uncontrollable spasms. With an abrupt jerk, Badda opened his eyes. His glance shifted back and forth like that of a crazed animal. As he crawled to his knees, he looked around the room like a person facing strange surroundings. In a state of bewilderment, he tried to create order out of chaos. His struggle was too much for him to handle. With a shudder, he fell to the floor unconscious.

The shadows of evening were cast in long lines across the floor of the West Tower when he awoke to the sound of a bluebird singing. The stale odor of dried sweat filled his senses as he opened his eyes. He slowly sat up, fighting past the pain in his body. As he tried to stand up, every fiber of his being was in rebellion. With a collapse of will, he sat on the floor with a hard bounce.

He studied the room in an inquisitive manner. It was the West Tower. He remembered visiting it as a youth. The room was mostly empty except for several tables, a large book and a man sitting in a chair. The man looked like Crossmore. The presence of the man in the chair awoke a series of memories and feelings. He remembered, as a youth, the excitement of visiting the tower as Crossmore's honored guest. Yet, the evening turned into a nightmare of agony and emptiness. The sweet smile of Crossmore had been transformed into an evil laugh. Badda remembered being drugged with poisoned drink and losing his ability to move and think. Then darkness surrounded him until the present moment.

As his thoughts cleared, Badda vaguely remembered the dramatic events of the past day. He could still feel the surging of memories pounding against the barrier of his mind. He remembered the fog of the unknown melting away as each new piece of his past was fitted into the vast puzzle of his life. He was overwhelmed and confused by his release from captivity. The freedom of choice had returned to him, yet he questioned what this would mean. Would freedom create joy or the burden of agonizing suffering?

He remembered his family, friends and events of his earlier life. Looking into the mirror, he saw his dirty, aging, neglected body. He then recalled the lean, beautiful body of his youth. He asked himself, "What has happened to me? What has Crossmore done to me?"

To his discomfort, the name Badda began to dominate his thoughts. The name was clouded with unpleasant images and feelings. He saw many eyes looking at him in terror. People turned away from him in disgust and fear. The odor of death filled his nostrils with the foul deeds of his own hands.

He shouted, "I am not Badda! I am no longer trapped in nothingness. I am free."

He then heard his mother's voice whisper, "You are Bobby. You are my special child."

Bobby exclaimed, "Yes I am! I remember! I am Bobby!"

A long silence followed this declaration. He forced himself to focus away from the awaking and to the present moment.

He finally stated, "I am hungry, lonely, dirty, sore and miserable."

As Bobby sat on the floor, he struggled to stand up and move. He soon realized he had lost part of his will to act. With massive effort he forced himself to stand up and begin walking. He staggered and stumbled. He felt like a baby trying to walk for the first time.

He stated, "I must escape from the influence of Crossmore. If I do not leave the tower, I will once again return to his control. I must escape this horrible place."

He ate a meal of dried food he found on the floor. He approached the door with caution, opened it and carefully walked down the stairs. At the bottom of the stairs he met a guard who stepped back from him in fear. This negative reaction continued when he entered the city. Bobby soon discovered he was a despised person. He carried the symbol of death and ugliness. A deep sadness overwhelmed him. His gentle nature was devastated. The positive values he had learned as a youth had been violated by Crossmore. He was a person marked with the curse of evil.

As he sobbed, he said, "What am I to do? Where can I go?"

The cold night air forced Bobby to seek shelter. After searching the alley in the north end of the city, he found a protected spot under a staircase. From his hiding place he watched people going home. In bitterness, he realized he had no home. He welcomed the cover of darkness because it protected him from people staring at him. Bobby's tear stained face drooped in sadness as he hid himself under a pile of debris.

The moon was shining over the city when Bobby awoke to the sound of footsteps approaching his hiding place. He was not concerned because everyone who saw him turned away in fear. Besides he was buried deep in the mound of garbage. The events of the past day kept racing through his mind with ever increasing frequency. He visualized each event with clarity. Like the roar of raging water, the cascade of ideas pressed him to the point of collapse. When he heard the footsteps stop in front of his hiding place, his mental anguish quickly diminished into the background. He could hear deep breathing and a hand probing into the litter. Bobby pulled himself deeper into his hiding place to escape from the unknown visitor.

Then a voice said, "Badda, you can not escape from me. I know you are in there. Make it easy on yourself and come out. You must face me."

Bobby froze. He could not move, think, talk or breathe. The stress of facing a new challenge caused him to drift into unconsciousness. He was only vaguely aware when rough hands grabbed him. The next thing he remembered was lying on a stone floor looking up at the ceiling. The dim light of a candle flickered from a table in the corner of a room. As he looked around, he saw the outline of a man with his back to him.

Without turning the man said, "So, Badda, you thought you could escape from me. After all these years, you should know you can't."

Bobby responded in anger, "My name is Bobby! Go away and leave me alone. You have destroyed my life."

The man slowly turned to face Bobby with his face hidden under his hood.

In a sweet voice the man responded, "So, Bobby has been reborn. What should we do about that?"

Bobby remembered hearing the man's voice in his past life.

As he rose to his knees, Bobby stated, "I have heard your voice before. You are not Crossmore. Who are you?"

A soft laughter flowed from the man. He responded, "So you think you have heard my voice somewhere else? Let me give you a hint. 'You are in great danger. Do not go.'"

Bobby's eyes searched the dark outline of the individual standing over him for a clue to his identity. Then a rush of tears poured down Bobby's face. He dropped his head to the floor in a respectful bow.

Bobby then said, "Thank you for coming to me. I was so hard headed as a youth. You told me the truth. I was too arrogant to believe you. I have done so much evil because I did not listen. What can I do to repay you?"

The man picked Bobby up from the floor.

He said, "You do not need to be punished for your mistakes. You have already paid the price. We must leave Neverly quickly. Follow me. You can repay me by your loyalty to people of the Empire."

Night Visitor

Magee and Norbert showed the stress of riding all day. Their throbbing legs, aching backs and saddle sores were causing a crescendo of complaints. Pacer had been concerned about the soft palace residents making the trip in the first place. Now, the group must deal with the possibility of traveling at a slower pace. With Crossmore's large army in pursuit, time was an important factor.

He would not allow anybody's soreness to slow down the progress of the group. He thought to himself, "Character is built by overcoming adversity. Now is not the time to threaten success by yielding to pain." He looked at Magee and Norbert with compassion, but also with the stern eyes of a leader facing possible failure and death.

By nightfall the group was ready for a rest. Fatigue and pain, in different degrees, distorted the faces of each traveler. The fading light of day revealed miles of flat terrain. The outline of the Sadden Mountains was the only contrast to be found in the broad expanse of the grassland and scrub trees. With the instincts of a seasoned outdoorsman, Pacer guided the group into the mouth of a ravine hidden in a grove of trees. Everybody in the group was surprised when the ravine appeared through the cover of trees. The gully was out of place in the flat, formless land. As the travelers entered the deep cut, they had the impression it had been gouged by an angry surge of power. The wedge in the earth disappeared into the horizon toward the Sadden Mountains. Towering walls gave the members of the group an uneasy feeling of being captured in a prison.

Pacer said, "We have arrived at our destination. We will set up our camp in the opening of the ravine. I do not plan to travel into the ravine because it could be a dangerous trap."

Magee and Norbert had to be helped from their horses with gentle hands. Both of them could not walk for several moments. They stood with discomfort etched onto their faces. Their legs were numb and raw from being wrapped around the fat horses in an unnatural position. As Magee finally started walking, she softly laughed at herself. She had always been a woman who took pride in behaving in a stately manner. Magee found great humor in contrasting her pathetic physical condition to the dignity she had always maintained in the palace. She also found delight at being thrust into an exciting adventure after many years of a passive, sedentary existence.

The camp was set up in a rocky alcove on the south wall of the ravine. Magee cringed at the cold dinner of hard bread and dried meat, eaten without the blessing of a fire. Pacer did not want any unwanted visitors to find their campsite. After guard duty was assigned for the night, each person quickly fell asleep. Coaldon was on duty when the light of the rising moon revealed the haunting landscape of the gorge. As the night progressed, the shadows and shapes cast in the gully by the moonlight created a mood of foreboding. His mind drifted into thoughts about the events of the past few weeks. Coaldon was especially delighted by the joy he shared with Noel. It was as if they had been friends all their lives.

As he glanced down the ravine, he saw movement among a pile of large rocks. At first, he let the motion pass as a figment of his imagination. He became alarmed when he saw more movement in the shadows near the camp. Coaldon barked like a blue fox to alert his companions. Pacer, Brother Patrick and Earthkin responded by slipping out of their sleeping blankets and drawing their swords. Coaldon explained to them he had seen movement in the rocks. Armed with this information the three warriors crept away from camp on their hands and knees. A half hour passed without anything unusual happening. Coaldon began to assume it was only his imagination that had triggered the alarm.

A grip of terror suddenly ripped through him as a large face appeared directly in front of him. The cold, gray eyes of his visitor burned with intensity and determination. With a quick move to his right, Coaldon tried to gain room to pull his knife. Before he could move his hand toward the knife, the powerful body of the visitor smothered him. Coaldon was quickly controlled by the raw physical strength and quickness of the intruder. He tried to struggle, but his captor's advanced fighting skills overwhelmed him. Out of desperation, he gave the warning call of a screech owl. A rough hand closed around Coaldon's mouth. Then silence covered the campsite like the presence of death. Magee, Norbert and Noel slept through the attack without any indication there was a problem.

Coaldon's captor quietly said, "Do not move or make a noise. You do not smell like the vile creatures invading my realm. You would be dead if I thought you were evil. What are you doing here?"

Before the intruder could say more, six powerful hands restrained him. The prowler gave an animal like scream of defiance as he was quickly bound by ropes and gagged. The scream awoke the three sleeping travelers.

The captive had the physical appearance of a dwarf with a short stocky body, powerful muscles, a round face, an unusually big nose and a large mouth with outsized teeth. The captive's eyes frantically darted back and forth between the seven faces looking at him. His panic increased as he struggled to gain freedom. His instinct to escape raged through his body as he twisted to break away from his bonds.

After the stranger finally yielded to his captivity, he carefully observed his captors. His body relaxed when his eyes finally rested on Earthkin's face. With excitement, he tried to speak but only grunts could be heard through the gag. Earthkin reached down removing the cloth from his mouth. The captive looked at Earthkin, saying several words in the guttural dwarf language.

Earthkin smiled, saying in the common language, "Yes, I understand your language. I am Earthkin, a dwarf warrior of the Clan Long Beard from great halls of Rockham. We are on a mission to save the Empire."

The captive responded, "I am Ripsnout of the Clan Hardstone. Our clan retreated to the deep caves in the northern Sadden Mountains during the First

Quarter Age. We have remained isolated out of the fear of being conquered. It is my understanding from ancient history that the clans Hardstone and Long Beard are close relatives. You might be my cousin."

Earthkin could not speak for several moments as tears ran down his face. He composed himself before he said, "The ancient legend tells the sad story of your clan being destroyed in the Battle of East Nome. I pray we can once again be family."

A long silence ended when Coaldon said, "I suggest we untie our new friend and greet him with the respect due a member of Earthkin's family."

At first Ripsnout responded to the hospitality of his guests with the restraint of a shy forest animal. All his life he had been taught not to trust anybody from the outside world. He debated if he should stay or run away. He knew his clan was being destroyed by the encroachment of the invaders. Many of his clan members had already died defending their homes from the beasts invading the subterranean caves. As he watched his hosts talk to each other, he detected honesty and caring. He found himself bonding in friendship with Earthkin. It was like finding an old friend after many years of separation.

He thought to himself, "I was sent by the elders to seek help from the outside world. I have wandered many days searching for an answer to the survival of my clan. Maybe I have been guided to these people. Maybe, I should trust them."

Coaldon said, going against his better judgment, "Sometimes we need to take a risk. Let's build a fire. I am cold."

Saying very little, the group gathered around the fire. With heat from the flames reaching into their tired bodies, everybody except Ripsnout and Earthkin drifted into sleep.

Ripsnout looked at Earthkin with a curious gaze. He said, "My clan needs help to escape from the wickedness that has invaded our land."

Staring into the flames, Ripsnout continued, "Do you think you could help my clan? We are slowly being destroyed by the war."

Earthkin responded, "I do not know what to say. We can talk to the rest of the group at day light."

Morning was greeted with groans from Magee and Norbert as they slowly started to move. The rest of the group was up and ready to begin a new day. Pacer pulled Magee and Norbert to a standing position with a gentle tug. Magee laughed softly as she walked around the campsite to loosen her sore muscles. Norbert did not find his aching body worthy of mirth.

When everybody was ready to continue the journey, Coaldon asked, "Do we need to discuss anything before we depart?"

Earthkin replied, "Our new friend has a question for us."

Shyly, Ripsnout looked around the group. He finally said, "I have decided to trust you. You are the first people any clan member has communicated with for many centuries. I was sent by my elders to seek help to fight the army invading our home. Would you consider helping us?"

Like all dwarves, Ripsnout did not use many words to communicate his ideas. The practical nature of dwarves did not allow for wasting time on excessive words. An old dwarf adage states, "Say it and be done."

Coaldon and Pacer looked at each other seeking counsel. Coaldon finally said, "We need to discuss this request as a group. What are your opinions?"

Noel's voice erupted with excitement, "We do not need to waste valuable time discussing this plea for aid. These people need our assistance! We will help them!"

Pacer laughed, "Your abruptness, caring and honesty are refreshing. I agree with you, but I believe this must be a group decision."

Coaldon responded, "At first, I thought our top priority was to reach Rockham. But now, I believe we should offer our assistance to the Hardstone Clan."

The silent nods of the group gave Coaldon the final decision.

Coaldon continued, "What do we do next? Maybe we should take counsel with Ripsnout."

All eyes then turned to Ripsnout for guidance. Ripsnout, because of his quiet nature, found it difficult to respond.

He finally said, "I accept your offer of help, but first you must realize you are in great danger. If you continue traveling along your current path you will be attacked before this day is over. Wicked beasts have invaded this land. I believe you have already been detected and an ambush is waiting for you. If you are going to survive, you must trust me."

Coaldon and Pacer tried to talk at the same time. Pacer won out, stating, "If we are to assist your clan, then we must first escape this new threat."

Ripsnout thought for several minutes before responding, "The best path into the Sadden Mountains is through this ravine. The ravine will hide our movements until we reach a secure route into the caves. If we travel quickly the beasts will be caught off guard. We must move rapidly."

Coaldon responded, "We place our well being into your hands. We can discuss the details of our involvement with your clan when we reach your stronghold. Now, we must travel with both caution and speed. I will leave a message written in high elf telling Topple about our plans."

The Bowl of Doom

With feelings of uneasiness Ripsnout looked at his seven traveling companions. He had never talked to an outsider before today. Now, these outsiders were willing to help his clan, plus trust him with their lives. Ripsnout wondered why the clan had remained so isolated. Maybe they had been wrong to hide from the outside world for all these years. Ripsnout remembered a fable of his clan telling the story about the appearance of the seven strangers. Their courage and guidance would bring the clan to a reunion with their past. He needed to have a long talk with his elders when he returned to the Homekeep.

Before the travelers mounted their horses, Ripsnout said, "We must travel quietly. Please do not talk or create any unnecessary noise. I will lead the way."

Ripsnout then started jogging up the ravine at a steady pace. Magee and Norbert were the first to mount their horses with the help of Coaldon and Earthkin. The two men grunted as they pushed the two groaning bodies onto their saddles. Ripsnout was out of sight when the group was ready to depart. Pacer took the lead with the intention of catching up with their guide. As the morning passed, the group made good progress up the long narrow gorge. Magee and Norbert knew there was no reason to complain. They were happy to have escaped from Neverly.

The journey was a fascinating expedition into an unknown world. The ravine became narrower and deeper as the group traveled up the channel. Over time, rocks and dirt had collapsed into the gorge making it increasingly difficult to travel over the rough surface of the ravine floor. The group was entertained by Sid's playful behavior. The dog seemed to enjoy the company of Ripsnout and the unique odors of the gorge. At noon Ripsnout led the group to a small spring in the wall of the gorge. Coaldon suggested the group take a short break to rest, eat and enjoy the taste of fresh water. Magee and Norbert dreaded the thought of getting off and back on their horses. The aches and pains of their abused muscles would be overwhelming. With bold courage and laughter, they literally melted off of the horses. Once on the ground they slowly walked around to increase the blood flow in their legs.

The break was short but refreshing. Ripsnout was tense as he observed the surrounding area. He was particularly interested in watching the top of the ravine. Ripsnout's nervousness caused Pacer and Coaldon to encourage the group to continue the journey. In a quiet voice Ripsnout said to the group, "I have the feeling we have been detected. We must be out of the ravine by nightfall."

Ripsnout again started to jog ahead of the group. He set a faster pace than in the morning. The terrain in the bottom of the ravine became more difficult to travel. Landslides from the steep walls of the gorge created obstacles that slowed their progress. The group made steady advance until mid-afternoon, when they came to a massive landslide.

Pacer looked over the pile of dirt and rocks with a critical eye. He said to the group, "We should be able to make it over the blockage if we walk across the face of the mound at an angle starting from the south side. We will need to lead the horses by hand because the surface of the mound is too steep for us to ride."

Leading his horse, Pacer led the way up the side of the steep mound with short even steps. The soft, loose earth beneath his feet kept breaking away, causing him to slide down the slope. When he reached the top of the mound, his high spirited horse exploded in frustration. The horse bolted away from Pacer and charged down the slope. After the horse loped down the pile of dirt, it galloped out of sight down the ravine. This left a distinct impression on the travelers. The members of the group knew the horses were essential to successfully complete the journey. With patience, the travelers lead the remaining horses over the obstacle. Pacer volunteered to walk the remainder of the way.

As the group prepared to continue the trip, they noticed that Ripsnout had disappeared. Coaldon responded, "We have no choice but to continue traveling in this direction. I just hope Ripsnout has not betrayed us."

At a quickstep march, the travelers maintained a steady pace for the remainder of the day. Yet, to everybody's uneasiness Ripsnout did not reappear. The towering peaks of the Sadden Mountains loomed over their heads as the sun dropped low into the west. The unnatural scar of the ravine opened into the broad expanse of a beautiful valley. A collective sigh of relief went up from the travelers as they left the claustrophobic prison of the ravine.

As the sun dropped low in the western horizon, Pacer led the group toward a large rocky formation under a tall, bowl shaped cliff. As the group walked across the valley floor, Sid's behavior changed. He lifted his nose, sniffing the air in a restless manner. Coaldon noticed that Sid's eyes kept looking toward the mouth of the valley.

Coaldon said in a loud voice, "Sid has detected something. We might have a problem."

The group set off at a run toward an outcrop of rocks. Upon arriving, Sid started to growl and bark. The growing darkness did not allow the travelers to see why the dog was so excited.

Pacer called the group together, saying, "I have found a trail leading into the rocks. It is too narrow for the horses to follow. Should we wait here with the horses, or let the horses go and follow the trail?"

Before anybody could respond, the boom of a large drum could be heard in the distance. This was followed by the scream of many voices. The beat of the drum increased as the invading force spread across the valley like ants. To Coaldon, the sound of the voices was only too familiar.

He was the first to speak, "Our unwanted friends have come to greet us. I never imagined trogs would be found in this part of the Empire.

The arrival of the trog army made their decision easy. Pacer said, "We have no choice but to release the horses and defend ourselves."

Working quickly, the group removed the tack and freed the horses. Earthkin led the way down the winding trail extending into the rock formation. Sid walked next to Earthkin as the group stumbled along in the darkness. Then for some unknown reason, Sid started leading the group. As his nose sniffed the ground, he seemed to follow a preordained path.

The journey through the maze of rocks was interrupted by loud shouts behind them. The warriors knew the trog trackers had picked up their scent. It would only be moments before the trogs would be chasing them. To everyone's satisfaction the moon rose in the east. Its soft light filtered into the jumble of rocks revealing the path. At a narrow section of the trail, Coaldon, Brother Patrick and Pacer told the group to continue while they attempted to slow the pursuit of the trogs.

The three warriors anxiously waited until they heard footsteps rushing down the trail. The men leaped in front of the invading force with their sword blades flashing in the moonlight. Death awaited the unsuspecting and unprepared trogs. Wounded trog bodies piled up on top of each other as new victims were pushed into the killing zone by trogs behind them. The arms of the three warriors ached with fatigue when the trogs finally stopped their advance. Never had Brother Patrick or Pacer experienced such carnage.

Coaldon said to Pacer, "I believe this should stop their attack until morning. Hopefully by then we will find a way to deal with our unwelcome visitors." Pacer nodded as the three men walked into uncertainty.

It was easy for Pacer to follow the trail left by their companions. As he moved through the maze of rocks, he was fascinated by the grandeur of his surroundings. The soft moon light cast a mysterious aura over the vast formation.

He thought, "The forces of nature must have been guided by the hand of the One Presence to fashion this colossal labyrinth. Only the celestial artist could have created the sheer cliffs into such an exquisite masterpiece."

As Pacer became immersed in this beauty, the memories of the massacre faded.

After a long walk through the narrow passageway of rocks, they entered into a large bowl-shaped arena. They could see the cliff wrapped around the enclosure. They found the arena deceptively large. It was obvious a large crowd of people could gather in the immense space. At the far end of the natural coliseum a small fire greeted their arrival. The three warriors were welcomed by their companions with eager voices. The warriors described the results of their victorious battle.

When Earthkin finally spoke, his news was discouraging. He stated, "I have searched the bowl, but could not find an escape route."

Coaldon responded, "We will need to wait until daylight to reexamine the area to find a way to escape. I suggest we rest for the remainder of the night. We will need to be ready for the challenge awaiting us."

On the following morning the deep, resonating beat of a war drum awakened the group. The slow steady cadence meant the trog army was being summoned to prepare for battle. The booming sound of the drum had an irritating effect on the travelers.

As they sat around the fire eating breakfast, Pacer stated, "We will face death unless we can find a way out of here. After we eat, I want each of you to search for an escape route. We might try to go back the way we came in, but I believe the passage way will be guarded. If we do not find a way to escape, I suggest we defend ourselves from this position against the cliff wall."

The group carefully searched the arena but was unsuccessful in finding an escape route. Everyone gathered around the fire in a mood of desperation. In the distance, the war drum increased in cadence. As the group debated what to do, their attention was drawn to the entrance into the coliseum. Beasts with tall, lean bodies ran into the bowl. These creatures had long narrow faces, with large eyes, big ears, wide mouths and broad foreheads. Their ugly heads stood on top of powerful, hairy bodies with long legs and gangly arms. From ancient books, Pacer recognized the beasts as geks. The gek's evil eyes intently searched the valley to find the victims of their blood lust.

Yells of excitement erupted when they spotted the small group huddled against the far end of the arena under the towering cliffs. The geks laughed with sarcasm when they saw the small group huddled together. The far side of the bowl soon filled with an army of Geks and Trogs. They chanted, "Crossmore! Crossmore! Crossmore! Victory! Victory! Victory!" These chants were in unison with the beating of the war drum. With the authority of slave drivers, the geks started to whip the trogs into a state of frenzy.

Without warning, the trogs and geks became quiet and subdued. The beating of the war drum stopped as the trog army separated down the middle to form a walkway. The trogs fell to their knees, bowed and touched their foreheads on the ground. There was complete silence as a giant gek wearing a purple robe slowly walked through the trogs to the center of the arena. The huge gek looked with arrogance and contempt at the seven lonely people standing against the cliff wall. The beast gave a loud mocking laugh that echoed around the bowl. It then raised a clenched fist into the air as a sign of conquest.

In a loud booming voice, the beast said, "Our Great Lord Crossmore sends greetings and compliments. He is impressed with your courage, wisdom and skills. You have done well in challenging his power. He wishes to offer you the opportunity to escape from your imminent death. He will grant you freedom, but only under one condition. You must release Noel to me. Lord Crossmore has a deep love for this intelligent, beautiful damsel. He wishes to share his life with her in heavenly bliss. She will be queen of the Empire with the power to help lead it to a new glory. If she is not released immediately, I will crush you. You will not escape me."

Coaldon stepped forward with the confidence and deportment of a mighty warrior. Pacer, Brother Patrick and Earthkin stood in a line behind him with swords drawn. With dignity, Coaldon slowly drew his sword and pointed it at the giant gek. In a calm voice he responded, "I am Coaldon of Rocknee, the Hand on the Sword. I am a man of few words and commanding actions. I accept Lord Crossmore's compliments with gratitude. He is man of greed and dishonor. I therefore reject your offer of freedom in exchange for the enslavement of my sister Noel. Let the battle begin!"

A bolt of light raged out of the tip of Coaldon's sword, striking the giant gek in the chest. The beast evaporated into a cloud of smoke and dust. The trogs and geks jumped to their feet in shock and dismay. They watched Coaldon, but did not take action. Their leader had been destroyed.

Another large gek stepped forward from the crowd to take control the trog army. Coaldon did not hesitate to destroy this gek in the same manner. The half elf stood in defiance of the army cowering before him.

Coaldon knew the trogs would be unable to attack until they had a new leader. The trog army needed the control of a royal gek in order to attack. He realized his strategy would only temporally delay the assault. He waited impatiently for a new leader to emerge from the ranks of the geks. He felt a sense of futility as he observed the trogs changing from passive observers to vicious fighters. The trogs were forming battle lines in anticipation of the command to strike. Coaldon tried to identify the new commander, but to no avail.

Coaldon turned to face his companions. With nobility, he raised his sword in salutations to his sister and friends. He then turned to confront the advancing army with an unnatural calm and serenity. His eyes blazed with the determination to defend all that was good. The trogs were once again being whipped into a frantic emotional state by the geks. As they beat their swords and shields together, the attack lines continued to advance across the arena.

The arena was suddenly filled with a loud, rumbling sound that caused the trogs to halt their attack. Coaldon glanced back to see a door open in the face of the cliff. Out of the opening a large company of dwarves surged forth, screaming guttural war cries. The trogs had faced these battle cries and warriors in the past. The dwarf attack meant death and carnage. The trogs started to retreat in panic.

The dwarves formed three lines across the floor of the arena. The warriors in the first line carried bundles of lightweight spears. As the first line took position, they began throwing spears at the trogs with pinpoint accuracy. The second line of warriors was composed of archers. Upon command, the archers shot arrows into the trog army in wave after wave of skilled marksmanship. The last of line of dwarves attacked with pike and sword. The front line of the trog's advance was laid waste by the dwarves' assault. The trogs and geks turned and stampeded across the arena running over and crushing their own rear guard.

As suddenly as the dwarves had appeared, they also retreated back into the cave. Ripsnout in light armor rushed up to the seven travelers, waving for them to follow him. Without hesitation, the group pursued the dwarves into the dark cave. When everybody was inside the cave, the door was closed and a large metal latch lowered in place. Heavy breathing and the pungent odor of sweat filled the narrow confines of the passageway. Silence saturated the pitch-black darkness of the cave. In uncertainty, the dwarves and humans stood together.

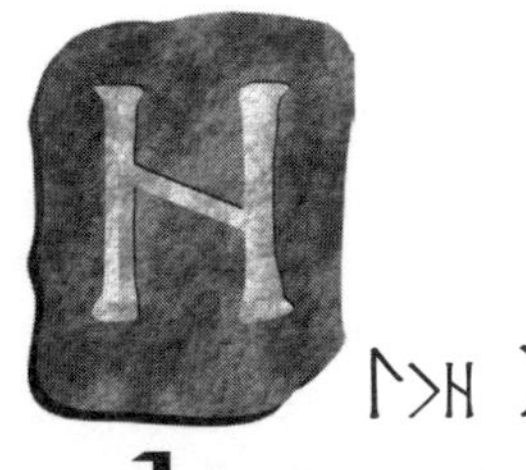

The Homekeep

A spontaneous cheer erupted from the warriors. A grim faced dwarf declared, "A job well done, my comrades! We have once again demonstrated our superiority! It is too bad we do not have more soldiers."

After lighting a torch, he bowed to Earthkin, saying, "I am Turrock, the commander of the Dwarf 2nd Brigade. I welcome you to the Kingdom of Hardstone. Your rescue has been worth the long, difficult journey through the mountains. I will be your guide on the trek to the Homekeep. Please feel free to talk with me if you have any questions or concerns. We will leave several guards to protect our retreat. I expect the trogs to break through the stone doors by nightfall. We will block the tunnel to prevent their invasion into this section of the mountain. It is important for us to leave immediately. We will rest at the Hall of Wonder."

Earthkin bowed, responding, "Thank you for your hospitality. You arrived just in time. Any later and we would not be sharing this conversation. Several of my companions are very tired and sore. Please consider their needs as we travel. Also, the humans will need light to assist them in walking through the dark passageways. Again, thank you."

The dwarves provided the humans with torches, plus words of encouragement. The passageways were wide with flat, even floors. The smooth, gleaming surfaces of the tunnel walls were a masterpiece of craftsmanship. The construction of these tunnels reached far back into antiquity, long before history was recorded. Yet, the workmanship clearly spoke of the devotion of the ancient dwarf communities.

The group walked at a leisurely pace for several hours before entering a large cavern named the Hall of Wonders. As they traveled, Earthkin shared stories he had heard about the cavern. Yet, his words did not express the splendor they experienced. The floor of the cavern was as smooth as glass with many crystals embedded in the clear surface. The torches illuminated what seemed to be millions of small points of different colored lights. These lights offered the sensation of waves flowing through the floor. Several times Coaldon almost lost his balance as he became mesmerized by the actions of the living dynamics of the rippling beauty.

The dome shaped room had several doorways entering from different directions. The ceiling of the cavern was truly a wonder to behold. Gems of every size, shape and color refracted the light of the torches in bands of radiant grandeur. Each movement of the torches created a new wonderland of magnificent colors and beauty. The seven guests looked in awe at the ever changing prisms of twinkling lights.

Earthkin proclaimed, "I have been blessed by entering this room. I can tell my children the gift of this special place. Some day I will return." The rest of the group agreed with words of praise and admiration.

Magee and Norbert were the first to find a place to rest. Their minds spun in bewilderment at the rapid series of events they had encountered over the past several days. They were in a near state of collapse. Noel, on the other hand, was animated by the expedition. She grew more energized with the advent of each new and exciting event. Noel had been held prisoner long enough; she was ready for travel and adventure.

She was first to notice the weakened condition of her two guardians. She said to the group, "I do not believe Magee and Norbert are capable of traveling any further today. They need to regain their strength."

Earthkin approached Turrock saying, "We need to rest before continuing."

Turrock responded, "There is a sleeping area next to the cavern. I will leave two warriors to be your guides. It is necessary for the army to return to the Homekeep to provide protection. I will visit with you when you arrive." Turrock turned, gave several commands and the army disappeared into the darkness.

The seven companions slept in a small room with water flowing from a small fissure in the wall. The floor was dusty from lack of use, but offered what the travelers needed, a place to rest. After a long sleep the group continued the journey with renewed energy and determination. They walked for many hours through an unending series of passageways and junctions. The travelers could see many tunnel entrances along each passageway. Noel, using her vivid imagination, tried to visualize what it would be like to explore each tunnel.

As Pacer and Coaldon traveled through the tunnels, they tried to remember the many turns and junctions, but after a short time they became disoriented and lost. Whereas, Earthkin had the innate ability to memorize each step of the march.

Their arrival at the Homekeep was a major event in the history of the Hardstone Clan. The dwarves greeted the outsiders with restrained excitement and hesitation. The members of the Hardstone Clan were happy to receive help. Yet, the arrival of the strangers was a painful signal that change had descended upon the clan. They were afraid of losing their simple life by the assault of the outside world. The invasion of the trogs had violently shifted their focus away from holding onto the past to finding hope in the future. It had been too easy for the clan to cling to yesterday, rather than confront the uncertainty of life. The members of the clan realized it would be necessary to face danger in order to survive.

Upon arrival at the dwarves' Homekeep, the guests were shown to their quarters. The guests noticed the dwarves' Homekeep was a maze of large domed caverns, connecting passageways, home dwellings and businesses. The Homekeep was a busy hub of children and adults involved in the everyday activity of life. Each family group contributed to the survival of the whole clan by sharing a particular skill or talent. The dwarves' economy depended on acquiring food and raw materials from under the mountain and from the topside world. The stability of the family group made it possible for the clan to survive for many centuries. Trips to the topside world to harvest natural products were necessary. The closure of the topside world, by the trogs, had caused the fabric of the dwarf society to deteriorate.

The dwarves provided a delicious meal of roasted nuts, moss greens and boiled deepwater roots. At the end of the meal, Earthkin received a message inviting him to attend a meeting of the Council of Elders. His exclusive invitation meant the humans would be curtailed in their contact with the dwarf community. At the meeting, Earthkin encouraged the council to allow his companions free access to the Homekeep. After a long discussion between Earthkin and the elders, it was decided that all seven guests would be allowed to participate in meetings of the Council of Elders. It should be noted that the dwarf society would only allow elders to speak during the formal council meetings. Elders were men elected to the council by the vote of clan members. This system of leadership was established in the ancient origins of the dwarves' common history.

The clan was summoned to the council meeting by the throbbing sound of several community drums. The Clan of Hardstone relied on the Council of Elders to provide the leadership necessary for the clan to survive. The members of the clan granted great authority to the council's decisions. As dwarves entered the meeting chamber, they talked in excited voices. The outsiders were surprised by the large number of dwarves attending the meeting. The arrival of the guests into the cavern created a loud stir of conversation. As they walked to the front of the meeting room, little children rushed out of the crowd to touch a human and hurry back to the safety of their mothers. Sid wandered among the children creating screams of happiness and delight. Each of the visitors, including Earthkin, experienced the sensation of being an honored guest, plus a novelty of unique character.

When everyone was seated a frail, old dwarf entered the cavern followed by six elders. The Council of Elders slowly walked to the stage in front of the room with steps reflecting the heavy responsibility they carried. They formed a line in front of the community, bowed to the audience and sat in large wooden chairs.

The old dwarf said in a dignified voice, "I, Rolfe of the Family of Stone Chip, welcome each of you to this important meeting. It is with joy I present our seven guests for your acceptance and appreciation." The outsiders stood, turned to the crowd and gave a deep bow.

Looking at the seven outsiders, Rolfe said, "Would each of you please introduce yourself to the clan."

Starting with Magee, the visitors stated their names and presented a brief history of their families. When Coaldon's turn came, he declared in a loud, clear voice, "I am Coaldon of Rocknee, the Hand on the Sword and heir to the throne of the Empire. Wastelow, through the power of Crossmore the Wizard, deposed my grandfather as Emperor, killed my parents and imprisoned my twin sister. I stand before you offering my assistance. I invite you to join us in fighting the evil scourge infecting the Empire." It was obvious to Coaldon that the audience was both surprised and impressed by his statement. The clan did not expect to have an outsider with Coaldon's status as their guest.

In a sad voice Rolfe stated, "Thank you for your willingness to offer your help. It is difficult for me to admit our failure, but our recent history has been characterized by the fulfillment of our own selfish goals. The clan has retreated from the activities of the Empire out of fear and suspicion. This attitude has brought us to the point of impending destruction. We have no one to turn to for advice, support or assistance. Lord Coaldon, please tell us about the evil growing in the Empire."

Coaldon was shocked at being called Lord. It took several moments for his mind to regain enough composure to provide a brief summary of events. He explained the history of the great splendor of the Age of Seaborn, the violence of the First Quarter Age under the wicked power of Doomage the Wizard, the casting of evil into the Chamber of Oblivion by the Key of Ban, the peace and prosperity of the Second Quarter Age and the current reawakening of wickedness by Crossmore. He further explained that the Empire was in the Age of Change and being ruled by increasing confusion, hatred and violence. In conclusion he pulled his sword from its scabbard. As he raised it into the air a surge of electricity danced around the tip of the sword. The audience gasped in disbelief at the display of power.

Coaldon declared, "This is the elfin Blade of Conquest. Under its banner, we have the power to return the Empire to a time of peace and prosperity."

A long silence followed Coaldon's presentation. Finally, Rolfe stood and bowed to Coaldon. He stated, "It seems you have been guided to us in our time of need. The invasion of Trogs started many years ago. At first it was easy to drive them from our kingdom. Recently, their increasing numbers have imprisoned us in our world under the mountain. In great sadness, I state that half of our clan has been killed at the hands of trogs and geks. We do not know what to do or where to go."

Jumping to his feet, Earthkin declared, "I am Earthkin, an elder of the Clan Long Beard from the Great Hall of Rockham. I was overjoyed to learn that the clans Long Beard and Hard Stone are relatives. I extend to you greetings and good blessings. My friends and I have been commissioned by Brad, the rightful Emperor, to help free the land of corruption. I pledge to you, I will do everything in my power to assist you in your struggle. I offer to you the resources of the Clans of Rockham. All dwarf clans need to pull together for the common good."

After Earthkin's short speech, tears of joy ran down the face of Rolfe. In a slow, rough voice he continued, "What do we do now? We can sit here and wait for the end to come to us, or do something. Which do we choose?"

He stood in silence waiting for the clan to respond. It did not take long before a flood of emotions erupted in the meeting chamber. Loud shouts, heated conversations, and anger filled the room. The pent up memories of hopelessness, death and agony exploded into a demand for action. Emotions of this intensity only burst from clan members every two or three centuries. The clan's past history of stoic patience turned into a call for heroic deeds. Voices of determination escalated into nearly unanimous commitment to the future of the clan.

After the clan's emotional outburst had run it course, Rolfe responded, "I accept your insistence for action. It is my understanding that you desire to gain freedom and security. What actions do we take to achieve these goals? Do we fight? Do we hide? Do we travel to a new home? Do we seek advice? Do we join arms with other dwarves? Do we join the forces in the Empire to conquer Crossmore?"

The clan's emotional call for action had suddenly been challenged by reality. What price was the clan willing to pay to live in freedom?

Rolfe continued his speech, "It is now time for the council to begin its special meeting. As head elder, I formally call the Council of Elders into session. You are reminded that only the elders are allowed to speak."

The seven elders gathered at the large table and began a discussion that lasted for the remainder of the day. On a rotating basis, each elder stated his opinions and concerns. It was the responsibility of the council to examine the issue from every possible viewpoint. After a general overview, it was time to find an acceptable solution. As the debate continued, the content of the discussion became a rehashing of the same ideas from different perspectives. The audience passively accepted the repetition of each argument as a redefinition of the debate. Dwarves were unhasty people who had infinite tolerance. They would patiently wait for a consensus to mature after a long dialogue.

Noel sat through the discussion of the council with increasing irritation. Her robust nature had a difficult time listening to the same ideas repeated over and over.

At first she only twitched with annoyance, but after several hours her whole body pulsed with agitation. Finally, out of frustration at the clan's inaction, she jumped from her chair asking, "May I have the opportunity to speak?!"

The audience and council gasped in disbelief at this violation of council etiquette. She stood facing the council without wavering from her request. The council members talked quietly together before Rolfe answered.

Rolfe finally said, "Young lady, your impulsive interruption is a breach of the council's Code of Standards. This Code was established to protect the council from unnecessary disruption of its debates. We view your request with both shock and admiration. Your courage is a quality the clan will need to demonstrate in order to survive. Even though we are creating an uncomfortable precedent, we grant you the right to speak before the council. The Clan of Hardstone will need to face the future with the same boldness as you have approached the council."

Noel stood before the council in humility. The lessons taught by Norbert and Magee had been lost to her half elf nature.

She responded, "I apologize for my youthful brashness. I will speak briefly and to the point. I believe you must leave your Homekeep. Only death and destruction will haunt you in this place. I also suggest you seek help from the citizens of Rockham, plus offer your strength to the war against Crossmore. Thank you for your understanding and patience."

After Noel's very candid observation and recommendation, Rolfe decided it was time to end the session and allow the community time to think.

He said, "I believe that each of us needs to evaluate all that has been discussed. We will meet tomorrow at 12 hours to continue the discussion."

After the dismissal, the community members quickly left the room deep in thought. A glimmer of hope could be seen in the faces of the dwarves.

The seven outsiders did not talk about the meeting, but rather returned to their rooms, ate a cold meal and quickly fell asleep. The roll of drums woke the guests, calling them and the clan to the council meeting. Rolfe called the meeting to order with his gentle, yet firm voice.

He said with clear authority, "The council met early this morning to discuss how to proceed. The members have decided to break tradition by allowing the adult members of the clan to determine their own destiny. Since any action will have profound consequences, you will need to make the decisions. Also, we have decided not to allow any further debate. It is now time for action, not discussion."

After a brief pause to allow the community to absorb his statement, he continued, "If you are in favor of the following resolution, please stand and be counted. The majority will rule."

Rolfe questioned, "Do you believe it is best to leave the Homekeep and seek a new future?"

The dwarves looked at each other with hesitation and doubt. Then with uncertainty a majority of the community slowly stood up. For the dwarves to accept a change of this magnitude, required the community to recognize and accept the hopelessness of their future in the Homekeep.

Rolfe continued, "Please be seated. I declare the clan will leave the Homekeep. Do you believe it is best for the whole clan to leave the Homekeep together?" With less hesitation, a majority of the clan stood up.

Rolfe directed, "Please be seated. I declare the whole clan will leave the Homekeep as a group. Do you desire to go to Rockham?" This time all adults stood in total agreement.

Rolfe continued, "I declare we will travel to Rockham. It will be necessary to travel overland, because the old tunnels under the mountains are too dangerous. As clan leader, I declare we will leave for Rockham in three days. Will the following people please meet with me directly after this meeting to plan our escape: Lord Coaldon, Elder Earthkin, the Council, the brigade commanders and the head of the women's group. The escape committee will make the plans for our trip south. May the One Presence be with us. May we have the faith and courage to fulfill our destiny!"

ᛚ>ᚺ ᚲᚢᛟᛏᛉᚺᚺ ᛚᚢ ᛏᚢᚴᚴ>ᚺᛒ

The Journey to Rockham

The unprecedented journey of the Hardstone Clan would not be a haphazard event. Every detail of the trip was planned to help assure the success of the clan's migration. The clan's first concern was the trog army that controlled the northern sections of the Sadden Mountains. The Clan leaders held long discussions with the seven guests.

At one such meeting, Pacer stated, "Crossmore's greatest weakness is his tendency to delay. Even though he controls great power, he is basically a coward. His cloak of power compensates for his sense of weakness and vulnerability.'

Coaldon added, "Crossmore enjoys crushing and destroying people, but only from a safe distance. His army acts as his courage. He stays away from direct challenges or confrontations."

Pacer continued, "I suggest your escape plan needs to be based on Crossmore's sluggish response to a crisis."

Earthkin injected, "The wizard's need to control will limit the ability of the trog army to respond in a concise manner.

After a pause in the conversation, Ripsnout said, "We know that the large part of the trog army is hidden in the valleys on the west side of the mountains. Only a token force is stationed east of the mountains. I suggest we exit from the East Door onto the coastal plains."

Using these insights, the escape committee decided to follow Ripsnout's suggestion. The dwarf army would lead the way by making a lightning quick attack on the small garrison of trogs to the east. Once the enemy was eliminated, the Hardstone Clan would travel south to Rockham. It would be necessary to travel quickly because Crossmore would deploy a large army to chase after the fleeing dwarves.

The three days of preparation were a nonstop flurry of activities. Each person including the children was assigned tasks to complete. By the beginning of the third day, the community was ready to begin their march to Rockham. It was essential for the clan members to travel lightly. This meant it was necessary to leave behind many family treasures and heirlooms. Tears were a common sight as the moment for departure arrived. Before leaving, a contingent of dwarf warriors blocked all entrances to the Homekeep, except for the escape route to the east. Few dwarves looked back, as Rolfe led the way into an unsure future.

The dwarf army was successful in clearing out the token force of trogs. The trogs showed little heart in fighting the savage dwarf warriors. The coastal plain was quickly cleared of resistance, allowing the Hardstone Clan to begin its long journey south along the east side of the Sadden Mountains. The planning committee decided the clan would move faster if the community traveled during the day. The coastal plain was a broad expanse of tree covered rolling hills that gradually sloped to the ocean. An ancient road to the South had once carried the commerce for a prosperous economy. After considering different routes, the dwarves decided to take the road because it was the most direct way to Rockham. The old road was so well constructed it could still be used. An advance party of warriors cleared the roadbed of obstructions to allow for a rapid movement of the clan. Scouts fanned out in all directions to provide a constant stream of information about the surrounding area and any possible threats. The Council of Elders did not want to be surprised by any unanticipated problem.

The first two days of travel were slow, but productive. It took several days for the clan to become organized and establish a routine of travel. It was necessary to create a system of making and breaking camp, feeding the clan, providing for the needs of the young and elderly, and finding water. Throughout the journey, the camps were set up in the unsheltered areas to save time. The need for speed was the first consideration. The rapid moving trog army would soon be in pursuit of the traveling community.

The weather was pleasant for the first few days of the clan's migration south. The warm days of spring brought a celebration of optimism. The sky was filled with birds flying north to their summer nesting grounds. A joke circulated among the dwarves that the clan was going the wrong direction. It was the time of year to fly north, not flee south. The travelers also observed large war eagles soaring overhead in wide, lazy circles. The eagles would catch the wind currents and soar with the grace of stately dancers. The giant birds often made long, twisting, free fall dives that ended just over the heads of the travelers. At first the dwarves were afraid of being attacked by the birds, but later accepted the eagles with little concern.

Coaldon had a different feeling toward the visitors from the sky. The constant presence of the eagles was more than a coincidence or just a passing event. The war eagle's voices spoke to Coaldon in a disquieting manner. The eagles talked, yet he could only catch a vague outline of their conversations. Coaldon was determined to find a way to communicate with the mysterious and aloof eagles.

The clan made steady progress. Clan members took turns performing different camp chores. Magee, Norbert and Noel spent most of their time caring for little children who were frightened by the journey. The older children were oblivious to the dangers facing the clan. To them the migration was a grand adventure that demanded a festive response. Each turn in the road was a time to explore and discover something new. Most adults were both irritated and delighted by the energy and excitement of youth. They realized that the clan had become stoic, unmotivated and withdrawn. The history of the Hardstone Clan illustrated how easy it was to hide from the world. The clan was learning the empty satisfaction of hiding in fear and isolation.

The morning of the fifth day started as usual. The roll of drums awoke the camp before dawn to prepare for a long day of hiking. The morning meal was bubbling in cooking pots, while dwarves bustled about stowing supplies in back packs. The watchmen returned after a night of protecting the camp. Their tired faces matched their fatigue. Yet, not a word of complaint was heard from these warriors. The call to duty was stronger than any physical discomfort they might experience.

Each person was required to carry a backpack full of supplies. Warriors carried large, heavy packs while children carried only their clothing. As the long line of dwarves stretched down the narrow road, a light misty rain began to fall. The dwarves in general did not like rain in any shape or form. As the day progressed, the rain increased to a steady downpour. Even though the dwarves wore protective rain gear, they became depressed and irritable. By evening the mood of despair ruled the camp. Tents provided shelter from the rain, but not from the cold that penetrated deep into each body. Few fires could be lit because of the rain soaked wood. After a long, miserable night, the clan wasted no time in beginning the trudge down the deserted road. Walking warmed the cold, aching bodies. By late afternoon on the sixth day, the rain stopped and sunshine flooded the long procession of pilgrims. The necessity for the dwarves to leave the Homekeep did not soften the feelings of being lost, forlorn and lonely. Some dwarves felt a sense of gloom to the point of hopelessness.

To everybody's happiness, camp guards found a large supply of dry wood in the shelter of a rock overhang. The inviting blaze of fires could be seen in all corners of the campsite. The seven outsiders, like the rest of the travelers, used the fire to dry soggy clothes. After a warm meal of trail food, the seven companions sat in front of a fire with eyes focused on the flickering flames. As they gazed into the fire, the mesmerizing power of the flames created a soothing sense of tranquility. The enchantment of the moment covered the group like a warm blanket.

Coaldon was the first to break the charm engulfing his friends. He said, "I hate to interrupt your thoughts, but I have a few things to share. I am detecting a growing presence of evil behind us. It is not close, but it is drawing nearer. Earthkin, in the morning, would you please share this information with the elders? I expect we will have several days to get ready to fight. Also, how long will it take us to reach Rockham?"

Earthkin responded, "I imagine we are about half way to the city. It should take us at least seven days to reach the door of Rockham."

Coaldon continued, "Earthkin, do you know of a place in the immediate area we could use as a defensive position?"

Earthkin sunk deep in thought for several moments before responding, "As a youth, I was viewed as being strange because I enjoyed trekking into the outside world. As a curious child I explored this area. While investigating, I found a deep, narrow canyon about three days' march south of here. The canyon has steep cliff walls on the north and south sides that would be difficult to climb or pass. The river flowing from the canyon has cut a deep, rocky channel. This time of year the river is full to the banks with the spring thaw. As I remember, the narrow, rocky entrance into the canyon is only 30 or 40 strides wide. The floor of the canyon is covered with large boulders, making it difficult to pass through. If we find it necessary to fight, I would recommend this location."

Pacer responded, "We will talk with the dwarf commanders about the details of this defensive site. They need to start preparing for a battle with the trogs. I dislike being trapped in a canyon, but if that is the best defensive position we can find, so be it."

Coaldon concluded, "Tomorrow, it will be necessary for me to spend the day by myself. There are some important things I need to do. I have guard duty tonight so I will not see you until tomorrow night." As Coaldon disappeared into the darkness, his companions followed him with curious glances.

After Coaldon completed his guard duty far south of the campsite, he slept for several hours. At daybreak he ate a meal of hardbread and walked to a high, rocky dome in the west. He enjoyed strolling through the forest listening to the sounds of life and observing the beauty of spring. Coaldon had been so preoccupied with surviving, he had lost track of his intimate bond with life. He remembered the hours he had spent as a youth enjoying nature.

Coaldon climbed to the top of a rocky dome with relaxed strides. This position offered him a good view of the surrounding area. The haze of the ocean mist formed an outline on the eastern horizon. The snowcapped peaks of the Sadden Mountains to the west stood like giant guardians. In the silence, the mountains commanded, "Do not pass!" The fresh, lush green of spring leaves and grass formed a blanket in all directions from his throne.

Peace crept into every fiber of his body. This was a time for him to forget about Crossmore, trogs and dwarves. He sat with his back leaning against a flat rock facing south, protecting him from a chilly morning breeze. His cold body was slowly warmed by the morning sun. Pushing away the usual surge of thoughts, he dropped into a state of meditation. Free from distractions, his mind became like a pool of still water. This void of thought allowed him to be open to the delicate pulses of energy in the atmosphere. The first mental image to appear to Coaldon was Crossmore having a heated conversation with a subordinate. Crossmore kept yelling, "You must move faster! You must catch them! You must destroy them! Remember, I want the girl unharmed. I will not accept any excuses! If you succeed, your reward will be great power."

Crossmore suddenly paused in mid sentence as if he had been distracted. Coaldon saw Crossmore's hand extending towards him across the vast darkness of space. The reaching-hand carried a sword dripping with a black substance. The sword slashed back and forth as it approached him. Coaldon was not concerned until he felt the blade slice through the air near his head. He had to decide quickly if he was going to fight or to remain silent. It was possible Crossmore was only guessing at his location. If he did not attack, Crossmore might continue his search somewhere else. Assuming Crossmore was bluffing, he sat very still. To his delight, the vision of the sword faded away. He heard Crossmore moan in frustration as his presence dissolved into emptiness.

Even though his concentration had been broken by the attack, Coaldon returned to his meditation. He had the feeling that more was to be revealed to him. It was not long before a second vision formed in his mind. He saw the vague image of five people running to escape from an unseen enemy. The five shadows turned towards him with desperate eyes. The five people looked directly at him in disbelief. They pointed at him in wonderment, as if seeing a ghost. Then out of the dark fog many vague images appeared. As the five people turned to face the invaders, a bright light flashed and five images vanished into the haze. The vision was so vivid Coaldon came out of his trance feeling anxiety and fear.

Coaldon felt his body trembling as he opened his eyes. To his satisfaction, he was still sitting on the rocky dome with the warm sunshine caressing his body. As he raised his head, he came face to face with a large bird. The bird's yellow eyes stared at Coaldon without moving. The bird stood about nine hands high with black body feathers blending into a white crown. A large beak and cold penetrating eyes dominated its majestic face. Without any doubt, Coaldon knew the bird was a black war eagle. The eagle cocked its head to one side as it continued to stare at Coaldon. The bird spread its large wings in a wide sweeping motion, lifting it off the ground several strides. It then settled to the ground and refolded its wings. The eagle spoke, "I am Blackwing, chief of the Northridge family of war eagles. I extend to you greetings and good blessings. It is my privilege to meet with you and offer the assistance of my family. I watched you grow up in Lost Valley. I can trust you to honor the gift of my service. How may I help you?"

At first, Coaldon found it difficult to speak. He finally said, "I am accompanying the Hardstone Clan in their escape from Crossmore's army. You could help by providing us with information and being a messenger. I need to know how many days journey the trog army is behind us. I also need to send a message to the elders in the dwarf City of Rockham."

The eagle shifted back and forth on its powerful legs in a nervous manner before it answered, "I will do this for you. You must remember that eagles have no desire to become involved with the problems of people. We watch with great humor and sadness, the stupidity of your kind. Only in unusual circumstances will we intervene in the affairs of people. The reason I offer my assistance is out of respect and obligation to your grandfather. You must agree to certain conditions. First, I will only talk with you. Second, you must be alone when we talk. Last, I will only meet with you in an isolated location."

Coaldon questioned, "I agree to your terms. I am curious how you know so much about me?"

The eagle laughed in a crackling voice, as it answered, "We have carefully observed you for the last 18 years. You are a person of destiny."

Coaldon responded, "I never imagined I was the center of attention."

The large eagle nodded its stately head in understanding.

Coaldon followed, "When will you start helping us?"

The eagle paused as it looked into the north. It turned back to Coaldon as it responded, "The trogs are about three days' march behind you. You will need to find a place to defend yourselves very soon. If you will write a message on paper, I will deliver it to Rockham. I will leave for Rockham as soon as you give me the message. I will meet with you tomorrow afternoon in a location you select."

Coaldon dug a piece of paper and a pencil from his travel pouch. In the message he explained the current circumstances of the Hardstone Clan, gave their present location and appealed for help. Blackwing carefully tucked the message into a claw, spread his great wings and gracefully flew away into the southern sky.

Coaldon had been so consumed by the events of the day he lost track of time. He realized by the position of the sun it was mid afternoon. He would need to hurry to catch up with the caravan before dark. He hated to leave his perch, but he knew he had duties to fulfill. As he trotted through the shadows of the forest, his mind reviewed every detail of the day. He was especially concerned about the vision of the five individuals being attacked. He wondered if Topple had been a part of the group.

R

Topple and Associates

Topple knew it would take several day of hard riding to catch up with his friends. Topple, Hilda and the two apprentices had not traveled far from Neverly before a sense of urgency flooded the wizard. From past experience, he knew this sense of anticipation required his immediate attention. The voice of foreknowledge forced Topple to face a choice between leaving Neverly and the need to respond to the mysterious intuition. He decided it would be best to talk with Hilda about his dilemma.

Topple led Hilda and the apprentices into a grove of trees in a deep ravine. Hilda questioned, "Why are we stopping? We need to hurry if we are going to catch up with the group."

He said, "Hilda, there is something I need to share with you. I feel we are overlooking something. What could it be?"

Hilda had a puzzled expression on her face as she gazed at Topple. She knew it was out-of-character for Topple to be so overly concerned about anything. He was experiencing something unusual for him to be so somber. She finally responded, "Let's rest here while you deal with your forewarning."

The four riders dismounted allowing Topple time to reflect on his premonition. Sitting by himself he drifted into an ever deepening state of contemplation. Soon he was oblivious to everything, except for the swirl of fog filling his mind. At first Topple heard an unrecognizable jumble of voices blending into a meaningless noise. It was like listening to all the voices he had ever heard passing before him at high speed. The noise stopped as suddenly as it started, leaving only the sound of one voice. Topple saw himself as a student sitting in the library of the long abandoned City of Mazz. He was listening to words from the Book of Wisdom. The book magically spoke the written words of prophecy to him. He remembered being required to memorize many passages. Later in life he discovered that these verses were important. Shadows of these prophecies often reached into current events to influence his judgment. He learned to pay close attention to his inner voice.

As the vision continued, the center of his attention focused on a single verse. The prophecy stated, "In the City of Neverly, the foul beast of death will be transformed into a new life. As the source of evil sleeps, the escaping beast will step into the future through a door from the past. A strong guiding hand will provide shelter for the trembling, lost child. By prompt action the lost will be found."

Topple emerged from his vision as if hit by a powerful bolt of electricity. The jolt caused him to shout and give a sudden jerk. Never in his long life had he experienced such a demanding summons. As he looked around, he felt sweat running down his face and his heart rapidly pounding. Topple's reaction was not only a surprise to himself, but also to his companions.

With a twinkle in her eye, Hilda responded, "You looked utterly silly when you jerked and shouted. Just to think a man of your wisdom and age acting in such a manner. You should be ashamed."

Before she could say another word, Hilda found herself flopping in the air about 30 strides above the ground. She yelled, "I am afraid of heights! Let me down this very moment!" Hilda realized that she had said the wrong thing when she abruptly fell toward the ground. Her scream violated the quiet of the secluded grove.

Of course Topple stopped her free fall just before she hit the ground. With the tenderness of a new mother, he gently lowered her to the earth.

He then said, "Hilda, you looked so immature screaming. You should be ashamed of yourself." Hilda was so overcome by the emotions that she could not talk.

Topple laughed saying, "Has the cat got your tongue? For the first time in my life, I have actually found you speechless. Let us celebrate!"

Before Topple could say another word, Hilda jumped to her feet, gave a shout of frustration and tackled Topple. They came to rest in a cloud of dust with Hilda sitting on Topple's chest. At this point the two apprentices were laughing at the comical performance. It took several moments before their loud roars of laugher died down to a jolly bout of teasing and bantering. Topple's serious mood had been transformed into a celebration of life. The four companions had found joy in the simple treasure of one another.

After Topple's encounter with Hilda, he took a moment to collect his thoughts before sharing his vision with Hilda and the two apprentices. He concluded his story by quoting the words of prophecy. He then stated, "I believe the verse has something to do with me."

Hilda responded, "Yes, I believe you are right. We need to discover the meaning behind the riddle. The verse has something to do with Neverly and a foul beast.

It is important to recognize that the beast goes through a transformation. I have the impression the beast will be freed from the bonds of enslavement. So, let's get started. Who is the foul beast?"

One of the apprentices answered, "There are only two people in Neverly that I would consider to be beasts, Crossmore and Badda. I do not think that Crossmore will ever be transformed, so I would suggest Badda."

Topple followed, "Who is Badda?"

Hilda answered, "Do you remember a young man named Bobby who disappeared many years ago? Well, I recently discovered that Crossmore had cast a spell over him and created Badda."

Topple said, "Yes, I do remember the arrogant young man. He was fascinated with Crossmore's magic. It looks as if he got more magic than he wanted."

Hilda continued, "The phrase 'the source of evil sleeps' might relate to the spell we cast on Crossmore. If all this is correct, we will need to go back to Neverly to find Badda. He will need our help when he opens his eyes and takes his first new steps."

Both Hilda and Topple knew it would be dangerous for them to return to Neverly, but this prophecy had now determined their destiny. Returning to their horses, they rode back to Neverly. Leaving the two apprentices to watch the animals in a sheltered area near the river, Topple and Hilda approached the East City Gate. Under the cover of magic they entered the city disguised as two merchants. It did not take long for them find Badda walking around the city in a state of perplexity. They followed him until he hid under a staircase in a pile of garbage. When Topple approached Badda, he could see fear on the man's face. After Topple talked with Badda, he discovered a transformation had taken place. The man had been changed from Badda to Bobby. Bobby was truly an infant needing protection. He yielded to Topple's fatherly guidance with trust and relief.

Hilda and Topple wasted no time in leaving the city with Bobby. They rendezvoused with the two apprentices and traveled the rest of the night. After a short break the group decided it was best to travel during the day in order to reach Dooms Ravine as soon as possible. Topple assumed Pacer would camp in the shelter of the narrow gorge. After several hours of hard riding, Topple led the group through a cover of trees and into the ravine. From the evidence left in the area Topple determined the seven travelers had camped for one night in the gorge.

Topple called the group together and explained, "While the group spent the night, they met a dwarf. There was a brief struggle, but then they departed with the dwarf up the ravine."

At this time Hilda noticed a piece of paper hidden under a rock. After reading it she said, "Coaldon left us a message. It is written in high elf to protect it from being read by anybody else. The message reads, 'We have met a dwarf from the Hardstone Clan. He has requested our assistance in fighting an army of evil creatures that invaded their tunnels. We have decided to go with the dwarf to his Homekeep. We will travel in the ravine to escape from the beasts occupying the west side of the Sadden Mountains."

Topple responded, "I remember stories of the Hardstone Clan disappearing from the face of the earth. It was assumed the clan had been destroyed by Doomage the Wizard. This is wonderful news. But, it is bad news to hear about the creatures invading the mountains. This sounds like the work of Crossmore. He has opened the door into the Chamber of Oblivion a little wider, allowing more evil to infect the Empire. We need to make a decision. Do we follow our friends up the canyon, or do we take another route to Rockham?"

Hilda answered, "We have found ourselves in a difficult situation. We can travel south to Rockham over the plains, but I am afraid we will be detected while moving across open country. Coaldon's message indicates that if we travel east we will face an unknown enemy. Maybe we should travel around the north end of the

Sadden Mountains and take the coastal plains to Rockham. It is much longer, but it might be safer."

Topple let his thoughts wander as he considered the different possibilities. He knew there was no right answer. Yet, no matter which way they chose to go, the One Presence would use their decision to create the greatest good. He finally said, "I do not know which direction to go. I recommend we rest here until we find an answer."

Hilda nodded in agreement as she gathered wood to build a fire. It was not long before a fire was burning and a hot meal of meat and roots was cooking in a small pot.

After eating, the wizard found an isolated place in the ravine to clear his mind. As he relaxed, he detected the sound of many feet running toward them from the southeast. He kept hearing loud, gruff voices yelling, "Keep running, you maggots! Run! Run! Run! We must catch them! Faster! Faster!"

Topple abruptly stood up, walked back to the fire and stated, "We must depart immediately. We are in danger."

The five travelers mounted their horses in haste and set a rapid pace into the dry wastelands of the northeast. They followed an animal trail that steadily climbed into the high hill country overlooking the plains to the south. After many hours of travel, the group stopped in a grassy meadow to rest the horses and eat a cold meal. From this location they could see the outline of the Sadden Mountains in the southeast and the mist shrouded plains to the south and west. The sun was low on the horizon as the five travelers contemplated their next move.

Topple stated, "The horses are tired and hungry. We also need to rest. I believe we have gained a large lead on whoever is following us. I propose we spend the night in the shelter of the grove of trees to our east."

Everyone was in agreement except Bobby. He responded, "I want to keep traveling. I want to get far away from Crossmore."

Hilda answered, "We understand your desire to escape, but we must rest." With his eyes filled with fear, Bobby finally nodded his consent.

The uneventful night passed in peace. The light of day came too soon for the small caravan of travelers. While the sleepy eyed group prepared to leave, the wizard walked up to the crest of a hill to check the area for any unusual activities. He returned in a hurry. He stated, "A large army is about five hours travel behind us."

Bobby started to shake in panic. He shouted, "They are after me! They are after me!"

Topple soothed, "Relax Bobby. We have fresh horses, a good night's sleep and a long lead. They will not catch us."

The group traveled at an easy trot for most of the day. It was important for them not to overwork the horses. Their hairy, four legged friends were the key to escaping the pursuing militia. They took several short breaks to let the horses graze. As their trek turned toward the east, the northern foothills of the Sadden Mountain range slowed their progress. It was necessary for the travelers to climb over ridge after ridge to reach the coastal plain.

Days passed into nights as the group finally conquered the obstacles of the northern foothills. It was midday when the travelers finally rode onto a hill top and viewed the coastal plains. A broad expanse of trees unfolded before them like a green blanket. With a strong sense of accomplishment, they assumed the worst was over. They decided to ride to the forest far below before making camp.

Topple was first to notice a blanket of smoke hugging the tree line. He raised his hand, commanding, "Stop! Something is not right."

The joy of the group was short lived when they saw movement in a large meadow. Topple guided the group to cover in the rocky shelter. Leaving their horses to graze on fresh spring grass, the five adventurers crawled to the edge of a hill to get a better look at the movement in the forest. As they studied the activities below them, they felt a sense of despair.

Topple quietly said, "Those ugly beasts are called trogs. They are the foot soldiers of Crossmore's army. We have arrived just in time to find them blocking our way. I wonder if they are part of the army that was following us? Maybe they are waiting for our arrival."

The other members of group were speechless at this discovery. A steady stream of trogs marched out of an opening in the mountain, joining a large horde already assembled. Topple explained to his companions that the tall hideous creatures directing the activities of the trogs were called geks. From their hiding place, the small group spent the rest of the afternoon watching the massing of the trog army.

Finally, a large drum carried on a cart rolled out of the tunnel entrance. A tall gek standing at the side of the drum held two large clubs in its hands. With a slow, formal motion the gek raised the clubs over its head and began to pound the drum in a slow, steady rhythm. The deep resonating sound of the drum could be heard on the hill where the five companions were watching. At the sound of the drum, the geks used whips to force the trogs to move. The army of trogs formed into units and marched south to the beat of the drum. As the trog army stretched out in a long line, the drum beat faster, forcing the trogs to trot. After the large army disappeared into the forest, wagonloads of supplies pulled by horses followed the advancing force. At nightfall the last of the wagons lumbered into position in the long caravan moving south.

After hours of silent observation, Topple stated, "We need to make camp."

Topple's comment jarred his companions into facing the reality of their situation. After a short search for a suitable campsite, they settled in a narrow rock crevice.

After setting up camp, Hilda was first to speak, "It seems our enemy is in a hurry. It is obvious the army is not interested in us, but concerned about something much more important. I wonder if the trogs are chasing after the dwarves. "

Topple responded, "It would be my guess that the dwarves, plus our friends, are fleeing to the south, probably toward Rockham. By the looks and size of the trog army, the dwarves are in trouble. I would suggest we follow the army to determine how we can help."

Hilda commented, "The trog army may or may not be following the dwarves. We need to determine why the trogs are marching south."

Bobby looked at his four companions with an agonized expression on his face. He blurted out, "I need to talk with you! As I watched the trogs below us today, I began to experience faint images of the dreadful things I have done for many years. In my youthful conceit, I allowed myself to be trapped into a life of wickedness."

Bobby's eyes rapidly darted back and forth with signs of anxiety.

He continued, "I feel a flood of anger and guilt. I do not know what to do. Should I run away and hide? Should I stay with you? How can I deal with my feelings of remorse?"

When Bobby had finished talking, he hung his head. He had been reawakened, but now he needed to confront the consequences of his past life. Bobby was a lost soul with no rudder to guide him into the future.

With a sorrowful face he continued, "I want to do what is right. I want to do penance for my sins. As a youth, I remember the Monks talking about finding forgiveness. Maybe I should turn to the One Presence to discover the purpose for my life."

For a long time Bobby's eyes stared into the fire in deliberation. No one in the group said anything to interrupt Bobby's thoughts. Finally, he looked up with a peaceful expression on his face. He stuttered, "I – I – I feel much better now. I want to stay with you. Somehow, I will find a way to offer my services to the people of the Empire. I will not be a burden to you, but rather I will do what is right and good."

After Bobby's reconciliation, the group rolled into their sleeping blankets and slept soundly throughout the night. By morning a misty rain cast a mood of despair over the travelers.

As they mounted their horses, a downpour soaked the group. Not having a better alternative, they decided to follow the trog army. Topple assumed the trogs would not have scouts watching the rear flank. Everybody, except the wizard, was hesitant as they rode off the hill, through the trog campsite and followed the wagon tracks.

In spite of the rain, Topple's mood had changed from serious to merry. He seemed oblivious to trogs, danger or wet clothes. He whistled, sang and made constant comments about the beauty of the new day. Several times he stopped his horse, looked into the distance and chuckled.

He finally said, "The stupidity of the trogs is no match for the beauty of this fine rainy day. Oh yes, faith in the Source of Life is like standing on the security of a rock; so let us go forth and sing a song of joy. Did you hear the story about the warrior's mouse who could not find his tail? He forgot to cover his rear. Ah! Ah! Ah! Zippy do, Zippy do, a path to do, to do a step in time. Not to do ahead or hind, but now to do, do in time. Ah! Ah! Ah!"

Topple continued all morning with a constant barrage of songs, verses and stories. Topple's infectious joy almost made the misery of traveling on a wet day a pleasant experience.

By the end of the day, the rain had decreased and signs of the trog army were increasing. The litter of animal waste and garbage left the foul scent of corruption. The forest was unnaturally quiet and devoid of life. It was as if the birds and other animals were hiding from an unknown predator. The haunting silence added to the aura of gloom dishonoring the beauty of nature.

Topple was the only individual not influenced by the oppressive sense of defilement covering the forest. Over the centuries the wizard had learned to focus his full attention on the Master of Life. His trust in divine providence offered him the peace to face problems with confidence, even joy. Unfortunately, he was alone in this. Not even Topple's stories and songs could dispel the sense of collective oppression.

The wizard only compounded the distress by stating, "We have been detected. Our presence has penetrated the fog of evil blanketing the area. We have disrupted the vibrations of hatred that energize the trog army. A search party has been sent to find us. It will be easy for them to detect our aura. I have neglected to cover our presence with a shield."

The negative mood of the group was openly revealed by his revelation. The group's sense of misery hit Topple like a hard punch. He commented to them, "I have the feeling each of you is being poisoned by Crossmore. Peace is a fruit growing from the stability of faith. You can look to the Tree of Life or be held captive by the power of doubt. What do your choose? Remember, choice determines destiny."

Screaming voices in the distance interrupted the quiet of the night. Each member of the group suddenly felt like a forest rabbit being hunted by a lion. Topple shouted, "Release the horses and only take what you absolutely need. The chase has begun. I can use magic to hide our goodness from the eyes of evil, but we must use wilderness tricks to hide our physical scent."

Topple spent the night leading his companions southwest toward the mountains. They walked up the middle of a bubbling stream flowing from the west. Then they went over a rocky ridge top and passed an open meadow into a steep walled channel. The bottom of the gully looked as if a flood had recently washed it clear of everything except a floor of river rocks. Topple led the group up the gully several thousand strides; then they walked back down the middle of the creek flowing through the narrow gorge. The light of the moon helped them find footing in the rugged terrain.

When the sun rose in the east, Topple led the group into a densely forested area. They found shelter under the cover of a thick canopy of trees. The sound of the pursuing trogs had disappeared. The demand for sleep became paramount as each person drifted into a restless slumber.

At midmorning the companions awoke to the sound of Topple's voice. The wizard said, "We have caused a real stir in the mind of Crossmore. I have decided to confront him as he searches for answers to our mystery."

Hilda responded, "Come off it, little brother. Crossmore will most certainly discover our location. I do not think this would be wise?"

The wizard smiled, "You under estimate my powers, ancient sister. This will be most entertaining."

Topple sat on the ground with his back to a small tree. As he shut his eyes, a deep state of calm encompassed his mind. He spoke into the dark void of his thoughts. In a deep solemn voice he said, "Crossmore, someday you will pay for your sins. Your evil ways are injecting hatred into the Empire. Go away!"

Crossmore's reaching-hand appeared in Topple's vision. Crossmore, with an enticing voice, said, "You humor me, little jester. Your comedy makes me laugh with the delight of a child at play. You have taken advantage of my good nature for the last time. My generosity has been wounded by your lack of compassion. It is not I who brings wickedness into the Empire, but you. You are creating disharmony by going against the established order. Give up your foolishness. I invite you to combine forces with me. Together we will have great power."

Topple smiled saying, "The joke is on you. You will be consumed by your counterfeit ideas. The poison of your words will return to you as total barrenness."

Crossmore answered, "My old friend, you speak with vacant words and tired ideas. My power fills me to the brim with exaltation. We must talk about reality, not philosophical jargon. I have the power. I have the hand of destiny."

Topple did not answer, but cut off communications with Crossmore. As he ended this encounter, he felt the presence of another person growing in his mind. Through a dense fog he detected Coaldon sitting on a rocky dome in bright sunlight. Topple reached out to touch Coaldon, but only found the emptiness of an impenetrable mist. When anxiety flooded him, he decided to end his reflection.

He opened his eyes to find his companions looking at him in bewilderment. He discovered that both of his visions burst into reality at the same. To their right, Crossmore stood before them with a troop of trogs. To their left Coaldon sat on the rocky dome looking at them with an inquisitive expression. In disbelief, Topple's companions pointed at Coaldon in wonderment. The group's attention quickly shifted to Crossmore as he started to rush toward them. As Topple jumped to his feet he pointed his hand at Crossmore. A blinding flash of light shot out of Topple's hand, surrounding Crossmore in a raging orange flame. The blaze was so intense Crossmore and the trogs dissolved into thin air. Both visions vanished into the bright sunlight of the afternoon sun.

In sarcasm, Hilda erupted, "Well, great wizard, what did you accomplish? That was stupid. You have made things worse. Next time think before you endanger us."

In false humility the wizard responded, "You are right. I am sorry, but wasn't it a grand show."

He continued, "I used more power than expected. I need to rest, but we cannot wait. We must leave immediately. I believe it best for us to return to the road and follow the army. That will be the last place they will look for us."

Dark Storm Clouds

It was dark when Coaldon arrived at the dwarf campsite. The light of flickering fires spread across a large meadow. He knew his friends would be on the southwest corner of the encampment. As Coaldon walked through the sea of tents, he detected a change in the mood of the dwarves. The aura of the silent camp had the subtle feeling of anticipation and tension. He was greeted by his companions with words of welcome and unspoken looks of curiosity.

For a long time he sat next to the fire without speaking.

Finally, he said, "The trogs are only three or four days behind us. We will need to prepare for war."

Pacer responded, "I think it is important to meet with the War Council this evening."

Earthkin injected, "I will talk with Rolfe, immediately."

It was not long before they heard footsteps approaching the camp. When the members of the Council appeared, the shimmering light of the campfire illuminated their grim faces with an eerie cast of foreboding.

In a gruff voice Rolfe stated, "Coaldon, we have waited for your return. Earthkin relayed your message about the approaching trog army. What have you learned today?"

Coaldon looked into the eyes of each dwarf before responding, "I have confirmed a large trog army is rapidly approaching from the north. We either find a place to defend ourselves, or be destroyed. This may sound bleak, but it is the truth. Earthkin told us about a deep, narrow canyon several days march south of here. This location might be an ideal place to build a defensive perimeter. At this point we do not have many choices, so I propose we accept Earthkin's suggestion. Further, I advise we divide the community into two groups. One group will rush ahead at a quick march and prepare the canyon for battle. The other group will set a slower pace to meet the needs of the noncombatants. A small contingent of warriors should stay with the slower group"

Rolfe responded, "When we decided to travel to Rockham, I never thought we would face such danger. Yet, I know we must be positive. Self pity will only limit our potential to survive. A vision of success will create the power for victory."

He continued, "Well, what should we do?"

The members proceeded to discuss the strengths and weaknesses of Coaldon's plan. After a full debate Rolfe called for a vote. Coaldon's plan was accepted with hesitation. They felt their small world was slowly being torn apart.

Rolfe declared, "Turrock, Earthkin and Ripsnout will lead the advanced force. I will guide the slower group. I will call a meeting of the community tonight to share our decision. The advance party will leave at sunrise tomorrow. May the One Presence be with us."

Later that evening a drum roll called the dwarves together for a meeting. Rolfe stood before the gathering with an air of confidence and determination. In a strong voice he declared, "The trog army is fast approaching us from the north. We are in great danger. Our only hope is to defend ourselves in the tradition of our great history. The council has decided to build a fortification in a narrow canyon several days south of here. It will be necessary to split the community into two groups. The warriors will go ahead to build a wall, while the remaining community will follow. We will only succeed if each of us makes the needed sacrifices. Be strong like the rock of your bones."

The revelation sent a surge of apprehension through the community. Yet, the dwarves were quick at finding the inner strength to be resilient. Their conquest of previous challenges had hardened their character and filled them with determination. The following morning each group assumed its new responsibilities without question. Coaldon, Brother Patrick, Pacer and Earthkin were assigned to go with the advanced group.

Noel protested not being included in the lead party. She proclaimed, "I believe I can do more good by helping the advanced group."

Pacer responded to her, "We will need to travel light and fast. Be ready for a tough go."

With a gleam of fortitude, she stated, "I can do it! It maybe a difficult task for a soft palace dweller, but I am ready for the challenge."

Pacer followed, "We are concerned about your endurance, but if you can bear the physical stress, please join us."

The lead party traveled at a quick march for 12 hours. After a short sleep break, they continued their trek without stopping until they reached the canyon. It took 24 hours for the lead party to complete the trip. Several times during the long trek, Noel wondered why she considered going, yet her fortitude helped her endure the demands of the expedition. With pride and sore feet, she walked into the canyon with the large troop of warriors. Her accomplishment was admired by her traveling companions.

Upon arriving in the canyon, the army surveyed the area to determine what needed to be done to build an adequate defensive fortification. The warriors divided into three teams to construct the barrier. The teams rotated their activities between rest, sleep and work. Their strength and willpower could be measured by the rapid construction of a stone barricade. The high, stone wall was built across the narrowest section of the canyon. Ramparts provided protection, while allowing the warriors room to fight. Large stones were lifted into place to form an intricately designed wall. The outside of the wall was relatively smooth, allowing few hand holds. Even though the wall was hastily built, it demonstrated the dwarves' innate ability to work with stone. The dwarves believed the wall would withstand the assault of many attacks.

Noel realized she was not physically ready to carry large, heavy rocks. Wisely, she chose to gather supplies to make weapons. Using a sharp sword, she cut and stripped the bark from piles of long, straight hardwood branches needed to make spears and arrows.

The wall was not their only line of defense. The river on the north end of the fortification flowed brim full with cold spring runoff. The trogs' fear of water would stop them from using the river to attack the dwarves. The sheer cliff, on the south end of the wall, created a natural barrier. After forty eight hours of continuous labor, the wall was completed with a small passageway in the center, allowing the dwarves to enter and exit the canyon. The passage would be closed when the battle began.

The final activity was to make extra weapons for the battle. Under Noel's direction, the warriors gathered thousands of branches from hardwood trees to make weapons. Little time was wasted in transforming the raw wood into lethal weaponry.

Finally, Ripsnout and Turrock granted the warriors a well deserved rest in anticipation of the battle. Scouts were sent out in all directions to detect unusual activities in the area. While the dwarves worked in the canyon, they kept an uneasy eye on the black war eagles flying in lazy circles overhead. Only Coaldon knew the real importance of the eagles. The dwarves also noticed Coaldon would leave his work group and then return several hours later. The warriors were curious about his strange behavior.

Yet, they had little time to think about such a minor detail.

As warriors rested, Coaldon sat on a tall rocky knoll in full view of the camp. The warm afternoon sun massaged everyone's tired bodies into a sleepy state of relaxation.

The camp suddenly came to full alert when a large shadow passed overhead. The warriors leaped to their feet ready for action. A magnificent war eagle flew low over the camp and landed on the knoll with Coaldon. With astonishment, the dwarves watched Coaldon and the giant eagle talk. Coaldon reacted to the eagle's message with excitement.

When the great eagle flew away, Coaldon ran down the hill and into camp, yelled, "To arms! To arms! The slow group is only six hours' march from here. The front of the trog army has almost caught up with them. We must take immediate action."

The sound of a horn echoed around the canyon as the warriors gathered their weapons, put on protective leather armor and formed fighting units. The muster only took minutes. At Turrock's command, the dwarf army ran out of the canyon in an orderly, disciplined manner.

Noel decided to stay in the canyon and prepare for the arrival of the clan. As she watched the warriors leave the canyon, she realized they were a deadly fighting machine. The dwarves inner strength and confidence would create fear in the hearts of any opponent. She noticed that superiority radiated from the very center of their souls. In her thoughts she described the warriors as a lethal-surge-of-destructive power.

It only took three hours of running for the warriors to reach the front line of the slow group. The warriors did not pause to talk, but maintained their quick march to reach the end of the procession. Coaldon noticed the members of the slow group were at the end of their endurance. Slumped shoulders and pale faces told of their desperate situation.

As the warriors reached the end of the line, they could hear the shouts from the trog army. The dwarf army advanced until they reached a dense growth of trees and underbrush. At Turrock's command the army dissolved into the forest, setting a deadly ambush. The long line of dwarves hidden on both sides of the road would attack the unsuspecting trogs with demoralizing violence. In the evening light a large group of trogs and geks came into view. Blood lust forced the evil army to look toward the fleeing prey, not to the side of the road.

The piercing sound of a horn sounded when the front units of the trog army entered into the ambush zone. The first unit of dwarf warriors rushed forward, throwing spears into the startled throng of trogs. The wedge shaped lines of the attacking dwarves pinched the trog army into a churning mass of confusion. The second unit of dwarves formed a line behind the spear brigade. Upon command, they released a cloud of arrows into the confused trog army. The destruction of the trogs was massive. The cries of misery grew into a roar of agony.

The last unit of dwarves to attack carried long, sharp pikes. The first two attack lines parted, allowing the pike brigade to rush forward. With the pikes held in a horizontal position the warriors attacked directly into the center of the trog army. After the initial attack, this unit retreated twenty strides and attack again, driving the long pikes into the panicked trog soldiers. Upon command, the pike unit again retreated twenty strides and held its position. The spear unit then passed through the pike line attacking the trogs with swords. The archers continued to shoot arrows into the center of the trog army with care not to hit a dwarf swordsman. The sudden and lethal attack by the dwarves was so effective the front edge of the trog army retreated in panic and disarray. The geks lost control of the fleeing herd of desperate trogs. The battlefield was littered with the wounded bodies. The black cloud of death covered the area with a foul odor of wretchedness. The geks offered no assistance to the wounded trogs.

At the sound of a horn, the dwarves stopped their attack and retreated toward the procession of noncombatants. The dwarves learned from past experience that fighting 100 to 1 odds was an exercise in futility. It was necessary to use the weaknesses of the beasts to their advantage. They knew trogs were slow witted beasts. Therefore, the dwarves developed a fighting strategy based on lightning fast, surprise attacks. After inflecting maximum damage, the warriors would then retreat from a battle before the trogs had the opportunity to reorganize their massive army. This battle would go down in the history books as the Battle of the Exodus. The Four-Line-Attack-Method, developed by the dwarves, had never been seen by the military officers of the Empire. Many commanders would use this attack strategy in later centuries.

After retreating from the battle scene, the dwarf warriors were not concerned about the trogs' being able to organize for a counter attack. It would take at least half a day for the geks to round up trogs from their hiding places in the forest. When the dwarf soldiers caught up with the slower group, they provided a rear guard. It was midnight before they arrived at the fortified canyon. The long procession of dwarves filed into the canyon in a haphazard manner. The hole in the wall was filled with large stones and guards stationed on the wall. The turmoil of the battle and escape had created a high stress level within the dwarf community. After satisfying their immediate needs, the emotionally charged dwarves talked late into the night. As the emotional energy drained from their bodies, a quiet atmosphere of sleep finally shrouded the camp.

The confined area of the narrow canyon provided the community with a sense of security. They found it uncomfortable to be surrounded by open space. Dwarves found security in the protection of their tunnels.

The new day greeted the community with bright sunshine and a gentle morning breeze. Even though the dwarves faced immediate danger, a casual environment permeated the campsite. Dwarves leisurely strolled through the camp performing their usual chores. It was midday before they were ready to prepare for war.

When the community gathered for a meeting, the warm afternoon sun showered down on the assembly. Green grass and leaves provided a pleasant backdrop.

The community became quiet as Rolfe stood up. He declared, "We must be thankful for our narrow escape yesterday. Yet, our focus must not be on yesterday, but today. We will soon be fighting a battle that will determine our very existence. Each of you will be given duties to perform before, during and after each battle. Dwarves will be wounded and dwarves will die, but this must be expected. Your courage is an important part of our success."

Rolfe dismissed the assembly with his personal blessing.

The camp became a beehive of activities. Assignments were handed out, and the preparations for war began. Coaldon and Noel did not approach the wall until late afternoon. The brother and sister did not want to view the opposing army until they had time to reconcile their own feelings. With reluctance they walked up the steps leading to the rampart and stood overlooking the open expanse of land to the east.

The area, in front of the canyon mouth, had been a broad meadow of green, lush grass surrounded by dense forest. With a gasp, both Noel and Coaldon were speechless at what they saw. The beautiful meadow was blackened and corrupted by swarms of trogs moving like a disturbed ant hill. During the past 18 hours the meadow became the center of the trogs' universe.

The individual units of the trog army were organized around a regimental flag and tent. Geks, with whips, drove the trogs in what seemed like a maddening exercise in orchestrated turmoil. Directly in the center of the war camp sat a large drum surrounded by a small group of geks wearing yellow robes. The Royal Gek, wearing a purple robe, walked around the drum in a stately manner. The beast finally stopped, pointing its arm toward the war drum. Using two large clubs, a gek started pounding the drum at a fast tempo. Without hesitation, individual regiments of the trog army rushed to form rank and stood at attention in front of their company flags.

When the drum stopped beating, the trogs and geks fell to their knees and bowed their heads to the ground. The Royal Gek began to rant and rave in a loud voice, using dramatic body gestures. Upon finishing its speech, the beast entered a large black tent in the middle of the encampment. When the Royal Gek disappeared into the tent, the drummer began to pound the drum at a slow steady rhythm. At this signal, the trogs dispersed to their regimental campsites.

The sun was setting in the west when Coaldon and Noel withdrew their attention from the activities of the trog army. The captivating events of the enemy's camp had an over powering effect on them. They realized the conquest of Crossmore was a challenge requiring the combined efforts of many people.

The war drum boomed all night long. The constant beat had an unsettling effect on the dwarf community. Within two weeks the clan had gone from the familiarity of their Homekeep into a noisy, chaotic war zone. After a lifetime of quiet existence in the bowels of the Sadden Mountains the constant throbbing of the drum was disturbing. The morning greeted the haggard faced dwarves with a seemingly impossible task - survival. Yet, hope characterized the faith of the community.

In preparing for war, some people made arrows, other shaped spears, still others made bandages for the wounded. Strong women carried rocks to the top of the wall to be thrown as weapons. Several husky women volunteered to work on the wall during the battles.

Midmorning, the drumbeats stopped and an uneasy silence filled the area. After a long pause, it started to beat at a fast tempo. This created a nauseating sense of anticipation in the dwarf community. The trogs started to scream in what seemed to be an endless assault on the minds of the dwarves. From the top of the wall, the warriors watched as the trogs formed attack units. The narrow canyon would only allow small strike units to fight in the canyon. Additional trog assault units waited in line ready to take their turn in attacking the fortified wall.

When the drum beat increased to a steady roll, the first unit of trogs attacked. They rushed up the narrow canyon with a single minded purpose to kill and destroy. As the enemy approached the wall, dwarf archers mowed down the first row of trogs like a blade cutting through grass. Before the first assault unit arrived at the wall, it disappeared into a cloud of black smoke. This method of attack went on for hours. Unit after unit of trogs stormed the wall, causing little damage to the dwarf defenders.

At mid-afternoon the drummers returned to a slow beat, indicating the end of the attack. The canyon entrance was clouded with the black smoke of death. As the dwarves evaluated the results of the day, they took no pride in their success. They knew the trog army was only testing their defenses. The death of a trog meant nothing to the geks. Every trog would be sacrificed to destroy the dwarves.

The dwarves spent the rest of the evening preparing for the following day. After a restless night, the community was ready to face another day of fighting. The trogs attacked at sunrise with a new strategy. Rows of trog archers, without shields, formed lines in front of the wall and began shooting arrows at the dwarves standing on the wall. In return, the dwarf archers shot a steady stream of arrows at the defenseless trogs. The dwarves' effectiveness was greatly limited because of their need to stand behind large war shields. The dwarf archers were forced to shoot arrows from around the corners of the shields, thereby reducing their accuracy.

Dwarves who carried supplies to the warriors on the wall used shields to protect themselves from the lethal barrage of arrows. The trog archery assault lasted an hour before the infantry units began their attack. At the command of the gek masters, the trog foot soldiers rushed at the wall in unending rows. The strategy of using arrows and infantry at the same time had a devastating effect on the dwarves' defenses. Their need to protect themselves from the arrows, plus defend against trogs climbing over the wall was nearly impossible. Many times trogs used ladders to reach the top of the wall before they were turned back by the heroic efforts of the dwarves. At noon the trog army retreated to its campsites in an orderly manner. The ground in front of the wall was littered with the garbage of war. The air was rank with the foul stench of evil.

Leaving three sentinels on the wall, the exhausted dwarf warriors staggered into the camp. Eight dwarves died from battle wounds, but countless more had cuts and abrasions needing immediate care. After receiving medical attention and a hot meal, the warriors rested for several hours.

The next attack came late in the afternoon. For two hours the trogs assaulted the dwarves with arrows and infantry. At dark the trog army was summoned back to their camp. The dwarves did not suffer a single casualty in the afternoon fighting, but were faced with a dwindling supply of weapons and reduced man power due to the wounded warriors.

Again, several guards were stationed on the wall while the warriors returned to camp for medical care and food. The violence of war created a depressing mood in the community. After the warriors had time to rest, a council of war was held. The moonless sky was a blanket of stars, when the members of the war council met around a blazing fire to discuss their plan of action.

Coaldon began the conversation, "Why don't the trogs fight at night? They would have a distinct advantage."

Pacer responded, "There are several reasons. First, trogs have poor night vision. It would be difficult for them to see the battle field in the dark. Second, the trogs and geks are arrogant. This is a cat and mouse game to them. They expect an easy victory."

In a more serious vain, Rolfe stated, "Even though we have destroyed regiment after regiment of trogs, they just keep coming with no end in sight. Our strength is limited and our ability to fight is waning."

The council members sat around the fire watching Rolfe.

Finally Earthkin said, "We must not lose hope. Even though the situation looks impossible, we must maintain faith."

Turrock added, "I suggest we transfer our attention from doubt to success."

Rolfe closed his eyes to clear his mind from the violent images of war.

He stated, "I agree. My mind is still running on the tension of the day. In fifteen minutes we will declare a time of meditation. Everybody, including children will spend an hour creating positive thoughts about our future."

When the community focused their thoughts on success, there was an obvious change in the camp atmosphere. The dwarves fell asleep with an attitude of positive expectation for the following day.

The war drum greeted the dwarf community with another day of war, death and bravery. The trog archers once again formed their ranks and began to shoot arrows at the wall. The trogs were not skilled at archery, but rather compensated by shooting a large numbers of arrows. Volume, not accuracy, was their method of winning a battle. The assault by the archers was once again followed by the attack by the infantry. The trog army intensified their attack by forcing more regiments to rush the wall. The larger number of trogs assaulting the wall forced the dwarves to push their endurance to the maximum. Time and time again, the trogs were on the verge of over running the wall when the dwarves rallied to push them back. During this attack ten dwarves died with many more warriors being wounded. The number of defenders on the wall had dwindled. Several women filled combat positions on the wall. Using swords, they attacked trogs trying to crawl over the wall. The warm noon sun did not offer any encouragement to the weary defensive force.

The trogs pulled back to their campsites to regroup during mid-afternoon. The once powerful dwarf soldiers were at the end of their endurance.

Coaldon considered using the power of his sword to strike a blow at the royal gek, but decided to wait for the appropriate time. For the present, he would depend on conventional fighting skills.

The defenders staggered off the wall happy to still be alive. After a brief meal, most soldiers collapsed on the ground and immediately fell asleep.

The beating of the war drums increased during late afternoon, indicating a new assault was imminent. The dwarf militia, with depleted ranks, once again mounted the wall. Before the army attacked, the trogs and geks stood out of archery range taunting the dwarves with laughter, jeers and screams.

With a taste of victory on their lips they began to chant, "Your end is near! You will die! Your end is near! You will die!"

The trogs increased the speed of the chant until they were at an emotional frenzy. With the archers leading the attack, the narrow canyon was once again clogged with a massive assault by the trog infantry.

The trogs were determined to make this the last attack on the dwarves. Total destruction was the vision energizing the trog army to batter the wall like an angry tidal wave. The attack pushed such a large number of trogs at the wall they literally stood on each other trying to reach the top of the barrier.

Many women mounted the wall to replace the dwindling number of warriors.

Standing shoulder to shoulder with the warriors, the women fought with a courage honoring their dwarf heritage. The dwarves pushed trog after trog off the wall until their bodies ached with fatigue. They finally understood their end was drawing near. Only a miracle could save them from the unending number of trogs marching up the canyon.

A Reunion

Topple, Hilda, Bobby and the two apprentices traveled several days without encountering the trogs. The group found it necessary to set a fast pace to keep up with the advancing army. Topple had the haunting feeling they would soon be plagued by trogs. Yet, the wizard's perpetual smile and positive attitude did not betray any sense of concern.

After several days travel, Topple felt guided to leave the road and hike along the east slopes of the mountains. The members of the group were happy to leave behind the foul remains and odor of the trogs. On the evening after leaving the road, they set up camp in a thick grove of trees. After the others had gone to sleep, Topple and Hilda sat next to the campfire in a state of readiness. Both of them received a premonition that something unusual was going to happen during the night. They looked into the fire waiting for a mysterious revelation to unfold.

While sitting in quiet anticipation, they listened to the sounds of the night.

In a soft voice Topple reflected, "It is interesting how the power of life provided the energy to feed the perpetual restlessness of nature. Life is constantly striving to fulfill the imprinted need to survive."

Hilda followed, "I often feel this throb of nature. It seems I have spent most of my life waiting to find answers to unknown questions. I guess tonight is no different. Each moment provides the next piece in the giant puzzle of my life. I believe we can only enjoy the beauty of life right now. Yesterday's beauty is too late; Tomorrow's is too early."

As Topple and Hilda sat in front of the fire, they allowed the sights, sounds and smells of life to caress their spirits into a peaceful harmony with their surroundings. In the distance a sound interrupted the events of the night. This noise caused the shy forest animals to pause in quiet respect for the approaching being. The soft steps of a two legged creature approached the campsite in steady, unhurried strides. Topple realized this sudden silence meant the new arrival had gained the sympathy of the forest creatures.

A shadow glided from the underbrush and stood directly in front of them. The flickering light of the fire exposed a withered old man with a long gray beard who was dressed in an old tattered black robe. The hood of the robe mysteriously hid the face of their visitor. From under his hood, two sad haunting eyes probed the very souls of Topple and Hilda. Without moving the old man stood like a statue watching them. The presence of many centuries resonated through him. The piercing eyes of the old man finally came to rest on Topple. The eyes did not reveal anger but rather an unfulfilled plea for help. The wizard had the impression the stranger's body only covered his emptiness. This person was the hollow remains of a once powerful individual.

In a gentle tone, Topple said, "Greetings, my friend. Please join us at our campsite. We offer you a meal and the warmth of our fire."

Like a thought searching for a way to speak, the old man only stood gazing at Topple. As the man watched, Topple cooked a small pot of trail food and dried fruit into an aromatic meal. He handed a bowl of the hot meal to their guest. The old man took the dish and rapidly consumed the meal without hesitation or waste. He held the bowl in his hand without knowing what to do with it. Hilda reached out, took it from him and touched the person with a gentle, caring caress. Hilda's touch created a ripple through the man as if a powerful need had been satisfied.

The more Topple watched the man the more his curiosity became aroused. As he considered this strange event, the wizard became aware of an unusual pulsation coming from his travel pouch. He had forgotten about Coaldon's Gem of Watching. He tossed it into his travel pouch upon leaving Neverly. He pulled the Gem out of the pouch and held it up to the firelight. The Gem had an uncharacteristic red tint and vibrated in rapid motion. Not knowing what to do with the Gem, Topple was about to put it away when Hilda grabbed his arm.

She suggested, "Why don't we invite Cando to join us. He has been stowed away for a long time. He might enjoy an escape from the Gem."

Topple held the Gem in the air, requesting, "Cando, please join us!"

Cando erupted from the Gem in an explosion of multi-colored sparks. He circled the camp in wide loops and erupted into a loud burst of laughter. Looking at the old man in disbelief, Cando floated over the fire creating a luminous image of shimmering radiance through his ghostly shape. An energy source inside of Cando's spirit grew into an expanding throb. The glow from the campfire was amplified through Cando's vaporous spirit into a dazzling, bright light. As this power expanded in Cando, the old man's eyes turned bright red. The light from his eyes were so intense Topple and Hilda could see the features of his bearded face under the cover of his hood. With increasing intensity, flashes of electrical energy shot back and forth between Cando and the old man. The surge of power was climaxed when a brilliant burst of lightning shot into the night sky. A loud clap of thunder echoed in the rocky valley when Cando and the old man were united into one being. The evil magic separating Cando's body from his spirit collapsed releasing a powerful blast of energy. Cando the Wizard was once again whole and fully present in the world.

The three sleeping companions were awakened by the commotion. They joined Topple and Hilda to watch Cando's reunion. They observed this blessed event with astonishment. They were delighted when the new Cando began to dance around the campsite in uncoordinated leaps of joyful celebration. As he stumbled around the camp he threw his arms into the air and shouted meaningless phrases at the top of his voice. When he finally saw Topple, he tackled him with a hug of joy. As Cando's energy drained away, the excitement of the moment shifted into serenity. At the conclusion of his last explosion of celebration, the old wizard fell to the ground in exhaustion.

Cando never raised his head but drifted into deep sleep. At this point Topple said, "We are again in trouble. The energy released by Cando's reunion has attracted the attention of many creatures in the area, including the geks. It will only be a short time before representatives from the trog army will pay us an official visit."

Hilda responded, "I suggest we ask Cando for assistance. His body has lived in this area for a long time. Maybe he can guide us to safety."

They allowed Cando to sleep for an hour before Hilda awoke him with a gentle nudge. He opened his eyes, looked around and sat up with a surprised reaction. It would take time for the two entities of Cando to learn to work together.

Topple said, "Cando, my old friend, we need your help. The trogs will be searching for the source of the energy surge. Do you know of a way we can escape?"

Cando was quiet as he considered the question. After what seemed a long time, he responded, "I never imagined I would ever be made whole again. Thank you for your help in completing this most special event."

Topple nodded, saying, "It is our pleasure to assist you. This event has been written in the Books of Time. We did our part in fulfilling your destiny."

Cando replied, "My body has roamed these mountains for centuries. All these years the wood elves and animals of the forest have protected and fed me. This area is my home. I know its many secrets. I find the invasion of the trogs a violation of nature's beauty and sacredness."

After a pause he continued, "Yes, I will help you. We can use a long forgotten tunnel both to escape and to take you to the dwarves. I watched the trogs chase them into a canyon. I can take you to the dwarf community if you desire."

Topple nodded in agreement as he responded, "We accept your generous offer.

We must hurry if we are to escape from the trogs."

Cando moved and thought in disjointed confusion as he learned to function again as a whole being. It took several minutes of walking before he regained his coordination. At first the group had to travel slowly because of darkness. They were happy when the moon crested in the east, offering a soft, pale light to guide their steps. Cando led the group up a wide valley and then into the rocky gorge on the northern slope of the mountain. The sound of Trog voices in the distance helped motivate the group to walk faster. The light of a new day revealed a ravine blocked by a massive landslide. Cando did not hesitate as he guided the group through a maze of twists and turns into the tower of jumbled rocks. The opening to a tunnel appeared before them after they passed between two tall pillars of jagged stones. The shouts of trog voices could now be heard clearly. It would only be moments before they would be attacked.

As the last of the group entered the tunnel, a large gek followed by many trogs ran toward the tunnel entrance. Topple turned to see the trogs only a few steps behind him. With a twinkle in his eye, Topple raised his hand and released a surge of magic. The leading gek suddenly ran head long into an invisible barrier. The trogs following the gek piled on top of their leader creating havoc.

Topple quietly said, "Go away. Please do not bother us. We are on a walk in the woods looking for mushrooms. You are causing us much distress."

Throwing trogs in all directions the gek erupted from the ground. The beast spoke in a voice of supplication, "Lord Crossmore, I have your enemies trapped in a tunnel. I need your help to capture them."

In an instant, a black cloud fell from the sky forming into the image of Crossmore. As Crossmore raised his hand to release a blast of magic, Cando pulled a large rock from the tunnel entrance. A rumbling avalanche sealed the tunnel entrance. Many years ago, Cando discovered that the original inhabitance has built this defense. By pulling out the rock, an avalanche would seal the tunnel.

The group could feel the searing heat of Crossmore's magic trying to penetrate the rock barrier. Topple laughed in glee knowing Crossmore had once again failed to destroy them. The wizard could feel the fury of Crossmore's frustration and rage.

The group sat in the tunnel to catch their breaths before starting their underworld journey. Prior to beginning the trek, Cando handed each person several torches to be used during the hike. The rest of the day they walked through a seemingly unending series of well constructed tunnels. Cando did not slow his pace for the next twelve hours. As the members of the group passed countless junctions and corners, they became disoriented. Topple was the only member of the group who enjoyed the journey. He viewed each new passageway as if it were a new and exciting adventure.

Hours passed into hours, with mind boggling boredom. It was impossible to measure the passage of time in the blackness of the tunnel. When the end seemed unattainable, a faint light appeared in the tunnel ahead of them. The light grew in brightness as they approached the opening. The group greeted the smell of fresh air with happiness and relief. The entrance to the tunnel was well hidden within a dense grove of trees. As the travelers stepped out of the cave, they heard the distant screams of death, the rapid beat of a war drum and yells of fighting men. Hilda, Bobby and the two apprentices ran down the narrow canyon to discover the source of the noise.

Looking at the unusual characteristics of the landscape, Topple and Cando leisurely walked down the canyon. As the two wizards approached the battle scene, they stopped to observe the events unfolding before them. They saw tired, bloodied dwarves and humans pushing an endless stream of trogs off the wall. As Coaldon fought the unrelenting waves of the adversary, he felt the presence of Topple behind him. He turned to see Topple nonchalantly waving at him. Coaldon did not have time to wave back because several trogs were ready to scramble over the top of the wall.

Topple cocked his head to one side and said to Cando, "Let's have some fun. We need to teach the trogs some manners. It is not polite to interrupt people when they are greeting each other."

Topple and Cando casually strolled up the stairs and peered over the edge of the wall into the frantic faces of the trogs. Around the two wizards the dwarves grunted and groaned as they fought off the never ending rush of trogs.

Topple said to Cando, "I think it is time for the dwarves to take a rest. They look tired. These trogs are not playing fair."

Both wizards raised their hands in the air, pointed at the black tent in the middle of the enemy's encampment and released bolts of lightning. As the searing heat of the lightning hit the tent, it vanished into a cloud of smoke. When the tent dissolved, the trog army stopped advancing. Topple and Cando destroyed the Royal Gek who controlled the collective minds of the trogs. The battle stopped as the trogs stood staring at the dwarves on the wall. They moved in a random order waiting for a command to tell them what to do. The geks realized it was worthless to try to motivate the trogs until a new commander had gained power. Topple knew a new royal gek would assume control after a short period of infighting among the geks.

The dwarves stood in awe at the blast of energy from Topple and Cando. The appearance of the wizards offered the dwarves a new mystery to comprehend. It was not enough to be dislocated; but now they also had seen the power of magic for the first time. The dwarves did not know if they should be afraid or celebrate. The answer to this riddle would need to wait because survival was on the top of their agenda. They needed time to regroup before the next assault.

Resolution

The violent sounds of war gave way to an eerie calm. The war drum was quiet. The trog army had stopped its attack. The two wizards were the sources of the Royal Geks destruction.

The dwarf defenders stared in disbelief at Cando and Topple. It was only in children's stories that any reference had been made to wizards. The dwarves thought the stories of these robed masters of magic were only fantasies. Now standing among them were two jolly wizards. With radiant happiness, Topple and Cando walked along the rampart shaking hands with the dwarves and joking about the immobile trogs.

There was a warm reunion between Topple and his long lost companions.

Topple chuckled before saying, "Gentleman, you look pathetic. You are just too serious about your work. I recommend you get more bed rest, eat better food, drink more water and get involved in a good hobby. By the way, have you noticed the trogs in front of the wall? I do not approve of their rude attitudes. I must teach them better manners."

Even though Topple was tired from his use of magic, he still had the energy to share his exuberance for life. As he stood on the wall, he waved at the gek master. His big smile and excited waves caused a group of geks to rush the wall in a frenzy. With a twinkle in his eyes, Topple made a sweep of his arm toward the geks. A small burst of blue flame shot out of the wizard's fingers hitting each gek on the forehead. The flames rolled around the geks' heads tattooing their faces with bright, colorful bands of flowers. The terrified geks stood transfixed in fear as fireballs shot down their arms and blasted out their finger tips. In panic, the geks ran through the throngs of trogs. The grim faces of the dwarves awoke into broad smiles as they watched the frantic geks disappear into the distance.

Topple turned to Cando saying, "I am hungry! Let's go find some food."

With a nonchalant attitude, Topple and Cando strolled off the wall and into the dwarf community. By nature Topple was more out going than Cando. As Topple walked through the community, he greeted each person with a warm smile and handshake. According to Topple, nobody was a stranger. At first the dwarves were restrained, tending to shy away from the strange individuals who commanded lighting. The children were the first to warm up to his outgoing personality. Then, like the breaching of a dam, the whole community opened their hearts to Topple's positive and joyous celebration of life. The dark cloud of gloom and despair hanging over the dwarf community began to vanish as Topple shared his joy in life.

After a hearty meal, the population gathered around a warm, inviting fire. The first event of the evening was to mourn and bury the bodies of warriors dying in battle. A time of silence was declared; several speeches were made; and the bodies were buried under a rocky ledge. It was the tradition of the dwarves to bury their dead under the protection of solid rock. The ceremony provided a time for the dwarves to honor the sacrifices of the deceased and to band together in a common goal, the survival of the clan.

When the dwarves returned to the common fire pit, Topple pulled out his flute and played a series of sacred songs. The beauty of Topple's music helped transform the mood of the dwarves from a feeling of grief to an occasion of acceptance. The focus of the community shifted from pain to hope. Their faith in the One Presence was more than an acceptance of ideas, but also a claim to the promises of trust and peace.

Topple ended his impromptu concert with an ancient dwarf song about two lovers who were reunited after a time of pain, separation and war. The music helped release the tensions caused by the violent events of the day.

Rolfe stated, "It is time to rest and sleep. Tomorrow we must once again prove our right to exist. I want to have a short meeting with the War Council after this assembly is dismissed. I declare this gathering full and whole. Good night."

The members of the Council of War crowded closely together near the fire in an attempt to keep their conversation private. There was no reason to burden the community with the grim realities the Council needed to debate.

Rolfe said, "The arrival of Topple and Cando has given us hope for another day. We now know there is a tunnel entrance in the canyon. Do we continue to fight, or do we attempt to escape into the tunnels?"

Earthkin responded, "You left the Homekeep because of the trogs' invasion. I am afraid an escape into the mountain would end with the same results. It is my opinion that a large group of dwarfs traveling in unknown passageways would be a disaster. Foul creatures are known to live in the deep recess of the mountain. Your passage might draw their attention."

Earthkin's statement created the catalyst for a lengthy debate about the different options available to the community. Before making a final decision, the council received a report from the guards on the wall. The lookout reported the trogs were returning to their camp in an orderly fashion. A new Royal Gek had taken control.

The Council agreed there were only two realistic options. They could either fight or flee. The Council finally decided they would fight for one more day before retreating into the caves. Fighting the trogs under the mountains might be a disaster. As the members of the war council walked back to their individual campsites the slow beat of the drum resumed. The booming of the drum was a reminder of the unseen reality in the valley.

The next morning the geks wasted no time in beginning their attack. The change of command caused delays in the communications between the gek master and trog slaves. The trogs attacked the wall with limited effectiveness. It was not until early afternoon that the attacking army regained its former efficiency. The dwarves noticed the number of trogs in the valley had been reduced. This observation did not create a false sense of hope. The defenders were still outnumbered at least fifty to one. Early in the day, Topple and Cando used up most of their magical powers slowing the advancement of the enemy. They were now observers to the passing events of the battle.

An intense, concentrated attack by the trog militia, under its new commander, forced the dwarves to use up most of their energy to resist the tide of destruction. It soon became obvious to the dwarves the trogs were about to over run the wall. Rolfe was ready to call for retreat when he heard a rush of air over his head. To everybody's surprise, twenty black war eagles swooped down picking trogs off the top of the barricade with their powerful claws. Time after time the large birds attacked, using their fierce yellow talons to dislodge trogs from the wall. The trog arrows bounced off the eagles' feathers.

Even though the eagles' intervention helped slow the trogs' assault, the ability of the dwarves to continue fighting was reduced by the effects of fatigue. Each dwarf and human fought as if moving in slow motion.

Coaldon knew he had to do something to save the community, but he was surprised by the absurdity of his behavior. Something guided him to go beyond logic and to take extraordinary personal risk.

Coaldon declared in a firm voice, "It is now time for me to take radical action. Impulsively, the young warrior left his position and jogged toward the north end of the wall. Without any hesitation, Coaldon threw himself headlong into the raging river. Pacer gasped at Coaldon's actions, but could do nothing because of the trog onslaught.

Coaldon went into shock when his sweaty body hit the cold water. As he sank, his muscles cramped, not allowing him to move. He saw bubbles in the churning torrent and heard the roar of water flowing over large boulders. Twisting and turning, he tumbled down the river like a helpless log. He held his breath, but his lungs burned with the need for air. He floated down the river for what seemed like an eternity. From the corner of his eye, he saw a large rock only seconds before he slammed into it. Pain shot through his frozen body. The force of hitting the rock pushed him toward the shore. To his relief, the intense pain broke the grip of his paralysis. With a desperate effort, he threw his hand out to grab for an obscure object over his head. He was able to grasp it with one hand and pull himself to the surface. As his head cleared the surface, he gasped for breath and saw a low hanging tree. With the rushing water ripping at him, he breathed deep and seized the branch with his other hand. He climbed up the limb and pulled himself onto to the rocky shore line. He did not allow time to recover, but forced himself to scale up the steep bank.

Looking over the bank, he saw the rear of the massive trog army to his right. He detected no signs of trogs searching for him. Now, he needed to decide what to do.

He thought, "The only way I can gain time for the dwarves is to destroy the Royal Gek. After Topple and Cando's attack, the geks moved the Royal Gek's tent to a new location. I wonder where it is located? I assume it is in the rear of the camp."

The distant sounds of war, accompanied by the boom of the war drum, provided a backdrop to his unusual situation. Muffled screams and the clash of metal reaffirmed the importance of his mission. He was surprised when he heard the trumpet of horns blending into the general turmoil of the war.

He thought, "The dwarves must be using the horns to summon their last vestige of resistance. I do not have much time."

Then out of the corner of his eye, he noticed the trog soldiers were being formed into units and marching to the south.

"No matter what is happening, I must find the Royal Gek."

Upon closer examination, he saw the top of a large tent on the far side of the flat meadow. He knew the tent was too far away to use the power of his sword. He had to get closer. Yet, if he walked across the meadow he would be detected. Waiting for the cover of darkness might be too late for the besieged dwarves.

To his shock, he heard footsteps approaching from down river. With a quick motion he rolled under the cover of dense brush. Through the branches of the undergrowth he saw a gek wearing a yellow robe patrolling the river bank. With slow steps the guard ambled up to Coaldon's position. The gek did not seem to be concerned about anything.

He considered, "The gek's yellow robe might be the disguise I need to get across the meadow."

He grabbed a branch, giving it a quick jerk. The gek's attention was drawn to the brush with the hope of an easy meal. The beast thought a rabbit or fox would provide an excellent dinner. With casual steps, the gek slowly crawled into the undergrowth anticipating finding a small animal, not the tip of Coaldon's sword. Before it could even react, death came quickly.

Without hesitation, Coaldon put on the robe and pulled the hood over his head. Using the rangy strides of a gek, he walked toward the large tent. The attention of the trogs and geks were on the war, not on a lone individual wearing a yellow robe walking across the meadow. He stayed away from any geks or trogs who crossed his path. He stopped when he stood on top of the knoll overlooking the tent. Several guards patrolling the tent became aware of him, realizing he was out of place.

Shouts alerted guards to a possible threat. A small platoon of trogs, under the control of a gek, ran toward Coaldon. Coaldon drew his sword, dropped to one knee and point it toward the tent. Consolidating his energy, he sent a blast of lightning through his sword toward the tent. The rush of energy was so intense it produced a clap of thunder. He felt strength drain from his body.

Upon impact, the bolt of lightning dissolved the tent into a puff of black smoke. Beasts standing in the general vicinity of the tent were also destroyed. Upon seeing the trogs become disoriented, he knew he destroyed the Royal Gek. The charging gek stopped when the trogs lost focus. The gek paused to determine if it wanted to attack the great warrior by itself. Fear of Coaldon caused it to ran away.

Coaldon looked toward the canyon, hoping this would give the dwarves time to regroup and make one more stand. Glancing around, he realized he had not considered his own escape. He thought, "Now what do I do? Which direction should I go? I am in a real mess. No matter which way I go, I will face death. I might as well start walking toward Rockham. Why not?"

Wearing the yellow robe and hood, he ventured into the churning mass of the trog army.

In the mean time, the dwarf warriors fighting on the wall also heard the sound of the shrill horns. They were slow to respond. At first, they believed the bleating horns were only a figment of their imaginations. When Topple and Cando heard the horns, they casually walked to the top of the wall. The battle on the wall raged on as the two wizards watched movement on the southern edge of the meadow. The attention of the trogs attacking the wall was diverted by an unknown disturbance. The beat of the war drum slowed as the focus of the trog army slowly shifted to an emerging threat.

A wave of silence moved from the center of the trog war camp toward the new battle zone. The fighting at the wall stopped. At this point, the eagles withdrew from the battle and flew away.

Standing on the wall, Earthkin raised his arms in triumph. He yelled, "The dwarves from Rockham have come to rescue us."

On the southern edge of the meadow, row after row of Rockham dwarf soldiers swiftly emerged from the trees in regimental formation. The attack was so sudden the trogs and geks were caught unprepared. Archers and spearman led the dwarves' attack followed by swordsmen. They attacked in short, rapid strikes. The swordsmen would retreat allowing the arrows and spears to inflict more damage. This advance and retreat strategy was effective. The lethal offensive was so successful the whole southern section of the trog army collapsed. Young dwarves moved in from the rear carrying arrows, spears and other supplies needed by the warriors. They also cared for the wounded and dying. As the deadly dwarf army advanced, a dense black cloud rose over the new battlefield.

The Royal Gek withdrew the army from the canyon to defend against the new assault. The early success of the dwarves was short lived. As more trogs were thrown into the battle, the southern dwarves were forced to retreat back toward the forest. The attacking dwarves were slowly overwhelmed by the shear numbers of the trog army. The geks decided to counter attack using flanking assaults. They saw the dwarf army was too small to stop attacks from the side.

Earthkin's hopes were dashed when the Rockham army was forced to retreat. The dwarves were successful in performing frontal attacks, but could not counter the flanking assaults by the trogs. The dwarves soon discovered they could not retreat fast enough to stay ahead of the trogs advancing on their flanks. The dwarves realized their danger too late. Only a miracle could save them.

Everyone's attention was suddenly drawn to a bright flash of light that came from the rear of the trog camp. This was followed by a clap of thunder that echoed up and down the canyon. The trog army once again was released from the power of the Royal Gek. The advance of the evil army came to a halt. The trogs stood in anticipation of the next command.

Pacer yelled, "Coaldon has killed the Royal Gek!"

When Earthkin came to his senses, he realized the opportunity offered to the dwarves trapped in the canyon.

He ran down the wall yelling, "Breach the wall! Breach the wall! We must join the dwarves from the south before the trog army regroups! We must hurry!"

Earthkin's words cut through the minds of the warriors like a sharp knife. They instantly understood the truth to his words. With renewed hope, the warriors quickly opened a hole in the wall. Leaving the canyon was a terrifying leap of faith for the dwarves. The members of the clan would walk directly into the milling throng of the trog army.

Topple, with the dignity of a grand lord, was first to exit through the wall. He enjoyed the privilege of waving his arm forward to begin the march out of the canyon. The wizard's poise and confidence generated an up beat mood of assurance for the people following him. Even though the community was facing death, many dwarves smiled as they watched Topple stride forward with an overly dramatized show of noble character and bearing. He used his magical powers to clear a path through the harmless mass of trogs. Following behind him were the weary warriors. With trembling hope the remainder of the clan formed a long line behind the soldiers. The column moved slowly out of the canyon. The dwarves' bodies were weak, but their determination was still strong and unbendable.

The dwarf soldiers from the south were astonished when the trogs stopped fighting. This event was beyond all understanding, but accepted without question. They cheered when they saw the clan members filing out of the canyon. A unit of Rockham dwarf militia was sent to assist the escaping clan. Without hesitating, they pushed a swath through the trogs toward the canyon.

Under the leadership of Topple, the escaping community advanced into the churning mass of trogs. The dwarves were surrounded by trogs. The beasts were so close the dwarves could reach out and touch them. The dwarves were repulsed by the trogs' foul odor and grotesque appearance. The trogs' mouths hung open with green slime drooling down their faces. Large, yellow eyes uttered their dull and limited intelligence. The trogs stared at the passing dwarves with hostility. As they hiked through the mass of trogs, the dwarves felt small and vulnerable. The trogs would easily destroy them if a royal gek regained control. This could happen anytime.

The two dwarf communities joined forces and blended into one unit without words or show of emotion. A series of trumpet blasts gave the command for the dwarf regiments to regroup and prepare for orderly retreat. In a secluded area, a work detail quickly prepared the earth for the burial of the dwarves dying in battle. A short ceremony was held to give honor for their ultimate sacrifice. With wary eyes on the trog army, the dwarves then made a hasty exit.

The need to travel rapidly put extra stress on the weak. Warriors gladly volunteered to carry the wounded and feeble. The survival of the whole required a sacrifice by each individual. Mental and physical toughness was a prerequisite for being a dwarf. The dwarves accepted this challenge with courage and a sense of duty.

The faint beat of the war drum indicated a new Royal Gek had assumed power. It would not be long before the trog army would be in pursuit. As the group moved south, they were thankful the trogs were slow in mounting their attack.

Many ambushes were set by the dwarf warriors to slow the spearhead of the trog army. The hit and run ambushes were triggered as the advanced units of the trog army chased its prey. The trogs blundered into one ambush after another. Following each attack, dwarf warriors melted into the forest to regroup for another ambush. These attacks were so effective the trogs became leery of rushing ahead without considering the consequences. The further south the dwarves retreated the fewer trogs they encountered.

After a twelve hour forced march the dwarves realized it was necessary to rest. A good defensive position was located; the rear guard was strengthened and campsites were set up. Little was said while meals were prepared and consumed. This was not an occasion for the formal introduction of the clans, but rather a time for sleep and recovery. The rear guard spaced itself out over a large area to gain the greatest advantage over the trogs. When the dwarves encountered trogs, they continued to use rapid hit and run tactic. The effectiveness of this strategy forced the trog army to stop its advance.

After a several hour rest the clans returned to an orderly retreat south. The pace for the remaining journey to Rockham was slower and more responsive to the needs of the travelers. The desire of the trog army to fight evaporated like smoke in the wind. It was speculated that Crossmore was content to gain control of the northern end of the Sadden Mountains.

The disappearance of Coaldon was viewed as a tragedy of war. It was assumed he died when he destroyed the Royal Gek. Yet, a hint of hope glowed in the eyes of his friends.

ROCKHAM

Without hesitation, Coaldon walked into the horde of trogs wearing his gek robe. His fatigue caused by his attack on the Royal Gek made it difficult for him to push his away through the horde of unrestrained trogs. Their random movement created constant jostling. As he continued, a tree appeared directly in front of him. He climbed into the lower branches to rest.

His view from this position was spell-binding. The aimless movement of trogs reminded him of ants. They darted this way and that way with motion seeming to be the determining force. As he watched this ballet-of-bafflement, the uniqueness of his situation became obvious. Even the rank odor and filthy appearance of the trogs did not interfere with his fascination. Mesmerized, he continued to watch until he once again heard the beating of the war drum.

It was apparent a new Royal Gek had taken control. The trogs lost their distracted appearance and started to move in definite directions. The eyes of the beasts became alert and focused on fulfilling their mission.From his perch in the tree, he watched the beasts moving toward the south end of the meadow.

He questioned "Why are the trogs moving away from the canyon? Maybe the horns were from the dwarf army arriving from Rockham."

Climbing higher into the tree, he saw the wall in the canyon had been breached and the dwarves were no longer in the canyon.

"Isn't this interesting? I must find a way to rejoin my friends. I assume they will be traveling south and the trog army will be pursuing them. I could conceal myself as a gek in the middle of the army. Later, I can escape."

He pulled a soggy piece of bread from his pocket and ate it with relish. With renewed strength, he was ready to go.

Dropping from the tree, he followed several trogs to a meeting point for their regimental unit. Upon arriving, the trogs were hastily organized into rows and columns. A roar of excitement arose from the trogs when their master gave the command to begin marching. The unit trotted toward the south, chanting depraved war songs.

After several suspicious glances from trogs, Coaldon decided he needed to be more realistic in playing the role of a gek. So with a look of authority, he assumed an official stance. He walked with his shoulders back, head high and a look of determination. To reinforce this aura of dominance, he asserted himself by moving with an arrogant swagger. His conceited stride demonstrated he was ready to fight anybody who might challenge his authority. With his sword in hand, he jogged in formation with the army.

Coaldon knew from past experience the dwarves would be setting a series of ambushes. The dense trees and underbrush were ideal for the dwarves' hit and run fighting style. After several hours of marching, he heard the clash of the first ambush. The blast of horns was followed by the savage war cries of the dwarf attackers. The clash of metal and the scream of dying beasts ended as suddenly as it began. One ambush after another continued for hours. The sounds of the ambushes came at different locations along the front of the trogs' advance.

Coaldon noticed the beasts slowed to a walk. The soldiers were showing growing signs of uneasiness at the possibility of being ambushed. The trogs were anxious because they could not see their opponents. Their agitation increased as the sounds of unseen battles grew closer.

The trog unit Coaldon was following finally blundered into an ambush. He was conveniently located at the rear of the troop when the sound of horns introduced the dwarves' attack. The lethal assault was so sudden and violent, the beasts fought with bewilderment and incompetence. Coaldon was not prepared for the retreating herd of trogs stampeding toward him. He had to turn and run or be trampled under foot. This confusion offered him the opportunity to blend into the underbrush. He decided it was a good time to escape. He chose to move east toward the coast to hide from the probing eyes of the geks.

He debated if he should remove his yellow robe. If he took it off the trogs might kill him. If he left it on the dwarves might attack him. Weighing the advantages and disadvantages, he decided to remove it. He would be more obscure by showing his own earth colored clothes. He used the primitive strategy of dodge-and-hide to avoid contact with the trog army. Several times he was only steps away from geks looking for retreating trogs but managed to remain concealed. After several hours of evasive actions, he was free of the geks.

As the darkness covered the land, he found a small creek bed cut deep into a gully. Crawling under a large pine tree, he slept. With hunger becoming a concern, he spent an uncomfortable night. Wild images kept ravaging his slumber. Tossing and turning in his sleep, he dreamt he was desperately struggling to escape from a watery tomb. The grave of churning water held him tightly on a journey down a raging river. He saw his hands thrashing to grab an object just out of his reach. Over and over he attempted to grab the elusive thing dangling before him. With his lungs exploding for the need of air, he saw the hand of death reaching for him. Erupting from the dream, he found his hands gripping a branch over his head. Sweat soaked his clothes.

In relief, he listened to the soothing sounds of the night. The first crickets of spring joined the animals and insects of the forest as they sang the serenade of life. Unable to stay awake, he drifted into a second dream. This time he found himself in a crowded building surround by many grotesque creatures. Their reaching hands began to tear at his flesh. By pushing and shoving, he was able to race ahead of their pursuit. With gasping breaths, he climbed a tall tree. The beasts' eyes were suddenly drawn away from him and toward an enemy on the horizon. Losing his balance, he fell from the tree, tumbling out-of-control. Looking down he saw grotesque creatures stampeding after an obscure prey. In an attempt to escape from falling, he spread his arms. To his relief, he began to fly over the top of the forest with unbelievable freedom. He dived, rolled and soared through the air with the majesty of a great eagle. The elation ended when he saw Noel running to escape from the claws of a giant monster. Noel was in a state of terror. With fear gripping her face, she looked up at him. He heard her pleading for help. Finally, out of exhaustion she tripped and fell to the ground. The monster picked her up and laughed with great satisfaction.

Exploding from his dream, Coaldon felt uncontainable anger and hatred. Never in his short life had he ever experienced such extreme emotions. He calmed himself by saying, "I have more important things to do than be concerned over silly dreams. It is more urgent I find food. I remember the dwarves of Lost Valley showing me how to find gopher roots. Eating these roots could keep me alive. I gain nothing by sitting here and talking to myself."

The light of the new day helped bring hope back into his life. The misery of the night was soon washed away by the healing power of the sun.

Fair weather accompanied his journey. At first, dense foliage and fallen trees made it difficult for him to make his way south. It was not until the evening of the first day that the forest opened into a broad coastal savanna. The tall grass plain was interspersed with many groves of trees. Over many centuries, the weather and water created gentle rolling hills. He was happy to be able to find an ample supply of gopher roots. Fortunately, the bitter tasting roots satisfied his hunger.

The second and third days went by without any concerns. Coaldon enjoyed this time of freedom and the beauty of the savanna. The wind blew the tall grass in waves across the expanse of rolling hills.

While munching on a gopher root, he thought, "I believe the dwarves will escape from the trogs. The hit and run attack strategy is very effective. It will not be long before the trogs will give up. Yet, this is only the beginning of the real war. The events of the past few weeks have confirmed to me the need to take bold action against Crossmore. We must find the Key of Ban. I do not believe we have the resources to conquer Crossmore without help. Using the Key of Ban seems to be the only way we can overcome his evil power."

Looking to the west he asked, "I wonder if Noel and my friends are all right."

On the fourth day, while enjoying the early morning sun, he detected movement on the western slopes of the savanna. A small group of travelers was rapidly moving south along the boundary between the grasslands and forest of the highlands. The group was too far away to see if they were humans, dwarves or trogs. His curiosity compelled him to investigate in case gek soldiers had been sent to create havoc. Setting off at a jog, he approached the group at an angle from behind their position. He felt confident they would not see him as he drew near. After fours hours of jogging, he determined the group was composed of ten trogs and two geks.

Stopping to take account of the situation, he thought, "This does not look good. Crossmore must have some unsavory plan in mind. They are moving faster than I had anticipated. At this rate it will take me half a day to catch them. I must hurry!"

Late in the afternoon the unit turned west into the trees. Coaldon feared they were heading toward the dwarf community. He considered, "If the dwarf community is to the west, they could be attacked. I should offer my assistance."

Elsewhere, the newly formed dwarf community was hiking toward the City of Rockham. The two dwarves clans had blended into one community with little trouble or hesitation. Their long separation did not offer any barriers to their union as one people. The journey offered time for the dwarves to share their unique histories. Understanding and cooperation developed on a person-by-person basis.

Norbert and Magee demonstrated robust fortitude by enduring the harsh conditions of war and travel. The two soft palace residents had been transformed into tough outdoorsmen with a strong sense of independence. Their gentle character was helpful in creating an environment of trust between the clan members. They gained the respect of the dwarves by working with the children, elderly and wounded.

As for Noel, her life of imprisonment in the palace helped her appreciate the need for cooperation and freedom. She was learning that true power was based on giving, not receiving; cooperation, not controlling; and understanding, not dominance. Even though Noel had the potential to successfully accomplish many things, she showed little common sense for surviving outside the walls of the palace. With youthful optimism, Noel was convinced she could survive most situations with the skills she recently gained.

On a particular evening, the camp had been set for the night and everyone warned to stay within the camp perimeter. Small groups of trogs had been seen during the day. It was early in the evening when Noel decided to go for a walk. Confident there was no real danger, she followed a small, noisy stream east through the forest toward the grassy savanna. It would not be dark for an hour so she felt she had plenty of time before returning to camp.

She found it delightful to be by herself. Enjoying the peace of the moment, she threw her arms out, turning in a wide circle. The sound of the rippling stream and the chatter of the forest animals filled her senses with peace. She shouted, "This is a wonderful day!"

With eyes on the setting sun, she started to walk back to the camp. As she entered a dense grove of trees, she felt a chill go through her body. She realized the sound of forest creatures had stopped. The blanket of unnatural quietness made it difficult for her to breath. Her half elf senses screamed with alarm. Turning, she began to run wildly through the forest. Before she took twenty steps, she was knocked to the ground by a blow to her head. She did not remember anything until hearing guttural voices arguing. A small fire revealed trogs and geks sitting under the ledge of a stone embankment. The light of the fire, illuminated the swarthy, distorted faces of her captives. The odor of their dirty, slimy bodies was overwhelming. Nausea gripped her stomach.

She listened to a loud debate.

"She must be the one."

"No! If she is, why would she be roaming in the forest?"

"Maybe, she's stupid."

"Lord Crossmore would want to know that we have captured a human female."

"I do not want to mess with her. She is so ugly. She makes me feel ill."

"The only way I like man flesh is dead. Ah! Ah! Ah!"

"We will be heroes if she is the one."

"Lord Crossmore will bestow great prestige upon those who capture her."

"Go ahead and report her to Lord Crossmore, but if she is not the one, I get to kill her."

"You have a deal."

"I will contact Lord Crossmore. He will soon be here."

Upon hearing this, Noel screamed, "You cannot do this to me!"

A gruff voice commanded, "Keep her quiet."

Out of no where, a rough hand slapped her across the face.

"That should shut her revolting mouth."

A burst of resentment boiled inside Noel. The shock of the blow sparked the release of a mysterious dormant power. Noel felt a new strength awaken deep within her being. A surge of energy vibrated through every fiber of her body. At first she was frightened by the intensity of this newly awakened attribute. Later, the rush of excitement melted away into a pleasant sense of confidence. It was not long before she heard a rush of air enter the camp. Looking around, she saw the trogs and geks bowing with their foreheads touching the ground. Their heads were pointed toward the shimmering image of Crossmore. They did not move out of fear of triggering his wrath. The link between Crossmore's image and his physical presence in Neverly was inseparable. He was equally present in both places.

He smiled, proclaiming, "What a pleasant surprise! It is with devotion to your beauty, I am pleased to once again greet you. I have missed you. I was saddened when you were captured by my enemies. Now, everything is all right."

With contempt she responded, "I was rescued, not captured. I was happy to escape from you."

With a gentle smile, he responded, "You are so beautiful when angry. You are now free from your enemies and safe with me. They have lied to you. You can now return to the protection of the palace. I will take good care of you, my dear."

In revulsion she exploded, "Go away! Leave me alone! I do not want to go to the palace!"

In a soothing voice, he swooned, "I must be firm with you for your own good. You need a strong hand to guide you. Some day you will thank me."

His reaching-hand firmly grabbed her by the arm. When he was ready to pull her across the boundaries of time and space back to the palace, a jolt of resistance broke the authority of his grip. She had resisted his magic by her own will. With command, he declared, "So, you have gained new powers. Like any good parent, I need to demonstrate my authority over you."

Noel gasped in pain when Crossmore once again grabbed her arm. He increased the force of his magic to control her. Once again she was able to resist his commands. Their struggle of wills lasted until Crossmore backed off to reconsider his strategy.

With anger in his voice, he proclaimed, "My child, the game is now over. You will now join me in Neverly." Noel was not prepared to suffer the grip of Crossmore's full power. Like a flood of red hot pain, she felt his anger. In agony, she collapsed into unconsciousness.

Before he could complete the transfer of Noel to Neverly, he was struck by a raging bolt of energy. The searing heat of the assault burned deeply into his being. Releasing his hold on Noel, he turned to face the source of the attack. Coaldon stood with his legs in a defensive stance and his sword in the ready position.

Crossmore stated, "It is nice to have a family gathering even under such difficult circumstances. You misunderstand what I am doing. I have come to help Noel gain a better life. She is meant to live in the luxury in Neverly. Do you want to join us?"

Coaldon could barely control the anger throbbing in his body. His rage poured into his sword. Surges of blue flame rolled around its tip, creating a resonating thunder.

In an attempt to gain the advantage, Crossmore suddenly raised his hand to attack. His attempt was quickly met by Coaldon's retaliation. A sizzling, cracking blast of energy ripped from the tip of the sword with the intensity of Coaldon's anger. The power of the strike violently slammed Crossmore into the stone embankment. Coaldon experienced the burning desire to destroy Crossmore. He wanted to punish him for all the evil he created in the Empire. He would show no mercy.

Without thinking, he released another blast of lighting. It struck Crossmore with such force that his life force nearly collapsed. Crossmore had never experienced such pain in his long life. Coaldon's hatred multiplied the power of the sword.

Awaking, Noel watched the battle between Coaldon and Crossmore with amazement. She was stunned by the aura of energy filling the area. At first she was numbed, but quickly recognized Coaldon's great danger. She was transfixed watching Coaldon's uncontrolled anger.

Noel said to herself, "Coaldon has become that which he has dedicated to conquer. Crossmore has infected him with his deadly poison. I cannot allow Crossmore to destroy him. Coaldon would win the battle, but lose the war. Crossmore might die, but he would return in the embodiment of Coaldon's failure".

Coaldon was ready to make the fatal blow when Noel's voice interceded.

He heard, "Coaldon, this is not the way to respond. Anger will only create more anger. Your hatred will only be a stain on your life. Do not darken your soul by allowing revenge to control you. Your justice will only invalidate the gifts you have been given. Please, for our sake, allow life to claim its own justice."

The darkness of his anger yielded to Noel's voice. Like the rush of a strong wind, Coaldon was drawn back into the reality of the moment. He struggled to release himself from the rage attaching him to Crossmore. Noel's words drew his attention to his great peril. He had been on the verge of self destruction. With determination, he slowly released his cramped grip on the sword. As the sword fell to the ground, he collapsed into the shadows of an empty cavern. A swirl of unrecognizable images streamed through the endless space of his mind. At first, he tried to gain control of the passing events, but was soon overwhelmed. It was impossible to manage the unimaginable volume of events rushing passed him. He either submitted to the providence of life or face unrelenting pain. His mind and body relaxed as he yielded to the will of destiny. Peace then surrounded him with a warm glow.

Assuming he was dead, Crossmore floated in a dark void. Then with a gasp of pain, he was thrown into the wall of his chamber in the West Tower. He lay for hours before he could move. In a weak voice, he stated, "She saved my life. There remains hope for me."

After a pause he whispered to himself, "My enemy is very strong. He will need to die before Noel can be my reward."

The energy enveloping the area of the battle quickly evaporated. The cloud of heaviness and fear dissolved into the mist of the early morning light. The trogs and geks did not want to become the focus of Coaldon's wrath. With shouts of panic, they charged into the undergrowth. The noise of their crashing through the forest soon melted into sounds of the new day. A brisk morning breeze rustling through the trees blended into the rippling sounds of the cascading stream and the chirping of many birds.

Coaldon was awakened by a touch on his shoulder. He opened his eyes to see Noel's smiling face. As he slowly sat up, he recognized the stone embankment where he battled Crossmore. To his surprise, he was greeted by Pacer, Topple and Earthkin. In a feeble voice he said, "You are a welcome sight. I am happy to find you, rather than the trog army."

Looking at his three companions, he asked, "How did you find us?"

Earthkin followed, "I will tell you the story at a later date. Right now, we must hurry. The trogs may return with reinforcements."

While eating a meal, Coaldon briefly told the story of his adventure.

He concluded, "I have never experienced such anger. The thought of Crossmore taking Noel to Neverly was more than I could handle. My emotions magnified the power of the sword. I hope this is the last time I lose control of myself. It was Noel who saved me. I am happy to be here."

Pacer stated, "I do not think Crossmore will take his next encounter with you lightly. I am greatly relieved to have both of you back with us."

Topple injected, "I heard the rumble of your sword and felt the blast of your attack. It was wise not to have killed him. I believe he would be more dangerous dead than alive. Hopefully this will slow down his plans for conquest. We need more time to find the Key of Ban and prepare for war."

Earthkin declared, "Both of you must be more careful. You are important to the future of the Empire. We could socialize for a long time, but we must catch up with the Clans. We have spent a full day looking for our lost sheep."

With long strides, Pacer led the way. After a long trek, the small group intercepted the dwarves. The clan rejoiced when the tired group joined the caravan. Sid and Coaldon had a rousing reunion including the usual excitement and rough play. The story of Coaldon's and Noel's exploits rapidly spread through the dwarves' camp.

After several days of traveling, the end of the journey could be seen in the mountains towering over the Echo Valley. The entrance into the underground City of Rockham was located in a long, narrow valley providing a buffer of protection.

Noel and Coaldon were invited to be part of the greeting party representing the Empire. The closer the clans came to their destination, the more excitement bubbled among the travelers. A cloud of dust on the horizon was the first sign of people in the area. To everyone's surprise they saw four horses galloping toward them. Only vague outlines of the riders could be detected at this distance. A mood of anticipation and exhilaration gripped each person in the procession. The ordeal was almost over.

The four riders dismounted, walked forward and waited in the bright afternoon sun. Coaldon made out the outline of two humans (one male and one female), one dwarf, and one elf. Coaldon had been excited about arriving at the city but remained rather passive about this meeting.

This attitude changed when he recognized three of the people waiting for them. Without hesitation he grabbed Noel's hand without thinking. He ran forward in long strides, dragging Noel along like a rag doll. He enthusiastically greeted his grandparents in an embrace. While this reunion was taking place, Noel stood at an uncomfortable distance waiting to be introduced. Coaldon finally came to his senses, turned to Noel and invited her to join in the celebration.

As Noel stepped forward, Coaldon said, "Noel, I introduce you to your grandparents Brad and Ingrid." At this moment, nothing more could be said. After the initial glory of the celebration passed, it was time to draw other people into the circle.

In a formal fashion, Grandfather Brad turned to Coaldon and Noel saying, "I introduce to you Starhood the Elf, Grand Advisor to the Elfdom of Talltree and father to Princess Starglide."

Coaldon was caught by surprise at the stately introduction of Starhood. His mind was so consumed by the emotions of the reunion it took several moments for the introduction to register. Coaldon became silent and motionless as he struggled to comprehend the full meaning of his grandfather's words. The veil of confusion finally parted with a burst of understanding. Like a bright light erupting in the darkness, he grasped the simple words of his grandfather. His body became rigid as he looked at Starhood and then at his grandfather.

Coaldon blurted out, "Did you say that Starhood was the father of Starglide?"

Grandfather Brad responded, "Yes, you are correct."

In childish innocence Coaldon stuttered, "Starglide was my mother. Th - th - then Starhood is my grandfather."

Grandfather Brad responded, "Yes, you are again correct. I am sorry we have kept this secret from you. We did not want to overload you with information at your birthday party. Please accept my apology."

Coaldon and Noel stood in a state of paralysis as their thoughts absorbed the new information. Then, like the release of an arrow, they both shot forward to greet Starhood with unrestrained emotions. Coaldon and Noel were not just blessed, but were double blessed. The celebration of their family consumed them for the rest of the day. As they basked in the glow of their happiness, they were only vaguely aware of the events culminating in their arrival at the City of Rockham.

The fourth person of the greeting party was the Lord Shortshaft, head of the Rockham Council of Clans. His short, broad, muscular body outlined his long, gray beard, deep penetrating eyes and face of cavernous wrinkles. The quiet power of his self-confident, calm presence and dignified poise radiated with the wisdom of ages.

The long procession of the Hardstone Clan and warriors snaked into Echo Valley. The entrance to the valley was a narrow bottleneck leading to the doorway into Rockham. The tall, massive wall guarding the mouth of the valley was constructed of large blocks of white granite. The outside surface of the wall was perfectly smooth and reflected sunshine like a mirror. The large metal gates in the center of the wall were so skillfully crafted they could be opened by one person. The black, hard metal of the gate had been forged deep in the mountain. The metal would resist any known force of nature or magic.

After the procession passed through the gate, it proceeded to the end of the valley. A large crowd of Rockham citizens greeted them with solemn and stately respect. In silence, Hardstone Clan remained separated from the people of Rockham. The blast of a trumpet, the roll of a drum and the cry of a sorrowful voice declared a time of mourning. Before a reunion could take place, it was the tradition of the community to mourn the dwarves who died in battle.

Earthkin, Rolfe and Lord Shortshaft walked forward in slow, somber steps into the space separating the two groups. In loud, clear voices Lord Shortshaft and Rolfe took turns naming the warriors dying in battle. When they finished, a spontaneous, loud, mournful cry of grief erupted from the dwarf communities. A cloud of despair extended for a long period of time. Death was never easy to face and reconcile. After the grief had been released, a slow beat from the drum was accompanied by the chant of a deep male voice. The chant told the stories of great warriors who died protecting the clan.

When the chanting had ended, Topple stepped forward with his flute in hand. As if standing in the silence of death, he played the flute with feeling and reverence. The tone of the flute both caressed and enthralled the members of the community as if overcome by the very essence of divinity. The melody of the songs wove a tapestry of peace into the hearts of everyone sharing in this time of grief. When

Topple finished playing, the mourners awoke from a cloud of enchantment and allowed healing to grip their souls. Then in a voice of authority Lord Shortshaft declared, "We have honored the dead, now it is time for the living to live. Let us rejoice in the blessings of life."

The two groups then merged into a single community. Family members greeted family members; strangers welcomed strangers; friends embraced friends. The celebration continued as food and drink were loaded onto large tables near the entrance into the mountain. The Council of Clans decided to hold the reunion in the valley as a neutral ground for the two groups to meet and share.

As the festivities continued, Coaldon threw off the burden of worry and concern. He was enjoying the sense of security offered by his new environment. As the festivities grew to an end, Topple approached Coaldon with a sly smile on his face.

He giggled as he said, "Are you ready?"

Coaldon with a puzzled look on his face responded, "Am I ready for what?"

Topple pointed to the sky saying, "Up there! Are you ready?" Coaldon looked into the sky, but only saw a beautiful sunset in the western sky. He looked at Topple with irritation etched on his face.

Coaldon continued, "I do not understand what you are talking about!"

In a dramatic fashion, Topple looked into the sky and waved his arms in a wide circle over his head.

He then looked at Coaldon, saying, "Are you ready? If you are not, I recommend you get ready."

At that, Topple fluttered away into the crowd like a butterfly looking for a flower to visit. Coaldon was faced with the frustrating dilemma of what to do. He knew Topple did not play games when it came to warning people about an upcoming event. He debated if he should continue to mingle in the crowd or be alert to possible danger. He became restless, so he walked away from the crowd and into an open space in the middle of the valley. Without realizing what he was doing, he withdrew his sword from the scabbard. He acted out of instinct. A hush came over the community as one person after another became aware of Coaldon's unusual actions. Coaldon was joined by his companions in anticipation of the unknown occurrence.

The orange and yellow colors of the sunset were suddenly replaced by churning, billowing, black storm clouds. These clouds did not move like a normal storm, but rushed toward the valley as if directed by magic. When the swirling cloud covered the valley, a clap of thunder introduced the approaching presence of evil. A black gloved hand reached from the cloud creating panic among the dwarves. Without hesitation, most clan members rushed into the safety of the tunnels.

It was not long before the valley was only occupied by a small contingent of dwarves, wizards and humans. Crossmore's booming voice echoed off the steep walls of the valley, saying, "My, you look so nice and cozy. Unfortunately, you are not nearly as safe as you might think. My army will soon visit you. Ah! Ah! Ah! Seeing all of you together is such a disappointment. You look like helpless rats captured in a trap. Noel, you disappoint me. You have made a poor choice. I will change your mind. Just wait and see."

Changing his attention, Crossmore thundered, "Badda, why did you leave me? I miss you. I welcome you with the open arms of a loving father. Please join me."

In fear and trembling, Bobby yelled, "I am no longer your property! I am my own person! I do not want to be your slave!"

In a sweet voice, Crossmore answered, "Your mind has been corrupted by the false whispers of your companions. Do not believe them! They are only using you for their own selfish purposes. You will be safe with me."

A shadow of doubt crossed Bobby's face as he looked at Coaldon and Topple with suspicion. Crossmore's enticing words were enchanting Bobby's mind. Bobby struggled to determine whom he could trust. Finally, Bobby raised his head, straightened his back and faced Crossmore.

He yelled, "Leave me alone! I will die before I become your servant!"

With a tone of frustration and anger, Crossmore declared, "Badda, I will grant your wish!"

As his black-gloved hand reached toward Bobby, Topple raised his hand to challenge him. Crossmore's hand froze in mid-air. The air in the valley pulsed and throbbed as Topple and Crossmore confronted each other in a battle of wills. Like combat between two giants, the opposing forces clashed against each other. The battle of magic grew into a stalemate. With a sudden release, Crossmore pulled his hand away from the battle for Bobby.

In a booming voice, Crossmore said to Topple, "Little man, you are determined. I am amazed you waste you time and energy on this pathetic group of rubbish. Your greatness is way beyond the character of these lowly creatures. It must be difficult to tolerate such common and depraved people. You are welcome to join me in fulfilling the fate of the Empire."

Topple only looked at him with an empty expression of boredom. Words were not necessary to reveal his answer.

Crossmore turned his attention to Coaldon. As Crossmore observed Coaldon, he laughed, saying, "You have caused mischief across the Empire. After our last encounter you must feel important and powerful. You need to realize, I allowed you to look good for the sake of your sister. I was in full control all the time. In truth, your worthless sword is only a meaningless toy. I permitted you to experience false hope. It humors me to see you take such pride in yourself. Ah! Ah! Ah! I find you disgusting. There is no glory in the performance of your pitiful tricks. I will enjoy punishing you for interfering with me."

Coaldon controlled his emotions as Crossmore belittled him. With calm deliberation, he allowed the sword to sizzle and rattle with energy. A red glow charged the end of the sword. Coaldon would not attack the wizard out of resentment or anger. He did not want to fall into Crossmore's trap of answering evil with evil. The glow from the Blade of Conquest forced Crossmore to retreat from an encounter with Coaldon. He was seeking to find a weakness in the armor of his opponents, not to suffer the pain of Coaldon's attack.

Crossmore then turned to Brad who was carefully listening to Crossmore's words. The wizard said to him, "I am surprised you would waste your time challenging me. You have proven you are incapable of being emperor. Your weakness was demonstrated when you allowed Wastelow the Miserable to assume the throne. If you could not even withstand Wastelow's feeble powers, how can you expect to conquer a Lord of my stature and supremacy? You are weak and you will always be weak. Go away, little child and play with your toys, because you are no match for me. In the future you will not be dealing with me, but rather with my magnificent army. You shall taste the bitter fruits of your battle against me. It will be better for you to hide like a cowardly creature rather than face me. I will find you and destroy you. Until we met again, may you properly anticipate the agony I have prepared for you."

In a flash, the black cloud and the hand disappeared from the sky. Only silence remained. The impact of Crossmore's visit was both enlightening and frightening. Any romantic visions of easily defeating Crossmore dissolved like salt in water.

They walked off the field knowing the war had only just begun.

As the group ventured into the entrance to Rockham, Coaldon declared, "United we stand, divided we fail. We must work together to regain our freedom. It is our duty to find the Key of Ban. The Key of Ban will be the doorway to conquering the forces of evil."

ᛚᚲᚺ ᚺᛉᚨ

Glossary

Historical Time Periods:

- Age of Seaborn ....Before the First Quarter Age (Time of Prosperity)
- First Quarter Age ....A time of evil and war
- Second Quarter Age ....A time of peace
- Age of Change ....The era of Coaldon of Rocknee

Badda..Mindless servant of Crossmore
Black Mountains........................Location of Lost Valley and the Outlast
Black Mist ....Evil presence controlled by Crossmore
Black Wing.................................Leader of the Black War Eagles
Blade of Conquest......................Coaldon's elfin sword with the power of Blessed Acts
Bobby..Badda
Brad Rocknee ....Exiled Emperor of the Empire
Brother Patrick ....Warrior monk from the Monastery of Toms
Cando the Wizard.......................Wizard whose body and spirit were separated by magic
Cave of Hope ....Location of the Key of Ban
Chamber of Oblivion..................Location of imprisoned evil spirits
Coaldon Rocknee.......................Grandson of Ingrid & Brad and son of Rodney & Starglide
Crossmore the Wizard...............Wizard to Emperor Wastelow
Dod, Doria, and Rosa................Farmers north of Grandy (Duke of Slownic)
Doomage the Wizard.................Evil wizard of the First Quarter Age
Earthkin....................................Dwarf warrior of the Long Beard Clan of Rockham
Gem of Watching........................Possesses the Power of Correct Actions
Hardstone Clan ....Dwarf clan living in the Northern Sadden Mountains
Homekeep ....Home of the Hardstone Clan
Ingrid Rocknee ....Wife of Emperor Brad
Key of Ban.................................Elfin book with the power to control evil
Long Beard Clan ....Earthkin's clan in the City of Rockham
Lost Valley ....Childhood home of Coaldon located in the Outlast
Monastery of Toms....................Located in the Wasteland of the Outlast
Neverly......................................Capital city of the Empire
Noel Rocknee.............................Coaldon's twin sister
Outlast ....Wilderness in the Black Mountains
Pacer ....Scout for Emperor Brad (Duke of Paulic)
Raff and Paggy...........................Friends of Coaldon who live in the Village of Grandy
Ripsnout ....Hardstone clan member
Rockham ....Dwarf city in Southern Sadden Mountains.
Rodney Rocknee ....Father to Coaldon and Noel

Rolfe	Head of the Hardstone Council of Elders
Sadden Mountains	Mountain located in the eastern part of the Empire
Starglide	Mother to Coaldon and Noel
Sid	Coaldon's dog and friend
Shortshaft	Head of the Rockham Council of Elders
Slownic River	River flowing past the City of Neverly
Starhood	Grand Advisor to the Elfdom of Talltree, father of Starglide
Strong Edge	Coaldon's Magic knife that bonds him to Starhood
Sword of Truth	Elfin sword owned by Dod
Topple the Wizard	Happy-go-lucky wizard
Trogs and Geks	Crossmore's evil soldiers
Village of Grandy	Located on Rolling River
Wastelow the Emperor	False Emperor of the Empire
Wandering Folks	Wood elves, stone walkers and free dwarves
Westmore, Land of	Location of the Key of Ban